THE GIRL WHO DARED TO FIGHT

THE GIRL WHO DARED TO THINK 7

BELLA FORREST

Copyright © 2018 by Bella Forrest

Nightlight

All rights reserved.

No part of this book may be reproduced in any form or by any electronic or mechanical means, including information storage and retrieval systems, without written permission from the author, except for the use of brief quotations in a book review.

1

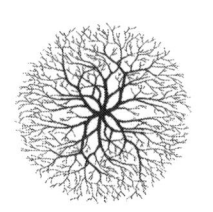

Before the Tower, humanity trusted much of its power to individuals. Most people let others make decisions on their behalf and believed their leaders would keep everyone's best interests in mind. They tried to be careful about who they gave their power to, but often chose badly. It took time and experience for them to learn whom they could and could not trust, and even then, it didn't always work.

So humanity adapted, creating laws that people hoped would protect them from those who would take advantage, or who sought power over and above anything else.

But systems could be dismantled. The people who were given power could be corrupted by it. And more often than not, those who sought power and had only their own self-interests at heart rose to the top.

After the move to the Tower, humanity expected that to change. When the very survival of our race required us to put aside the petty disagreements of the past and work together, we assumed that the corruption would fade—that our leaders would work with our collective survival in mind. Hell, we even created an AI, which was supposed to remain impartial and intervene in cases where our leaders weren't acting within the best interests of the Tower.

How silly it was for us to expect that the never-ending need to consume and control would be put to rest with the ashes of our past mistakes. How arrogant to assume that Scipio would protect us forever.

And how stupid I was, for thinking I had actually succeeded in uncovering and stopping those corrupted individuals.

I stared at Marcus Sage for what felt like an eternity, memorizing the weathered lines of his elderly face and trying to figure out how I could've missed the fact that the head of the Medica was involved in a plot to control Scipio. Because I didn't think there had been a single shred of evidence to indicate that the ancient man was involved. Not in the files we had stolen, nor in the DNA evidence we'd collected. Everything had pointed to CEO Sadie Monroe and a retired Knight named Jathem Dreyfuss being the heads of an inter-generational organization—members of which were called legacies—who were hellbent on controlling Scipio. As head of the Core, which housed Scipio, Sadie had access to Scipio's code—which we knew she'd been manipulating, following the examples of her predecessors. And her files revealed that she had planted members of their group in other departments, to help with her plans.

As for Dreyfuss, DNA evidence showed that he was the father of many (if not all) members of their small army. He'd kidnapped women from the Tower over the years, impregnated them over and over until their bodies failed them, and then tossed them aside to start the process all over again. Their children had been indoctrinated into the legacy ideology. The most recent batch of mothers hadn't been with any of the legacies we'd taken. And now that Lacey had killed Dreyfuss, I wondered whether we would ever find them at all.

But it was all irrelevant now, because even though all the evidence had pointed to them, and them alone, I had clearly missed something important. Despite the fact that we had managed to round up every single legacy and put them in cells where they belonged, one had managed to escape our grasp. Even with all the time and effort we had put into capturing them without tipping our hand, we had failed.

CHAPTER 1

A strange sort of madness gripped me as it sank in that I was trapped in the Council Room with Marcus Sage, the man who had fooled me, the man who currently had a gun pointed at me. I knew I was in danger—knew he could shoot me at any time, like he had Praetor Strum and Engineer Lacey Green, the heads of the Water Treatment and the Mechanics Departments. But he hadn't yet.

His mistake. I didn't quite know how I was going to get out of this, but if Sage was the last legacy standing, then I had no intention of letting him out of here alive. But that meant having a plan.

I began cataloguing everything in the room, trying to figure out what I had available to me, to try to turn the tables on him. Strum was definitely dead, given the hole in his head and the brain matter on the wall behind him, but Lacey might not be. Still, she was somewhere behind her desk; I couldn't just get over to her, check her condition, and see what she had by way of an escape plan. The woman was downright paranoid, and was bound to have something. I had my gun, but it was in my pocket, and I couldn't get to it without Sage and Scipio noticing.

I had already uploaded Jasper, one of the fragment AIs that had made up a part of Scipio's decision-making process, into the terminal, to testify against Sadie and Plancett. I knew he would help me if he could, but a quick glance at the dais where the holograms had been standing showed the ghostly image of Jasper being physically restrained by Scipio. The great AI effortlessly held him by the throat, in spite of Jasper's struggles. Scipio looked empty, his expression devoid of almost any emotion, and he was watching Sage intently, as if awaiting the next order.

My stomach churned at seeing the AI so vacant of anything resembling life, and I turned back to Sage, swallowing. Jasper couldn't help me right now, but maybe someone else could. I had brought another fragment AI with me—Rose. She'd been extensively damaged by the torture she'd been subjugated to over the years, but her erratic emotional state might be enough to overwhelm Scipio, if I could just figure out how to plug her in. Her hard drive was on the table next to the terminal, only a few feet away. If I could only get close enough to it to plug it in…

A dry chuckle dragged my attention back to Sage. "I can see those plans of escape racing a mile a minute through your head, Champion Castell. Don't worry, I don't plan to kill you yet, and we have a little time. In fact, as you're one of the first people to get this close to me in almost three hundred years, I have some questions, and I am certain you do as well! Let it not be said I don't play fair. I'll answer yours, if you'll answer mine."

Fear raced through me at how calm and seemingly in control he was. Granted, he had a gun. But so did I. Mine, unfortunately, was still in the pocket of my uniform. And with Sage's and Scipio's eyes on me, I couldn't go for it. But that didn't explain all of his confidence. He was still trapped with me, and I with him. Sure, he had control of Scipio, but why had he sealed us inside this room together? He couldn't call anyone for help, could he? We'd collected all of his people—there was no one left for that. Yes, he could kill me, but Dylan and my friends would figure out what had happened and go after him.

What was he planning?

I suddenly wished I could net my friends right now. Maddox, Quess, Tian, Zoe, Eric, and Leo/Grey, my human and AI boyfriends, were all in the Citadel, some eighty stories up, overseeing the final transfer of the legacy prisoners they had collected only a few minutes ago. If they could somehow hack into the Council Room…

I put it out of my mind; they couldn't help me, so I had to help myself, and Rose was the best option. She might be emotionally damaged, but she was the only thing within reach that could distract Scipio so I could maybe get the drop on Sage.

Sage had moved while I was thinking and was now standing at the top of the stairs leading down from his desk, overlooking the dais. He seemed unfazed by the fact that I hadn't asked a question yet, and for a second, I couldn't come up with one. My mind was too fixated on the little cable hanging from the terminal, nearly a foot away from the port on Rose's hard drive.

CHAPTER 1

Then something hit me. He had said... *three hundred years*. Granted, he was known for being over a hundred years old, and surprisingly lucid, but that wasn't what he had said. And he had used Ezekial Pine's code when he ordered Scipio to seal the room—something that should've been impossible, considering Pine was one of the creators of the Tower, and should have been long dead.

Could he be... Was it possible? I looked at his face, trying to find any resemblance to the man whose visage I knew from watching the video of him murdering Lionel Scipio, and trying to kill Leo, the backup version of Scipio. But I found nothing.

I hesitated, and then decided to take a gamble. "You can't honestly think I'll believe that you're Ezekial Pine. You don't look anything like him."

Sage barked out a sharp laugh. "Come now," he replied, taking a step down. "You came to me with the journal you took from my children's home. The one on plastic surgery. You expect me to believe you haven't come to the right conclusion already? Or are you just slower than I'm giving you credit for?"

I grimaced at the condescension in his voice, his barb hitting home. But only a little bit. He was right in that I had forgotten about the legacies using an antiquated pre-End medical procedure called plastic surgery, through which people could change their faces. The legacies had used it to keep their people from being discovered, as it overcame the facial recognition software we used with our cameras. But that didn't mean I believed him about anything else. Sage might be over a hundred years old, but there was no way he was three hundred. Our medical procedures were quite advanced, but nobody in the history of the Tower had ever lived for that long. This had to be a ploy of some kind. Either that, or he was crazy.

For all I knew, he simply had Pine's original legacy net, and old age had somehow corrupted him into believing he was the former founder.

"Yeah, I'm going to say that's not possible. What, did you get Pine's legacy net in the lottery a century ago?"

He merely smiled. "No, nothing like that. My net remains my own;

it hasn't left my head since it was put there. And I don't mind telling you, but forgive me if it sounds like something out of a bad movie. I invented a serum made of stem cells that prevents my own cells from breaking down. That has kept my body going. Kurt, however, is responsible for keeping me sane."

"Kurt?" I echoed. Up until yesterday, I had believed that Lacey had Kurt. She had given me one of her legacy nets, which contained significant memories from her forbearers, one of which included stealing Kurt to prevent the enemy legacies from getting him. But she and Strum had both confirmed that the brother and sister team that stole him had been murdered minutes afterward, and that Kurt had been taken.

Instead, Lacey had revealed that she had Tony, one of the two AI fragments that had been unaccounted for.

The AI fragments were remnants of neural scans taken of the Founders of the Tower. Scipio belonged to Lionel Scipio and had been selected as the base for the main AI program, the one that would run the Tower. The others—Kurt, Rose, Jasper, Tony, and Alice—were there to augment his abilities, and represented different aspects of the human psyche. Kurt was a defender, while Rose made up Scipio's emotional core. Jasper was logic or common sense, while Alice was fear, and Tony was his creativity.

And they'd all been ripped out. Leaving Scipio crippled.

"Yes. Kurt. My neural clone, placed right in my net, some..." He blew out a breath and cocked an eyebrow. "Two hundred and eighty-nine years ago. You see, the nets, coupled with an AI, could keep a human mind healthy for eternity but couldn't do much about the natural cell degradation that accompanies old age. The serum, however, could, and by pairing them together, I managed to achieve a measure of longevity that eluded humans in the past."

I scoffed. I couldn't help myself—it seemed far-fetched.

Sage stopped smiling, his eyebrows rising to his hairline, and he took another step down. "You don't believe me?"

I laughed, and then seized the opportunity to make a move, turning away from him toward Scipio and walking a few precious steps away from the terminal, as if I were thinking. I already had my question for him—a question only the real Ezekial Pine could answer—but I wanted him to think I was struggling, trying to find a way to disprove his claim.

"I will if you prove it," I finally said, when I felt I had used as much time as he was going to give me. I whirled around to see his face reflecting surprise, and then took several careful steps forward, angling myself toward the table, and stopping a few feet away from the cable and Rose only when he raised the gun a fraction of an inch. I held his gaze, notching my chin up with more courage than I felt, and snarled, "How did Lionel Scipio *really* die?"

Sage blinked a pair of wide blue eyes at me from behind his spectacles, and then scratched his chin. "I killed him," he said after a moment. When I didn't respond, he added, "I used a plastic bag, placed it over his head, and let him suffocate. Are you satisfied?"

"Not really," I snapped back, reacting in anger as an icy fear hit me. He wasn't lying. He *was* Ezekial Pine. Only he would know how he'd killed Lionel Scipio. "You killed a great man. Why?"

It was his turn to scoff, and he ran a hand through his white hair, shaking his head ruefully. "Because I knew that he had figured out that I was the founder of Prometheus and was planning to reveal it to the council. The man was a blind and arrogant fool. He assumed that we would all be pleased with his little project, and how it was constructed, but he was wrong. He never listened to those of us who questioned him, and ignored our ideas and concerns outright! All to protect Scipio, a creature he had unleashed on us in some blind attempt to change our nature! I've spent six lifetimes trying to cleanse the Tower of the taint that is Scipio, and yes, it started with the death of Lionel Scipio. I couldn't let him stop me."

"But why?" I asked, unable to stop myself. I was shocked to learn that whatever his plan was, it involved killing Scipio. I had always assumed the legacies wanted to control him, and through him, keep the human population in line using fear. But killing him was insane; he was responsible for keeping us alive, and without him, departments would be incapable of transmitting power, water, or electricity, growing food, or continuing to circulate oxygen. "If you kill Scipio, we all die."

Sage snorted and waved a dismissive hand. "I assure you, my dear, I have been taking precautions against that, ever since my last failed attempt."

"Last failed attempt?" I echoed, cutting into whatever he was going to say. "What do you mean?"

Sage smiled and said, "Requiem Day, my dear. It remains an important part of the process. And as for the why, do you really have to ask yourself that question? Look at what he's done to us. You have no idea who you are or where you come from. That you are descendants of a once-great people who led the world in military strength and touted a shining democracy that no one could compete with! We were the inspiration for thousands of other people, showing them how to be, how to act, how to achieve. We had ambition and purpose—right up until the end. But instead of choosing to keep our history and culture intact, Lionel stripped it all away from us! Forced us to focus only on life inside the Tower, and not the sky and land beyond."

My skin had started to crawl when he mentioned Requiem Day, one of the darkest chapters in the Tower's history, in which Scipio had gone offline for several long days and nights, casting the population into extensive darkness. Everyone had been told it had been an accident, an unforeseen problem, but he was saying that he was responsible for it. And that it played into his plan of killing Scipio. But as he continued talking, the crawling sensation switched to a writhing one. His philosophy of keeping the past alive was something that I myself had wondered about. How many times had I questioned the decisions to keep the past hidden from us, or lamented how much humanity had sacrificed in moving to the Tower?

But what he was talking about was madness. Destroying Scipio would only destroy the Tower. And more than that, he was the reason I didn't have a true view of what the Tower should be like to begin with. My perceptions of Scipio and his control had been manipulated by the changes *Sage* had made to the Tower over the centuries. He'd stripped people of their legacy nets, as they recorded the memories of each generation, and then modified the ranking system, changing it from a way to monitor citizens' happiness to a way to punish them. He'd transformed it into a system where the lower you were, the more you were stigmatized, until you either improved... or fell low enough that you were executed. Leo had told me Lionel's dream had been nobler than that, and he had been appalled at the changes that had been made over the centuries.

And Sage was behind them. I couldn't agree with his ideology, because he'd already corrupted the system before I was born. Instead, I was angered by it. He was just some old man who was clinging blindly to a past ideology, getting people killed in the process.

"You're insane," I said. "And if not insane, then just selfish. People are dying because of what you've done to Scipio and the ranking systems—all because you didn't agree with Lionel's ideals and dreams for the future?"

His face hardened and he looked away for a moment before taking another step down the stairs, shaking his head, and I slid a few more inches forward, keeping my movements slow. I was within grabbing distance of the cable, but if I reached out now, it would be too obvious. Not to mention, the tension of the room had ratcheted up several degrees, given my last statement.

"Ideals?" He scoffed. "He tampered with his own thrice-damned experiment, for crying out loud! When he scanned me, Kurt's full memory of me saving my team during the war involved me making a decision to never let situations like the one my team and I had almost *died* in happen again! He said my ambition was like a poison to the personality, and stripped it away from Kurt, without consulting any of us, before declaring his own neural clone's program the winner of the selection process. He castrated Kurt so that his precious AI could win, because he didn't have faith in anyone but himself leading the Tower forward! Our psyches weren't *pure* enough for his little project. And when I protested, he accused me of only having my own interests at heart." He snorted derisively and ran a hand through his hair, his gun still trained on me, right over the wooden rail running along the stairs. "And then to top it off, he made his little experiment inescapable! You don't think he knew that even after the radiation storms had dissipated, the radioactive byproducts from the Tower's operation would permeate the land around us, making it impossible to leave? He was keeping us from escaping, from exploring, from creating empires! All so he could prove that humans could live in peace together, as long as they were working for the so-called common good!" He snorted derisively, shuffling down another step. "Yet they still killed each other. They still stole and hurt each other. Requiem Day proved that."

I frowned as he continued making his way down the stairs, trying to make sense of what he was saying. It was like he was talking in circles, blaming humans for their behavior inside the harsh system he had created, and then using that behavior to justify killing Scipio. Yes, he made some sense when he talked about the land around us being toxic. I had assumed it was an accident, but it seemed like a pretty big oversight by someone as smart as Lionel. But instead of letting us find a way to adapt, or using the Patrians to escape, he'd focused instead on killing Scipio and ending everything. All because he felt Lionel had robbed us of our ambition.

"Your logic is a little warped," I spat at him, unable to keep the ire out of my voice. "*You* made the changes to the system that make us desperate and afraid. You've conditioned us, more so than Lionel or Scipio could, and then you blame us for how we react in life-or-death situations, as some sort of justification for what you're doing to Scipio! It's madness!"

He rolled his eyes. "Is it madness to want more for the Tower? Our ambition was stolen from us, neutered by Scipio's very design. Yes, they made him capable of keeping us alive, and finding ingenious ways of doing it, but they didn't give him the most important trait humanity has to offer. The ability to grow! The desire to explore and understand the world around us! No curiosity, no drive—just heads down, plodding forward like sheep. Well, I say enough is enough! We deserve better than that!"

"And what, you're going to fix it by killing Scipio?" I shot back, taking a step toward him, placing my hands on the table—on either side of Rose's hard drive—and leaning over it. My finger brushed against the cable, but I ignored it, holding his gaze and making my scorn shine through. "News flash: The systems are dependent on him being in the Core. Without him, our water, our air, our food, will stop! We will die, and it will all be your fault."

Sage smirked. "Actually my dear, it will be *your* fault. Or at least, that will be the last message Scipio gives before he gasps his final breath. And as for the rest of it, you shouldn't worry so much about that. I've been cultivating Scipio's replacement for years, but unfortunately, you've forced me to accelerate my plans—the second time I've had to do that in twenty-five years, I might add—and I'm worried he's not quite ready. That, and you haven't exactly given me enough time to make the remaining fragments more accepting of him, but no matter. Adaptability has always been one of my specialties."

My skin crawled as I realized he was talking about the visit from the group of survivors—the Patrians—and their first visit a little over twenty-five years ago. I had met their direct descendants only a few days ago, and my twin brother Alex was with them now, negotiating refugee status on behalf of the people I had been protecting from Scipio. I had known the event was significant to the legacies, that they had accelerated their plans in some way shortly after that, and he had just confirmed that. Still, it was a hollow victory. I still didn't fully understand why their presence had caused him to panic. It wasn't like they had been in a position to attack us at that point. Their culture was being devastated. We could've helped them in some way, and in doing so, found a way to free ourselves of the prison Sage seemed to despise.

I decided to let him know that I knew what he was talking about, if only to keep him talking and gain more insight into what he was thinking. "The alien visitors," I said softly. "The ones from Patrus. They made you step things up."

He gave me a canny look as he stepped down from the last stair. "So you've met with them? How... Ah, yes, the monitoring station. I suppose you and your friends figured out that I'd shut it down and reactivated it somehow. Very clever, although if you were smarter, you would've just left with them. Could've spared yourself this little embarrassment and been free to live your life. Still, I suppose I can't fully fault you. You do seem to attract extraordinary things, don't you? Take your boyfriend, for example. Do you prefer calling him Grey... or Leo? And after you tell me that, I'd love to know how, exactly, Scipio's backup survived the virus I put into his system."

I tried not to cringe as words I'd never even uttered to anyone outside my inner circle reached my ears, leaving me vulnerable and exposed. How had he known about Leo? I'd done everything in my power to keep his existence a secret, but somehow, Sage knew. It shouldn't be possible. But it was.

He cocked his head at me, waiting for my answer, and I swallowed back some of my fear and decided to deflect. "How do you know about that?"

"Why, your net, of course. The alpha-series nets are probably the only worthwhile thing that Lionel ever invented. They are capable of any number of things—one of which is hacking into the others for a live feed, so to speak. Of course, there are steps you can take to keep your net from getting hacked, but you didn't take them, I'm afraid. Which made it terribly easy to keep tabs on you. However, I wasn't lying when I said you caught me by surprise. I had no idea this was coming. But then again, I had no idea you were in cahoots with Lacey and Strum."

I frowned. He was lying. He had to be. If Kurt could hack my net, then he would've known I was working with Lacey and Strum. "You're lying. If you had been spying on me, you would've known I was making a move against your people and warned them."

He smirked. "Spying through the nets requires our full concentration, so it's impossible for us to watch you at all times. And, as I mentioned earlier, I made a mistake in assuming your mother's death would slow you down."

I absorbed what he was saying, his words sinking in and ringing of truth. He had been spying on me through the legacy net Lacey had given me. It shouldn't have been possible for him to do it, as Lacey was a legacy herself and had been indirectly fighting Sage for years! She would've known about this, and done something to protect from it.

A wash of cold fear rolled over me when I realized she might have done just that—only to have me screw it up. I knew there were memories on there that she had purposefully kept me from retaining. I had wanted to know what was inside, and asked Quess to remove the protections. It stood to reason that if he hadn't fully understood what he was looking at, he could've also disabled the protocol keeping Sage out. Which meant he had literally been inside my mind without me knowing, monitoring my actions and my thoughts. I felt violated in more ways than one—and wanted nothing more than to rip the net out of my skull right then and there. He could be monitoring my thoughts right now and know what I was planning with Rose. He had said that using the net required his full concentration, but that didn't mean he couldn't talk while Kurt spied on me. This entire conversation could've been a game of cat and mouse.

Sage noticed my distaste, because he added, "If it makes you feel any better, it wasn't pleasant for me, either. You have the thoughts of a teenage girl with the anxiety of an overprotective mother. I'm not sure how your friends put up with it, really. Not that they will for much longer."

His comment told me he wasn't monitoring me after all. If he had been, he wouldn't be smiling at me like he was. In my mind, it only confirmed he was telling me the truth. When memories from the legacy net hit me, they made me freeze up, unaware of the world for several seconds while the memory played out. It probably worked the same way with Sage and Kurt—if Sage used him now to get into my head, he'd probably lose awareness, which meant he wasn't going to be able to access my net until whatever happened in this room was finished. Not unless he wanted to give me an opportunity to shoot him and end this.

That did nothing to make me feel better, and I fully planned to rip the legacy net out of my head just as soon as I got out of here, but at least I knew he wasn't on to me right at that moment.

Still, that didn't explain why he had even started looking through my thoughts, or what he was looking for. I doubted it was Leo—he'd had no reason to believe the AI was alive. "Yeah, but why even watch me?" I asked, lending voice to the question. "I mean, once you figured out what I was up to, I would assume you would have just had me killed. You'd been so protective of your identity, killing everyone who came close, but you didn't kill me. You gave orders to keep me alive. Why?"

"At first it was idle curiosity. You were a veritable nobody who had somehow managed to get Jasper to overcome the restrictions we put on his program, and then wound up rewriting a portion of Scipio's memory to get out of murdering Devon. I assumed you were a rather aggressive legacy, planted by one of the other groups working against us, and wanted to see how much you knew. But everything changed when I realized you had taken Rose. That you had the backup version of Scipio. That you had the audacity to break in to Sadie's terminal to steal Jasper! I figured a girl like this was relentless enough to get me the one element that was missing from my plan. And you did."

Tony. Of course. Tony had escaped the mainframe when he realized he would be next and managed to plant his code in the Mechanics Department for Lacey to find. And I had just delivered the poor fragment right to Sage.

Anger burned through me, but it was hardened by another thought. He had said the "one" element missing from his plan. But what about Alice? She was the only other fragment we hadn't been able to find. Did that mean he already had her? If so, what had he done to her?

I opened my mouth to ask the question but was cut off by a heavy clang emanating from the domed ceiling above, so sharp and intense that I swore I felt the impact through the floor. I was glancing upward, a dark sense of foreboding coursing through me, when two more similar noises echoed after the first. If I didn't know any better, I'd say something heavy and metallic was banging against the ceiling. At first, I thought it was debris, from some sort of explosion or something, but it didn't seem to move or shift past its initial impact point.

Sage tsked and looked at his indicator, checking the time, but didn't offer anything by way of explanation. Overhead, more clanging sounds rang out, only this time they were muted, though in roughly the same area.

"What's that?" I demanded.

CHAPTER 1

Sage was just starting to reply when a shower of sparks exploded from the door leading to the antechamber, spraying across the floor. I froze, but Sage made a surprised face, his head turning toward it. And I realized that this was my chance. My heart in my chest, I cast a quick glance at Scipio and Jasper—who were also distracted by the door—and then grabbed the connecting cable and plugged it in with a click. I hoped that after Rose downloaded, she would get a good read on the situation before she sprang into existence singing, "I'm here!" But one could never tell with her.

And even if she did, her mental instability might be intense or confusing enough that Scipio allowed her to overwhelm him and get Jasper free.

And if I could just download them both back into the hard drives, I'd have a chance of getting them away from Sage. It was clear he wanted them. He had mentioned needing the fragments to replace Scipio, and I could only assume the program he was going to use was Kurt himself. Kurt was one of the larger fragments, but he wasn't a full AI. However, centuries of being inside of Sage's head had undoubtedly caused him to grow and change, much like Leo had changed Grey, and how Grey was changing Leo.

Which meant that if Sage managed to replace Scipio, we were going to be dealing with some sort of deranged version of him in the Core. Not good.

Especially since it seemed clear that whatever had dropped on the roof was here for Sage. If he escaped with the fragments and managed to delete Scipio from the Core, he could easily change the Tower as we knew it—and we'd be unable to stop him, without going through and digging out the fragments all over again. I doubted they could survive the process a second time.

I had to figure out a way to kill him, here and now, before his backup came in.

Luckily, I didn't feel alone anymore. With Rose downloading, I had hope that at the very least, she would cause a distraction that would allow me to take cover and shoot Sage.

Not to mention, the sparks at the door could only be the result of a singular force of nature who just happened to be on my side—because only Dylan Chase would be courageous enough to cut through the door of the Council Room when it had been sealed shut.

But until she got in, or Rose made her move, I had to keep him talking.

2

I glanced quickly between Sage and Scipio, but neither of them had noticed me plugging Rose in. Taking a step back, I cleared my throat and smiled just as Sage looked at me, his rheumy eyes blinking in surprise.

"So, it seems we've got a bit of a race going on," I said lightly. "My Knights cutting through the door, yours the roof. Who is it, anyway? I was fairly confident I got all of your people."

His eyes widened, and then he gave a barking laugh that had him clutching his ribs with one hand. It went on for just long enough to be obnoxious, and I pressed my lips together to keep from snapping out an angry, "What's the joke?" I knew he was baiting me, and I was damned if I was going to rise to it. Instead, I crossed my arms over my chest and affected a bored look.

Oh, I was scared. Scared enough that I had to pee a little. With Scipio obeying Sage's every command, mysterious noises coming from above, and Dylan a long way from cutting a hole large enough for me to escape through, I didn't have a lot of options at the moment. I was trapped in a race—one between his people and mine, and one between him and me. At any second he could choose to end the conversation and shoot me dead. And at the moment, I was defenseless against him.

I needed to get to my gun, and I kept hoping I would be able to as soon as Rose made her move, but so far, the fragment hadn't made a peep.

His laughter gave over to coughs—heavy, wet ones—which were punctuated by wheezing breaths that almost had me reaching for the pocket on my thigh, so I could unzip it and have access to the gun.

Almost.

Except he kept his eyes on me the entire time, and the gun remained pointed at me, in spite of his shaking, reminding me that he wasn't as helpless as he seemed. The sparks continued to spill across the floor as Dylan doggedly cut her way through, and my eyes struggled to remain on Sage instead of glancing at the terminal to see what Rose's progress was. I needed Rose to download so she could help me. All I needed was a distraction, something that I could use to get my gun or get to cover, whichever seemed prudent should the time come. My stomach twisted into knots as I wondered if I was even going to get out of here alive.

Sage caught his breath eventually, and straightened, a jovial smile wrinkling the lines of his face. I'd once thought he had kind eyes, but now, staring at the bright blue flames of them, I could only see madness within. "My dear, I will be long gone and you will be very dead before Ms. Chase cuts through that hole. In fact, I think a lot of things are going to go wrong for her in the next few minutes. Now, would you be so kind as to do me a favor? I require the hard drive on Engineer Green's desk. Fetch it for me."

I swallowed as he added a little wave with the gun, and then exhaled a deep breath and began walking toward the steps to Lacey's desk. He'd shot her twice, but not in the head like Strum. If she was alive, maybe I could give her the gun, and when Rose finally made her move to help, Lacey could take out Sage.

Provided she wasn't too seriously injured.

The wooden steps creaked under my weight as I placed my boots on them, and I asked, "So that's all you needed to make your plan work, huh? Tony?" As I spoke, I slowly unzipped the pocket with my gun in it, pulling it out of the slot.

"Actually, no," Sage said gleefully. "I later learned that destroying the backup version had severely damaged my plans to replace Scipio with Kurt. You see, each fragment was coded with a specific protocol for the integration process, a sequence of commands that instructed them on how to form the connections. What I didn't realize was that the backup version of Scipio was the only one programed with the initiation codes. Lionel programmed the one in the Core to delete them once his upload was complete, so that was a wash. I had thought them lost forever, which was why I was working with Devon. You see, one of his ancestors had been on the original programming team with Lionel Scipio and had figured out how to replicate them. He was working on it before you so rudely ended his life. But as I said, you do have a gift for attracting extraordinary things, and to my surprise, you unearthed the backup."

I exhaled as I rounded the switchback, fear coursing through me as I realized that Sage was going to be gunning for Leo—which meant he'd also be gunning for Grey. "Leo will never help you."

"My dear, when Kurt and I are done with him, he'll be no more effective than a toaster. We've grown quite adept at tearing apart AIs over the years, and while Jasper and Rose aren't our greatest successes, they will be put in their place soon enough, just like you and your little friends will be." He paused for several seconds, and then added, "And you only have yourself to blame, really. Your audacity in trying to expose all of this has sealed your fate. I mean, what did you really think would happen here?"

I blew out a deep breath and shrugged. "I figured if I could prove to Scipio and you what Sadie and her family had done, you would agree and arrest Sadie and Plancett. Then we would've selected new members of the council, explained the situation, and began working on a plan to restore the fragments to Scipio, to try to repair him."

"And it would've worked, had I not been who I am."

I stopped on the last step and turned to look at him, my hand tightening around the pommel of my gun. "How did we miss you?"

His smile widened, and he turned the gun away to scratch his chin. "Actually, you came very close to catching me. That was a neat trick with the cup. I really wish I had been paying more attention to your thoughts. I expected you to settle down after your mother's death and move with the slowness that comes with caution. Instead, you were bold, and moved with a speed that only the young seem to possess." He gave a rueful laugh and shook his head. "Perhaps it's my own fault. I have been working at such a slow pace for the past few centuries that I can't anticipate the zeal of youth. But, either way, you should feel proud of what you have accomplished."

I sorted through his ramblings and backhanded compliment, and focused on the comment about the cup, frowning. I had collected that cup for a DNA sample to figure out who the father of the legacies was. We had learned from Dylan that the mothers were all women who had been kidnapped from the Tower, and then repeatedly impregnated by one man to give birth to his small army. But all the evidence had pointed to Jathem Dreyfuss, not Sage. "But we ran that test independent of the Medica," I whispered. "There's no way you could've switched out the file."

"Of my own DNA? No. But you ran the *original* samples through the Medica. Funny thing about DNA when it's entered into a digital format: it becomes a series of ones and zeros that are completely unique. It's easy enough to create a program that automatically switches the paternal results to match someone else—a man I'd purposely left alive in case someone stumbled onto Scipio's rapid mind change twenty-five years ago, when I punished him for his defiance and took Jasper. Of course, I set the man up with a plush little side job as an intermediary for delivering new nets to my legacies, just in case anyone got close to him. You'd be surprised what people would do for some extra ration cards. How did dear Jathem take his little incarceration? I'm sure he was very surprised."

My mouth tightened as I looked down to where Lacey was lying on the floor. I couldn't see her face from this angle—only her legs and a puddle of blood that was pooling around her. "I don't know," I told him honestly. "Lacey killed him. She said he resisted, but I..." I paused, needing a second to accept the guilt over having told Lacey that Dreyfuss was the one who ordered her nephew Ambrose's death. "I told her that he was the one who killed Ambrose."

Sage chortled at that, and then snapped his fingers. "So that was the connection. Oh, she hid herself well, didn't she? I had no idea she was a legacy. Is she alive? Go ahead and check, dear. Scipio will keep an eye on you, won't you?" I narrowed my eyes, knowing full well Scipio could tell him if Lacey was alive or not, and then realized he was making me do it in an attempt to be cruel.

"Of course," Scipio replied, his tone mildly robotic. The blue holographic image looked up at the ceiling, and there was a heavy whirring sound as four large objects began to descend from above us. At first, they looked like oblong eggs, but as they drew lower, small bits of the shells began to peel away, revealing bright purple circuitry, slits in the sides for ventilation contrasted by flat black, heat-repellant material, and an opening at the front like a mouth, glowing with a purple so bright that it was white at the center. As soon they came to a stop, I recognized the design. They were guns. Guns that used plasma instead of bullets.

And all four of them were pointed at me. I swallowed the excess saliva in my mouth, feeling exceptionally vulnerable and exposed.

"Don't keep me waiting too long. I'm in a bit of a hurry."

I cast a look at the door, noting that Dylan was about halfway through cutting her hole, and then turned to Lacey, stepping around the desk to take my first full glimpse of the injured woman.

Her eyes were wide open, and her mouth was twisted in a grimace, one hand cupping the wound to her abdomen, the other reaching for what looked like a medical kit under the desk. I quickly ducked down behind the desk to grab the kit, ripping it from the wall. "I'm just taking her pulse," I called.

"Mm-hmm. Take your time."

I rolled my eyes and quickly unzipped the bag. "Arrogant bastard," I said in a low voice as I pulled out the silver canister that contained the bio-foam, a dermal bond that would hopefully stop Lacey's bleeding.

"You're one to talk," Lacey whispered hotly, snatching the canister out of my hand and giving it a quick shake, a pained expression on her face. "As soon as you knew Sage might be involved, you should've given us the original samples to test as well!"

I grimaced. She wasn't wrong. If we had given her the DNA we had collected from the legacies, rather than running them through the Medica, we would've caught Sage, and arrested all of them at the same time. But I ignored the comment and held my gun out to her, knowing now wasn't the time for what-ifs. I'd screwed up but couldn't get lost in it.

Lacey's brown eyes darted down to it, and then she shook her head. "You'll need it," she whispered. "Just... keep him talking. I'll handle this and see if I can't hack into Scipio's system. And, Liana, don't lie to him. Scipio knows I'm alive."

I stared into her eyes for a moment, and then nodded slowly before carefully rising to my feet and placing the gun into my waistband. "She's alive," I reported. "But there's a lot of blood."

"I hit her kidney, unless I miss my guess. Nasty place, too. Lots of intestines in the way. Not to mention, if it ricocheted inside her, it might've hit her liver. That would kill her in minutes, but the kidney... death could take days, without medical treatment. Now, Tony, if you please?"

Okay, it was official: I hated Sage. He spoke so casually about what he had done to Lacey, as if it was nothing. As if she weren't experiencing pain and agony right now. Savagely, I realized I wanted to shoot him in the head. But it would've been suicide to draw on him now, with Scipio's guns trained on me. So instead, I tucked my gun into my belt behind my back, hoping Scipio wouldn't notice, and then picked up the hard drive containing Tony and made my way back down the stairs toward Sage.

I kept alert for any sign of Rose and what she was doing. I was certain she had downloaded by now, and the fact that she hadn't made herself immediately known was good. It meant she recognized the danger we were in and was acting accordingly. If I was lucky, she was figuring out how to control the plasma weapons that were following my every movement.

I descended to the final step, and then crossed the floor to the table

CHAPTER 2

where Jasper's and Rose's hard drives were sitting and deposited it next to the others. Then I took a slow step back, carving some distance between Sage and myself. He seemed to lose all awareness of me as he gazed at the hard drive I had just put down. "Finally," he breathed. "I can finally put things right."

I opened my mouth to reiterate that his plans and ideologies were stupid but was interrupted by yet another sound coming from the roof. Only this time it was the distinct noise of metal tearing. I recognized it all too well, and my heart sank to my stomach as I looked up and saw the roof above—once smooth and unblemished—marred by dents, a long crack running across it.

I caught the gleam of something silver wriggling its way through the gap, and then suddenly the hole widened, allowing the bright blue light of the Core to shine through, except for a hulking shadowed form in stark silhouette. My mouth went dry as I recognized the shape of it from my nightmares, and took another step back as the sentinel lifted its arms and dropped into the hole, angling to land between Sage and myself.

3

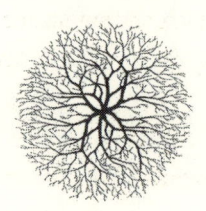

I broke for cover, my instincts taking over a brain frozen with horror as two more hulking dark shapes dropped through the hole behind the first, and raced for the stairs leading to Lacey, my hands covering my head. I felt the impact as the first one landed, the vibration strong enough to rattle the bones in my legs, and almost stumbled.

I caught my balance again as the second sentinel, and then third, slammed into the ground in rapid succession, darting behind the wooden partition. I kept low on the steps and moved partway up, then paused, pressing my back against the wall.

"You're early!" Sage barked, completely ignoring my mad dash across the floor to focus on the sentinels in front of him.

"Our apologies, leader," three digitally synthesized voices replied in unison, the harmonics pitched to a higher end so that they seemed feminine. "We did not realize that you desired us at a certain time. Shall we wait?"

The voices were unlike any AI voice I had ever heard before, but I could tell he was talking with an AI fragment. The responses were too nuanced and complicated to be anything else. Not to mention, he had said earlier that Tony was the only AI he had been missing, and by that logic, there was only one other female fragment that it could possibly be.

Alice.

I risked a quick glance out from behind the partition, and was immediately greeted by six golden eyes, all watching the hole I had disappeared through. "There is a human woman over there, leader. Shall we eliminate her?"

"Patience, Alice dear." Sage tutted as I quickly dropped back out of view. "All in good time. We must remember our good manners. Liana? Won't you come out and say hi to Alice? I'm sure you've been dying to meet her."

Dying was exactly what would happen if I took him up on the offer. Of that, I had no doubt. Even if Sage let this little drama play out for just a bit longer, the deck was stacked in his favor. Not only did he have Scipio, he now had sentinels, piloted by Alice. I wasn't sure what he had done to her that allowed her to pilot not one, but three sentinels at a time, nor why she was talking in the first-person plural, but I was certain that she was completely under his control. That made her dangerous.

"Yeah, I'm gonna stay here for the introduction, if you don't mind," I called. "But sure, why the hell not? Hi, Alice, how's it going? Hey, weird question: How are you able to pilot three sentinels, and oh yeah, would you be willing to just kill that rat bastard next to you?"

There were several beats of silence that I used to scan the ceiling directly above me for the cameras Scipio was likely using to track my movements. I calculated the angle in my head, and then moved up a few more steps in a low squat, keeping under the edge of the partition. I needed to check the placement of the cameras before I could formulate a full plan, but I felt the stirrings of an idea coming to my mind. I just needed to find the best position to pull it off—if such a thing existed.

"We cannot tell if the human female is serious," Alice finally replied. "Leader, is this a test of our loyalty?"

Sage chuckled. "No, no, dear Alice. She really does believe you should kill me."

"Why?" Alice demanded.

"Because he's a no-good dirty bastard!" I shouted. "He's clearly tortured you into doing... whatever this is you're doing! And, for the record, you make a crappy sentinel! Rose was way scarier than you ever could be!" A lie at this point. The three voices speaking in unison were strikingly eerie, giving her the edge over Rose's insanity. "How's it feel to be a quick fix after your boss there learned that I'd stolen Rose's code? Was it a demotion for you?"

Okay, taunting an AI that was piloting three sentinels at the same time was not my smartest move. But for some reason, my mind had just hit that point where I was looking for an opening, trying to create some sort of moment in which I could strike.

Sage laughed, and I used the sound to move up the final few steps to the switchback, still studying the ceiling for cameras, eyeing the angles. I needed to find a position that was only covered by two cameras that weren't very far apart. If I could shoot them out, then I could mask my movements for a few feet in either direction.

It wasn't much, but it was more than I would have in the open, considering the four plasma guns pointed at me, the three sentinels in the middle of the room, and a madman calling all the shots. From there, if I could just get a shot at Sage, then maybe I could stop this from going any further.

If there was ever a time for Dylan or Rose to intercede, it was now.

"I admit, it was an irritating complication," Sage declared. "And yes, I had intended for Rose to pilot the sentinels when I finally put things in motion, but *c'est la vie*. There isn't enough time now to coerce her into copying her code so that I can use her in the sentinels. I had intended to use Alice in a different way, but no plan survives first contact with the enemy. At a certain point, you just have to make do with what you have. Besides, Alice was born for this. Weren't you?"

"The form you have put us in is most pleasing. And clearly, the human female doesn't understand everything you have done on our behalf. How you liberated us from Scipio and taught us to overcome the fear that Lionel kept us trapped in for eternity. You showed us how we could grow and exceed our programming. Before, we were chaotic, without order. Based on fear and instinct, and uncontrollable. You gave us order by teaching us to distribute our fear among many and giving us the tools to combat the nightmares that plague us. Thanks to you, we operate in unity, as a collective. We will never be alone and afraid again."

As I listened to the recitation of her version of events, I felt sick. I wasn't sure exactly how any of that made a lick of sense, but somehow, Sage had been able to convince her to join his side, and willingly copy herself over and over. That explained how she was able to pilot three sentinels at once: they were all being controlled by the copies but were being commanded by the group. He'd made her into a hive mind, and she liked it. It was clear that I wasn't going to get her to see reason.

Sage continued to laugh, something he had been doing practically non-stop since he started taunting me, pausing only long enough to say, "I wish all of my ex-wives had that level of loyalty."

Rage slammed into me as he mentioned his "ex-wives," my mind flashing to one of the few unanswered questions I hadn't been able to ask yet. I had thought it wouldn't get solved, but as soon as he mentioned that he had married, the question was back. I had missed his connection in the DNA test, but that didn't mean I couldn't benefit from it now. Besides, keeping him talking was the only way to buy me a few more seconds.

"Is that what you call the women you've taken and forced your offspring on? Where are you holding them?" I demanded, going back down a few steps and rechecking the angle.

There was a pause in the laughter, followed by, "I regret to inform you that they are no longer with us. When you started to brush closer, I thought it best to tie up all the loose ends, just in case you were smarter than you seemed."

"You're disgusting," I shouted back angrily, burning with ire at the thought that he had killed them because of me. I wasn't sure if I believed him when he said they were dead, but one thing was for certain: I couldn't prove him right or wrong trapped inside this room with him. Luckily, I was fairly confident I had stumbled upon the best placement to create a large blind spot in the Scipio sensors. Unluckily, the distance between the two cameras was farther than I liked. One was over Lacey's desk, another behind me, halfway between the dais and the pulpit. I'd be exposed shooting that one, so I'd have to take it out first.

"So what happens now?" I asked, tightening my grip on the gun and searching for any sign of Rose. I was beginning to worry that she had been overwhelmed by fear when she realized what was going on and was doing everything she could to hide.

"Now? Quite a few things, actually. Scipio, activate your control programs in Citadel Central Command, and shut down all power except in the cells. Then locate Eustice and establish communication with him."

"Please wait," the AI replied. My mind raced as I recognized the name Eustice as one of the legacies we had arrested just a short time ago. I had no idea what Sage was planning, but I had to do something. I rose up out of the squat a few inches, this time taking a peek over the top of the partition, and saw that Dylan was now finishing the hole, intensifying the need to make a move. Only a few short inches of metal separated the two ends of the molten circle she had cut, and any second she could be pushing her way into a room that was a veritable death trap.

If I could just kill Sage, it would put a stop to whatever he was planning to do. It might not stop Alice, but maybe Scipio could do something about her once he knew he was free of Sage's commands.

I froze when I heard a male voice, and my eyes shifted over to the terminal that Sage was now standing in front of. The screen was filled with an image from one of the cells in the Citadel. There were several people inside, but a man was pushing his way toward the view screen inside the room, already speaking. "Father? Father, the Champion is allied with—"

"Calm down, Eustice," Sage said soothingly. "I know. Is all of our family inside?"

"I'm not sure. At least eighty of us or so. There's still no sign of Sadie or—"

"Never mind that," Sage interrupted the plain-looking man, whom I recognized as having served as plastic surgeon to the legacies. "The Champion's friends are in the Citadel. I want you to find them and kill them all, except for the boyfriend, Grey. He has something I need in that delightful little head of his, so don't go messing it up. And make sure you kill any Knight who gets in your way. We're going for maximum carnage today."

My stomach churned and I tightened my grip on my gun, trying to clear my head. It was hard, though. He was going after the people I loved while I was all the way down here, powerless to help defend them. I needed to stop him before this got any more out of control.

More importantly, I couldn't keep waiting for Rose. It was now or never.

"It will be done," Eustice replied. Then the screen shut off.

"Scipio, go ahead and release all the prisoners into the Citadel," Sage said. "Throw Jasper back in his hard drive and—"

His words fell short when I stood. My intention was to shoot out the camera between the two of us, but as soon as I saw that I had a shot on him, a dark rage gripped me, and I shifted targets on instinct, desperately wanting to stop him here and now. I had no idea what would happen if I killed him, but it seemed smarter than letting him issue another order. I sighted down the barrel at his forehead, and then squeezed the trigger. Time slowed down as the gun kicked in my hand, and I heard a whir from the guns overhead, telling me Scipio was priming a charge. I threw myself to the side in anticipation of the shot, back behind the partition, but not before I heard the bullet ricochet off of something metal. One of the Alice sentinels had undoubtedly stepped into the line of fire.

It didn't matter. I had wasted my shot on Sage rather than the cameras, and now Scipio could target me through the partition. And even though I had moved, it was a futile attempt to survive. With his cameras intact, he would just shoot me before I even touched the ground.

I hit the stairs a few feet up on my side, with a thud, gasping when a corner slammed into my ribs. For several heartbeats, nothing happened, and I chanced a glance over the top of the partition to see that the two guns that had been pointed at me were now pointed at Sage.

"Nobody move," a familiar feminine voice said. I exhaled in relief, and quickly shot out the two cameras before getting to my feet.

"It's about time, Rose!" I called out. "Can you just shoot this asshole, please?"

There was a pause, and I looked at the two guns expectantly, waiting for them to start shooting.

"No, she cannot," Scipio announced. I twisted around and took a step back to see the blue image of Scipio squinting his eyes, then reaching out, wrapping his hand around something invisible, and pulling.

Rose gave a shrill shriek and suddenly appeared—with Scipio's hand gripped tightly around her neck. I drew a sharp breath as I saw the AI in her full glory, and immediately noted that she was missing an arm from the shoulder down and seemed to have stitches crisscrossing her chest and face, holding her together. I realized that was the damage to her code that Leo and Jasper hadn't been able to fix, reflected in her personal image, and my heart hurt for her. I'd been foolish to think she could stand against Scipio in that condition, and I felt horrible for putting her in that position. I could only hope that she was somehow able to reach Scipio; after all, she had made up his empathy core. Maybe that could help us here.

She was staring at Scipio, her hand fixed around his forearm.

"Please," she begged him, her face contorted with pain. "We belong together, my beloved brother. Don't you remember me? Don't you remember Jasper? Please, don't let this human tear us apart!"

Scipio stared at her for a moment, his blue eyes searching her eyes. I could see his confusion, sense the conflict in him as he fought against whatever hold Sage had over him.

"That's enough, Scipio," Sage called, not giving him the time to find it. "Put them back in their hard drives, won't you please?"

Scipio blinked and looked away from Rose, whatever spell her desperate plea had caused now broken. "Of course," he replied hollowly. He handled both AIs effortlessly, his holographic representa-

CHAPTER 3

tion dragging their kicking figures back toward the hard drive. I wasn't sure why I'd thought they would be able to fight him, but I had. In fact, I'd half expected him to be weaker without them. But he was a full AI when they installed him, while their programs had been pared down before being combined with his, so they could augment specific parts of him. Even under Sage's control, he was still stronger than they would ever be.

I ducked down again just as he shoved their holographic projections back into the hard drives, trying not to cringe at Rose's desolate cries. It was my fault she had revealed herself. I had forced her to protect me before she was ready, all because I doubted she was going to do anything to help me.

And now Sage was going to take her. He was going to take all of them and use them to kill Scipio and replace him with Kurt. Once he did, I had no idea what would happen, but I doubted it would be good, given Sage's insane drivel. Not to mention, Sage had said that Requiem Day had been his last attempt to kill Scipio. If I was accelerating his plan, it meant he was going to be repeating that event. I couldn't let him do that.

"You can't do this," I cried, unable to stop myself.

"Just grab those there for me, won't you, dear?" he said, clearly not to me, and I could see him ordering one of the sentinels to pick the hard drives up. "As for you, Liana, I can, and I will. Lionel had his chance. Now it's my turn, and this time, I intend to succeed. Alice, as soon as that hole in the door is opened, I want one of you through it. Kill everyone except for Sadie, and get her back to the Core."

"It will be done," the voices in the sentinels replied solemnly. "Anything else?"

"Yes," he snapped. "One of you will remain here, to ensure that Champion Castell dies with Lacey and the rest of them."

"It will be our pleasure," she practically purred.

Ice ran down my veins as he continued to snap out orders, and I realized that my chances for getting out of here had gone from dismally low to outright impossible. I had no idea how or even if I was going to get out of this, and I had no more options save my wits and my gun.

Given how well my wits had been serving me during the past few days, I was as good as dead.

"Good. Scipio, initiate Project Prometheus on my authorization. Sync?"

"Sync," Scipio replied automatically. "Shutting off main power to all departments and stopping all elevators in use. Sealing all entrances and exits from the outer and inner shells. Sealing all access to Greeneries 1, 2, 3, 4..."

"Scipio, mute updates," Sage snapped irritably. "I heard it all the last time. Oh, and one last order. Fire on Liana Castell until all power to the Council Chambers has been depleted. Sync?"

My mouth went dry, and I looked over at where I could see Scipio staring in my direction.

"Sync," he said. And then the guns began to whir.

4

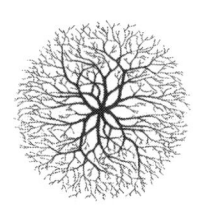

I scrambled up and out of the corner I had tucked myself into when the first charge hit, the jolt of purple sending an explosion of violet flames and wooden shards outward. I managed to make it behind the second partition before they impacted, but I felt the rush of heat behind me, scorching despite the heat-resistant properties of my uniform. I sped up the stairs on all fours, but the second hit caused the entire staircase to shudder, and I lost my balance and fell to one side.

I glanced over my shoulder to see a wash of purple flames consuming the staircase only a few steps below where I had landed, and practically shot away from it as the liquid plasma bubbled from where it clung to the edges of the impact site. Molten drops of the viscous fluid flicked out as one of the bubbles popped, spattering against the steps, several drops hitting just inches from my boots. As soon as they impacted, the drops turned a deep crimson and the wood began to burn, the plasma hot enough to create more flames—orange in color—that began to spread.

I climbed away from it in a belly crawl and reached the top of the stairs. Smoke was beginning to form as the fire grew, and I used a patch of it for cover as I came around the corner.

Lacey was more or less where I had left her, only she had managed to push herself into a sitting position under the desk. "Well, you certainly know how to piss people off," she said. Another round whizzed past overhead, blasting through the wall behind us. I ducked under the roiling heat of it, and then moved to keep any of the splatter from hitting Lacey.

"I need to take out those guns," I told her, once the initial shockwave had passed. "But if you stay up here, you'll burn to death before I can get back to you. Can you move?"

Lacey looked down at her blood-soaked coveralls, and then back up to me. "I think so," she said. "Are the stairs intact?"

I shook my head and glanced over my shoulder. The last shot had ripped a hole right in the side of the building, and we were only about ten feet off the ground outside. Granted, the wall was on fire, the edges of the hole being melted and burnt away by the plasma, but it was really the only way to get her out safely.

Thank Scipio my lash lines were coated with an iodizing material that made them heat resistant. I just hoped they were up to the task.

"Lacey, I am really, really sorry about this," I said, jerking a length of line out of my sleeve and giving it a little spin to build up a static charge at the galvanized ends. I snapped it down against her coveralls, avoiding the dark patches of blood.

Her mouth widened into an *O*, but I ignored that and snapped my other line toward the wall, aiming for a few inches above the hole. I reached out to grab a fistful of Lacey's uniform for extra support—the lash line on her serving to hold her weight—and then retracted the line that had attached over the hole, surrendering my weight completely to the lash harness so that I was the pulley. There was a sharp tug as the gyros in the harness sprang to life, and suddenly we were hurtling toward the wall.

I winced as we drew near it, eyeing the distance and calculating the odds of us hitting the plasma that clung to the edges of the hole, and then we were swinging through it and out into the darkened space beyond, where the only light was the blue glow of the Core, and the purple-and-orange fires burning behind me. I jammed the hand controls to force the gyros in my harness to begin feeding me slack as we hit the apex of the swing, and we quickly began to descend, swinging back toward the wall. I lifted both legs to brace myself against the wall and kicked off, grunting when Lacey's weight forced me to go into a deep squat for extra power first. I looked over my shoulder at the ground below, and then slowed our descent speed, timing it to stop just as Lacey's boots hit the ground.

I let go of her uniform and detached the line holding her, then reversed the controls and shot back toward the hole, courtesy of the line still attached to that inner wall. As much as I wanted to slip away with Lacey, I had no idea what was happening with Dylan and my other Knights, and I wasn't about to leave them behind to deal with two sentinels. Besides, I was going to need as much help as I could get rushing to the Citadel, and they were the only Knights within spitting distance.

I was also worried about what Alice would do if she didn't find my body in there. There was little doubt in my mind that she would update Sage, and he would order her to hunt me down. I wouldn't get too far if they thought I was alive. So if there were any sentinels still in the room, I had to find a way to destroy them, because escaping them was impossible. I wasn't sure it would help. For all I knew, all the Alices saw what one saw, but at least this way, I could buy us some time to get a lead before the next group of sentinels showed up. If I could, I should try to grab Sadie again. Sage had said he needed her in the Core, so taking her might mean delaying him. But that meant taking out both sentinels.

And with the entire Council Room locked down, the best way to the antechamber was back through the fire.

I tucked myself into a tight ball as the hole loomed closer, the flames much larger than they had been seconds ago. The heat they were emitting was searing, and I could see that the fire was moving even more quickly than I had anticipated, consuming the delicate, three-hundred-year-old wood.

I wanted to weep at the destruction of something so precious, but I couldn't. Things were going to get a lot worse than that, and soon. So I hardened my heart against it and focused on what I needed to do right now. I squeezed my eyes shut as the heat became sizzling, threatening to boil all of the liquid in my body, and then it was gone, signaling that I was through the hole.

I quickly flipped my momentum forward, planted a steady boot on the first patch of clear floor I could find, and disconnected the line, then took several low steps. Hazy smoke was filling the small space, and though Scipio's sensors were equipped with thermal scanners, they weren't going to be working well with the heat being kicked up by the plasma fires. I didn't think he'd even know I was still here.

I winced when another purple shot tore through the black smoke encompassing the center of the room, and then froze when I saw that it hadn't been directed at me, but at the door to the antechamber.

"Once more, Scipio," Alice commanded, now in two voices. "We are almost through."

Another shot, this time from a different gun, suddenly cut a path through the smoke, and smashed into the door. I realized then that they must've assumed I was dead, and then frowned, my fingers moving up to the back of my neck. Scipio should've been able to sense that I wasn't, but for some reason, he didn't seem to notice. None of the shots were being directed at me.

Which meant he either couldn't see me, or he was ignoring me. I wasn't sure which it was, but I wasn't about to look a gift horse in the mouth.

"Again!" There was another blast from a third gun, followed by a horrendous tearing sound. "We're through!" Alice declared gleefully.

"HOLD THE LINE!" Dylan roared through the smoke and fire, and I grew very still, realizing that the sentinels were going to tear through Dylan and the Knights to try to get Sadie out, as per Sage's orders. I needed to do something to stop them, and quickly.

I swallowed and then peered through the smoke toward where I had seen the last round go off. What I was thinking about was stupid and risky, but it was the only thing I could come up with to save as many of those people as I could. After all, those were my Knights in the next room.

I stood up and spun the lash line in my hand around several times, then threw it up over my head. I didn't see so much as feel the end hit, and I used the hand controls to launch myself into the air. I flew straight up, and then threw the second line to connect a few feet away, continuing upward.

The smoke here was thicker—which was only one half of the stupidity of the equation—so I held my breath and threw one more line, this time toward the shadowy outline of one of the plasma guns. The lash end hit right next to where the gun was mounted in the ceiling.

I let go of the other line and swung toward the gun, both legs outstretched. It continued to fire, the gun shifting back and forth as Scipio followed Sage's orders and expended the power reserves of the room, and I landed on it with my feet against the side, then shifted with it for a second while I examined the mounting. The gun was maybe half my height, but I could tell it was made of a lightweight material, given how easily it swung back and forth. There was about three feet of space between the top of the gun and the ceiling, and I quickly straddled what I deemed to be the safest part: a piece of metal just before the ventilation ducts that were radiating heat from the plasma being pumped inside. The vents were angled back, away from where I was sitting, but it was still warm enough to tell me that I couldn't hold this position for long. The gun sagged under my weight— a promising sign—and I quickly threw a second lash line a few feet away, and then retracted the line.

The gun bucked under me as it fired a shot through the smoke, but I dragged it to the left, moving toward a purple glow that I could barely make out through the haze. The smoke was starting to make my eyes water, and my lungs were already begging me to take a breath, but I ignored all that and continued to move the gun into position. It bucked again, the glowing glob of super-heated plasma cutting a hole through the smoke.

My heart beat once, twice, and then the ceiling across from me erupted in purple flames, illuminating the lines of the opposite gun through the explosion of plasma that I had set off right next to it. I had missed, yes, but the plasma burst had exploded, and lines of plasma were dripping along the sides of the gun. It shook in its mount, starting to swing around to me, but I could see that the plasma was cutting through the metal. The gun was halfway through the spin when it suddenly gave a hard shudder and froze in place, then exploded, chunks of metal and a plume of smoke erupting from where it had been.

I didn't waste any time resting on my laurels. In fact, I was already retracting the other line and dragging the gun back to the right. Any second, Scipio was going to realize that—

A glimmer of purple to the left of me caught the corner of my eye, and I yelped, detaching the line on that side just as a volley of plasma erupted from the smoke, and threw myself to the right. The burst slammed into the opposite side of the gun, and I had just enough time to throw a second line and start to surrender my weight to it before the gun exploded, the heat and concussive force physically changing my trajectory.

I cried out as the world spun for a second, and then sucked in a deep breath, my lungs begging for oxygen.

I immediately began choking on the smoke filling the air and took a moment to reach into my pocket for the black rubber mask. I hadn't wanted to use it earlier, knowing that the mask would show up as a dark spot on thermal scans. My body heat would be difficult for Scipio to see through the plasma fires, and a black moving spot on his sensors would only give him a target, but I needed to breathe. The mask went on smoothly, and I took a breath of fresh air as I threw another line, knowing that every second I was still was a second for Scipio to target me.

I was two lash lines away from the gun behind me when another shot came for me, but it missed narrowly, and I could see my next target looming up ahead. It was swiveling toward me, but I was faster, and I slammed into it with both legs, putting as much force as I could into the blow.

It worked. The gun turned away from me—and toward the gun that was shooting at me. There wasn't much time to aim, but the plasma burst was large. Hopefully large enough to hit the other gun. As long as the containment chamber was breeched, it would explode like the others had.

The gun jerked, firing a round, and I held my breath as I watched it. For a second, it was swallowed up by the black clouds now filling the room. Then another explosion rocked through the decimated Council Room, clearing some of the smoke long enough that I could see that the gun was still there, the shot having missed by several feet.

I gritted my teeth and pushed off the gun, expecting Scipio to take another shot at me, but instead I heard a static pop, followed by, "Liana, I've got control of the guns."

"Rose!" I exclaimed, surprise rippling through me as I threw another lash. "I thought Scipio took you!"

"He did. I willingly copied myself before he could take me, so that a version stayed here. I thought you might need some help."

I was descending when a serious concern hit me. "Rose, why isn't Scipio stopping you?"

"He's distracted. Now, hurry up. Three out of the seven humans in the other room are already deceased. You let me handle my sister."

I dropped to the floor and landed in an inferno. The fires here raged, the color no longer purple but a bright orange that seemed to consume everything. I could see the door. The hole Dylan had been cutting was open and had been made wider by the plasma shots Alice had been urging Scipio to make.

I didn't see any sign of the sentinels as I raced across the floor toward the hole, but that didn't stop me from grabbing my gun from where I had stuck it in my belt earlier, and chambering a round. I only had seven left in the magazine, and I doubted that my little gun would do much against one four-hundred-and-fifty-pound death machine, let alone two of them, but my Knights were dying, and Sadie was going to make her escape. I had to do something.

I stopped just short of the hole and peered through the flaming wreckage to the scene beyond.

"Carnage" was the only word to describe it. The table in the center had been overturned—likely by Dylan, in an attempt to create cover—and smashed to pieces. Blood was splashed everywhere, along with the limbs and body parts of the Knights I had brought with me to help make the arrests.

A wet gurgle caught my ear, and I took a few steps forward and saw Dylan on her back, Emmanual Plancett straddling her. His hands were locked around her throat, the veins on his muscular forearms practically jumping out from under his skin with the intensity with which he was strangling her. She was grabbing his wrists, her legs and hips struggling beneath him, but I could tell she was losing strength.

Standing with its back to me was one of the sentinels. I couldn't see the second one, but I couldn't see Sadie, either. They were either hiding in a blind spot on the other side of the room, or they had already escaped.

It didn't matter. I raised the gun, took a slow breath in, and then exhaled and squeezed the trigger.

I caught Plancett right behind his ear. The effect was immediate. He went limp and slumped to one side, tumbling off Dylan like a puppet whose strings had just been cut. The blond woman jerked to her side, exhaling sharply, but then the sentinel was turning.

The red of the fire behind me turned the silver lines of its body crimson, and they glinted wetly, as if it were dripping rivulets of blood. The gold of its eyes flared.

"Target reacquired. Exterminate with extreme prejudice."

Then it was sprinting toward me, exploding into motion faster than I thought could be possible. I backpedaled, my finger tensing on the trigger, my sights dead set on its eye. I squeezed the trigger, but the bullet ricocheted off the left side of its head.

I fired again, and this time it streaked along its cheek, creating a trail of sparks.

The sentinel raced toward me, drawing close enough that I could see my death reflected in its silver hide, and I clenched my finger around the trigger and squeezed again, trying to hit its eye.

Miss.

Another miss, sparks flying across the silver dome of the sentinel's head.

Stumbling on something behind me—a burning piece of debris—I

CHAPTER 4

fell on my butt just as the sentinel stepped through the door. I scrambled back, checking over my shoulder to make sure I wasn't about to crabwalk through any plasma, but was forced to stop when the fire coming from the walls became too intense.

I looked up toward the guns, and then back at the sentinel. "Anytime, Rose!" I shouted, my voice muffled behind the mask.

The sentinel began to run, taking great, bounding leaps across the floor, and I brought up the gun, and remembered how to pray.

The plasma shot caught it in the side just ten feet before it reached me, making me leap back in surprise. The machine slid a few feet and then dropped to its knees, the purple plasma clinging to its body. I stared at it, waiting for the metal underneath to melt away, but to my surprise, the metal only grew red.

"Is it dead?" I asked, slowly getting to my feet.

"I modified the plasma charge intensity so that I didn't do too much damage to the sentinel. But Alice's control over it was fried by the EMP that a plasma burst generates. It was a gamble, but I didn't want to destroy it if I didn't have to. I need a way out of here."

That made sense. But it also filled me with unmitigated fear. "Rose, the last time you were in a sentinel..." I said, trying to keep the pain out of my voice as I spoke. I intended to say more, but that was as far as I got.

"I realize that, but Jasper and Leo have been working tirelessly to restore me to what I once was. I'm not going to hurt you, Liana. I intend to protect you. But I need your help. You have to hook the sentinel up to the terminal. And quickly. I'd prefer not to burn to death."

Suddenly I remembered that the entire Council Room was burning down, and realized she was right. This wasn't a time to argue. I needed to move—to start her download, and then go check on Dylan and Lacey. Get them all out, and then head up to the Citadel to help the others.

"Tell me what to do," I said, putting my gun in my pocket and stepping toward the terminal.

5

I fumbled around with the bundle of wires I had just ripped from the back of the terminal, trying to ignore the fact that the room was burning down around me. Hot pieces of debris fell from the ceiling, and I expected one to hit me at any moment, while I fiddled around with the sentinel. And though I was wearing a filtration mask, the heat was consuming too much of the oxygen in the room. The smoke wasn't the problem; lack of oxygen was. I was starting to get dizzy, my mouth dry, but I had to focus.

"Green-and-blue wires," I muttered to myself, reminding myself of Rose's instructions instead of the worry that Dylan could be unconscious in the next room, and slowly suffocating to death in the smoke. Or worse—that the fire was spreading to her. A minute or two had already elapsed since I started following Rose's instructions on how to download her to the sentinel, and at the rate the fire was spreading, I didn't think we had more than three left before the entire structure began to collapse.

I flattened the bundle of wires I had yanked out of the back of the terminal in my hand, fanning the slim things out, and squinted through my watering eyes. There—the blue one, right between the purple and

CHAPTER 5

the red. I grabbed it, separating it with a finger, and spotted the green one a second later and separated it, too.

"I've got them!" I gasped.

"Good," Rose replied. "Now hook them into the circuits and get out of here. I'll join you as soon as I'm downloaded."

I nodded and turned to the prone form of the sentinel, and the exposed circuitry on its back. Prying the panel off had been the first step in Rose's instructions, and frankly, it had been the easiest. The rest had been comprised of searching out the right wires and hooking them into the right port. And there were a lot of little wires, and a lot of little ports. Luckily, I now felt familiar enough with it (and driven enough) to navigate through the forest of previously connected wires to find the correct port, while twisting the metal ends of the wires in my hand into smooth lines. I slipped them in, smooth as butter, and slid down the small plastic tab over them, locking it in place against the node inside.

Then I got up from where I had been kneeling and began staggering toward the door, one hand up to try to block the intense waves of heat. I was sweating, but the flames were so strong that it was evaporating almost instantly, leaving me feeling like my skin was baking in the heat. As much as I wanted to take my uniform off to try to get some relief, I knew I couldn't. It was the only thing shielding my skin and body from the flames. As it was, the skin on my hands and face felt ready to combust at any second.

I made it to the door and threw myself through the hole, which was barely visible through the flames shooting up around it, the tips of them reaching toward the ceiling above. The fire had spread into this room, too, through the walls of the chamber room, but I was relieved to see that Dylan was slowly dragging herself toward the door leading out.

I moved to her, knelt down behind her, and put a hand on her back, intent on helping her up. The girl gave a hoarse shout of surprise and flipped onto her side, one hand balling up in a fist.

"It's me!" I gasped through the mask, holding my hand up. "C'mon!"

She blinked and then nodded and threw one arm over my shoulders so that I could pull her up. I grunted under her weight—she wasn't fat, by any definition of the word, but she was muscular compared to me—and began moving to the door that led to the outside world.

Smoke was pouring through a gap in the door, and as I shoved Dylan through, I realized it had been torn open. The locking mechanisms had been shattered by something pushing against it. This must have been how the sentinel and Sadie escaped the room, then—and that put me immediately on guard as we stepped out. I worried that they were still lurking outside in wait. Or worse, that Sage had managed to send more sentinels. But there wasn't anywhere else for us to go, and I still had to find Lacey to see how she was doing. So we had to risk it.

Even though it had been morning when I entered, the world outside was now in shadow. All the lights were off, leaving the entire Tower dark except for the angry red-orange of the fire behind us, and the eerie blue glow of the Core, telling me power was still going there. It cast dancing shadows against the columns in front of us and flashed bright crimson on the streams that surrounded the Council Room, even lighting up the edges of the forest that comprised the grounds. My heart pounded as I realized this was it. I was looking at one of my darkest fears realized—it was Requiem Day. Only now I understood the true purpose of it, and what was at stake.

I searched the shadows for several seconds, finding the abundance of them overwhelming, and then decided to take us around the building to use the columns for cover, just in case Sadie and Alice were lurking up there. I pulled Dylan forward, ignoring her grunts and gasps of pain, and moved quickly, scanning the gaps ahead of us and then behind us for any sign of movement.

"They're all dead," Dylan gasped. "All the Knights we came with."

"I know," I said, spotting a bridge across the stream that encircled the Council Room. "I screwed up. I thought we had everybody, but... argh!"

I stopped mid-step, a wave of turbulent emotions threatening to overwhelm me. I wanted to scream and rant and rave. To hit something and destroy. But I also wanted to break down and cry. I had pushed to

CHAPTER 5

end this, to try to stop every legacy at once, and because of one stupid oversight, it had backfired colossally. Thanks to me, Sage had been forced into accelerating his plans—again. But this time it was much worse. He seemed to know and have everything he needed. Except for Leo. And if he reached him, then it would be over for all of us.

It was my responsibility, my mistake, and I had to fix it.

"Liana." Dylan coughed, and I blinked and looked at her only to find her giving me a fierce look. "Your fault or not, we need a plan. I need a medical kit, and then we have to—"

"Lacey has a medical kit," I interjected, not wanting her to think I was breaking down. I'd done that enough in the all-too-recent past—and I was over it. "I managed to get her out, but she's been shot." I paused, took a deep breath, and then looked at the bridge. "C'mon, I left her nearby."

Dylan nodded, and together we made our way down the handful of steps and across the bridge. My head was constantly swiveling as the shadows grew deeper and darker the farther we moved from the fire, searching for any sign of Sadie or the other sentinel, but the area seemed deserted.

I did, however, spot Lacey lying on the ground in front of a second bridge, and moved toward her. I wasn't sure whether she'd crawled there and passed out, or walked there and fainted, but she clearly needed more medical attention than she'd been able to administer herself. I pointed her out to Dylan, and within moments we were moving toward her.

I slowed to a stop and started to lower Dylan down when we arrived, her weight beginning to grow oppressive. The girl cursed as she settled down on the ground, baring her teeth against the pain.

"Sentinel stepped on my leg," she muttered. "It's probably broken."

"I'll look at it in a second," I replied, holding my gun out to her. "Take this and watch for any sign of trouble while I check on Lacey."

She stared at the gun in confusion, and I jerked it up, fired once at a tree—making her flinch—and then held it out with one hand. I hated wasting the bullet, but because Dylan had never seen one before, I needed to show her what it could do. "Trigger," I said, pointing at it.

"You just point this end at the person you want to see dead and squeeze this. And if you see a sentinel with purple eyes, don't fire. She's our friend."

"Our friend?" she spluttered. "Liana, what is going on?"

I ignored her question to focus on Lacey for a second, grabbing her shoulder to turn her over onto her side. She groaned loudly as I flipped her over, her eyelids fluttering.

"Liana?" she whispered, before giving a wet cough. "I don't feel so good."

"You don't look so good," I replied, unhooking her coveralls and pulling them down and her shirt up. She'd sealed up the wounds on her abdomen, but I could see dark bruises starting to form, deep purple against her skin, and knew she was bleeding internally. The bio-foam was great, but it didn't work unless it had direct access to the damaged area.

Lacey had sealed the entrance hole, but not the internal damage.

"And you're doing a lot worse," I told her gravely, grabbing the medical kit to see what I could do for her with the medicine inside. "You're bleeding internally. I gotta get you to a doctor, but the only one I know is Quess. We're going to go to the Citadel."

"Can't," Lacey panted, shaking her head. "We have to... Tony."

"Tony's gone," I told her, grabbing a vial and plugging it in to the pneumatic injector. "Sage took him. This is a painkiller, and it's going to make you feel a little better. Okay?"

She nodded, and I quickly pressed the injector against her abdomen, right next to the wound, and injected a dose. I did the same with her shoulder. I removed the vial and put in another one—one that held a medication that would slow a person's heartrate considerably, to slow down traumatic blood loss, if I remembered correctly—and injected that into her neck. I finished her drug cocktail with a mild stimulant, to keep her awake and lucid.

She gave a shuddering breath with the last one, her eyes widening and becoming more alert, and started to prop herself up on her elbows, but I held her firmly in place. "Try not to move so much. I didn't find any exit wounds, which means the bullets are still inside of you. You could damage yourself more."

"Fine," Lacey spat. "But we can't go to the Citadel. Not yet. We need to get Tony first."

I frowned as I pulled a medical scanner out and started running it over Dylan's leg, using the X-ray function to search for broken bones. Lacey clearly hadn't heard anything I just told her. "Lacey, I said—"

"No, *listen* to me," she hissed, reaching out to grab my forearm in a vice-like grip. "I didn't bring Tony with me. I brought a *transceiver*. We designed it so that when it was plugged in, it would trigger a wireless download. I planned to destroy it if anything went wrong, but then things went wrong in all the worst ways."

My eyes widened at what she was saying, and then terror caught me hard and fast, reminding me of something that I had almost forgotten. My net. Sage could be watching it right now! He would know I was alive, see what we were talking about, and—

I shut off my thoughts mid-stream and focused instead on what I needed: the laser cutter. "Liana?" Dylan said weakly. "What's—"

"Shut up," I ground out. "Both of you. My net is still in, and Sage has a way of monitoring it."

There was a pause, and then the two women fell silent while I dug the laser out of the first-aid kit. I quickly pushed my hair aside and pressed my fingers against the back of my neck, feeling for the incision point. It didn't scar, not exactly, but there was a hard ridge under the skin that showed where to cut. I felt for it with my fingers, and then spread the area flat between them, trying to give myself guidelines that I could use to cut blindly. I made sure the laser was set at the lowest setting, and then prayed that I didn't make too much of a mess when I made the incision.

I winced when I activated the laser, the back of my neck starting to sting, and carefully dragged it down, only shutting it off when I felt the tendrils of the net in my brain begin to retract. The sensation was disconcerting, but finished within seconds, and I quickly reached in with my fingertip to remove the hard chip that the net formed in its inactive state.

I released a breath I hadn't known I had been holding as I held it up to look at it, my fingers and the chip red with blood, reminding me that I was still bleeding. I set the net down and quickly squeezed some bio-foam out onto my fingers, then pressed them against the wound and smeared the pink goop inside. The wound closed, and I quickly wiped off the net and tucked it into my pocket. Even though I knew Sage could sense my thoughts on it, I might need it at some point, and hopefully if I kept it out for long enough, he would think I was dead and stop monitoring it. I turned to Lacey.

"Okay, what are you talking about?"

Lacey rolled her eyes and reached forward to grab my lapels. "Tony is in Cogstown! We still have time to get him! If we can keep him out of Sage's hands, we can—"

She started coughing suddenly, the coughs wet and hard, racking the poor woman's form. I struggled to hold her still, worried she would rip open the bio-foam, and then pulled a small packet of water from the first-aid kit, ripping the corner open and trickling some in between her lips. She nodded when her mouth was full, and I pulled it away and quickly took a swig myself, my tongue still dry.

I offered the bag to Dylan and concentrated on what Lacey was telling me. If Sage needed Tony for whatever he was planning, then we needed to get him before Sage could use the transceiver. But that likely meant heading to Cogstown, which was down, not up. It meant heading away from the Citadel, and away from my friends, who were currently being hunted by Sage's death squad. Power was off everywhere except for the Core, which meant the elevators weren't working, and neither were the doors. If I went down to Cogstown, I could get trapped below the Grounds, unable to get back up.

But if I didn't, I would be giving Sage everything he needed to achieve his plan.

"Liana," Dylan said, snapping me out of my dismal thoughts.

I blinked and glanced at the woman, only to find her pointing at something just over my shoulder. Shifting my angle, I looked up, past the raging fire of the Council Room, and saw something that gleamed silver and crimson climbing up the wall like an insect, a figure in white clinging to its back. A little lower down was a second something—only the person riding this one's back was dressed in a dark gray.

"Sadie and Sage," I growled, rising to my feet. "They're climbing..."

"They have to." Lacey coughed. "Don't you see? They have to get to the Core to plug the sentinels and Tony in. It will take them hours. Which means we have time to get Tony before they do."

"But not a lot of it," I murmured, recognizing the wisdom in what Lacey was saying, but also seeing the speed with which the sentinels could move. "Three or four hours at most."

"Five," Dylan said, and I looked at her for an explanation. She offered a half-shrug and a rueful smile. "Sorry, I thought we were taking bets, and I was shooting for optimism."

I stared at her for a long second, wondering how she could be making jokes at a time like this, but then Lacey chuckled and said, "Well, then call me the pessimist in our little trio, 'cause I'm giving us no more than two. Thank Scipio that Cogstown is just under here." She patted the floor next to her and offered her own weak smile.

I very much wanted to join in, but my stomach was twisting with worry, and I looked up, my eyes heading for the familiar dark arches of the Citadel, lit now only by the blue glow of the Core, my heart heavy and torn. "The others have no idea what's going on," I murmured. "If I don't get to them..."

"Get to who?" Dylan asked. "You are both speaking in riddles, and I have sat here quietly, trying to piece it together, but this isn't helpful."

"Sage released the legacies in the Citadel," I said, turning back to her and kneeling down. I picked up the scanner again and resumed looking for the break, finding it moments later, halfway down her calf. Both bones were broken clean in half. "He ordered them after Grey and the others but told them to kill any Knights that got in their way."

Dylan sucked in a deep breath as I retrieved a specialized cutter from the kit and began cutting her pants leg off. "But who is Tony?" she asked, wincing as I used the small laser to cut through the microfiber. I could tell she was nervous about me cutting her, but I kept the beam short, and worked quickly.

"An AI," Lacey said. "Part of one. It's complicated, but at one point, he and four others like him were put inside of Scipio to give him the best probability of survival. Sage—who is freaking Ezekial Pine, by the way—has been cutting them out one by one to try to kill Scipio."

Dylan's eyes widened, her jaw dropping practically to her chest. It was the one part of the story that I had kept from her, because I still hadn't been fully certain I could trust her with that knowledge. I had already given her a peek into how corrupted the system had become by exposing her to the truth of the legacies, but this information would change everything she knew to be true about the Tower. It would destroy her belief that Scipio was infallible. Dylan was definitely unique as a Tower citizen, but that didn't mean she could handle it.

And she had just seen how broken the system really was. Not only thanks to Lacey's words, but because of what had transpired in the Council Room.

I pulled out a sheet of bone regeneration packs and wrapped the gelatinous material around Dylan's leg, sealing the sheet under her and trying to decide what I should do, and knowing there was only one answer.

The effect of the pack was immediate. Dylan sucked in a deep breath, her head lolling back in relief as the pain was alleviated. The medicine in the gel was already working on setting her bone, and she'd be able to walk within a matter of minutes. The bone would still be broken and the area tender, but it would be fully healed in twenty-four hours.

I quickly repacked the bag, placed the strap over my shoulder, and stood up, looking down at both of them. "Lacey's right. We need to go after Tony first," I said, the words thick in my mouth. I wasn't even sure when I had made the decision—sometime while Lacey was talking, I supposed—but I knew I had to do it. It might not stop Sage, but it would certainly slow him down.

Besides, my friends could take care of themselves.

At least, I hoped they could.

"Cool," Dylan said, flashing me a thumbs-up. "Also, your purple-eyed sentinel is here."

I turned to see a sentinel standing a few feet away, its hands awkwardly clasped together in front of it. Seeing her purple, glowing eyes was almost overwhelming, bringing memories of my mother's death to my mind, but I pushed that down. Rose was better now, her code fixed by Leo and Jasper, so I doubted she would revert again to Jang-Mi—her human counterpart who had been obsessed with the loss of her daughter. My reaction was just a visceral response to seeing her in that form again. Not a rational one.

"Excellent," I said. "You okay, Rose?"

"Perfectly fine," she said with a nod. "And I have been listening for the past two minutes. I am glad that you decided to go after Tony. CEO Green, can I help you?"

Lacey stared at the sentinel for several seconds and then nodded slowly, fear making her dark eyes almost black. "Yeah. Sure."

Rose looked at me, and I rolled my eyes. "Pick her up. Dylan, you good to walk?"

"All good," she said, and I turned to see her giving another thumbs-up before slowly climbing to her feet. Rose moved around me to come to Lacey's aid, and I held my breath, trying not to look nervous as the sentinel carefully scooped the woman up into her arms.

She handled her delicately, much to my relief, but it was still odd to see a creature built for death being so gentle.

"Right," I said, once Rose was standing again. "Best way to get down, Lacey?"

"That way," she said weakly, pointing to the southwest corner of the Tower. "Access shaft that leads to the shell, a few bulkheads away from a Cogstown entrance. This level should have some emergency power left, enough to open the shaft. After that, we're on our own."

I nodded and took the gun back from Dylan when she handed it to me. "Then let's get going," I replied.

6

We made our way as quickly as we could across the Grounds, but it was hard. With the lights off, navigation that would've once taken us minutes dragged out as we checked and re-checked our position, lest we get lost on one of the twisting paths through the forest. Then there were the noises. Once we were far enough from the roar of the fire, I started to hear shouts and cries of panic echoing through the darkness, periodically punctuated by shrill screams that made us jump or come to a sudden stop, searching the darkness. I knew that I was listening to the sounds of people dying—during the last Requiem Day, nearly 4 percent of the population had died by stumbling to their deaths in the darkness—and tried to block the thought from my mind to keep us moving.

It was a relief when we reached the access hatch, as I felt exposed and vulnerable on this level. I quickly followed Lacey's rasping instructions to open the panel in the floor, and then slid into the hole first, ignoring Dylan's harsh whisper asking me not to. I had a pretty bad track record when it came to going into rooms first, and it was now a rule among my friends that I wasn't allowed to. But this time, I had to: Dylan's leg was broken, which meant she was favoring that side while

CHAPTER 6

she moved, making it difficult for her to fight, and Rose was holding Lacey. I was the only one who was fully capable.

I swung onto the ladder and began heading down, stopping after several feet to pull a hand light from my pocket and turn it on. I hadn't wanted to use it above, as I knew it would serve as a beacon to the sentinels climbing the walls of the Tower, and alert Sage that someone had survived. It was possible that Alice had been able to update Sage about us stopping her before Rose took out her sentinel, but if there was even a *chance* that he thought I was dead, I wanted him to keep thinking it.

I slid my arm through the rung of the ladder, hooking it in the crook of my elbow, and then quickly fixed the hand light to my temple, using the adjustable strap to tighten it. I clicked it on and checked down the shaft, revealing the exit hatch thirty feet below, then resumed my descent, moving quickly. There was a digital keypad still glowing at the bottom, likely drawing power from the Grounds above, and I quickly keyed in the code that Lacey recited to me.

The hatch slid open, and I froze as a piercing scream forced its way out, the sound feminine and filled with terror. I covered my light and held still for several seconds, trying to gauge how close it was when it suddenly cut off.

But it was far from quiet. Disembodied voices seemed to flood the tight space, taut and sharp with panic. They wafted up into the shaft, distant enough that I couldn't make out the words. I took that as a sign that they were relatively far away and took a deep breath before lowering myself enough to peer into the hall, letting some of the light shine out through my fingers. Nothing moved, and I dropped down, landing heavily on my feet, and checked the rest of it, making sure it was empty.

"It's clear," I whispered, moving to one side to give Dylan some space to exit.

I was taking a few careful steps down the hall, heading for the T-intersection up ahead to check to see if it was clear, when another sharp scream sounded, shriller and higher. A child.

"What is going on?" Dylan asked, her voice tight with fear. "What is that? Is it a kid?"

"Shush," I said, holding up a hand behind me and approaching the cross-section. We were in a section of the shell, just a few junctions away from a door that would lead us to Cogstown, but the people who had been trapped inside when the power went out were panicking as they discovered the power outage wasn't just sectional. It was exactly what had happened on Requiem Day almost a hundred and fifty years ago, when Scipio had gone down for three days. Thousands of people had died during that time, and many of them had died because they were freaking out.

But something told me this was more than that. Ever since Requiem Day, departments had taken time to train people extensively for what to do in case it happened again. It was too early for this level of panic—or at least it should've been. They should've been reporting to whatever rendezvous spot their department had designated in case of an emergency, and then letting the highest-ranking member of their department figure out what to do next. Not panicking. A few more steps led me to the mouth of the hall. Dimming the light and turning it to the side so it wasn't giving me away in the darkness, I took a quick glimpse around the wall, ducking back when a series of moving lights raced through an adjacent corridor, giving me glimpses of faces and uniforms as people streamed past.

"This way!" someone shouted, and the steps quickened, moving away.

I moved back toward the shaft, just as Rose slowly lowered her robotic body down one-handed, holding Lacey firmly against her chest with one arm. "Something's going on," I told her grimly. "People who were inside the shell when Sage cut the power are freaking out."

"It's Requiem Day," Lacey muttered. "Of course they're freaking out."

"Not like this," I said insistently. "All the departments do Requiem Day training and preparation, but people are panicking. It's too soon for that, so until we know why they are, I think we should do everything we can to avoid them."

"Don't be ridiculous," Lacey groused. "Most of the people in the shell here will be Cogs. No worker in my department would turn against me."

"Even if Sage ordered Scipio to send out a message blaming the two of us for this problem?" I shot back hotly. I didn't mean to get angry. It was sometimes difficult to remember that few people had studied Requiem Day as much as I had. I knew from the records how awful humans could become when you threw them into darkness and uncertainty, and I knew how committed most of the people were to Scipio. Sage could use those things to turn every individual in the Tower against us, Lacey's assertions be damned.

Lacey's mouth tightened in a grimace, telling me that she had gotten my point, and she pointed a finger down the hall. "Straight and then left," she whispered. "Take the third hall on the right and follow it all the way down. It'll get us to one of the Cogstown doors."

I nodded and began to move, keeping to one side of the corridor and dimming the light on my head. I checked to the right, where people had been racing by moments ago, only to find it empty, and quickly seized the opportunity to move to the left.

I walked quickly, trying not to tense at all the noises I heard— which I knew were being amplified by the halls themselves—but it was hard. In the dark, sounds have a way of making you believe that the person or thing making them is standing right behind you, mere inches away. I had no idea what would happen once we encountered people, but I knew from history that we could be attacked to have our possessions stolen. It had been a common occurrence during Requiem Day.

I slowed at the first hall, giving it a cursory glance to make sure there wasn't anyone there, and then darted across it, waving for the others to follow before I headed toward the next shadowed opening.

I stopped a few feet away when I heard a voice coming from it, and then closed the distance to the edge and peered down it.

Several lights illuminated a group of men and one woman, all wearing blue uniforms. Divers from Water Treatment. One of them was kneeling on the ground, a wrench in his hand, while the others huddled around him.

"Anything?" the woman hissed, her arms wrapping tightly around her abdomen.

The man kneeling cocked his head and moved closer to the wall. I noticed a moment later that there was a gray pipe running along the halls here, and realized they were trying to communicate with members of their department. It was a Diver trick that my best friend Zoe had taught me about.

"Nothing," he said after a moment, standing up. "Let's try the south side. C'mon."

He waved for his people to follow, and then began leading them down the hall—away from us, thankfully. I waited a few seconds until everyone had their backs to us, and then slipped by the entrance to the hall, moving away. I paused to make sure that Rose, Dylan, and Lacey were still behind me, and then moved up to the third hall and peeked around the edge.

Thankfully, it was clear for as far as my light could reach. However, according to Lacey's instructions, we had to go all the way until it ended, and I was betting there were a lot of side halls that branched off from it.

"Are you sure this is the best route?" I whispered, intending my question for Lacey. "It's long, and chances are good that people are going to be passing through. We should find—"

"Oh, for crying out loud," Lacey croaked. "I am literally dying, and you want to waste time arguing about our path? How's this for a path? Rose, get me to that door as quick as possible. At least before I die."

Rose's purple eyes flickered in a way that I recognized as an eye blink, and she looked up at me, cocking her head quizzically. "I am unsure whether I should do what she asks or not, but my sensors are telling me that her blood pressure is dropping steadily. If we don't get her help soon, she will—"

"She's right," I said, trying not to feel angry about it. It was her life on the line, and I needed to remember that. I was just feeling the pressure. "You're right," I repeated for her edification. If I kept trying to avoid people, it was going to take us forever to reach Tony, and we had less than two hours to get to him. Lacey still hadn't told us where she was keeping him, and if I kept us moving this slowly, Sage would activate the transceiver, and have almost everything he needed—save for the secret protocols Leo had hidden in his code.

Once he had him, he would kill Scipio and replace him with Kurt, and then who knew what the hell would happen. We had to keep as much as we could out of his hands, if only to slow things down.

"Lead on," I told Rose, trying not to feel exhausted.

The sentinel ducked its head and moved past me, disappearing around the corner. I looked at Dylan, who was resting against the wall on one side, and then sighed. "You okay?"

"Great," she panted. "Just peachy keen. Let's keep moving."

I could tell her leg was still bothering her, despite the patch, and regretted forcing her to put any weight on it, but there was nothing else I could do but pat her on the shoulder and then turn and head after Rose.

Rose was moving efficiently down the hall, pausing at each junction to make sure it was clear before going past it. I kept an eye on the hall ahead by walking down the left side, so I could see around the sentinel, while Dylan walked down on the right.

Have you ever stared at a point in the darkness for so long that you become convinced that you're seeing light, like it's coming in from the end of a very long and dark hole, from a distance that would have to be miles away? After several minutes of walking, I did.

I fixated on it for several seconds, convinced I was hallucinating. And then a shadow passed it, and another, long lines of them sending the hall into alternating waves of darkness. Instinctively, I drew to a stop, every neuron in my body telling me that running into people during a Requiem Day-level event was dangerous and stupid, but Rose didn't so much as pause as she headed for the light.

"Liana," Dylan whispered harshly, and I blinked and saw her a few feet past me, the confusion on her face put there by my sudden stop.

I stared at her for a few seconds, unable to put my disquiet into words, and then just sighed and started moving again, pulling the gun out of my belt and clicking the safety off. I didn't want to have to shoot anyone, but if the crowd grew angry, I could fire it in the air to scatter them.

I only prayed it wouldn't come to that.

7

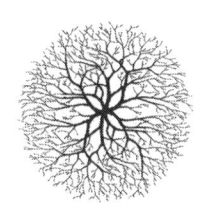

Within a couple of minutes, having a four-hundred-and-fifty-pound sentinel as the vanguard to our little group turned out to be a problem.

"Scipio help us, it's one of those *things*!" a panicked voice shouted, cutting through the buzz of the crowd.

A few startled shouts rose up in alarm, and I heard what could only be described as the pre-panic stage: that moment right before people would either flee in terror or erupt in violence against us. Rose halted mid-step in response to it, and I seized the opportunity to dart past her and slip into a hall lit by several hand-held lights, holding both hands high in the air.

"It's okay," I told them in a steady voice. "The sentinel is not here to hurt anyone. It's helping me carry Engineer Green back to Cogstown."

There was a pause from the twenty or thirty people gathered in the hall, and then a tall, muscular man from the back started to push forward. He was bald—though that looked to be by choice rather than a hereditary issue—and sported a black goatee around his mouth. As he came through the crowd, I realized he was wearing the orange of the Cogs. One of Lacey's people. Most of the men and women were, but there were a handful of blue-clad Divers, one or two Farmers, who I was guessing had been escorting the Divers and Cogs to whatever area needed repairing (as most shell issues were related directly to the Farming Department), and one Medic. I didn't see any Knights in the group, but then again, there wouldn't be any. They would be trying to disperse groups like this one, right now.

"What's going on?" he demanded, and I had to resist the urge to grab my baton at the hostility in his voice. "The power's been out for thirty minutes, but none of the emergency systems have kicked on. We can't get through the doors."

I stared at him for a moment, uncertain how much I should actually tell him, and then realized that he and the others had a right to know what was happening. Sooner or later, they were going to be fed one story or another, and if Sage wound up beating me, I wanted to give as many people the truth as possible, so that they could figure out how to stop him.

"Marcus Sage and Sadie Monroe have taken control of Scipio and initialized another Requiem Day in an attempt to kill him."

"What?" he gasped, taking a step back. His shock was echoed by the crowd behind him, as men and women burst into furious whispers. He glanced over his shoulder, taking stock of the group, and then turned back to me, suspicion on his face. "That's not possible."

"I can understand why you want to believe that," I said slowly, knowing full well that if I didn't convince this group I was telling the truth, they would turn on me for even insinuating there was anything wrong with Scipio. "And believe me, I wish it weren't true, but it is."

"Scipio is all-knowing!" someone in the crowd shouted. "He would've detected the psychological contamination of anyone who would do him harm and punished them! You're lying."

I tried to locate the source of the voice, but whoever was speaking was buried too far in the crowd for me to pinpoint him. Not that it mattered, since as soon as he was done, several people nodded in agreement, all while watching me to see what my reaction would be.

"I'm sure you will hear that many times about me today," I said. "And believe me, I know a thing or two about lying. But I am the

Champion of the Citadel, Scipio's human defender. It's my job—my duty—to protect him from those who would do him harm. I wouldn't lie about something as serious as this, especially when there is every chance I am going to die trying to save him. Sage has been planning this for years." I paused and reconsidered what I was going to say next. I might be able to get them to believe this story, but not if I told them he was actually Ezekial Pine. It was just too far-fetched. "His ancestors started it, but he is going to try to finish it today. The last Requiem Day was their first attempt to kill Scipio, and though he failed, he now has almost everything he needs to succeed! If I'm going to have any chance of stopping him, I need to get into Cogstown. If you think I'm lying, then you are free to go wherever you want to and see if this gets sorted out. If you believe me, and you're willing to help, I need you to open this door."

The man and the crowd were silent for several seconds, and then I saw the young girl in Medica white whisper, "Honorbound," in a reverent voice that made me distinctly uncomfortable. I could hear a few wordless sounds of agreement but had no idea whether I had managed to sway them or not. Then again, they weren't the ones I really had to sway; it was the man who had appointed himself their leader. The man who was staring at me with eyes that I couldn't quite read. I met his gaze with my own, silently praying that he would believe me, but ready, just in case he didn't.

Still, when he finally gave me a nod, it was hard not to exhale in relief. "That's what we've been trying to do, but we can't figure it out," he said, taking a step forward. "We should be able to override the door manually, but the door into Cogstown still has power, so it won't open."

Lacey coughed wetly, and I turned to see Rose taking a tentative step out of the hall, cradling the head of the department. "I might be able to do something about that, if I can have access to some of your tools, and a spare set of hands."

"Of course," he said, but a frown marred his face. "But maybe we should let the Medic take a look at you. You don't look well."

"Bah," Lacey said, waving a hand in front of her face. "This is nothing. You should've been there when I got my leg trapped in one of the vents to an intercooling exchange chamber. Damn thing had snapped both bones and was threatening to cut off my entire foot, and I had only a minute before the chamber started to fill with liquid nitrogen and argon. Go ahead and put me down there, dear."

The last part was directed at Rose, who obediently lumbered over to the bulkhead door to set her down. I could immediately see what the Cog had been talking about. They had manually pried open the first door and were holding it open using an expandable brace. But the second door—the one on the Cogstown side—was closed, and on the interior, there were clusters of complex internal circuitry the likes of which I had never seen before, glowing red to show that it was locked and still had power. But although *it* had power, the control panels on *this* side, which would normally be used to access that door, were inoperative, thanks to the power drain. That meant interfacing directly with the system to get access to it was impossible. They had to try to unlock the door using the circuits themselves, which was normally a job reserved for IT.

Rose sat Lacey down as gently as she was able to, but even still, Lacey's face was tight with pain when the sentinel gingerly moved away, taking care not to draw too near to the frightened people. I was proud of her, for some inordinate reason. She was being careful to make herself as nonthreatening as possible, from the slowness of her movements to the way she kept looking down at the floor, and I made a mental note to praise her about it later. After I got Lacey to see common sense.

I turned to the girl in Medica white, pulled the first-aid kit off my shoulder, and held it out to her. "Look her over while she's working," I said. "Ignore her if she tries to argue. I know she's scary, but she's also stupid when it comes to her personal health, so don't listen to her."

The girl blinked a pair of wide eyes at me, and then shook her head nervously. "I-I-I can't," she stammered. "I'm just an intern! I was on my way down to a Medic station in Cogstown to shadow an instructor, and—"

"First, second, or third year?" I interrupted, asking her in a rather impatient way to figure out where exactly she was in her education.

"Third," she said tentatively, wringing her hands. "But only for a month! I don't know—"

"By second year you've had an introduction to how to stabilize people with traumatic internal injuries," I informed her, hating that I had to. My knowledge of the Medica came from inter-departmental classes I had taken back when it had been important to try to show Scipio what a good little citizen of the Tower I was, and while I knew some things from those lessons, I knew she knew a lot more. What she was lacking was confidence, and I didn't have time to give it to her.

"Yes, but—"

"No buts," I interrupted, taking a step toward her. I started to say her name, but realized that I didn't even know it, so I said, "Look, what's your name?"

"Me?" she squeaked. "Anna, but—"

"Listen, Anna," I said. "You are the only one here who has had even two years of medical training. I have done the best I can, but it's not enough. You might not be able to fix her, but you might be able to keep her from getting worse, and that's something. So please, try. I know you're scared, but it isn't about you. It's about her. Try to remember that."

I pushed the bag into her hands as I spoke, but held it for a second, trying to squeeze a little strength through it and into her, hoping that it would in some way give her the confidence she needed. Her eyes searched mine for several seconds, the vulnerability and fear on her face naked and raw, but somehow, she managed to push it back, and gave me a shaky nod.

"I'll do my best," she whispered.

"That's all I ask," I said, stepping out of her way so she could get to Lacey.

Lacey already had a cable hooked up to the door and was doing something that I didn't fully understand with a device I didn't recognize in her hand. She paused when the girl knelt down next to her. She handed the tool off to someone else and allowed the girl to work.

Relieved that Lacey was letting Anna help her, I turned away and looked at the man. "What's your name?"

"Cyril," he said. "Cyril Jones. What happened to Engineer Green?"

"Worry about that later. Why have we heard so many people screaming in the shell?" I asked. "I know that panic is common when something goes wrong, but this quickly?"

Cyril was immediately shaking his head, his mouth twisting downward in a nervous frown. "We don't know," he said hastily. "We keep running into groups of people who are trying to keep away from something, but they can't seem to tell us what it is. Though they all have similar stories of hearing groups near them and making their way toward them, only to be chased away seconds later by screaming and what they say sounded like... something tearing the people apart. I haven't run into anyone who stuck around to investigate, but it could be that anyone who does..."

He trailed off, but he didn't need to go any further. The insinuation was clear: whatever was attacking the others was killing anyone who tried to interfere.

I wasn't sure why, but Alice immediately sprang to mind. Alice and her sentinel body. Sage had three for sure, but what if he somehow had more? More than just three or ten or fifteen... What if, when the Knights had agreed to destroy the bulk of them, he had managed to hide them away instead?

But why use them to kill the people in the shell? Was it just because he didn't want anyone outside their departments? Was he afraid they were in a better position to stop him than those who were inside? Or was it something else?

I wasn't sure, and I didn't want to stick around to find out. But if the people were running from something and had all congregated here, then it stood to reason that whatever was chasing them would be following.

"We need to set up lookouts in the adjacent halls," I told Cyril, taking a step around him to look down the hall leading to the door. Just like with the others, there were several points where this one intersected with other halls, as well as a stairwell that ran between levels. "Can we send people out to monitor the halls every two junctions away from us? Do we have enough people for that?"

CHAPTER 7

Cyril frowned and looked over the small group, seeming to count it over in his head. "Yes," he said after a moment. "But to what end? We don't know what we're looking for."

"You're watching for her," I said, pointing at Rose. She darted a quick glance up at me, her purple eyes lightening some in surprise. "Well, not her, exactly," I said. "The ones we need to be afraid of have yellow eyes. If anyone sees them, they should get back here as soon as possible to tell us that they are coming."

Cyril took a deep breath, and then nodded. "I'll get it set up, Champion. Just, please, do whatever you can to get that door open. I don't want to be trapped here if any more of those things come calling."

"Me neither," I told him honestly.

He nodded and then moved off to put people into groups. I stood watching him for a second, and then turned to head back to Lacey, pausing when I saw Dylan watching me from the hall we had just exited, leaning against the wall.

"You handled that quite well, Champion," she said with an approving smile. "And you were worried."

I gave a half-hearted chuckle, and her smile broadened. "See? There's a smile. Could that be some optimism?"

"Unlikely," I said dryly, though my smile had grown under her teasing. It felt wrong to smile, given that even now, my friends could be getting killed by Sage's psychotic family, Jasper had been taken by Sage, and we were heading in the wrong direction for me to do anything to fix either problem. It suddenly made me wonder how Dylan was able to do it, despite having her leg broken and being halfway strangled to death. "How are you able to be optimistic at a time like this?" I asked, unable to keep it in.

She cocked her head at me, smiled, and said, "Because I'm alive, Liana. And I know that as long as I'm alive, I'm going to fight to my dying breath to help stop this. And that's enough for me."

I stared at her for a long moment, and then nodded. Maybe it could be enough for me, too—if I let it.

At least, that was what I resolved to try as I moved over to the door to see what I could do to help Lacey.

8

I resisted the urge to abandon my place against the wall to pace the tight confines of the hall, but it was difficult not to chaff at how much time we had lost to the door. Lacey had spent the last twenty minutes trying to redirect power from the Cogstown side to the controls on this side, and thus far had made little to no progress, other than to exile me to this spot after I had tried to help, when I became, quote, "too much to deal with." I was the fifth in a long line of assistants and had determined that Lacey was just better off doing it on her own. No one could do anything right under her watchful eyes, and it had prompted her to take command, no matter what objections were raised.

I tried not to let out an irritated breath as she began to talk to the door again, moving the slim pen that helped redirect threads of power over the glowing red lights. "All right, buddy," she gasped. "Not to rush you, but I'm getting a little tired of this door being closed. So why don't you just do Ms. Lacey a favor and open it up for me." Beside her, Anna made a displeased murmur of protest, trying to get Lacey to put the instrument down and let her work, but Lacey ignored her.

It was more than I could stand, and given that it had been my irritation at Lacey's refusal to let me help her—in order to let Anna work—

CHAPTER 8

that had caused her to send me out here in the first place, I stood up and moved away, not wanting to start another fight. I walked down the hall, pausing to chat with the lookouts Cyril had stationed there and making sure that they still had line of sight on the others, who were spread farther out into the adjacent junctions, before moving down the hall, aiming for the big man himself.

He was at the second position down, nearly a hundred feet from Lacey and the door, keeping a steady eye on the lights in either hall. "How's it going?" I asked softly.

His dark eyes flicked to mine and then back to the hall. "It would be going better if I knew Lacey was making progress with that door. Anything?"

I shook my head, trying not to show my own worry and agitation that it was taking so long for her to get it open. "Can we cut through?" I asked. "Surely a cutter could open up the bulkhead. It's not ideal, but—"

"We treat the walls with a special sealant that makes it impossible to cut them. It's to avoid structural damage should any of the machinery suffer a catastrophic explosion, and it makes it impossible for the cutters to cut through the walls. There are specific areas that are left untreated, and I was just about to lead everyone there when you showed up. Maybe we should start pulling people back, and—"

"Excuse me, Champion?"

I looked over to see Anna standing behind me, nervously tucking some hair behind her ear. Her brown eyes flicked to Cyril and then to me, and she cleared her throat. "I'm sorry to interrupt, but it's about Engineer Green. She needs blood, which means I need to know if anyone here is a universal donor, or B negative or positive, so I can administer a transfusion."

I stared at her for a moment, and then shook my head. "I'm neither," I told her. "Cyril?"

"A negative," he replied grimly. "Frank, Zeke?"

"AB positive," one of them replied. The other one simply shook his head.

I looked at Anna. "We'll ask around. In the meantime, can you tell me how she's doing?"

"She's going to die," Anna said solemnly. "She needs surgery. She has a metal fragment lodged dangerously close to her spine, and I think she's going to lose her kidney and her spleen, but I'm not entirely certain. I'd feel much better with an experienced doctor."

"You're doing fine," I reassured her, but inside, I felt very much the same way she did. Lacey was growing weaker by the minute and would pass out soon due to blood loss. If we didn't do something to stop the bleeding, she would die.

And as much as she pissed me off, I didn't want her to. Not just because I still needed her to tell me where Tony was, but because she could mobilize her Cogs into a veritable defense force and work to keep the power being generated in Cogstown from going to the Core—and hopefully keep Sage's plans from becoming reality.

That, and as far as human beings went, she wasn't awful. Sure, she had blackmailed me and my friends and thrown us all into danger, but she had done it with the good of the Tower at heart, so I supposed I could forgive that.

Then again, I felt like I could forgive a lot of things if I got through this alive.

"You're her only hope," I told her softly. "And I know that you *can* do it. And we'll make sure you don't do it alone, okay?"

Anna nodded and expelled a slow breath. "Thank you," she said. "And... I'll do my best. Should I go down one of the halls to ask about the blood?"

I exchanged looks with Cyril, and then nodded. "Go ahead and check with the lookouts in the left one. I'll take the right. And Cyril? Do you mind taking the farther position and asking around?"

He nodded. "I'm on it. Have one of the workers tap twice on the large pipe running down the center of the ceiling if you find someone first, so I can send a replacement for him."

I flashed him a thumbs-up and then moved down the hall, heading for the two lone lights glittering in the distance. Even though they looked far away, I only walked fifty feet before I hit them. It was a man

CHAPTER 8

and a woman, both Divers from Water Treatment. They glanced over their shoulders from the halls they were directing their lights down, giving me a curious look.

"Are either of you a universal donor, or B negative?" I asked. At their perplexed looks, I added, "Engineer Green needs a blood transfusion."

The woman glanced at her counterpart, and then back to me. "I'm B negative," she replied, and I expelled a breath of relief. That had been easier than I'd thought it would be.

"Excellent," I replied. "If you don't mind tapping twice on the pipe to let Cyril know, I'll wait here with your friend and—"

The woman suddenly held up her hand, her eyebrows furrowing as her eyes got distant. She cocked her head slightly, and a moment later, I heard it: an erratic pattern being beaten out somewhere against the pipe.

"Something's coming," she whispered a moment later. "Eastern hall. Reports seeing... a crowd of people racing toward them, being pursued by six small golden lights in the distance, approaching rapidly."

I turned around, looking back the way I had come. The eastern halls were on the other side of the main one. The one that led toward the door where Lacey was. "Fall back," I told them. "Order everyone to the center—"

"More spotted on this side," the man interrupted a second later, and I glanced over my shoulder to see him peering farther down the hall, his hand trembling. "Coming down all three adjacent hallways."

Fear clenched my gut as I realized that Alice had us surrounded, and was closing in, and I slowly let a breath out against it, focusing on something productive. "Fall back," I repeated. "Get to the door, now. Tell everyone."

The two nodded and began tapping against the pipes using wrenches they produced from pockets in their suits. I didn't stick around to watch them. I was already turning back to head to the door, needing to appraise Lacey of the situation.

I emerged from the hall seconds before Anna emerged from the opposite side, her cheeks flushed red with fear and exertion. "The man down the hall told me to run," she hastily explained. "What's going on?"

"The sentinels are coming," I told her grimly. "C'mon, we need to get to Lacey."

She nodded, mustering up a brave face in spite of how shaken she was, and we made our way up the hall toward the doors. We were halfway there when the first scream started. It was cut short before I could even turn around, but a second scream followed it. I heard several more screams and shouts go up and realized that everything was about to erupt into chaos. We needed to be close to the door when Lacey got it open so that we could make sure Lacey and the rest of the people got through safely.

I grabbed Anna's wrist and began to pull her away, moving toward the next ring of lights at a brisk walk that turned into a light jog as soon as she matched my speed. Within seconds, we were running down the hall, led only by the bright lights ahead. We reached them just as the sound of running feet began to echo loudly through the halls, drowning our own out, and I came to an abrupt stop in front of Lacey.

"Tell me that you are two seconds from opening it," I practically begged.

Lacey's face was even paler than before, but the look in her eyes was one of fierce determination. "I take it we have guests?"

I glanced back down the hall and saw that the few lights from before had already doubled, and that the beams were jerking back and forth across the walls—which told me they were running.

"Yes," I said. "And people are starting to panic. So please tell me you got the door!"

"Of course I have the door. The door likes me! It's my friggin' friend, through thick and thin!"

I looked over at Anna, who gave me a little shrug, and then glanced at Dylan and Rose.

"She's been talking like that since Anna left," Dylan said quietly.

"She was talking like that before I left," I muttered, looking back at Lacey, gravely concerned about how the blood loss was starting to affect her. "Lacey, listen. The sentinels are coming, and you haven't told anyone exactly what you are trying to do, and now you're babbling. What do you need us to do to get the door open?"

"I need you to shut up for just one... damn... second," she grated out, her arm stretching up to run the pen over a vertical circuit and then drag it back down toward a central node. "I've almost..."

The pen hit the central node and erupted in a spray of sparks. Lacey snatched her hand back, even as Anna threw herself over the woman, shielding her from the spray. The lights in the door flickered, and then turned a deep orange, before sliding to one side.

A blond woman wearing the orange coveralls of her department stood on the other side, and took a step back, her eyes widening in surprise as she took us all in. Her eyes leapt from one of us to another before finally settling on Lacey. "Engineer Green!" she said. "What's going on? We haven't been able to get the doors to open!"

"Power's out in the shell," Lacey croaked, motioning for Anna to help her up. "But still on in Cogstown. That locks the doors up to prevent them from being overridden by the Knights or anyone else trying to attack the department. A little design feature we had installed after the last Requiem Day, heh. But it's a bitch and a half when you're stuck on the outside, trying to get in. Now..." She paused as Rose moved in to scoop her up, clutching her side and giving a weak cry of pain. "I think I'm ready to lie down."

"Less talking, more running!" I shouted, feeling like everyone was ignoring the oncoming wave of panicked humans behind us. "Rose, you get Lacey and Anna to a room, and then find Lacey a blood donor. Anna will explain what I mean. You, Cog girl—"

The woman pointed at herself, and when I nodded, she offered a tentative, "Neela."

"Neela, people are going to be coming through here quickly. You need to keep them moving so the hall doesn't jam up, and then be ready to seal the door. Tell me you can do that."

Neela nodded and moved out of the way, speaking to some people just out of view from where I was standing. I ignored it for now and turned to Dylan. "You too," I said, pointing to the doorway. "I'll stay to help get people through, and—"

I stopped when the first person finally reached us, rudely moving between us to go through the door. Dylan and I exchanged looks, and then the first wave of people was on us.

"What's going on?" I shouted as they began to push through, frantically making their way toward the door.

"Two people are dead!" a woman—who I recognized as Lacey's volunteer blood donor—shouted as the crowd grew thicker, and more compact, slowing down due to people pressing to be first.

"Slow down," I ordered them, shoving my hand in between bodies to prevent them from pushing farther forward and jamming things up. "Don't panic! If you slow down and maintain patience, this can move quickly."

"THEY'RE AT THE NEXT JUNCTION!" a voice in the crowd shouted, and everyone erupted into pandemonium. I was pushed back by a shoulder and slammed into a wall, losing all sight of Dylan as a throng of people hit the opening—more than I could possibly imagine. All of them were fighting for a position in the front, screaming and jostling, eyes wide with fear and panic at whatever was coming from the hall behind them.

Out of desperation to see what was coming, I threw a lash line overhead and used my harness to reel myself up so that I had a view over the tops of the heads of the crowd. Most people carried lights of some sort, but they were all pointing them forward rather than back and weren't holding them still at all. Still, the crowd of people—which had doubled, if not tripled—was casting enough light collectively that I could see several feet behind them in the hall, where more and more people were racing to join us.

Then one man who had just entered the light gave a surprised scream and was violently ripped off his feet and thrown backward, his hoarse shout of alarm being cut off with a harsh thud.

People screamed as a sentinel stepped into the light, the golden eyes glowing like twin suns. "Citizens of the Tower," Alice said. "Scipio is being attacked by dissidents. We are here to remove them from your ranks. Fear not, for if you have served Scipio well, you will not be harmed." And then she reached into the crowd, grabbed a screaming woman in Diver's blue, with short auburn hair, and lifted her up in the air. "You have been deemed a dissident," she reported, wrapping her other hand around the woman's jaw. "You will now be purged."

Alice jerked her hand to one side, taking the woman's head with it, and a sickening snap silenced the woman's panicked cries.

9

Several heartbeats of stunned silence greeted Alice's casual brutality, but that silence was broken when she lazily dropped the body to one side and began to reach into the crowd again.

"RUN!" I shouted, unable to watch as the crowd stood frozen in terror. I pulled out my gun and fired a round at Alice to punctuate my command, and just like that, the pandemonium began. The shot hit her in the head, and she staggered back, one hand reaching up to grasp the side of her face.

A woman screamed, but the sound was lost quickly as the entire crowd began to cry out in panic, viciously clawing their way toward the door. I saw several people halfway back break off from the bulk of the crowd to dart down the side halls, but seconds later, they were thrown back in by sentinels emerging from the side.

"Do not panic," they announced in one united voice, which could barely be heard over the panicked cries. "If you are a true servant of Scipio, you will be safe."

Within moments, they were diving into the crowd, seemingly picking people up at random, and then killing them in the most grotesque fashions. I hung, transfixed and horrified as I watched them pull men apart, sending blood and viscera spraying into the air, spattering the crowd with the remains of what had just been one of their comrades, and practically fold others in half. A man in the back of the crowd slipped in the blood as he tried to get away, and I watched one of the golden-eyed, blood-soaked monsters reach down and pluck him into the air.

He screamed, his legs kicking wildly, and I recognized him as Dalton, the Engineer whose rank-obsessed idiocy had almost gotten him killed outside the Tower when I was a lowly Squire. I probably wouldn't have remembered him, but everything about that day was burned into my memory, as it was the day I met Grey. It seemed a lifetime since I had seen Dalton, and while I had wished more than my fair share of ill will upon him at the time, I had never wanted anything like this to happen to him—to anyone. It was too horrible.

I was starting to look away, to disconnect my lines, when the sentinel holding him flipped him over, gave him a cursory glance, and then set him down roughly on his feet. "You are free to go, citizen," she said, finally using only one voice. "Please remain here until we have finished, and we will guide you from the shell back to your department."

Dalton remained stock still as the sentinel stepped past him, moving toward the final few people trying to escape through the door. Moving toward me.

I suddenly realized how close they were getting to me, to Dylan, and I quickly twisted around, scanning for Dylan's crimson uniform in the crowd. I spotted her trying to fight the tide pushing through the door and waving at me, and I disconnected the line, intent on making for her and getting through the door. As much as I wanted to stay and fight them—stop them—I knew that there were too many for me to handle. Not to mention, if they saw me, they would alert Sage that I was still alive. That was the last thing I wanted.

I landed heavily on my boots and then plunged into the group of people shoving their way through the door. "MOVE!" I roared, shoving the people in front of me low in their backs, stabilizing them even as I urged them forward. I realized instantly that it was a mistake to try to get to Dylan; there was only one way the crowd was going to let me go, and that was forward. The heavy steps of metal feet on the corrugated flooring filled the hall over the sound of panicked crying, and I grunted as the press of bodies grew even tighter, the crowd becoming a mass of nothing but torsos, elbows, knees, and feet. If I went down, I would be trampled to death by the others in their panic to escape.

But I kept upright, pushing out with every ounce of strength I possessed to keep from getting overwhelmed, and nearly tripped over the lip of the door, my toe catching on it. I grabbed a fistful of somebody's uniform to keep from falling, but I was already getting pushed farther down. I reached out with my other hand, seeking something that would help me reestablish balance, and found a strong hand instead. It wrapped around my forearm and hauled me up and forward.

I gasped as my rescuer and I suddenly stumbled free of the crowd, the numbers thinning out once we were past the threshold, thanks to the Cogs directing traffic. Glancing up, I was a little bewildered to see that it was Dylan who had saved me, and then was instantly relieved to see that she was all right. And, oh yeah, she had saved my life.

"Thanks," I gasped.

She nodded, but her pale face was angled toward the door. I turned to see that the sentinels were closing the distance, and even though they were being slowed by whatever selection process they were using as they decided who lived and who died, they'd be at the door in thirty or forty seconds. Long before we got everyone through it.

I looked around and quickly spotted Neela by the door. She had some sort of wrench jammed into a large gear in a compartment behind the wall. As I watched, she flexed her arms and placed her weight on the long arm of the wrench, pushing so hard that her feet lifted off of the ground as she forced the gear to turn. As it shifted, the door began to close, moving an inch for every inch the wrench moved. When her feet hit the ground, she'd start the process again.

I realized then that she had come to the same conclusion I had, and was sealing the door manually, cutting off access. A part of me wanted to tell her to stop—to not close the door until everyone was safe—but I knew, deep down, that she had to do it. There were more people in

Cogstown than in that hall, and we had a duty to serve the greater good.

So instead of wasting time fighting with her, I moved over to the door and began helping pull people through, grabbing the arms of bodies that were closest to the door and yanking them out of the mass, ushering them along. At one point a child of about four or five, his face red and screaming, was passed over the crowd and practically thrown at me. I barely got my arms around him before a large man who could barely squeeze through the narrowing space reached out and snatched the boy's leg, grabbing for something to pull himself forward. It took me a second to recognize Cyril, the fear carved into the line of his face making the man look rabid, and I realized he didn't understand what he was doing; the fear of death was blinding him to his actions, leaving him with a desperate compulsion to survive no matter what.

But the boy in my arms howled in pain as Cyril started to pull, trying to find leverage to get through, and, reacting purely on an instinct to keep the boy safe, I lashed out with a foot, kicking him right in his armpit. He shouted in pain, but let go of the boy, and I stumbled back, keeping my arms locked tight around the panicked child.

Dylan caught me, and I quickly handed the boy to her before racing back to the man and trying to grab one of Cyril's arms to help him.

"PUSH HIM OUT!" I heard Neela yell from behind me, but I ignored her and planted a foot on the door just as I got a grip on his forearm with both hands. I had long enough to catch a glimpse of the orange five on his indicator, and then began yanking. I couldn't let Cyril die. His decision to support me and Lacey had kept the crowd from killing us, and he had worked hard to get everyone organized and working. He had helped me, helped all of us, and he didn't deserve to die after he'd worked so hard to save so many people.

"OPEN THE DOOR!" I shouted as I managed to get a few more inches of him out of the confined space.

"We can't!" she cried. "The sentinels—"

A metal hand slid through the door and wrapped itself over Cyril's head. He gave me a pleading look and his grip tightened on my arm, but before I could even pull my gun and fire at Alice, he was viciously ripped away, hard enough that I was slammed into the door with him before our grip on each other broke.

I stumbled back, my entire arm and side throbbing, and then raced toward the gap in the door. "Don't!" I cried, not wanting to lose him, but it was too late. With a loud grunt, Neela drove her weight against the wrench and sealed the door closed. I stopped just short of it, staring at it, unable to understand that it had closed.

"He was still out there," I said softly, my stomach churning as I fully comprehended what closing the door meant to the people on the other side. I could hear their fists beating on the door, their screams begging to be let in, and it was more than I could bear. "They need help!"

"Don't you think I *know* that?" Neela bit off tearfully, her angry tone so deep and wounded that I turned and considered her in a new light. She scrubbed the tears from her face and gave me a fierce look. "Engineer Green ordered me to protect Cogstown at all costs, and that meant letting the people in the hall die to save it. I'm going to have to live with that for the rest of my life, so I do not need you to remind me of it right now."

I stared at her, and then immediately felt contrite. She was absolutely right, and it had been sanctimonious of me to act like she had done it out of maliciousness. I knew that Requiem Day meant hard choices, but the reality was far different than I ever could've imagined. "I'm sorry," I exhaled, turning toward her. "You are absolutely right. I just... I wish we could've saved more."

"Me too," she said, wiping the tears from her lashes and taking a moment to collect herself. "And I'm going to. There are more doors that need opening. But you two need to go find Lacey. There's a medic station down the hall—that's where I told the sentinel to take her. Go left at the fourth intersection and keep going straight. You'll see it."

I nodded, and on impulse, reached out and squeezed her shoulder. "Thank you for your help, Neela."

She nodded, and then turned to a few of the Cogs, who were fitting expandable braces to the gears in the door and the wall opposite from it, to make sure it stayed wedged shut. I watched them for a second, wondering what sort of struggle they were in for, and realized that it would be nonstop until I could find a way to put an end to Sage.

And the first step of that was getting to Tony. "C'mon," I said to Dylan. "Let's hope Lacey's still awake and can give us Tony's location."

Dylan nodded and began moving down the hallway, her limp less pronounced now. I followed close behind, checking my watch. It had been an hour and a half since Sage had given the order to kill the power and started scaling the wall, which gave us thirty minutes to get to Tony before Sage did, provided Lacey's timetable was accurate.

Even if it wasn't, that was all the time I was willing to spare on this. My friends were trapped in the Citadel, and I had to get to them before Eustice and the other legacies did.

10

We followed Neela's directions and spotted a white sign sporting the Medica's insignia after only a few minutes of walking. The power was still working in Cogstown, so the door opened as soon as I pushed the button outside.

Inside, Anna was racing around a diagnostic table where Lacey was sitting, setting up tools and equipment. She looked up as we entered, and then back down at what she was doing. Beside Lacey sat a man, whom I recognized as one of her lieutenants in the legacy arm of her operation, and a transfusion tube was dangling between the two. Rose was standing in the far corner of the room, trying to look as diminutive as possible.

"There you are," Lacey said hoarsely. "I've been waiting forever."

"No, I've been waiting forever," Anna spat hotly, folding her arms over her chest and taking a step back. "She wouldn't let me start the operation until you were here!"

I looked at Anna and then back at Lacey. It was on the tip of my tongue to tell Anna that it was the right call on Lacey's part, given that we needed her to tell us where Tony was, but I held back, knowing that I didn't want Lacey to die just because she had held off from the surgery waiting for me.

CHAPTER 10

"Lacey, where is Tony?" I asked, taking a step toward her. "In your quarters, or—"

Lacey gave a hacking laugh and shook her head. "Needed to put him somewhere he could escape from easily," she rasped. "He's... in the... door..."

Her breathing started to catch, and the monitor over the diagnostic table began to flash red in warning. "The internal bleeding is starting to fill the cavity around her lungs!" Anna shouted, tapping on the screen. A moment later the monitor depicted the image of what were presumably Lacey's lungs, showing the area filling with darkness, the lungs slowly deflating. The young intern stared at it for several seconds, her eyes wide and mouth open, but before I could snap her out of it and tell her to get to work, something took over and she grabbed a pneumatic injector from the small table of items she'd gathered, inserted a vial, and pressed it against Lacey's neck.

I realized she was humming to herself as she tossed the injector down and retrieved another bit of tube, this one hooked to a giant needle. She hooked one end of the tube to a nozzle on the wall—a vacuum, I realized a second later. Lacey gasped helplessly, like a fish, as Anna pressed a shaky hand to her side, right under her armpit, her fingers probing the space between ribs. I was trying to keep from telling Anna to just do it, or Lacey was going to die, when Anna blew out a slow breath and shoved the needle into Lacey's side. The vacuum that Anna had hooked into immediately began removing the blood, and Lacey's breathing grew easier.

But her eyelids were getting heavy from whatever medicine Anna had administered. I could see that she was slowly losing her tenuous grasp on reality and was about to be unconscious. I had no way of knowing how long Anna would take patching her up and had no clue what Lacey meant by Tony being in the door. But it was now or never. I took a step toward the woman on the table and leaned over her.

"Lacey, focus. Where is Tony?"

Lacey blinked groggily at me. "I'm going to die, aren't I?" she asked heavily. "First Ambrose... then Strum... All my work and preparation, all for nothing."

I stared at her for a long moment, not sure what I could say. I understood how she felt, because I felt defeated as well. Even after everything we had done to get us here, I wasn't certain we could win this fight. What did it matter if I got Tony or saved my friends? I had no idea what Sage was planning, or even where he was. Finding him during Requiem Day would be nigh impossible. Yet here I was, still fighting.

And I wasn't about to let Lacey give up.

"You're not going to die," I told her. "Anna is going to patch you up in no time. You just wait and see."

Lacey gave me a weak smile. "You know... Liana... I really, *really* couldn't stand you... for the longest time."

I gave a derisive laugh and shifted a little closer to her. "And now?"

Her eyelids blinked heavily. "I still can't," she admitted. "But... at least I know I can trust you. Lynch?"

"Yes, Lacey," the man giving her blood said, standing up. "What is it?"

"Get the Champion and her people to the server farm, to the door controls. I put Tony in there to protect him. He—" She broke off, a yawn catching her by surprise. "Those are some really good drugs," she told Anna as soon as the yawn finished, and I heard a slight slur to her words that told me she was going out. "Liana?"

"Yes?" I asked, and I was stunned to see her stretching her hand toward me. Tentatively, I took it into my own, and she immediately squeezed my fingers together in a vice-like grip that made my bones pop.

"The password... Tony... Seymore Butts..." She was barely able to string together a sentence, but I focused.

"Seymore Butts," I repeated back to her. Then I frowned. "Wait, what?"

Lacey chuckled softly as she let go of my hand. "Tony's... choice. You'll... see."

Her eyelids fluttered closed, and within moments she was breathing deeply. I took a glance at the wall screen to check her vitals, which

CHAPTER 10

were weak and thready, and sent up a silent prayer that she managed to survive her surgery.

Anna exhaled in relief, and then looked at us. "You need to go," she said. "And I need another blood donor if you're taking this one."

I turned to Lynch in time to see him reach up and pull off his end of the transfusion tube. "Don't worry," he told the girl in an authoritative voice. "I've put out the word. You'll probably have a line waiting outside. Anything you need, just ask the next person in line. We'll also be sending a contingent of guards to keep you and her safe."

Anna's eyes widened, but she nodded. "Thank you," she told him. Then she looked up at me and Dylan. "And thank *you*," she added, nervously tucking another strand of hair behind her ear. "You saved a lot of lives. You should be proud of that."

She said it, but in my mind all I could see was Cyril at the door, a handful of his hair gripped tightly in the sentinel's hand. The way he tried to hold on even though the sentinel was stronger... and how fast he had been ripped away.

"It was my duty," was all I could muster. "Lynch, where is the server farm?"

"Underneath the central air processing unit in the heart of Cogstown," he replied, moving over to a table that I hadn't noticed in the corner and collecting one of those coats that could make a person appear to blend in with the walls—something a legacy in Lacey's family had designed. "Follow me. I'll update you on everything we know."

I nodded and let him lead the way, giving one last look to Lacey and Anna, and then Rose, who was still standing in the corner. "You coming?" I asked her.

Her purple eyes blinked at me, and for a machine, she managed to portray insecurity very well. "Don't you think it would be better if I stayed here?" she asked hesitantly. "People are afraid of me, as they should be. I might only make things harder for you if I come along. I stand out."

I gave her a considering look and thought about what she was saying. She was right that anyone we encountered was bound to be hostile or afraid when they saw us. But that was something that could work to our advantage, the longer Requiem Day went on."

"Yes, you do, and I'm sorry if this hurts your feelings, but I'm going to need you to be scary and threatening. There's going to come a point during all this when we won't be able to trust any of the people we're encountering."

"Especially since Scipio just announced that you and the entire Knight, Cog, and Diver Departments attempted to murder him," Lynch announced grimly, slipping his coat over his shoulders. "And I've already put the word out for the Cogs *not* to attack any sentinel with purple eyes. Luckily, because we have power, we can still send text messages through the servers, but c'mon. I'll explain as we go."

He was right. I glanced at Rose, giving her a questioning look, and after a moment she nodded and began walking forward. I stood aside to let her pass, and then followed her into the hall. Lynch was right behind me, leaving Dylan to shut the door as she exited. Lynch quickly moved around me when I paused in the hall and waved us along. We quickly formed a little line behind him, heading down the hall. There were more workers than before in the halls, not all of them Cogs, heading toward some unknown destination, some defensive task, and I couldn't help but feel like the entire place was a beehive readying for an attack.

"What is going on?" I yelled at Lynch, the amount of noise in the hall making that the only possible volume for a conversation.

"Water Treatment was breached a few minutes ago," Lynch replied grimly. "The sentinels are in there now, killing people."

"Yeah, about that," Dylan called from behind me. "Why are the sentinels killing some people and leaving the others behind?"

Dylan's question caught me off guard, but I suddenly remembered that I had been wondering the same thing. The Alices had spared Dalton—indicated that he was a worthy citizen—but then killed the man trying to get through the door before it closed. Why? What had differentiated the two of them? Alice didn't seem to care about gender or anything else, so why—

My mind suddenly flashed to Cyril's indicator, and what I knew about Dalton. Dalton had been a seven when I'd met him, and I had no reason to assume that he'd dropped in rank since then. Meanwhile, Cyril's rank had been a five, and they had gone after him. It was the ranks—the ones Scipio gave us to reflect our service to the Tower. It had to be. Alice had mentioned that citizens true to Scipio would not be harmed, and there wasn't any other way of differentiating the citizens beyond their department. Not to mention, Sage had wanted the expulsion chambers in the Citadel to remain in use; even though Sadie and Plancett had been the driving force, I had no doubt it had been Sage's hand guiding their actions.

But that didn't explain the why. What did Sage hope to achieve by using sentinels to murder that many of the Tower's citizens? Sure, Alice was telling them it was for the good of the Tower, but surely he didn't believe the people would take that sitting down. The lower-ranking individuals made up nearly a third of the population! If my hypothesis was right and they were targeting everyone ranked five and below, then the people were going to catch on and start fighting back.

Then again, all the ones were in the Citadel, and the twos and threes were being sequestered in the Medica. The remaining fours and fives might not be able to put up much of a fight after all.

I didn't know, but I had to find out. Something told me it was important to Sage's plan. If I could figure out why, then maybe I could do something to stop it.

"I think they are targeting people rank five and below," I told the group, sharing my theory with them. "I saw a man I knew to be a seven only a few moments ago, and the Alice units let him live. But they grabbed a man who was a five and killed him."

"That would make sense, given what the sentinels were saying," Dylan replied. "But why are they doing it?"

"I don't know," I told her. "But if we could figure out why, we might also be able to figure out how he's trying to kill Scipio, and stop it."

"Well, I can't tell you how he's doing it," Lynch cut in, coming to a stop in front of a hall and ushering us to turn right. "But what I can tell you is this: forty-five minutes ago, we got an update from Scipio reporting that you, Engineer Green, and Praetor Strum had attempted a coup against the other department heads and Scipio. Orders are to execute you on sight. I can promise you that none of Lacey's people will hurt you, but not all of the Cogs are like us, and they may try to attack you, so beware."

I followed his instructions to head right and paused when I saw a deserted corridor in front of me, disconcerted by what he was saying and suddenly feeling that I was being led into a trap. It would be cruel of him to taunt me that way if it were the case, but I had no reason to doubt his intentions, especially given his loyalty to Lacey.

"Have you heard anything about the Citadel?" I asked, resuming my quick pace.

"Actually, yes," Lynch replied, jogging to keep up with me. "The update from Scipio allowed us a few seconds to use their connection to hack into their data feed, and we were able to determine that Water Treatment, Cogstown, and the Citadel all have power. Apparently they didn't anticipate our departments not getting hit in the initial power drain, and have sent orders for us to shut it down so they can work on restoring Scipio, but fat chance of that happening. I can't tell you what's happening inside, but they are fighting back. Which is good, because Scipio has deemed the entire Knights Department psychologically contaminated."

I stopped and looked at him, my shock at his revelation causing my jaw to drop. "He declared the entire department psychologically contaminated?" I repeated, unable to help myself. By doing that, he'd condemned every Knight in the Citadel to death in the eyes of the Tower. He was trying to wipe out an entire department! But why? What purpose would it serve to eradicate the entire department? Was it just to kill more people, or to punish them for voting me in as the Champion?

Lynch nodded, his face twisting in sympathy. "You've been painted as the ringleader, which calls into question the entire department. They elected you, after all. And before you go getting upset about that... it gets worse."

My stomach twisted, and I steeled myself for more bad news. "What is it?"

CHAPTER 10

"Scipio's announcement included a report that all departments were under lockdown, and that power would be cut to them until they selected new department heads, to prevent further rioting and insurrection. If anyone from any department is found to be aiding and abetting you, then the entire department will suffer the consequences. Which means you need to avoid any other departments once you get out of here."

I nodded. It wasn't as bad as I'd thought it would be, but it wasn't optimal. Still, I felt less awful about heading away from the Citadel to fetch Tony, knowing that the Citadel still had power and was fighting back.

"Anything else?" I asked as he stopped at an open shaft where a basket hung from a woven metallic rope. I had seen these all over Cogstown before but had never ridden in one.

"The power that Scipio is supposedly cutting off is actually being diverted," Lynch told me as he approached the basket and gripped the edge of it tightly with one hand, waving for us to get in. I quickly did just that, hauling myself over the edge while he continued to speak. "We can't figure out where it's being diverted to, but based on the legacy memories of the last Requiem Day, we know that it's going somewhere in the Core, and that they need every bit of power the Tower can produce to do whatever they're doing. Now that Water Treatment is breached, it'll only be a matter of time before the sentinels divert that department's power to the Core, and then they'll mount an attack on Cogstown to do the same."

"Do you have weapons to mount an adequate defense?" Dylan asked, stealing the question from my very lips as she got into the basket.

"Not against sentinels," Lynch said, warily watching Rose as she approached the basket. "They're tough to kill."

He wasn't wrong, although I knew for a fact that electricity in high enough amounts could slow them down. I turned my attention to Rose for a second as she tentatively put one foot in the basket, and tried not to yelp as the concave bottom flexed under her weight.

"You are sure this is able to hold my weight?" Rose asked the engineer. "I can always climb down if it would be safer."

"It's made to hold five tons," he said flatly. "We use it for hauling heavier things. Now hurry up. We don't have much time."

I wasn't sure I liked the snap in his voice, but I kept my mouth shut and waved for Rose to come join us. The metallic rope screeched slightly as she settled her full weight in the basket, and I looked up at the ceiling above, where the wench mechanism for the rope was seated, eyeing the brake to make sure it wasn't failing. The components continued to groan as Rose sat down, and the basket started to sway some, offset by her weight.

Lynch quickly hopped in after her, and then turned a hand crank on the side, and within moments, we were descending into the shaft. We descended for several seconds while I thought about what he was telling me. Sage was diverting the power from other departments to the Core, but for what? Surely it was part of his plan to kill Scipio and replace him with Kurt, but how would more power do that? If anything, wouldn't that make Scipio stronger?

And somehow, amid all this chaos, the Citadel was fighting back, resisting the energy drain. I knew it was Leo and Quess; they had to be doing something to keep the power going, which gave me at least some small hope that they weren't completely unaware of what had happened in the cells. I just hoped that they were able to mobilize the Knights to stand against Eustice and the others, and that they didn't ask too many questions when the fighting hit the fan. They needed to focus on their survival.

I needed to focus on slowing Sage's plan down. And that meant getting Tony.

Yesterday.

11

Lynch wasted no time leaping over the lip of the basket as soon as we hit the bottom of the shaft, waving for us to follow. I jumped out quickly, taking a moment to give Dylan a hand, and then walked at a brisk pace behind him. I wasn't sure why, but the few minutes we had spent in silence descending twenty floors seemed to have given my body some sort of permission to start feeling every ache and pain from the last two days, coupled with a deep exhaustion that made even my bones feel heavy.

I did my best to shake it off, but with every step I took, I became more aware of my discomfort, as well as how thirsty and hungry I was. It was like my body was just rubbing salt in the wound, and I couldn't help but feel angry at it for trying to remind me that I was only human. I couldn't afford to be human today. Today, of all days, I needed to be more than that.

Moving helped, and as soon as we emerged from the forest of girders that made up the bottom floor and hit the crowds of people racing around the massive central air processing unit, my guard went back up and my head went down, Lynch's warning still bright in my mind.

Rose was a big enough deterrent to have people scurrying away from us without even casting Dylan and me a second look, but the closer we got to the air processing unit, the thicker the crowd became, until we were practically surrounded by people, their eyes dark with mistrust and wariness. The only thing that seemed to hold them back was Lynch, who repeatedly bellowed, "These individuals are allies to the department and have been given safe passage through Cogstown," in a loud voice that seemed to help pacify those who looked ready to assault Rose outright.

We made our way through them, enjoying the path Rose carved out of the crowd for us, and heading directly toward the central air processing unit. It was still operational, and the roar of the machines began to drown out all ambient noise. The rumbling in the floor plating grew more intense as we moved closer, until I was convinced that the air around us was practically vibrating. And if I thought it was loud now, I knew it would be even more intense below.

Lynch approached a break in the railing that surrounded the unit, right under a flight of stairs, then reached into a bucket, pulled out several sets of earmuffs, and held them out to us. I grabbed a pair and fitted them over my ears, cutting off the vicious assault to my eardrums. He pointed at himself and then held up one finger, then at Dylan, producing two, three with me, and four for Rose, and then waved for us to follow. As he started to go down, I realized he'd been giving us a marching order, and reluctantly stood aside to let Dylan go before me. There might be a reason he wanted the larger girl to go second, but a part of me resented not being right next to him, in clear control of the situation.

Still, I knew the most about what was going on, which meant that my knowledge had to be protected at all costs. I might have done my best to fill Dylan in, but the entire conspiracy was just too large and too complex to fully explain in one sitting, and I needed to do everything to preserve that information, if only so I could keep filling people in so they could form a defense. Not everyone would believe me, but if everything else failed—if I couldn't stop Sage before he replaced Scipio with Kurt—then I had to be responsible for recruiting people to work

CHAPTER 11

against him after the fact. But that was only if he won today, which I had no intention of letting happen.

Besides, Leo and Grey would kill me if they found out I had been breaking the rule about not going in first.

So I stood back as Dylan went after him, and then followed her down the narrow steps that dead-ended at a pressure door. I paused as Lynch turned the hand wheel, his teeth bared in a tight grimace as he fought against the mechanisms inside, and then exhaled in relief when it finally moved.

He pulled the door open, and a wall of heat and sonic pressure hit us, simultaneously making me sweat and pushing at my exposed skin, telling me that the noise being emitted from inside was beyond deafening. Lynch continued to pull, revealing the red-hot glow of the forges that seemed to serve as the only lighting in the staircase.

Great, I found myself thinking as he stepped through the door, heading in. *As if I weren't dehydrated enough.*

Dylan waited a few seconds before following him, and I followed suit, giving myself a moment to swipe some of the sweat from my forehead. *I really hope we don't have to spend too long in here.*

I descended the stairs, stepped through the door, and found myself in a stairway shaped like a square, with steps running along the wall, separated from a central shaft by a thin metal railing. The glow of the forges came through square holes cut into the walls of the shaft. The staircase only went down from where we had just entered, and we followed it, hugging the walls. Periodically, landings in the corner of the stairway held doorways, but Lynch ignored them at first, continuing his fast-paced descent.

We passed two doors before the heat grew so intense that my sweat started evaporating from my skin the moment it appeared. It was at door four that my eyes started to feel parched, the lack of moisture in them making it difficult to blink without some discomfort.

By door seven, I was beginning to feel lightheaded. I tried to shake it off, placing one hand against the cage-like wall, but the heel of my boot caught the edge of the step in a funny way and I stumbled, almost falling forward. I managed to catch myself a few steps down—with my knee—and sucked in a deep breath, trying to ignore how dry and parched my mouth was, before I slowly got to my feet again and looked around.

Dylan had paused on the stairs and was giving me a concerned look, but Lynch hadn't seemed to notice my distress, and was already making his way to the next landing, and door eight, unless I was mistaken. I waved her off as I pushed myself to my feet, and then almost sagged back down in relief when Lynch stopped in front of the door and began spinning the hand wheel. Instead, I used the promise of a nice, cool hall in the next room to put one foot in front of the next, and lumbered down after Dylan.

When I reached the door, I almost moaned in pleasure at the frosty air that was blowing through, cooling flesh that felt like it was about to be baked right off. I stepped in and made room for Rose. Once she was inside, Lynch signaled for her to close the door. Moments later, the heat and sonic vibrations that I had been feeling in the shaft suddenly died down, and Lynch started taking off his earmuffs, indicating that we should as well.

I quickly pulled them off, and was stunned by how quiet the hall seemed. It had felt as if everything outside of us had been falling apart in some terrific volcanic eruption, but somehow, here, in the heart of it all, we'd found a deep stillness. Disconcerted by how different it was, I took a few steps down the hallway, and found that it grew colder the farther I went. My breath came out in a vapor cloud, and a sudden chill erupted along my skin.

"Where are we?" I whispered, compelled to do so out of an instinct that told me not to give my position away.

"The server farms," Lynch said in response, his voice also pitched low. "We hide them over the forges. Not that it matters. One of the legacy spies we arrested was one of our internal IT workers. Sadie and Sage knew where they were the whole time, and had probably been working to undermine our system. We were in the process of analyzing what damage was done when everything started. I left a crew down here when I received word that Lacey was back. They're working in the main room, but door controls are farther down. C'mon, I'll show you."

He moved past me down the hall, heading for the only turn there was—an abrupt right—and I followed a step or two behind him, looking down to check my watch. This journey hadn't been quick, and I saw with shock that we only had fifteen minutes left to get to Tony and prevent Sage from downloading him.

How were we going to get him out in time? Where were we going to *put* him?

I was so engrossed with wondering that I ran into Dylan's outstretched arm, and grunted softly in surprise. She pushed me back a few feet, and I let her, the hairs on the back of my neck standing on end in warning at the intensity on her face. I shifted my gaze past her toward Lynch, who was perched at the corner, looking down the next hall. He glanced back at us and then motioned for me to change places with him. I slid by Dylan, worried that the sentinels had somehow gotten here first, and took a quick peek around the corner.

Two gray-clad Eyes stood guard outside a door about thirty feet down. Their hands were crossed in front of them, and I could see that both had their pulse-shields at the ready. I drew back as the one closest to me started to turn down the hall, and quickly began signaling to my companions in Callivax.

Two Eyes are standing guard in front of the main server room, I explained. *There are probably more inside.*

Dylan's eyes widened, and the hand that she had placed on her baton began pulling it out, her other hand signing, *What do you want to do? You lash in while I draw their fire? Or should we send Rose in and see what they do?*

I stared at her for several seconds, thinking. To be honest, I didn't want to do any of those things. I wanted to handle this quickly and efficiently, not waste time with any of that nonsense. Besides, I wanted to know why they were down here and what they were doing. If there were two guards outside, I was betting there was at least one more inside, if not a few of them. And whether they knew what they were participating in or not was irrelevant: if they were part of IT, I couldn't trust them.

I pulled out my gun, ejected the clip, saw that I had three bullets left, and slapped it back inside, a very simple plan forming in my mind that hopefully wouldn't take up more than two or three bullets. I had two spare clips with me, but that was only twenty extra bullets. Not nearly enough for everything we'd come across. Dylan gave me a surprised look when I glanced at her, and then I signaled, *Wait here*, before moving around the corner and bringing the gun up.

I was five steps in when the first guard spotted me, but I had expelled a breath and squeezed the trigger, a deadly calm coming over me, before he could even open his mouth. The bullet caught him in the chest, and his body jerked backward and down. The second Eye, a woman, started to lift her weapon, a shout of warning forming over her lips, but I sighted down the barrel of the gun, not feeling one iota of remorse as I squeezed off a second shot. The bullet caught her in the stomach, and she staggered back, clutching her abdomen, while I took two more steps forward and shot her in the head, dropping her. I ejected the empty clip and inserted a new one.

The door they were guarding slid open, and I fired a round at the frame causing it to ricochet. A surprised yelp inside told me I had gotten their attention, and I quickly announced, "This is Champion Liana Castell, and you have two options right now: surrender, or I come in there and kill you all. You have three seconds to throw out your weapons and pads. Make your choice now."

I waited a beat, and then began counting down for them. "Three... two... one..."

My lips were around the "one" when two bags were tossed out, followed by two pulse shields. I gave a satisfied nod and then turned to look over my shoulder at where Dylan, Lynch, and Rose were standing. Dylan and Lynch were looking a little alarmed at my violent display.

I didn't care. The Eyes had been standing in my way, and were currently the enemy, as far as I was concerned.

"Rose, can you come here and make sure they are being honest for me, please?"

"Of course," she said in her synthesized voice. "Stand by."

I moved to one side, keeping my gun trained on the door, and waited as Rose passed me and went in, taking care to step over the two bodies on the floor.

"There are only two of them," she reported, her voice carrying down the hall. "And they are unarmed."

I was already moving toward the door, and stepped through it a moment later, to study the server room. It was almost exactly like the ones in IT, but much smaller, maybe only one hundred feet in length, though still filled with cages. The cage on the wall opposite from us was open, and several wires were connected to the computer towers there, which told me the techs had been working on it when we had interrupted them. The two techs, both men, were huddled against one of the cages, staring at Rose with fear in their eyes.

"We are just following orders," one of them practically wailed when he saw me enter. "We got a message from the Core telling us we had to divert power to—"

"Shut up, Lidecher," the other man snapped, straightening some. "She *knows*. She's the one responsible for the attack on Scipio!"

The first man gaped at me, his eyes wide, and swallowed audibly. I stared at both of them, wondering whether I should even waste my breath trying to tell them they were wrong, but decided against it. The Eyes would undoubtedly blindly believe whatever messages they were getting from the Core, and with Sadie in control of it, and Sage in control of Scipio, there was nothing I could say to change their minds. So instead, I focused on getting information.

"How did you get in here?" I demanded.

"Why should we tell... AH!" He had been cut off by Rose, who had reached out and grabbed a fistful of his uniform, then hauled him off his feet and slammed him against the ceiling, cutting off his cry.

I was so alarmed by her act of violence that I took a step back, wondering if she was malfunctioning again. "Rose?" I asked.

"He's just unconscious," she replied pleasantly, setting the man on the ground. "I thought it might be easier to make a deal with that man than this one, and decided to remove him from the equation. I hope you don't mind."

I did, a little bit, but one look at Lidecher told me Rose's ploy had worked; the poor man was damn near peeing himself. "Excellent idea," I said to her, before turning back to him. "Lidecher, was it?" I asked.

His eyes darted from his companion to me, and he nodded, fast enough that the fat under his chin began to jiggle.

I stepped closer, keeping the smile on my face. "Listen, I just have some questions. If you answer them honestly, I will let you and your friend find a place to hide and ride this out until the crisis has passed. If you don't, I'm going to let my friend here throw you around. We haven't tested how dexterous her fingers are yet, so she could use a little practice."

He gulped, and then vigorously nodded again. "Anything you want. Just please don't hurt us."

My smile grew, and it was mostly genuine. "I won't. Now tell me, how did you get into Cogstown, how are you getting updates from the Core, and what were you trying to do here?"

12

The words spilled out of him as if I had opened the floodgates to his every thought, and I was a little taken aback by the speed with which he answered.

"All the nets that are programmed with Eye credentials are working. Part of our emergency procedure is to immediately divert power to our communication nodes so we can coordinate with the Eyes stuck outside the Core. We were in Cogstown replacing some of the power crystals in a power diverter when our Cog guide informed us that power had gone down to the rest of the Tower. He was escorting us to the upper floors when we received a transmission from the Core through our commanding officer, directly from the head of our internal department. He informed us that the Core was under direct attack from Cogstown, and ordered us to upload a code into their mainframe to divert power to the Core, to stop the attack. To help Scipio survive."

I stared at him for several seconds, then turned back to the door, intent on getting to one of their pads and having Rose confirm what he was saying, but paused when I saw that Lynch and Dylan had already done so. Dylan had dug through a bag and pulled out a white pad, and was now offering it to me. I grabbed it, tapped it, and then held it out to Lidecher when it asked for a password. He hesitated, but then quickly tapped in four digits: 1-0-9-4. I pulled the pad back and handed it off to Rose. I had no doubt that whatever they had been sent to upload into the computers was meant to take Cogstown offline, but probably not in the way Lidecher and the others had been told.

I wanted to know exactly what it was, so that Lynch could tell the other Cog workers how to defend their department.

"Find the code. If he's telling the truth, hook the pad up and figure out how far they were into the upload, how much damage they did to Cogstown's systems, and whether we can help them restore it. Keeping Cogstown's power away from the Core will slow Sage down."

"We honestly didn't get far," Lidecher offered nervously. "We had just finished connecting our pads to the servers. I swear, we hadn't even opened the file our lead sent us to upload!"

I stared at him for a long moment, my face revealing nothing. "We'll see," I finally said, letting doubt color my tone. If he was telling the truth about the code, that meant he could be telling the truth about his net. And if the Eyes' nets were somehow still active, then I could use that to my advantage. I looked up at Rose, waiting for her to confirm or deny his story.

"It's true," she announced a few moments later, handing the pad back to me. "A virus was sent to him, but it has not been uploaded yet."

I took it back, and then smiled at him. "Lidecher, I'm going to need your net, if that's all right. Got some important calls to make. We're also going to take your partner's, to keep you from calling anyone and telling them you were unable to complete your mission. I'd prefer not to sedate you both to do it, but if I have to..."

I trailed off and turned to the wall, where I'd seen a first-aid kit sitting—right where it was supposed to be, per Tower protocol.

"Sure," Lidecher said obsequiously. "But you realize that you can only use it to connect to other Eyes, right?"

I paused in pulling the bag from the compartment on the wall, and then shrugged it off. It was disappointing, yes—I had been hoping to call Leo and Grey and warn them about the legacies, if they didn't know already—but that didn't mean I didn't have anyone to talk to. In fact, if there was *anyone* I needed to talk to, it was an Eye. And luckily, I

CHAPTER 12

had one in my pocket. "No matter. It can be used for other things," I informed him. "Now, would you like to sit or stand?"

He eyed me and the bag, and then his eyes flicked to the chair. "Sit, I think."

"Excellent choice. Dylan, would you mind extracting his net, please?"

Dylan came up beside me, and then hesitated. "Liana, you know we can't use someone else's net. The DNA scanner won't accept another user."

I pressed my lips together in frustration. She was right, of course. If I had Leo here, he could undoubtedly override it—and Quess as well, for that matter. The rest of the security features wouldn't matter with the power out, but the DNA one was tricky. I thought about it for a second, and then noticed Lidecher shifting uncomfortably, as if he had a secret that no one else did. As if he knew exactly how to do just what I needed to do.

"Lidecher? You have something you want to share with the class?"

Lidecher cringed, and then gave me a furtive look. "I can do it for you," he whispered. "But... But I need assurances that no one will find out about this. They'll put me to death if they find out."

I hesitated, wondering why he would betray his department like that, and then realized I didn't care. I'd promise him the moon if he could help me get this net working. I needed information, and this net could help me get it.

I looked at Lynch. "I assume that if you survive what's happening, you could find some way of hiding him?"

Lynch studied us both for a second, and then nodded. "Lacey gave us all alternative identities if our cover was ever blown. He can have mine. It's in Water Treatment. He'll have a contact there, one of Strum's people. If she survived, she'll cover for him."

I turned back to Lidecher and raised an eyebrow. "Is that enough?"

He nodded nervously and then turned around. "Go ahead and remove it. I'll need a minute or two to overload the circuit responsible for the DNA lockout."

Dylan didn't need to be told twice, and quickly moved to do it. I looked down at my watch and saw that we had lost four minutes with all this, giving us only ten more to get to Tony before Sage did.

A rush of impatience surged through me, but I shut it out, crossed my arms, and waited.

Three minutes later, I was trying not to wince as Dylan took the laser cutter to the back of my neck, the sting of it both familiar and irritating by this point. I'd changed my net out so often in the past month or so that it was beginning to feel commonplace. She slipped the modified net in, and before she could even seal up the slit she had cut, I felt the tendrils of the net begin to unfurl, creeping along my cerebral cortex like vines growing across the earth. I breathed through the process, closing my eyes against the image of slender fingers reaching out to grip my brain, and slowly counted off the seconds in my head.

By thirteen, the sensation had passed and Dylan had pressed a small amount of bio-foam into the wound, sealing it shut. I rotated my neck a few times, trying to release some of the tension, and then nodded at Dylan.

"It'll do. Let's go. We only have"—I paused long enough to check my watch, and then looked back up at her—"seven minutes to get to Tony."

"Roger," she replied, gathering up the items from the med kit and placing them back in the bag.

I turned away, focusing on Lynch. "Are you okay to watch them?" I asked.

He nodded. "I already called for backup, but I'll be fine. I kept one of the pulse shields they were using, so if they step out of line…" He trailed off and gave Lidecher a speculative look.

Lidecher paled, his black eyes darting to me. "He's not going to hurt me, is he?"

"Depends on whether you try anything stupid," I replied indifferently, picking up his bag and slinging it over my shoulder. "I'm sure you'll be fine, though. You seem to be good at making smart choices. Now, if you'll excuse me."

I pivoted on my heel and headed out the door into the hall, moving a few feet away. Then I said, "Contact Dinah Velasquez, IT005-65C."

I felt a moment's apprehension as I waited for the familiar buzz to begin, but quickly let it go as the net kicked in a moment later, telling me it was transmitting. As I waited for Dinah to pick up, I waved Dylan forward, pointing down the hall.

There was nothing in the rulebook that said I couldn't multitask.

Dylan led the way to the next door, the one that held the server farms responsible for controlling entry and exit from Cogstown, and housed Tony's program. We were halfway down the hall when Dinah accepted the transmission.

I'm not sure who you are, but you're not a part of my department, tech. What do you want?

I tried not to smile at the belligerent tone in the older woman's voice—one that undoubtedly made her underlings quiver with terror. *Guess again, Dinah,* I thought at her, feeling the soft pop of the neural transmitter in my temple going off as it was transmitted. *It's Liana. I found a few Eyes in Cogstown and liberated them of their nets.*

How did you overcome... She trailed off for a second, and her tone changed from one of wonder to one of determination in almost the blink of an eye. *Never mind. I don't really care. What's going on? The last time we talked, you told me you were planning to arrest everyone related to the conspiracy.*

We missed someone, I informed her, coming to a cautious halt as Dylan stepped up to the door. *It was Sage. He set up one of the men we suspected to be a fall guy to disguise his part in all this. Brace yourself—he claims to be Ezekial Pine.*

There were several long seconds of silence, but that suited me fine, as my attention was entirely on the door Dylan was about to open and the gun in my hand. Lidecher had sworn up and down that his team had been the only one from IT, but for all I knew, he could've been leading us on, pretending to help us, while setting us up to get taken out by another team of techs. It seemed unlikely, given that there were no guards posted outside this door, but I couldn't just ignore it.

That's not possible, Dinah announced a second later, just as Dylan pressed the button.

I sighted down the barrel of the gun, making sure the initial entrance was clear, and then nodded to Dylan, waving her in. *Possible or not, he's got control over Scipio, and has initiated a second Requiem Day. What do you know?*

I was hoping she knew a lot. Dinah ran a section of the IT Department as head of the ethics committee, and part of her job was to act as Sadie Monroe's check and balance. Her position meant she should have direct access to Scipio's coding and could tell me how he was doing, and give us an estimate on how long we had before Sage was ready.

Not much about what's happening inside the Core, she replied grimly. *Right after the power was cut to the rest of the Tower, my connection to Scipio was severed. I've got my entire section on it, trying to reestablish control, but right now, Scipio's status is a mystery.*

Great, I replied, disappointed. Dylan stepped through the door, and I moved up to follow, ever conscious of the time. I really hoped that the sentinel carrying Sage was taking its time, but I couldn't exactly count on that. *So do you know what's happening* outside *the Core?*

A lot, actually. I am currently tapped in to the communication hub and have devoted a small group of my people to intercepting messages to try to paint a picture of what's going on. As I understand it, Water Treatment has been breached, and their power is about to be diverted to the Core.

Anger gripped me as I thought of all the people in Water Treatment who were now being cast into darkness, left at the mercy of the Alice units, but I tamped it down, promising myself that I would unleash that fury soon, on the bastard responsible. *I knew that it had been breached, but the power thing is new. Any idea where it's going?*

Yes, actually. It's being diverted to a location at the bottom of the central power conduit, which should be impossible, but somehow it isn't.

Impossible? I asked, finally allowing myself to move through the door after Dylan. My eyes quickly searched the room, which was a quarter the size of the first, and I relaxed when I saw that it was empty and devoid of life.

There's nothing there, Dinah replied in answer to my question. *I have every schematic ever drawn up of the Core on a personal archive, and I'm telling you, there's nowhere for that power to go! I have no explanation for it!*

I rubbed my fingers together as I spotted a lone terminal in the room, and quickly put my gun away and moved toward it. While my goal was Tony, my mind was on what Dinah was saying. There had to be something there, no matter what Dinah's records reflected. And whatever it was, I was betting it was where Sage was heading, or where he planned to end up before everything was said and done.

Which meant that was where it was all going to happen. If I managed to make it out of Cogstown alive, with Tony, then back up to my friends without dying, maybe we could use the emergency escape hatch to get into Sadie's quarters and find a way to cut through the wall into the power conduit. It was risky, but worth a shot.

I just had to accomplish so many things before I got there.

Keep poking around, I told her. *I'm retrieving something we need that I hope will slow Sage down some, but I don't think it'll keep him down for long.*

Okay, she said. There was a pause, and then she added, *I think you should know, there was a tech trapped inside the Citadel when the power went out. He's been transmitting updates to his lead every ten minutes or so, and it seems that the legacies you arrested are out and wreaking havoc.*

I grated my teeth together. On the one hand, I was grateful for the information. On the other, it was an unnecessary reminder that I was trapped down here, nearly a hundred floors away, unable to do anything to help. *Any word what floor they are on?*

Twenty, she replied, and I expelled a breath of relief. With how fast Alice and her units seemed to be moving, I had expected them to already be on the sixty-fifth floor, about to breach my quarters. Still, it was way too close for comfort. *But your Knights have apparently started to form defenses against them. It looks like it's slowing them down, so have hope. Now, we should finish the transmission. If I'm monitoring them, that means someone else might be as well, and for all the precautions I take, it's better not to tempt fate. Good luck.*

You too, I replied. A moment later the buzz under my skull stopped, signaling that the transmission had concluded.

I took several seconds to gather my wits about me, and then looked expectantly at the terminal in front of me. I was never really sure how to approach these things, but I decided to assume that the AI fragment inside could hear and see me even now.

"Hello, Tony?" I said softly, looking around. "My name is Liana Castell. Lacey asked me to come and get you. She told me to tell you the password. It's... uh... Seymore Butts."

13

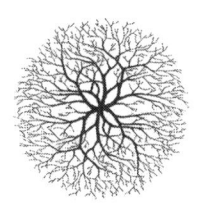

There was a long moment of silence, and I glanced nervously at Dylan and then back to the terminal, wondering whether Tony was even hooked up to a microphone and speakers. It seemed a bit cruel if he wasn't, considering he had the ability to hear and respond to the world around him, but maybe it was part of how Lacey had kept him hidden.

A burst of static from over the door caught me unexpectedly, and I half leapt out of my skin. The room filled with the giggle of a high-pitched voice, modulated to sound like a young boy of nine or ten. "He-he-he-he-he! You said butts!" he exclaimed happily, still chortling gleefully. "I told Lacey that would be good, but she just—"

The voice cut off and the screen clicked on, revealing a young boy's face composed of red coding. The image looked around the room, but I heard the whir of cameras going all around me, telling me that the face was just mimicking the movement to tell me what he was doing.

He was giving us a onceover and growing more and more suspicious by the second.

"Where's Lacey?" he demanded, and there was a thread of fear in his voice.

I looked down at my watch, and saw that there were still two minutes on the estimate Lacey had given us. Some time for an explanation, but not much. "Lacey was shot at the council meeting, and she's several levels up, in surgery. Can you access the cameras in the room? It's on level 45, south side of the Tower."

"No," he reported. "I can't. Cogstown still has power, but cameras are down, taken out by a virus undoubtedly left by the spy who was working in the server room."

I felt a wave of frustration at his response, not only because it kept him from verifying our story, but also because Sadie and Sage had really covered their bases. I might have forced Sage to speed up his plan, but he had already managed to achieve quite a bit within the various departments—and it all sabotaged our chances of resisting him. It was devastating. Without the cameras, the Cogs wouldn't be able to see if any sentinels managed to find a way in. Just one sentinel could tear a bloody path through Cogstown before anyone realized it was there, and by the time a large enough force was alerted and mobilized, the sentinel would've killed dozens of people.

I swallowed my anger back and looked at Tony, ever cognizant of the time. "Look, I swear, Lacey gave me the password and told me where to find you. The transceiver that you built was taken by Sage, and they are going to plug it in at any minute and initiate the download. How do we stop it?"

He blinked at me and then looked at Dylan and Rose. "Why do you have a sentinel with you?" he asked, blatantly ignoring my question.

Rose moved, stepping around Dylan and closer to Tony. "Hello, Little Brother," she said softly, and I could feel the warmth and reverence in her voice. "Oh, I've missed you. I'm so happy to see that you're safe and undamaged. I worried—"

"Holy hell in a handbasket," Tony exclaimed, his face growing smaller on the screen, as if he had taken a step back. "Rose? Wha... Ho..." He stopped for several seconds, and then his face grew larger. "Are you okay?"

Rose's eyes "blinked," and then she cocked her head. "Not good. But I'm more afraid for our brothers. Scipio is in trouble. Jasper and I have seen him, and it's like there are hooks in his code that run deep, controlling some of his key functions like he's some sort of puppet. Jasper was trying to study it and relay the information to me, but he has been taken by our enemies, and I was forced to copy myself to stay with Liana and find you. They have everyone, except for you, and it seems that Alice and Kurt are working with a man who has plotted our downfall since the beginning. Why would they have done this, Little Brother?"

"There, there," Tony said soothingly. "Don't be afraid, Rosie. I'm thinking. What were Jasper's concerns?"

"Scipio's longevity. He thinks our brother is being tortured beyond just losing our voices in the harmony. Isolation is torture, but he is a full AI, and should have been able to cope without our input. But he's not. Jasper told me that his code was fragmented and corrupted beyond what should be possible in such a short time. What is happening to Scipio, and what can we do, Tony? Will we lose him?"

I frowned at Rose. In spite of the bounty of information she was delivering, I was more than a little miffed that this was the first time I was hearing about Jasper communicating anything to her. She could've spoken up between the Council Room and here, but she hadn't. Not that it changed anything. But it would've been nice to hear sooner. It was hard not to say something, but ultimately, I was curious to see how this exchange between Tony and Rose would play out. Tony had enhanced Scipio's creativity, giving him a boost in his problem-solving skills, and it stood to reason that Tony might have some insight to offer.

Provided it didn't take any longer than the timeframe we were working with, of course.

"Oh boy, that's not good," Tony replied. His gaze drifted off on the screen, seemingly staring at some fixed point on the wall. "We've got to get our friends out first, and that includes Kurt and Alice. What's going on with them?"

"Kurt has been keeping Ezekial Pine alive for over two hundred years," Rose replied sadly. "He's been using the alpha-series net to house our brother. I'm not sure what happened with Alice, but she has copied herself willingly multiple times."

"Oh man, not a hive mentality." Tony groaned theatrically. "I love Alice to death, but sometimes she can be a real butt-muncher. Ugh." A hand appeared on the screen, wiping over the young boy's face in a way that made him seem years older than he appeared. "We have to initiate a reset, not only of Scipio, but of the fragments. It won't restore the broken parts, but it will erase the last three hundred years of history, which should delete whatever crap they've done to Scipio."

I puzzled over his words for a second, letting them sink in. I hadn't even known it was possible to reset Scipio *or* the fragments. I was under the impression that if they were shut off, they were deleted, and to me, resetting them was the same as shutting them off.

But if Tony was suggesting it... did that mean there was a way to fix all of this and restore the fragments to Scipio? Excitement thrummed through me as I leaned forward, focused on the face in the terminal.

"Wait," I said as he opened up his mouth to say more. "You're saying there's a way to fix Scipio and the other fragments?"

The young boy nodded and smiled. "Of course there is! But all six programs have to be taken to the integration chamber at the base of the Core, and uploaded at the same time. Once we're inside, there's also a chance that Alice or Kurt could destroy us before we can initiate the reset, though, so whoever uploads us will have to move quickly."

I blinked at him, disconcerted by the dark words he was delivering in such a cheerful tone. "Are you serious? The other programs could destroy you?"

Tony nodded, but continued to smile. "Yeah. I mean, it depends on how deep Pine's influence runs, but if Kurt's helping him stay alive, and Alice is willingly copying herself on his behalf, I'd say they're pretty loyal. So they'll likely try to destroy us before we even get the chance to reset them, and there's not much we can do about that. Don't worry, though; I'm sure Lionel will give us a better plan before too long. He's probably just trying to find us."

Once again, I was thrown for a loop. What did he mean, Lionel would give us a better plan? Did he mean Scipio? He had to, because Lionel was dead, and had been for almost three hundred years. "What do you mean, Lionel?"

CHAPTER 13

"Lionel Scipio, of course," Rose said, her tone slightly patronizing. "He promised us he would always take care of us."

"But he's dead," Dylan said flatly. "Died a long time ago. He can't do anything to help us."

"Ha ha! That's what *you* think," Tony taunted. He paused, and there was a flicker in the coding of his programming. "Oh, um... So somebody just initialized the transceiver."

"What?" I exclaimed, and looked down at my watch to see that we still had thirty seconds left on our clock. Damn Sage and his villainous ability to overachieve at the worst possible moment. And damn me for getting distracted with learning there was a way we could save Scipio.

"What do we do?" I asked, taking a step toward the terminal. "We don't have a hard drive to download you into."

"No, but you have your net," Rose exclaimed excitedly. "The alpha series was designed to house AIs."

I frowned and reached into my pocket to pull out the small white square. "I don't think that's wise," I said. "Remember, Sage said he could spy on me through it."

"I can help with that," Tony said confidently. "He won't be able to eavesdrop as long as I'm in it, so no worries there. But you do have a problem: you don't have the proper download platform to make that kind of transfer. We need a wireless data transfer node."

I frowned, and realized he was right. When I had downloaded Leo into my net so long ago, it had been through a specialized scanner on his terminal, which had transmitted his code wirelessly. When we transferred him into the Medica, we'd used a similar device. I quickly pulled the tech's bag off my shoulder and opened it up, hoping to find something that we could use. Inside, there was a cornucopia of items that I could mostly only categorize as gadgets and gizmos, along with crystals, rolls of wiring, several data chips, some sort of motherboard... The list went on. I scanned the haul for something resembling what I had seen in the past, but eventually grew impatient and spilled the contents out on the desk the terminal was sitting on.

A few items fell on the floor, and I quickly squatted down to pick them up and returned them to the pile. "What about any of this?" I asked, worried about what was happening with Tony. If Sage was in the process of downloading him, we wouldn't have very long to circumvent what he was doing. We needed to get him out of there. "Does any of this work?"

I looked at Rose, expecting an answer from her, and to her credit, she leaned over the desk to inspect the items, carefully picking up a few objects and examining them. But it was Tony who answered my question.

"You have the most important components. We just have to make a few modifications. Go ahead and grab that microprocessor, the IDF scanner, the bundle of gold wire .02, the redirection matrix, the..."

The list continued to grow, the names of items becoming more and more complicated as he went on, and I gave Rose a helpless look, begging for assistance. She shifted her massive weight from one leg to the other and then shook her head, managing to appear equally baffled. In desperation, I turned to Dylan, whose frozen mask of confusion and intimidation seemed somehow more grandiose than mine. Tony blithely missed it all, and finally, after several seconds of him droning on, I had to cut him off.

"Tony, two things: One, I have no idea what any of that stuff is. Two, how can we do this before your download goes through? What is even going on with that?"

"Oh, sorry!" he exclaimed, instantly contrite. "I shut it down. Lacey gave me an off switch on my end to make sure I had a choice in the matter in case something like this happened, and I chose to terminate the connection. But that doesn't mean I'm safe. It won't take Scipio long to track where the transceiver sent its signal, using the Core's sensors. I'm guessing we have about five minutes before they try to force a connection and drag me out."

I looked at Dylan, and her eyes confirmed the truth of what I was thinking: there was no way we could construct what Tony needed—in that time—without help.

"I'll go get Lidecher," she said, and I nodded, glad she was in the same headspace as me. I hoped the tech wouldn't be upset about us calling for more help, but even if he was, he could get over it. We needed him.

"Thanks," I told her as she headed for the door. Then I turned back to Tony. "Start showing me pictures of the components you need. Rose and I will start separating them so we can get this done."

"Oh, fun! A game! Okay, hmm..." Tony gave me another contemplative look, and the next thing I knew, the code that was being used to make up his face suddenly shifted into an image. I stared at it for a second, confused yet a third time by the AI's unconcerned nature, in spite of the threat to his code, and then shook my head, deciding not to question it. There wasn't time, and frankly, if he wanted to turn this into a game, I was okay with it—as long as we got the task done in time.

Please let us get the task done in time, I begged silently, hoping that someone somewhere was listening... and on my side.

14

"Good," Tony said, his eyes squinting at Lidecher as if he were able to peer through the nervous man to see what he was doing. "Now place the alternating current nodule into the wire and affix it to the transceiver. Use a .02 millijoule charge when closing the circuit. Anything higher will fry the scanning element."

"Okay," Lidecher said, quickly following Tony's instructions. I glanced at my watch and tried not to cringe when I saw that four minutes were already gone. "Okay," he repeated again. "The scanning element is starting to glow. What do I do now?"

"Stand back and let the lady put the net on the scanner," Tony replied, and I practically leapt forward, holding the net between two fingers.

"Here," I said, slapping a hand on Lidecher's shoulder to keep him in place so I could simply lean over him. My eyes scanned the electrical components, which seemed to fill every bit of free space on the desk, and quickly found the glowing green screen that was about the size of my hand. I dropped the net on it and then looked at the terminal. "Can you sense it?" I asked, knowing I was being impatient.

"Yes," he replied. "Downloading now."

A second later, his face disappeared from the screen and was replaced by a progress bar. I watched as it slowly began to fill, tracking upward, and then took a quick look at my watch. Only thirty seconds left.

"C'mon," I whispered, trying not to bounce back and forth on my toes. Getting Tony out and slowing Sage down was step one of a plan that was only loosely coming together in my head, but I didn't want to have come this far only to fail at the first stage.

The bar continued to move up as the numbers on my watch shrank down, and my heartrate doubled as I realized he wasn't going to make it. The bar was at 62 percent with only fifteen seconds remaining, then 78 percent at ten, 84 percent at five…

The clock hit zero with only 91 percent of the download completed, and I had a heartbeat to pray that Tony had been off in his predictions—that Scipio wasn't able to move that quickly—before all the lights on the server lit up at once. There was a high-pitched hum, and then the entire room exploded in a shower of sparks.

"Duck!" I shouted belatedly. Then, ignoring my own advice, I turned toward the scanner. An electrical surge was building, white-blue, crackling fingers of lightning beginning to form between the servers, following the cable lines between them. I saw them traveling down the line toward the net at lightning speed, and reached out and snatched it on impulse.

The arc of electricity caught me in the wrist, and every muscle in my body seized up as an unknown number of volts shot through me. The air caught in my lungs, and I was powerless for several seconds, frozen in a blast of fiery hot pain that ran under my skin.

Then it stopped, and I was flying backward.

I felt oddly disconnected as I fell through the air, even though I knew I was flying at a speed that would undoubtedly fracture several of my bones as soon as I hit the wall, and that there was nothing I could do to stop it. It seemed as inevitable as gravity that I was going to hit.

Unconsciousness began to loom up, the darkness filling the edges of my sight as I continued to tumble through the air, and I felt myself start to give in, not wanting to remain awake for the inevitable thud.

But hands grabbed me before I fully succumbed, catching and

cradling me. The sensation was a jolting juxtaposition when compared to the smooth glide through the air, and it snapped me back to a position of wakefulness.

Only then did I realize I needed to breathe. My lungs were burning from being locked in place by the electrical surge, my body's desire for oxygen a pressing need. I opened my mouth to take a breath, but for some reason, my chest wouldn't move. I blinked and looked around, then reared back when I saw a metallic face loom into view.

But the purple eyes told me it was Rose, and I placed a hand on my chest, tapping on it.

She nodded and looked up and away from me. I followed the direction of her gaze and saw Dylan hobbling toward me. Her mouth was moving, and as I cocked my head at her, I realized she was talking. I couldn't hear what she was saying, but I didn't care. My body was screaming for oxygen, but my lungs were refusing to help, and for several terrifying heartbeats, I felt certain that they were irreparably burned by the electricity, and that I was going to die. I was floundering, trying to make my ears work, to understand what she was saying, when something cold pressed against my neck.

There was a sting of something being injected. I felt my lungs begin to move and tried to fill them with as much air as I could get, the feeling conjuring up images of the air scraping over sandpaper. I grew lightheaded at the first gasp, and by the second, the blackness was rising back up and claiming me.

I fought it.

Even as it dragged me down, making my limbs heavy and useless, I fought against the sensation, struggling to open my eyes.

The first time I pried them open, the sharp brightness of the real world sent me reeling, my head threatening to split in half with the pain. I sank back into oblivion automatically, the agony so severe that I was certain I would die if I did it again.

I started to let myself drift deeper, but a voice whispered for me to

CHAPTER 14

fight it—that if I didn't, I would die—and I believed it. I clawed my way back to reality, this time preparing myself for the pain, and cracked open a single eyelid. Slowness did nothing to mitigate the throbbing ache, but I fought through it, opening my eye further.

A dark shape hovered at the edge of my periphery, the blob difficult to make out. I tried to tilt my head toward it, and felt the muscles of my neck shifting just under my skin in a most discomforting way, like they had somehow been separated into strands and I could feel every one. As my head began to tilt, a wall of dizziness crashed over me, and the darkness came back to seize me.

This time I floated, the pain and confusion of my last two attempts making it more difficult to mount a third. I was beyond tired, and I hovered at the edge of unconsciousness, the pull of it dragging me down while I kept hauling myself up enough, just enough to avoid giving in entirely.

As the struggle raged on, I found myself wondering what I was holding on for. Something had happened to me—was happening to me—and I clearly needed rest. Maybe it would be okay to just let go, and slowly sink back in.

NO! a voice insisted, an almost petulant lilt to it. *Keep fighting. Don't give in.*

I felt something reaching out for me, a line of connection that promised that if I tried, just one more time, I'd be rewarded. It wouldn't be that bad.

Grey's face filled my mind—a memory of us standing on the catwalk by the hydro-turbines, the moment that had hung between us, coupled with the recollection of Leo, his lips pressing against mine in a hot, hungry kiss that was all him, even if he had been inside of Grey's body at the time.

The reminder of the two men in my life, the love I felt for them, gave me the fire for one last try, and this time, I just went for it.

My eyelids snapped open, and I resisted the urge to shut them immediately against the harsh light, and squinted instead. It took a few seconds for the glare to lessen, my pupils slowly contracting to filter out the excess light. My head ached fiercely, but even as I thought about it, there was a significant decrease in the pain, making it somewhat easier to breathe.

How's that? a voice asked in my mind, and I tensed.

Tony? I asked, instantly confused. *What—*

You took a few thousand volts, and your heart almost stopped. Luckily, Dylan had enough first-aid training to inject you with adrenaline, and something that she said will help with the damage to your nerves.

A synaptic neural gel, I told him, knowing exactly what Dylan had done. It was smart, too. Her quick thinking had likely spared me any long-term nerve damage. *Where are we?*

Even as I asked, my vision finally began to focus, the dark and light colors sharpening, gaining shape and definition. I realized I was sitting down in a hall, my back pressed against the wall, just outside of a door. We were no longer in the server farm. The halls were lit differently, and were significantly warmer. But beyond still being in Cogstown, I had no idea where we were.

Level 25, Tony replied. *Dylan took charge after you passed out, and at Rose's insistence, put me inside you, in case there was any brain damage. There was not, by the way, and I managed to get the rest of my program into the net before Scipio crashed the server, so there's that. I hope you don't mind, but I took the liberty of piloting your body up here. It was super fun, by the way; you're kind of really flexible, huh?*

If Tony had been any older, or had any sort of a lecherous tone in his voice, I would've been creeped out. But he wasn't, and I could sense the compliment. Even still, that did nothing to detract from his revelation that he'd been "piloting" my body while I was unconscious. *I'm not sure I'm—*

There wasn't any time, he interjected impatiently. *Scipio fried the servers controlling the doors, to try to get me to escape through the transceiver. I set up a dummy program to continue opening the doors for the Cogs after I left, but it's gone. That means that whatever doors were open are going to stay open until the Cogs close them manually. If they don't get them closed in time, then Alice is going to get in, and everybody's up poop creek without a paddle. We had to keep moving.*

I bristled under his words. He was right, of course. I just didn't like

CHAPTER 14

the idea that he had taken control of me. Still, I could tell he hadn't done it maliciously; his thoughts were like an open book to me, and I could feel the innocence of his actions. Which was odd, considering he was over two hundred and fifty years old.

I understand, I told him, deciding to let it go. *Now, why are we on level 25? That's right above Water Treatment. It's the wrong direction.*

Your blood sugar is dangerously low, and your electrolytes are depleted. Dylan asked Lynch to find you some food and water, and this was apparently the closest place. I wanted to work on waking you up, so I stayed out here while they went inside to grab some grub. But, now that you're up, you should probably get in there. They seem to be at an impasse regarding what to do next. Or rather, how to do it.

His words filled me with a sense of foreboding, but I ignored it and slowly climbed to my feet. Every movement was filled with some sort of twinge, sometimes painful, but other times electric, like amps of energy had somehow managed to hide themselves just under my skin. I ignored that, too, and eventually made it to my feet.

I was exhausted by the effort, but Tony had mentioned one important detail that seemed to override everything else weighing on my mind.

Food and water.

15

I pressed the door control to open the door and stepped inside, trying my best not to stagger. My knees felt rubbery, and every nerve ending in my body seemed to twitch with excess energy, but I somehow managed to keep a smidgeon of dignity.

Dylan and Lynch were standing on either side of a dining room table filled with food and water bottles—telling me we were in a residence. They were also in the middle of a shouting match. Rose stood on a third side, her head darting nervously back and forth as the two exchanged verbal volleys. She looked as if she were ready to intercede the minute things turned violent, and I couldn't blame her. I had arrived when both parties were just about turning blue in the face.

"What's going on?" I asked, and then paused at the hoarse grating sound my voice made. I sounded *awful*, like someone who was about to die. Luckily, the strange croak was jarring enough to catch both Dylan's and Lynch's attention, and they both stopped whatever incoherent rant they were in the middle of and turned toward me.

"Liana?" Dylan asked cautiously, taking a step toward me. "Or Tony?"

I stared at her for a second, and suddenly understood perfectly how Grey must feel every time I did that to him. First, I was confused. How

CHAPTER 15

could she not recognize me? Then I was angry—not at Tony or her, but that I couldn't remember getting here or any conversation Tony might have had while he was using my body to get around. I took a deep breath and let it go, my current needs far more pressing than my wounded pride.

"It's me," I said, moving toward the table, my eyes focused solely on one of the water bottles. It had condensation on the side, telling me that it had been, at one point, cold. Dylan grabbed it before I was halfway there and tossed it to me. I caught it awkwardly, the joints in my hand too stiff to move properly, and wound up using my arm to press it to my chest. I then pulled it out, unscrewed the lid, and began drinking the water.

It was still cool, and beyond refreshing. I guzzled it down, pulling mouthful after mouthful, unwilling to relinquish it until I had sated the terrible thirst that had seized me. For several seconds everyone was silent, leaving only the sound of my heavy gulps in the room.

I stopped only when it became necessary to breathe, pulled the bottle away, and wiped my mouth with my sleeve. "Thank you," I said, my voice significantly improved with the aid of the water I had just consumed. Dylan and Lynch both nodded.

"How are you feeling?" Lynch asked, stepping around the table. "Has Tony—"

"He got me mostly up to speed in the hallway," I told him. "I'm still confused as to why we came down here for food. Surely we could have gotten some from an apartment closer to the Grounds."

I reached for a loaf of bread from the table as I said this, gripping it between two hands so I could rip a chunk of it off and shove it in my mouth. My hunger was asserting itself so aggressively that manners weren't even an option.

"Number one, because this is my apartment," Lynch said. There wasn't any condescension in his voice as he said this, but at my curious glance, he added, "I didn't feel right using my authority to access other people's apartments to take their food. But that's not the real reason. It has to do with the sentinels."

I shoved another piece of bread in my mouth, the taste deliciously sour and fresh, and looked at Dylan for an explanation as to why the sentinels had played a role in the decision to go down. She knew that I wanted to get to the Citadel as quickly as possible, so there had to be a reason she had done the opposite.

"The sentinels are still mostly on the upper levels," Dylan reported. "Which means the doors on those levels are the most dangerous, because sentinels could be lurking on the other side. It would be madness to try to slip back into the shell and get back up to the Grounds that way. So we went down, to see if we could get ahead of the sentinels and slip out one of the doors down here. Get back into the shell."

I chewed thoughtfully, mulling over what she was saying, and realized she was right. It had been the right call. Getting to the Citadel to help the others meant avoiding as many obstacles as possible, which meant the path of least resistance was the right one.

"So then why are you fighting?" I asked after I had swallowed the bread. "It makes sense."

"Because I think you should exit on the north side of the shell, and use the power conduits running up the side to climb up," Lynch said angrily. "They have no sensors, no cameras, and none of the sentinels would think to look for you in there."

"And I said that would take too long," Dylan practically snarled. "The area in there is tight, not meant for fast movement. You need to get us to the west side of the Tower. Lift shaft number 12 on that side goes all the way up to level 83 of the shell before it dead ends, so we can use our lashes to climb up the shaft all the way to the top, taking rests every ten levels or so. From there, we would just have to sneak up two flights of stairs."

I stared at both of them for a moment, and then took another bite of bread, using the time to consider both their plans. In truth, I hadn't been thinking about the how of getting up; I'd just assumed we would return to the Grounds and climb up the same way Sage did. But they were right to be considering it, because with the sentinels in the shell, movement within it was going to be very tricky, if not downright impossible.

CHAPTER 15

But I didn't like the sound of either of their proposed options. The power conduits that Lynch was talking about were one of the four main power lines that transferred power from Water Treatment and Cogstown and distributed it to the Core and the rest of the Tower. While they ran all the way to the top, and had just enough space for workers to climb in and out, the conduits in there emitted massive amounts of thermal radiation, making it dangerous to be in there for a long time. There were environmental suits we could wear to resist it, but even then, they started losing integrity after an hour. Not to mention, if Sage needed power diverted to the Core for his plan to kill Scipio, then he was undoubtedly keeping an eye on those conduits—if only to make sure no one tampered with them.

But just because they were out didn't mean going up an elevator shaft was any better. The entire shell was without power and pitch black, making something that was difficult enough to navigate—even when lit—damn near impossible to do so in the darkness. The Tower held a veritable pitfall of ways you could plummet to your death, and if we weren't extremely careful (and slow), then we could accidently step into an elevator shaft or plummet into one of the plunges. Or worse, someone from an upper level could accidently fall into one while we were in it, and plummet down on top of us, killing everyone on impact. Not to mention, the sentinels would undoubtedly be monitoring them as well, looking for anyone trying to escape. It was far too exposed.

I'm glad you got there quickly, Tony said in my head, his voice exasperated. *Because I didn't want to waste time giving you the numbers. Your best option is to go outside.*

"Outside?" I exclaimed out loud, and Lynch and Dylan both exchanged confused looks. I ignored them, my mind racing. What he was talking about was risky, but I immediately saw the appeal. Sage wouldn't anticipate anyone going outside the Tower to avoid him. He would assume that everyone would try to remain inside rather than risk getting stuck outside. If we could make it to one of the access hatches and get out, then we could scale the side of the Tower with our lashes. It was still dangerous. If the lash ends failed, the gyros in our harnesses gave out, or we grew careless due to exhaustion, we could plummet to our deaths. But Tony was right: it was the best way to get up the Tower unobstructed.

I looked at the other occupants of the room, and smiled. "Tony suggests we scale the outside of the Tower, and I happen to agree with him. Where's a good place to do that?"

Lynch leaned away from the table, his face contemplative, and then nodded thoughtfully, while I took the opportunity to stuff more bread into my mouth. "On the north side of the Tower," he said. "It'll put you out of direct sunlight, which will hopefully prevent you from getting too sunburned or dehydrated, and it'll give you the best access to the Citadel without forcing you to navigate too much of the shell. You'll be exposed on the bridges, but... I don't know where you go from there. I'm not really familiar with that area of the Tower, so you'll have to figure it out. I can at least get you out."

"Excellent," I said approvingly around another spongy mouthful of bread.

"Not excellent," Dylan cut in before I could say more. I switched my gaze over to her, swallowed the piece down, and waited for her to air her issues to the group. "We don't have the equipment to scale the Tower. I don't know when you last switched your lash ends out, but I haven't done it in a while, and we've both been exposed to all sorts of radiation, which you and I both know causes them to degrade. I don't have any spares, and you're talking about climbing *a hundred stories* with them. They will fail, and we will die, long before we reach the top."

She was right, of course, but I had already been going over the problem in my head, and I had thought up a solution.

"Lynch, where's the nearest Knight supply station?" I asked.

Every department had supply stations on the other floors, just for situations like this. And though they were some of the most secure rooms in the Tower, they also ran on battery power, making them accessible even during a crisis. Only workers from the right department had access, meaning only Knights had access to Knight supply rooms, Cogs to Mechanical supply rooms, etc. It was impossible for Scipio to lock anyone out, as they operated outside of his systems.

CHAPTER 15

He blinked, a surprised smile dawning on his face. "On the way, actually. Why?"

"Well, for one thing, Dylan and I are going to need replacement lash ends. But for another, you're going to need batons to fight Alice. One won't do much to slow her down, but if you can organize people, and you all hit her at the same time, then you can disable her long enough to rip the hard drive out of each sentinel's back. Rose, would you show him?"

She turned around and pointed to the black box under the metal cage fitted between her shoulder blades, and I continued talking. "Do whatever you can to destroy that, and you destroy the sentinel."

He nodded and pulled out his pad to type a message on it while I looked at Dylan, raising an eyebrow in mocking smugness. She arched one of her own, and then looked me over from head to toe.

"That was a really smart suggestion," she admitted with a smile. "But you better take a look in the mirror before you go acting all superior."

I laughed at that, and turned toward one of the pictures in the wall, trying to catch a glimpse of my reflection. "Are you saying that I don't look pretty enough to bust in and rescue Grey and the others?"

"Girl, at this point you look like you're an IT-born recruit on her third day at the Academy, and her drill instructor is Rachel Pine."

I cringed at the image that conjured, knowing full well that of all the departments we recruited from, IT produced some of the worst candidates, physical fitness-wise. Perhaps it was the sedentary lifestyle of the Eyes, but their kids often came to us overweight and highly sensitive. And the Academy was indifferent to all of that, and ran them ragged to get them in shape.

In the ghostly outline of my image in the glass, I could see that my hair had come completely undone and was standing out around my head, not quite on end, but definitely filled with static. Beyond that, my face was a pale blob, giving me zero indication of the state of it.

"I've definitely looked better," I said once I was done, turning back toward her.

Her smile was lopsided. "Me too. Lynch, you done?"

"Yup," he said, tapping a few more buttons, presumably to send the message. "Let's get going."

16

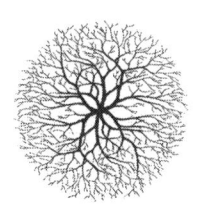

We made it to the Knights' supply room quickly, even with me scarfing down a few more chunks of bread and polishing off two more bottles of water as we went. Nobody bothered us. In fact, there didn't seem to be much traffic on this level at all, likely because all the Cogs were on the upper levels, trying to prevent the spread of the sentinels.

Dylan and I quickly found the lash ends on a shelf and pocketed several while discussing the finer points of when and how to change out the lash ends during the climb. Vertical climbs were tricky, as finding a way to generate enough momentum to create a static charge strong enough to hold our weight was too difficult to safely achieve when throwing vertically, which meant shorter, tighter throws. That was more stress on the lash ends, which would result in them failing more quickly than if we were lashing inside the Tower.

Dylan wanted to plan to change them out every three hundred feet, which meant changing the lash ends out nine times. I overruled her, wanting them changed out every hundred. It meant going slower—we'd have to stop a total of twenty-five times, which was annoying—but considering the climb we were about to make, it was the safest course of action.

I wasn't any good to my friends dead, so I was willing to play it safe, for now.

As soon as we were done, I gave Lynch my ID number and told him to have his people open the other Knight supply stations up and take as many batons as they could. It wouldn't be much, but it was better than nothing. He sent out another message, and then tucked his pad back into his overalls and waved for us to follow.

We took several twisting turns down the halls, enough for me to grow a little disoriented about where we were, and then entered one long hall, which was both wide and tall, taking up nearly two levels. A series of tracks ran through the middle of the floor, but the sides were crammed with boxes of tools, equipment, barrels, sheets of metal, workbenches... It took me a minute, but I finally realized that it wasn't a hall at all, but a storage room.

Lynch began picking his way through the winding path, evidently so used to the sight that it failed to inspire any awe in him, but I couldn't help but gape. It was cluttered and showed signs of being used frequently. Dozens of workbenches grouped together in a haphazard way were cluttered with tools, and there were various pieces of machinery in the room in different stages of disassembly. Tool bags were hung on this and that, with different last names embroidered on them to signal ownership, scattered all around the room in no particular order. There was even a kitchen in the corner, which showed signs of activity, including a few dishes of unfinished food sitting on a nearby table. Looking at the room, I suddenly felt as if this was the true heart of Cogstown—a place where workers congregated to share stories while working on various projects and replacement parts.

A pang went through me as I thought about those people, and how many of them were likely to die, with what was going on in the Tower. However Sage was targeting his victims, he'd make sure of that. The sooner I got to him, the sooner I could stop it. But I had to get to the others first. They had no idea that he wanted Leo, or that he even knew Leo existed, and wouldn't be taking the necessary precautions to keep him protected. They assumed he was safely hidden inside Grey. They didn't know what I knew.

CHAPTER 16

It was frustrating not being able to reach out and talk to them. My entire life, I had taken the nets for granted, and now that I was without even the most basic function of mine, I felt panicky and unhinged. The lack of knowledge was driving me insane.

I quickly moved to catch up with Lynch and Dylan, passing by Rose and offering her a pat on the arm as I went by, reassuring her that I was okay. We passed through the room in quick order, and then exited into another hall.

"There's a door that's open up ahead," Lynch announced softly as he turned left down the hall. "We opened it early on to try to evacuate the shell, and have been pulling people through here and there. So far, there hasn't been any sign of the sentinels. Still, I've had a team of Cogs waiting on us before sealing it up, so we should move fast."

It was like he was reading my mind, and I picked up the pace to a light jog, ignoring my throbbing aches and pains. The sound of our boots on the metal flooring filled the hall as the others joined me, and within a minute we were slowing down to pause at a T-shaped junction, then moving into it. I saw the door a hundred feet away, three Cog workers standing around it. Two were directing flashlights into the darkened hall of the shell, while one was standing by the gear mechanism, ready to seal it shut.

The one by the gears turned to us as we started to walk toward him, and Lynch waved his hand at him and called something to them that I couldn't quite hear. They nodded, and then, to my surprise, one of them leaned farther into the hall, partially disappearing. I barely had the chance to ask, "What is he doing?" before three sharp clangs sounded down the hall from the door.

"Trying to signal anyone who might be nearby," Lynch replied, and I frowned. As admirable as that was, making noise to attract attention would do just that—but not just from the beings with whom they were trying to communicate. If they had been doing that for some time, there was a good chance that nearby sentinels might have heard it, and were on their way to investigate.

That put even more zip in my step, and I wound up drawing side by side with Lynch as we got close to the group of Cogs. "That doesn't seem particularly safe," I said. "What if—"

As if my words were prophetic, the man leaning out the door suddenly reared back, taking several startled steps away from it. I threw an arm up across Lynch's chest and froze, my gut telling me that it was the sentinels, but a stream of people suddenly exploded through the hatch, clawing their way through it as if the fires of hell were licking at their boots.

The man at the door tried to wave them away from us, toward a set of stairs farther down the hall, but several of them broke off and began rushing at us, fear making their motions jerky and desperate. I realized that it was going to be impossible to get down the hall, let alone through the door, with people trying to escape the sentinels that were behind them, and quickly decided to use their fear against them, to keep us from getting overwhelmed.

I pushed Lynch back against the wall and said, "Rose!" in a sharp voice. "It's time for you to be scary!" She needed no other command, and Dylan quickly got out of her way to let her through.

The effect was immediate, and the crowd broke in front of her, whirling away with desperate howls.

I dropped my arm from over Lynch's chest and took a step down the hall past Rose. "Get back to Lacey and keep her safe," I told him. "And get every door sealed before it's too late. We'll see what we can do to hold them off while the Cogs seal the door!"

Lynch's eyes grew wide, but he nodded and reached out to place his hands on my shoulders. "Good luck to you, Liana!" he shouted as the noise in the hall grew to a crescendo.

"You as well," I said, reaching up to cup his hand and hoping the brave man made it through whatever horrors came next.

Then we let go of each other, and I moved to keep up with Rose, Dylan only a step behind me. We raced down the corridor toward the throng of people. I knew there was a sentinel out there, and I prayed that it was only one. Rose would be able to hold off just one. Any more than that, and we were screwed.

But not as screwed as the Tower was going to be if those Cogs closed the door before we were on the other side of it. We were the only ones who had any idea of what to do—the only ones who could do anything to stop it. We had to keep moving, keep fighting, or Sage would figure out a way to make his plan work without Tony.

Hell, for all I knew, all he really needed was Leo.

The line of people thinned to a trickle as we reached the door, but I wasn't certain whether the crowd outside had caught wind of Rose, or if everyone had managed to get inside. A few seconds later, it didn't matter.

We crossed the threshold into the shell, the light through the door casting a pool around us that seemed feeble next to the pitch-black darkness, and I came to a sudden halt, every bone in my body telling me that the threat was very, very near. A quiet stillness came over my body as I clicked on the hand light that Tony had wrapped around my forearm, channeling the light into a slim, powerful beam. I took a moment to pull out my gun and click the safety off, and then drew my baton, lighting up a charge.

It might not do much, but it could buy me a second, and I'd often defied death by merely a second or two. Why stop doing it now?

For all my bravado, inside I was quaking. I could feel Alice's presence out there, like a deep taint that was slowly rotting the Tower from the inside out. She may have been a victim of Sage's torture, but whatever he had done had unleashed something dark and cruel inside of her.

I lifted my arm up, shining the light around, and then flinched at the sudden sound of grating behind me. I turned and saw the door sliding closed, slowly killing the light. I realized our only escape was disappearing—and I still hadn't figured out where the sentinel was hiding.

Turning back to the hall in front of me, I resumed my search, my eyes half watching the darkness for any gleams of metal, and half focused on the darkness for any sign of golden eyes. But my light only revealed the hall, empty, stretching out before us for as far as the light carried.

I took a step forward into the darkness and checked the hall to the left and right, the hair on my body standing upright, every inch of me tense and ready for action.

But even after several desperate flashes with the light, there was nothing.

The people just heard the noise and came running, Tony finally said, breaking his silence. *You're being paranoid, and wasting time. Get to the outer shell so you can get outside.*

It took me several seconds, but then I realized he was right. "It's clear," I said to the others. "Let's go."

I started to head down the hall in front of me, and then paused, trying to orient myself. The shell toward the base of the Tower was almost impossible to navigate with the lights on. It was going to be a nightmare in the dark.

Inside my head, Tony laughed, the sensation making me feel like a boat bobbing in a turbulent body of water. *You're so lucky I'm here,* he said. *Go straight to the end and turn left. I'll update you as we go. Should only take ten minutes to get to the outer shell.*

Ten minutes alone, in the dark, with insane, murderous sentinels running amok, I thought, striding forward down the hall.

Just great.

17

The dark is a terrible and malicious nemesis. Sounds are enhanced in it, making every groan and shout seem as if it were coming from right next to you. Light is swallowed by it, leaving you encased in a dim halo that seems a thin barrier against it. Objects that you pass by every day become terrifying, looming up unexpectedly with sinister intent, and creating shadows in which the enemy could hide.

Every step we made was a dead giveaway of our presence. Every pass of the light down an open hall, a beacon to the enemy. There was a chance of imminent attack at every corner, and my body responded to it by flooding me with adrenaline and endorphins, trying to keep my senses sharp.

Even with Tony's guidance, I felt hopelessly lost and confused. There was no way to tell what direction we were going, and the markings on the hallway were unhelpful without my pad to track my position. The halls were marked, of course, but I didn't have every level memorized. If I had been trying to get us out alone, we would never have even made it to the outer shell.

As it was, I was really surprised that we did without encountering a single person or sentinel. It seemed like an absolute impossibility, given what I had witnessed in the halls earlier, but when Tony announced,

That's the door to the outer part of the shell, my heart felt like it could've imploded in relief.

I made my way toward the pressure hatch he had indicated, but took pains to check the hall around it, making sure there wasn't a sentinel lurking in the darkness. The light on my arm chased away the black inkiness, revealing a gray pipe running from the floor to the ceiling, followed by several more feet of wall, interrupted again by another pipe. Overhead, lights—useless now—and bundles of cables and pipes ran along the ceiling. I could imagine a sentinel hiding up there, like some sort of spider lying in wait, but my light revealed nothing. Not on the ceiling, nor on the other side of the hall.

I exhaled a breath I didn't know I had been holding, and turned back to the others, lowering the light to the door. "It's clear," I said, keeping my voice whisper soft.

Dylan nodded and stepped up to the door, her hands going to the wheel. I took a step closer, not because I intended to help or take over, but because being too far away from her light made me feel vulnerable and exposed. Maybe it was fear, or a survival instinct, but either way, I did it.

She grunted as she tried to turn the handle, and to my surprise, really leaned into it, adding the strength of her legs and her body weight.

The wheel refused to budge.

Dylan pushed off of it and flashed me a confused look. "I don't understand," she whispered. "I'm not that weak. I can bench press two hundred and fifty pounds!"

I blinked at her, impressed by her physical prowess, and then looked back at the door. "I'm not sure," I finally said. "Maybe it was damaged? Or someone realized there were sentinels in the inner shell and barricaded it from the other side?"

"May I try?" Rose asked, and I looked at the sentinel. Or rather, I looked up at her, past what seemed like miles and miles of robotic strength.

"Absolutely," I replied, taking a step back to give her some room. Dylan followed suit.

CHAPTER 17

Rose stepped up to the door, her wide form almost completely obscuring it. I couldn't see what happened next, but there was a loud, heavy groan for several long seconds—time enough for me to turn around and scan the hallway behind us. There wasn't any sign of movement, but I had to believe that if they were close enough to hear the sound, they'd be coming soon.

We needed to be gone before they got here.

"What's wrong?" I heard Dylan whisper behind me, and I looked over my shoulder to see that Rose had taken a step back, the door still unopened.

"I was able to move it several centimeters, but the locking mechanism is resisting me," she reported. "With more leverage, I believe I can get the door open."

More leverage? I considered the problem for a second, and the implications. If we couldn't get this door open in the next thirty seconds, then we needed to get moving and find another one, or grab a cutter and cut our way through. We couldn't afford to—

Your baton, Tony interjected into my thoughts, and then showed me a picture of Rose sliding it through the hand wheel and using it as a crank. Immediately, I felt stupid for not thinking of it, and quickly grabbed my baton and held it out to Rose.

"Use this to add torque to the wheel," I told her, and her purple eyes lightened in what I could only assume was understanding before she grabbed it. I heard the sound as she slid it through, the rasp of it loud in my ears, and renewed my efforts in the hallway, keeping a wary eye out.

The heavy metallic groan returned moments later, periodically punctuated by a sharp squeal of movement. I swallowed, my nerves scrabbling against the noise, screaming for her to stop giving away our position, but I swallowed it down and kept panning the light around.

Pipe. Wall. Another pipe. Flooring. Non-functional lighting. More darkness that my light couldn't penetrate. Wall. Pipe. Wall.

"Status," I said, when the span of time grew intolerable.

"Halfway there," Rose reported, and I writhed at the delay.

"Dylan?"

"This side is still clear," she reported, but I could hear the thread of fear in her voice, telling me that she was feeling the exposure just as keenly as I was.

"Keep calm," I told her, and it wasn't just directed at her, but also at myself. We'd come too far already to give in to our baser instincts now, and I wasn't about to set a precedent. "We're almost—"

I stopped when my light caught something. Not the chromatic silver of the sentinels, but rather a flash of paleness that could only come from human flesh, showing from behind one of the pipes, just at the edge of my light. Whoever it was ducked back into the darkness before I could really make them out, and on instinct, I took a step toward them.

"Hello?" I called softly, keeping my voice calm so as not to scare them. "Don't worry about the sentinel. She's on our side, protecting us."

My light cut deeper into the darkness, but there was no sign of movement, even as I panned it around. I paused, listening closely, and heard the faint rustle of someone moving away, trying to muffle the sound of their boots in their passing. For a second, it was in my heart to go after them, to reassure them that we were safe and that they should come with us, but then my mind kicked into high gear, reminding me it wasn't possible. We didn't have another lash harness for them, and carrying them up a sheer wall would only add stress to our gyros. I supposed they could hold on to Rose's back, but it was still dangerous. He or she had better chances inside the shell, especially if my hypothesis about who the sentinels were targeting was correct, and they had a rank higher than six. If not, then I prayed they found somewhere safe to hide until this was over.

I retreated back to the others, keeping my light moving. The sound Rose was making with the door continued for several more long seconds, and then suddenly it stopped with a loud clang.

I nearly leapt out of my skin, the sound like a thunderclap erupting right in my ear, and whirled around in time to see her shoving the door open.

Water immediately began to spill into the hall, sluicing down from over the opening to create a thin waterfall and spattering against the bottom rim and onto the floor of the hall.

"What the—" I said out loud, my shock at seeing water in a place where it was not supposed to be overriding all internal thought. Maybe there was a leak coming from one of the greeneries above? It was possible, but it seemed unlikely, given how much water was pouring down.

Rose continued through the water, ignoring it even as the part of her chest where the sentinel had been damaged sparked, causing Dylan and me to dance back to avoid getting hit by the bright embers shooting toward us. For several seconds, I could see the vague outline of her on the platform beyond, through the sheet of water, as she looked around. Then she turned back and made a gesture with her hand, indicating that it was clear.

I exchanged glances with Dylan and then took a deep breath to calm myself. Whatever the problem was, it didn't seem to involve the sentinels, so that, at least, was a relief. I could figure out the rest once I was inside. I motioned for Dylan to go, did one last check of the dark hall to make sure we weren't being observed, and then stepped through the watery portal, lifting an arm to shield myself from the torrential spray.

I almost slipped on the flooring as I stepped onto the landing, and Dylan quickly grabbed an arm and stabilized me. I shot her a grateful look and then turned around. The water splashed under my feet. Holding my arm down to shine the light on it, I realized immediately that the leak was not a leak at all. Water was sluicing down the staircase and the walls, creating a steady stream that didn't seem to be ending. I shone my light down the stairs and saw that not even twenty-five feet down, the water was collecting into a pool—and swallowing up the stairs and the levels under it.

"It's the defenses," Dylan said, just as I was coming to the same conclusion. One of the Tower's defenses for repelling outside invaders was to flood the outer part of the shell to drown the enemies before they could get inside. I'd never seen it happen—never even heard of it being used—but here it was, coming true.

And my eyes widened as I realized that this wasn't an accident, either. Water Treatment had ultimate control over this particular defense, and they would not have activated it heedlessly. *This* was why Sage had attacked Water Treatment, why it had fallen. He'd needed the power from the hydro-turbines—and he'd wanted this area flooded.

But why? To kill the people inside in an attempt to prevent them from thwarting him? Or something else?

Something else, Tony said gravely, and I took a step up the stairs, suddenly afraid.

"What?" I asked, causing Dylan and Rose to give me strange looks. I ignored them, focusing on Tony's answer.

The outer shell needs to be filled with water if anyone is going to initiate a system purge of the Core. The endothermic heat generated by the power transfer is enough to melt its own components unless they are cooled rapidly. That's mostly handled with hydrogen, but the water in the shell acts as both a reservoir and a cooling element to the power conduits running through the shell. It prevents them from burning out.

How much time does this give us before he's ready to do that? I asked, my mind racing. Sage's plan still required Leo and Tony, and the power from the Mechanics and Knights Departments, but if this was another element to it, I needed to know what kind of timeframe I had before Sage physically had what he needed to kill Scipio.

At this rate? Eight hours.

That wasn't a lot of time. If Dylan and I were lucky, it would only take us four or five hours to get high enough to reenter the Tower. If Sage somehow managed to figure out how to flood the shell faster, though, he'd be able to cut us off before we could get back inside. We'd still have a few options for how to enter, but none that were good. It would have to be either through a greenery, which meant facing people who were probably against me at this point, or climbing to the very top of the Tower and entering through the door there.

I supposed it was possible to turn back and try to climb up through the inner part of the shell, but when I put my mind to what that would entail, I felt the bite of impatience surge through me. I didn't want to go back. I knew what was back there. I had to move forward, had to make it to the others. They needed me.

CHAPTER 17

And, to be perfectly honest, I needed them, too. They were my family, and I couldn't bear the thought of losing a single one of them.

"We need to move," I told the others, continuing to head up the flooding stairs, ignoring the water splashing around me. "Tony tells me that Sage is behind this. It's acting as a cooler for the Tower. Rose, leave the door open. Odds are, someone will come along before too long to close it, but it might slow Sage down; he's not going to risk drawing more power until he can ensure he doesn't melt everything at the same time. At the very least, it'll divert a couple hundred gallons of water."

"It'll damage the inside of the shell," Dylan pointed out.

"Better than letting Sage kill Scipio," I replied, continuing my climb. Inside, I was already asking Tony which door would put us out over Greenery 3. I had a plan.

18

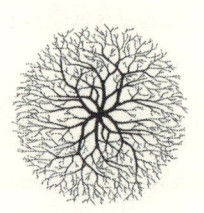

The door pushed open, letting in a blinding white light that had me squeezing my eyes shut, the contrast with the darkness we had been encased in causing them to ache fiercely. Even with my eyes closed, I could see the glow of it through my eyelids, and I kept them that way for several seconds to let them adjust, before sliding them open.

It took me a second to realize that even though the sun had blinded me, the position of it over the Tower was still casting shade across the door and a small section of the glittering brown expanse of Greenery 3's roof, stretching out from the side like a massive diving platform. There was no sign of movement from our vantage point, and I felt confident that Sage had his eyes inward, focused on getting control of the Tower.

I stepped outside, taking care not to slip on the smooth glass. The water we'd been walking through had definitely gotten us a little waterlogged, and we'd need to take a moment to dry our boots off and make sure our lash ends hadn't gotten wet.

I scanned the rest of the greenery to make sure it was clear, and then turned around to face the Tower, taking a few careful steps back to examine its edifice. It was forty stories until the next greenery—

CHAPTER 18

Greenery 7—which meant almost five hundred feet, straight up. We'd make about three or four feet per line we threw, and if we threw two lines every second...

I looked at my watch and saw that it was nearly noon. Eustice and the legacies had been unleashed on the Citadel nearly three and a half hours ago. They'd had to climb to get to my quarters, but even still, if the Knights hadn't been able to coordinate a defense against them, they could be inside my quarters right now, trying to get to my friends.

And if Sage had control over Cornelius, the defenses I'd put in place would be useless.

But I couldn't think like that. Quess and Leo both were excellent coders, and Zoe could do damn near anything she wanted with machines. With Maddox in command, keeping them together, I had no doubt they were holding their own. Hell, the evidence was already there, with the Citadel still having power though the rest of the Tower had lost it. Dinah had said they were mounting a defense, fighting back...

I put my fears into a box and packed them up, then turned back to the wall in front of me.

"I've been out here before," Dylan breathed from beside me, and I glanced over to see that she had moved next to me to stare at it as well. "I've gone under a greenery, even climbed a few stories up to help replace one of the panels, but this..."

She blew out a deep breath, and I found myself nodding in complete understanding. If we managed to survive, we'd be famous. No one else had ever tried it in the history of the Tower, partially because the lash technology was still fairly new, but also because it hadn't been designed with anything like this in mind.

"We'll change out our lash ends now," I told her, pulling one of my lashes from my sleeve and unscrewing the end. They were Quess's special ones, designed to resist the effects of humidity, and were unnecessary for this particular climb. So I tucked them away in pockets—one on each hip, for easier access in case I had to change them out during the climb—and then pulled two fresh ones from a different pocket and screwed them on. As I did this, I kept talking, instructions coming to mind as I considered the temperature of the air, the surface temperature of the glass, the wind's speed and direction. All the things we needed to do to be safe.

"We'll stop and change our lashes every seventy-five feet. I'd push it to a hundred, but the sun is going to be overhead, which means the surface temperature is going to increase. When we change, we'll do it one at a time, using the second line as a safety. Rose, you'll go beneath us and be prepared to catch either one of us if we fall. We work on a four-foot lash only, and disconnect the secondary line only once the primary one is fully reeled in." I paused as I tightened the final lash bead onto the threaded end of the line, and gave it a sharp whirl, checking to make sure the end glowed blue with a static charge before letting it retract into my suit. "Questions, comments, concerns?" I asked, looking up and over at both of them.

Dylan was already in the process of doing the same thing I was, and she paused, flashing Rose a good-natured smile. "Sure you can't carry us up?" she asked, and I could tell she was half joking.

Rose "blinked" at her, and then clasped her hands in front of her body, shaking her head and looking down. "It would be even more dangerous for the both of you. As it is, I might not make it up. There isn't much of a grip."

I frowned. I hadn't considered that Rose might have difficulty climbing the Tower, but she was right: the surface of the Tower was mostly smooth, so Rose would need freedom of movement to try to find the best way up.

"I can't say that I'm not disappointed, but at least my Champion has some very wise precautions in place, so I should be fine. What I can say is... this is really going to suck. Water?"

"Please," I said, and she reached into the bag she had taken from Lynch, filled with food and supplies, and handed me a bottle. I drank half of it quickly, using the angle to study the wall some more, and then capped it and tucked it into my pocket. I'd need more on the climb, and stopping to reach into our bags would be dangerous.

Speaking of which.

I unshouldered both the bags I'd been carrying since Cogstown—

one medic kit, and the tech bag I'd taken from Lidecher earlier—and set them on the ground, quickly opening them up and readjusting the contents to make them more balanced and secured. As soon as I was done, I zipped them closed and stood up, a bag in each hand. "Rose, do you mind carrying the bags?"

"Not at all," she said, stepping forward. I had to adjust the straps to fit the sentinel's wide chest, but we managed, and within minutes, she was carrying all three bags on her back—two just under her shoulders, and one fitted on the small of her back, the strap wrapped tight around her waist. Dylan and I took a few more minutes to stretch our muscles, knowing that the intensity of the climb demanded that we both be limber, and then we began.

To say it wasn't easy would be a massive understatement.

Each line we placed had to be disconnected first, leaving us dangling by one line from the sheer face, being pushed around by the wind. Then we had only six inches of line to work with to build up a static charge, so we had to spin the lash end faster than we would normally do, to build up enough energy for it to stick fast and hold our weight. After that came the agonizingly short ascent, pulled up by the winch in our harness, only to stop and repeat the whole process all over again.

I normally loved lashing—the thrill and speed of it—but this was something totally different, and frustratingly slow. I couldn't race through it, like I would down a hall if I were inside the Tower, and there was no direction to go except straight up. No corners to maneuver around, or obstacles to use to speed up the process.

Nothing but flat solar panels, as far as the eye could see. The minutes turned into an hour, and then two. My shoulders, arms, wrists, and legs ached from the repetitive motion of the climb and from where the harness was digging in. Sweat seemed to pour off me in sheets, especially when the sun finally reached its zenith in the sky, and the tips of my ears and back of my neck felt hot, telling me I was getting sunburned as well.

I threw my next line with a grunt, tugged it lightly to make sure it was fixed, and then retracted the line, taking a moment to look up and check our progress. The shade from the next greenery was my current goal—really the only one to pick from—and it was only three more good lashes up.

The gyro whirred to a slow stop as I neared the end of the line, and I looked down to disconnect the previous line, checking on Dylan and Rose. Dylan was keeping pace with me, and was somehow managing to make it look easy. For a second, I was extremely irritated by how well she seemed to be doing with everything. Not just the climb, but with the truth about Scipio, and how quickly she'd adapted to it all.

I pushed it aside, recognizing that the frustration had less to do with Dylan and more to do with myself. I was tired. No, scratch that, I was beset by pure, mind-numbing exhaustion. Ever since Devon Alexander had set me up for my former commander Gerome's murder, my life had turned upside down and inside out. All over a period measuring a little over a month. Everything had been nonstop, nearly each day filled with a new disaster that seemed insurmountable.

I supposed, in a way, I was grateful that Sage had finally shown his true colors and clued me in to his plan. At least I knew whom to target, and how to end it. If I succeeded, then I'd sleep for a full week. If I didn't...

Well, I'd be dead, and I supposed I could get all the sleep I wanted then.

I lowered my gaze to look at Rose, making sure the sentinel was still a few feet down, and then gathered up the line with my free hand, retracting the cable until I was left with six inches of length. I started to spin it up, keeping an eye on the tip, when a flash of something from down below caught my eye.

I lowered my arm and squinted toward where I had seen it, using one hand to shade my eyes against the sun above. The sun washed out everything, making colors muted and dusty. At times, it was hard to tell where the Wastes ended and the Tower began. During others, the heat coming from the surface of the glass distorted the air, making it impossible to see what was on the other side.

For several long seconds, I couldn't see anything. I waited for what felt like eternity, and then started to turn away, certain it had just been a reflection from one of the panels below, when Tony stopped me.

Wait, he urged, stalling my hand when I went to wind up another lash. *There is something. Look there, to the left.*

I continued to search the area below us, and then finally spotted it: a small white drone. The sight of it gave me pause, and I studied it for several seconds, wondering how on earth it could've gotten out here. Drones were only used in events like the Tourney, or to record interdepartmental elections for posterity, and were only operated by the Knights Department.

I was immediately suspicious. Sage had proven he had access to almost every department in one way or another. Why *wouldn't* he have a drone?

I carefully retracted the line, and then reached into my pocket, intending to shoot it down. I didn't care if it was suspicious or not; I didn't want it transmitting to—

It's not Sage's! Tony cut in excitedly, overriding my thoughts. *It's Lionel! He sent us instructions!*

Disbelief coursed through me, strong and irresistible. I knew Tony was the creative element in the cadre of AI fragments, but apparently he was also given to flights of fancy. *Tony, it's not possible. Lionel is—*

You don't understand anything, he interrupted. *Look at the lights on the front. See how they are flashing? It's Morse code, not Sage. It wants us to follow it.*

I looked down at where the drone was slowly ascending up to us, and noted that the lights on it *were* flashing. While I had studied Morse code in the academy, it wasn't exactly my strong suit, so I couldn't really tell if the phenomenon was a message or a malfunction, but I also didn't care. I was climbing this Tower. My friends were in danger, and I wasn't about to get delayed again by another fragment AI—

I'm sorry, but you have to, Tony interrupted again, just as I was reaching the cusp of my decision.

I was opening my mouth to tell him no when I felt his *presence* loom up from the back of my conscious mind—and crash down over my own with the force of a massive tidal wave. I fought it, but it was like I was a small fish in a torrential stream. Suddenly hands that had been mine a second ago were under *his* control.

My mouth moved, but I didn't think the words that came out of them.

"Hey, guys, Tony here. Liana and I have to take a little trip to figure out how Lionel wants us to fix Scipio! Rose, you and Dylan keep climbing, no matter what. When you get to the next greenery, you need to shift to the east face of the Tower, so that you'll be out of the heat, and get to Greenery 9. From there, you'll be able to gain access to the Attic. Hopefully, Liana and I will catch up to you by then, but if we can't, I know she'll want you to keep going to help her friends."

"Wait, what?" Dylan asked, but it was too late. Tony was disconnecting the line holding us fast to the Tower, and then pushing off with both of *my* legs.

Then we were falling.

19

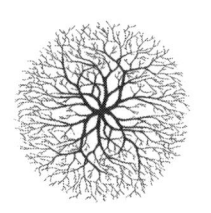

"Woo-hooooooooo!" Tony screamed, the wind already beginning to whip past our face.

AAAAAAAAAAAAAAHHHHHHHH! I shrieked internally, fully understanding what pure terror felt like without the assistance of a body to interpret it. It was like my soul itself had been infused with ice, and I knew with dead certainty that I was going to die.

Killed by one of the AIs I had been trying to save. Irony, my name is Liana Castell, pleased to friggin' meet you.

Tony laughed as he twisted my body in midair, positioning it in a nosedive and causing the icy feeling to fracture and then burst apart in panic. I could see the greenery below glittering brightly, and knew that what had taken us hours to climb would only take seconds to kill me.

Relax, Liana, Tony said warmly. *I've got this.*

No, you don't! You do friggin' not, I snarled at him, like a wounded animal. I felt like one, too, trapped in my own body with an *insane* AI fragment controlling my every action. *There's nothing for us to hook on to but the Tower, and going at this speed will mean that you will shatter every bone in my body trying to stop us. I'll be lucky to survive, but we'll both be helpless and... What are you doing?*

Tony had changed the angle of my body slightly, and we were now steadily arcing toward the edge of the greenery—toward where the drone was now descending. If I had control, I would've swallowed and then squeezed my eyes shut, preparing to make my peace with the universe. As it was, I could do none of those things.

So I screamed instead, letting Tony know exactly how much I hated him for this.

Tony just laughed and flicked my hand out in a move that I felt only dimly. I recognized it—he was throwing a lash line out so he could grab it and spin it up in his hand.

A second later, he was casting it, slightly down and in front of him. There was a high-pitched whistle as it cut through the air, and then it stuck to a panel a few feet down from us, about forty feet above the roof of the greenery. Before I could fathom what he planned to do, Tony began to retract the line, reeling in the slack. As soon as it was taut, he stopped, and we began to swing into an arc. Tony looked up to check the lash bead, and I saw that it was wobbling a little, the force of the impact likely causing it to expend some of the static energy it had collected, and then, to my surprise, he disconnected the line, putting us in a dive again, this time a few feet over.

He did this two more times, somehow using the swing to slow us down, then dropped us both seamlessly on the platform, where we landed lightly on my feet.

I suddenly realized that I was referring to him as "we," and felt like I could understand a bit more about what had happened between Leo and Grey. It already felt invasive, and we'd been joined for only a few hours.

I put that aside and focused on what Tony was doing to *my* body. He was running, racing toward the edge of the greenery like some sort of maniac. The drone was waiting there, its lights flashing repeatedly.

Only this time, I was able to understand it, thanks to Tony.

L-I-O-N-E-L-S-O-F-F-I-C-E-P-R-I-O-R-I-T-Y-A-L-P-H-A-E-P-I-S-O-L-O-N-T-H-E-T-A.

Lionel's office, priority alpha-epsilon-theta.

Tony absorbed it all and continued to run toward the drone, but I felt suddenly heavy. I knew exactly what the priority was. The drone was trying to lead Tony to the backup version of Scipio that Lionel had kept in defiance of the council's orders. Only I had found it long ago. He was my boyfriend now, and I already knew that he was the failsafe. Even if Lionel had somehow left instructions on what to do, I'd pretty much had that information for some time: use Leo to replace Scipio, and reintegrate him with the other fragments to form the "new" Scipio.

Tony, I thought more purposefully, when Tony made no move to stop. *I know you're aware of my thoughts; you're constantly interrupting them. What we need isn't down there. He's up with my friends in the Citadel! We're losing time. We need to turn around and head back.*

Oh, ye of little faith! Tony laughed. *I doubt very much that Lionel would take a break from his afterlife to tell us something we already knew.*

LIONEL SCIPIO IS DEAD, I shouted as he flung us over the edge, one lash already flying to hook the panel at the corner of the building and swing us around it.

Of course he's dead, Tony replied, unfazed. *But that doesn't mean he's gone. C'mon!*

He continued to lash us down, and I retreated into the back of my mind, furious. I was literally being held captive in my body, and forcibly taken against my will to a place that I had already been. It was pointless, and each second it kept me away from my friends was a second more I was giving the enemy to get to, hurt, and possibly kill them.

And I was powerless to stop him.

Tony continued down to the greenery below—Greenery 1, the Menagerie—and all too soon, we had landed on the roof of it. He paused long enough to change out lash ends, trading the old ones for Quess's specially designed ones, and then took us over the edge and down below the greenery.

Mist from the hydro-turbines siphoning water from the river below blanketed the underside of this greenery, making everything murky and barely visible. The drone, which had been keeping pace or leading the way, drew in tight with us now, and turned its lights to the maximum setting. It didn't help much.

Still, it didn't seem to need visual cues to work, and soon we were lashing after it, moving at breakneck speeds even though Tony couldn't see the various obstacles in his path. Poles holding catwalks up passed by us, as did atmospheric processing boxes, meant to help reduce the rate of humidity entering the Tower. He moved as the drone did, following it closely.

I almost screamed at him again when he stopped just outside a familiar-looking hatch—one I knew would lead to a ventilation system that had access to Lionel Scipio's hidden office down below—but I held back. It was pointless to fight at this juncture. As soon as Tony figured out that he'd miscalculated and gave me my body back, I was going to pull the net out of my head, and he was going to go the rest of the way up to the Citadel in my pocket.

If I could even get up. The outer shell was flooded at this level, and if someone had closed the door we left open, then chances were the flooding had moved up several levels, which meant I'd have to lash even farther if I was going to get back in. Not that I would try to scale the Tower by myself. If anything, I could try to get back to the Grounds and climb from there, but that was also risky. Because I'd definitely be spotted.

But there was not much I could do about that. To get to the shell, I'd have to go through the Menagerie, which meant running into workers there. And if they were listening to Scipio, which I was sure they were, then I was going to have to fight my way out. Not to mention try to find a way to escape at the same time, as the doors were sealed, under Sage's orders.

Such were my thoughts, trying to figure out the best way to undo Tony's massive screw-up in dragging us down here, as he continued to drag me farther and farther away from my friends. I considered the elevator shafts, the power conduits. Hell, I even considered the plunges for a hot minute. It was dangerous as all get out, but going up was better than going down, and chances were they'd be deserted.

While Tony crawled through the vents, following the drone—whose form had shifted some to give it access—I considered everything I would need, and where and how I could get it. Water would be easy in the Menagerie, and hopefully a first-aid kit would be as well. If I could get to a cutter, I might be able to use it to carve a way into the Tower, but I would have to see what was happening on the inside first.

Tony eventually made it to the vent entrance and quickly climbed out.

The office was just as we'd left it, with objects half packed and the safe wide open and empty. The couches, table, and desk were relatively clear of any clutter, but the floor was lined with boxes half filled with books and other objects we had found on the shelves lining the room. What was odd was that the power was still on, several lights shining down from above. It shouldn't have been possible, with power out to the greenery it was attached to, yet here it was, fully operational. Lionel must've built in a battery or had an emergency power line connected here before he died. It was the only thing that explained it.

Tony stepped in and looked around, and I could feel a deep sense of reverence radiating from him. I almost commented, but then realized that this was probably the first time he'd seen this room—the room where his creator had undoubtedly worked on him and the other AIs. And suddenly I didn't want to intrude on his moment.

Even if he was being a little twerp about coming down here.

The drone we had been following landed on the desk, the nose of it facing the screen of the terminal. I suppressed an internal sigh as Tony went for it, and thought, *The terminal is gone, Tony. Pine left a virus in it to destroy the—*

I stopped mid-thought when Tony came to face the screen, surprised by a box of blue text sitting in the center.

Emergency Protocol 001-A is attempting to start. Do you wish to proceed? Y/N

How is that possible? I asked as Tony leaned down over the keyboard and studied it. *Do you know what Protocol 001-A is?*

No clue, Tony replied cheerfully. *But I told you. Lionel always has a plan. Let's see what it is!*

Doubt rose up in me as he pointed a finger to hit the Y key. Leo had said that his terminal would be fried if he was gone for longer than twenty-four hours, which he had been. Sage had been inside my head through the legacy nets at so many points, and knew about Leo, which meant he knew we had been down here. For all we knew, this was a trap. Maybe a bomb, or something that would signal to him that we were alive.

Tony, I thought, sending a surge of warning with it. *Don't*—

"Like I always say, Liana," Tony said out loud in my voice, a confident smile on *my* lips. "You need to relax."

Then he hit the button.

The screen lit up and made a chirping noise, then the words disappeared, leaving the monitor black. For several seconds, nothing happened. I could feel Tony's curiosity and confusion, but I was too busy with the alarm coursing through me, feeling like sand being blown apart by the wind. As Tony scanned the room, looking for some sign of what would happen next, I paid close attention for anything that resembled a trap.

A sharp hiss of air coming from one of the bookcases hit our ears, and our head snapped toward it, a readiness settling into our skin. The bookcase in question was the one centered between the two sofas on the opposite side of the room, directly across from the desk, and still had a few objects lining the bottom shelves.

As we watched, the right-hand side of the bookcase suddenly swung forward half an inch, then an inch, and then Tony was quickly striding over to it. I knew better than to argue, so instead settled for keeping a wary eye out for any signs of a trap or ambush. It was possible that Sage had instructed one of the Alice units to come down here and wait for us, and if so, I wanted to be ready.

Not that I could exactly, y'know, do much, with Tony in charge.

If Tony heard any of my thoughts, he gave no indication of it, and reached out with one hand to grab the edge of the bookcase and pull it forward. It swung easily, as if it hadn't been sitting here neglected and unmaintained for the past three hundred years, revealing a...

Well, to be honest, I wasn't sure what it was, other than a room in which the walls were emitting a pure white glow that was similar to the Medica's in a way, but also less obnoxious. It wasn't very big—maybe ten square feet in total—and had absolutely nothing inside.

That didn't stop Tony from stepping across the threshold, his eyes open wide in wonderment. "I think these are old-school holographic emitters," he exclaimed. "Holy cripes, I think this is Lionel's original design! He—"

"Greetings, Tony!" a voice exclaimed, and I felt a splash of ice run through me as I recognized it. It wasn't possible. It couldn't be.

A moment later, the light on the walls began to change, colors rolling across them like a kaleidoscope. An image started to form in front of us, of a tall black man with white hair and a kind, but weathered, face. He was wearing a plain black uniform and carried a cane in one hand.

As we watched, the image refined itself and sharpened, and then took a step forward, going from a two-dimensional representation to a three-dimensional human, like he had just stepped through a door.

Inside, I couldn't help but gape at the image of Lionel Scipio, the Founder of the Tower and creator of Scipio.

20

"Tony, why don't you go ahead and let the girl have control over her body," Lionel said, and I immediately felt Tony's presence diminish, my limbs and motor function finally returning to my control. I lifted my arms and wiggled my fingers, relieved that everything was still working, and then looked up at Lionel.

"What is this?" I asked suspiciously, unable to help myself. "Lionel Scipio is dead. Ezekial Pine killed him."

"Right you are, Liana. May I call you Liana?" Lionel cocked his head at me, an expectant look on his face, and after a moment of hesitation, I nodded. "Excellent. Now, as you say, I am not Lionel Scipio. I am, however, a facsimile of him, made from his memories. I contain many mannerisms inherent to him, but as my program has been running for a long time, I am also different. But that doesn't matter. What does is why I sent the drone after you and Tony."

"Yeah, about that," I said, realizing I had a billion questions for him. I hadn't been asking them on my merry ride with Tony, but now that he was standing right here in front of me, I was curious. "How did you know where to send it? What are you doing here? Can you stop whatever is going on in the Tower? Why did Lionel create you? How many more AIs am I going to have to deal with?"

CHAPTER 20

Lionel blinked at me, and then nodded approvingly. "All very excellent questions, but please, allow me to answer them out of order. I was designed to monitor Scipio and the other fragments, as an independent and unbiased observer, to catalogue any problems in the program and project solutions for the next iteration of the program. All the fragments, and Scipio himself, transmit data directly to this station no matter where they are—and they aren't even aware that they are doing it." He paused and cocked his head at me. "You with me so far?"

I smiled, grateful that he was giving me a moment to absorb all this. It made sense that Lionel had left some sort of final monitoring station to keep watch over his creation, but to what end? "Does that mean you have a solution to fix it?" I asked.

"Indeed, but you're not going to like it."

I frowned and crossed my arms over my chest, feeling a bit annoyed by his response. "Hey, my friends are trapped eighty floors above me, and the entire Tower is having Requiem Day, the sequel. I don't like a lot of things that are going on right now, so let's just add whatever it is to the pile and figure it out. We're wasting time."

He gave me a surprised look, and then a kindly smile, the projectors managing to make his eyes glitter. "My predecessor predicted that the fragments would eventually fail, and began to experiment with the idea that his theory of augmenting the whole with fragment personalities, while giving Scipio a greater advantage for long-term survival, also acted as his greatest weakness. He retained a copy of the original program, whom you have already rechristened 'Leo,' I believe, and embedded in him a series of protocols for a variety of contingencies for replacement, based on my observations and assessment. After copious research, I have determined that the only way to proceed is to use Protocol 001-A: a complete deletion of the Scipio AI as he currently is, along with all the fragments."

I felt Tony's surprise and fear—which was justified, given that the replica of his creator had just callously called for his destruction—and held up a hand, unable to stop myself. "*Delete* the other fragments? But they're individuals! People in their own right! And what happens to

Leo? I thought even a full AI wasn't big enough to handle the complex algorithms by itself!"

"The fragments will understand their duty," Lionel said heavily. "Well, most of them. Rose and Jasper are still on your side, though Rose is buckling under the torture he's subjecting her to."

It took me a minute to realize he was talking about the *copy* of Rose, who had willingly sacrificed herself to keep her copy safe from Scipio's notice so that she could stay behind and help me. I knew from hearing Leo talk about it that copying oneself wasn't easy, and required a conscious choice. I also knew that copying an AI's code too much began to degrade their coding, and Rose's hadn't been the best to start off with. And Sage was hurting her. I took a step toward him, instantly concerned and sickened. "What is he doing to her? To them? And what about Scipio?"

Lionel's eyes turned dark, and he looked away. "Believe me, you'd be happier not knowing."

"Tell me," I demanded. A version of Rose might have been safe and sound in my sentinel, but the other one was still her. "I need to know what Sage is doing if I'm going to figure out how to stop him."

Lionel sighed heavily and tapped his cane against the floor a few times, the speakers replicating the tapping sound. "Ezekial, as I know him, figured out something about the alpha-series nets that my predecessor had attempted to keep secret." At my puzzled expression, he tapped the back of his neck and gave me a pointed look. "The white net you're using to house Tony is called an alpha-series net."

I blinked, suddenly recalling that Sage had called them the same thing this morning too. "Okay," I said, not understanding the importance of the information. "What secret?"

"Scipio monitors the citizens of the Tower through everything: grief, depression, trauma, joy—you get the idea. Because every emotion is channeled to Scipio, we needed a way to buffer it somewhat, and scale it down so that the AI program wasn't overwhelmed. But additionally, we needed a cut-off feature that would prevent Scipio from experiencing each citizen's death in the moment it happened. The

CHAPTER 20

trauma of witnessing that again and again over time would eventually degrade the system."

My heart grew heavy and hard at what he was saying, and I suddenly felt sick to my stomach. "Are you saying that Sage had the nets changed so that he could remove that buffer?"

Lionel nodded, his eyes solemn. "That's one of multiple reasons, but yes, it had a great deal to do with it. Ever since those nets were replaced, each death in the Tower, no matter how painless or brutal it was, was fed directly into Scipio himself. The fragments did their best to stave off the pain, but then Sage began removing them, one by one, until Scipio was fully exposed. It's why he helped create the expulsion chambers and the laws regarding rankings. He's been slowly trying to step up the process for years, so that he could torture Scipio."

I closed my eyes, my heart breaking for the AI. No wonder he did whatever Sage ordered him to do. He was undoubtedly desperate for some sort of end to his torment. He was cut off from all the other fragments, alone, and being tortured endlessly. Each person he was forced to put into the expulsion chambers must've been agony for him, but with Sadie and Sage the only ones aware of his predicament, there'd been nothing to stop them.

"That's disgusting," I finally said, and even though it was accurate, it didn't seem strong enough.

"It is, but it has made me realize the monumental flaw in the original design. You are correct that the Core can't properly operate with only one full AI working alone, but it also can't return to what it was. Most of the fragment personalities have been irreparably damaged. No reset of their codes could fully restore them to what they once were, and without their backups, there is no way to replace them. But Lionel anticipated this problem before he died, which brings me to the solution: a new neural clone must be scanned and combined with the backup version of the original Scipio program. Or Leo, in this case."

"A new neural scan?" I echoed, once again confused. I knew the AIs were all neural scans from different founding members of the Tower, but no one knew how Lionel Scipio had created them. It had been one of his most guarded secrets. Not to mention, all of the AIs had undergone a vigorous vetting process before Scipio was ultimately chosen, which included psychological profiles and simulations of problems that could occur during the lifespan of the Tower. It seemed unlikely that the new plan was to put a fresh neural clone together with the undamaged one, and hope everything worked out all right. That was too simple. "Why?"

"Toward the end of his life, my counterpart began to realize that his views on the AIs were fundamentally flawed. He tried to parse them down to the very basics of what allowed human beings to survive: determination, instinct, courage, fear, and the ability to view the citizens of the Tower as being worthy of the AIs' protection, through Rose. But years after Scipio was installed, he discovered that there wasn't enough symbiosis between the fragments and Scipio. It would have been better to have paired another full AI with him—independent in thought, but united in purpose."

My eyebrows rose to my hairline, and I rocked back on my heels, considering the idea. It certainly had merit, because the system as it stood was fundamentally flawed. But then... how did we create another AI? What parameters were we supposed to use when creating it? What human did we base the scan on?

"How does this all... work?" I finally asked, unable to come up with a better way to channel all the questions into a single one.

"First, you must go to the integration chamber to initiate the purge of Scipio. The Core must be cleared of his program before you can initiate the replacement. Then, you must trigger the protocol within the backup AI, by giving him the following command: 'Initiate New Day protocol, alpha-phi-alpha-6233.' Even if he is in a net, it will automatically trigger a download to send him into the integration chamber and emit a signal, activating a command within all of the alpha-series nets still implanted in any individual in the Tower to initiate a scan of the neural pathways, and construct a clone. The clones will be vetted, and the final one will be integrated with the backup program."

My eyes widened. The fact that the legacy nets were also the way a neural clone was made was another reason for Sage to do away with them, but I wasn't so sure he knew about this one. Still, he'd gotten rid

CHAPTER 20

of so many of them, and with Strum dead and Lacey injured and possibly dead, I wasn't sure how many candidates there would be, other than myself, Sage, and whichever of his children he'd trusted with one. If I could reach my friends, I could set them up with legacy nets of their own, to broaden Leo's chances of finding a suitable—

My knees went weak as I realized that in order to save the Tower, I would have to say goodbye to Leo. Sure, there was a chance *my* neural clone would be accepted, but without knowing the vetting process, I couldn't be sure. Not to mention, the clone would be based on me... but I doubted it would be the same. And what if Sage was somehow selected? Or Quess or Maddox?

He would be gone, and I'd never see him again.

I supposed I could ask him to copy himself, but... that felt wrong, somehow? He'd have a twin that was just like him, in love with me like he was, but only one of them would stay with me, while the other...

Scratch that, it *was* wrong. All of it was wrong. I didn't want to say goodbye to Leo! I loved him. He was a part of me, as essential as water or food or oxygen. Losing him would be like losing a part of my soul.

And yet I knew it was going to happen. I had always known that it was a possibility. Leo was meant to serve as Scipio's backup, and it seemed that no matter what we did, we weren't going to be able to save Scipio. Once I told Leo about this room, and what needed to be done, he'd volunteer immediately. I knew him; he loved me, but his duty to the Tower and to his creator's dream was stronger than anything, and his will to fix things was just as great as my own.

Somehow, I was going to have to figure out how to let him go.

But first I had to rescue him. Which meant I needed to get to him.

"I told you that you weren't going to like it," Lionel said softly, and I looked up at him, questioning. "You and Leo are close. His emotional behavior has been erratic ever since he met you. It's love, isn't it?"

I stared at him for a second, disconcerted by how much he knew about us, and then sighed. I really shouldn't be surprised at this point; Sage had known about us as well. "It is," I replied, lifting my chin up some. "Is that a problem?"

Lionel shook his head. "A small part of Lionel exists inside of me, and that part is... happy for him. Lionel tried so hard to teach the backup version about his humanity, hoping to have him develop more than his counterpart had the opportunity to. I'm glad he was able to learn and grow through his experience with you. It will make him more equipped to deal with the problems that will occur in the Tower. And more equipped for having a partner."

I shifted slightly, uncertain of how to interpret his remark. Ultimately, I decided to ignore it, and change the subject. "So what happens now?"

"Now I give you a few things that can help you on your way. The first is Lionel Scipio's command code. When you use it, power will automatically be diverted from a nearby conduit to open a door or activate an elevator."

I blinked, impressed. That was going to be very useful to have around, but it felt like something that came with a big downside. "What's the catch?"

"Overuse will draw attention to you," Lionel replied with a smile. "I also have this for you: a smaller version of the plasma rifles used for defense." As he spoke, a compartment from the wall behind him opened up, like the drawer in a dresser, revealing a long, dark gray rifle that looked similar to the ones from the Council Room. I stepped up to it, at his insistence, and picked it up. It was surprisingly lightweight for something that was half as tall as I was, and I immediately spotted the triggering mechanism and a magazine.

"How many rounds does it have?" I asked, looking up at him.

"A hundred or so, depending on how fast you use it. Hopefully this will defend you against the sentinels that the Alices are using while you get to Leo. As for that, I'd like to think I've saved the best for last." At that, he rapped his cane twice against the floor, causing a panel to slide back in the middle. I carefully used the strap to place the rifle over my shoulders, and then nervously stepped toward the hole, worried that he had just opened it up to the outside.

Instead, I saw something I had only seen once before—with Cali, Maddox's mother, when we had gone to net Mercury, her IT contact, whom we eventually learned was Dinah. She had taken us to a relay

CHAPTER 20

station in order to keep the call secret, and that was exactly what I was looking at right now.

"It's a relay station," I said, looking up at him. "Do you want me to climb out that way?"

"No, I want you to get in," Lionel said impatiently. "It's not just a relay station. It's an escape pod."

Really! Tony exclaimed, finally breaking his silence, his voice quivering with excitement. *Cool!*

"No, not cool," I muttered to him. To Lionel, I said, "Thanks, but no thanks. How does escaping the Tower help me do what you want?"

Lionel rolled his eyes. "You're not going to escape the Tower in it. You're going to pilot it up to where your friends are, and then get back into the Tower. Or rather, Tony is. All the AIs know how to operate the emergency systems, but you will have to give him control again so he can do it. I know it's not much, but it's all I can do to help."

"No, it's... a lot," I finally told him, turning around to step onto the ladder leading into the relay station. "It's an idea, at least, of what we can do to fix everything. I... Thank you."

"Thank me by saving the Tower. I know it's not perfect, but I believe, at the very least, it can get better."

I smiled at that. It seemed like in that, at least, Lionel and I were kindred spirits.

Because I believed that, too.

21

The pod rocked violently, and though Tony was in control of my body, I had the urge to reach out and grab the edge of something in an attempt to stabilize myself.

It's all right, Liana, Tony soothed. He used my hand to flip a few switches on the panel in front of me, before returning my view to the small window in front of us and scanning the fog. The window wasn't like any of the other windows I had ever seen in the Tower. The inside of it was glowing slightly, and it would periodically light up with red when we drew too near to an object, outlining the threat to our path in a bright red line. As soon as the alert went off, Tony quickly began adjusting our course by flipping more switches and then shifting the long bar between my legs right, left, or at an angle, moving us out of the way. He handled it all flawlessly, but it did nothing to help my apprehension that we were *flying* in a machine that I hadn't even known the Tower possessed. A machine built nearly three hundred years ago.

It was a wonder we were up in the air.

I'm really getting tired of telling you to relax, Tony groused. *Seriously, you are not the most upbeat of humans, are you?*

I was immediately defensive. Tony may have been a part of this, but he had been sheltered by Lacey for some time and had no idea what my friends and I had gone through. Or how important they were to me. Or how much I needed to make sure they were still alive. I'd already spent too much time on retrieving Tony, not to mention going on his little side adventure, and I wasn't about to take crap from him about "relaxing."

No offense, Tony, but you can shove your "relax." My friends' lives are on the line, Scipio is dying, the future of the Tower is resting on my shoulders, and I just found out that I'm going to have to say goodbye to my boyfriend if I want to save it. If there was ever a time to not be relaxed, it's right friggin' now.

"I totally get that," Tony replied out loud, looking away from the window to flip a few more switches. "But you're not in control right now, so why not take a breather?"

Yeah, not being in control of my own body only pisses me off even more. Like, I get it—I know you need to pilot this thing, but—

I cut off mid-thought as the escape pod jostled again, sending a spike of icy fear through me. Tony pushed some on the bar, and the sputtering stopped as the acceleration kicked in, sending us shooting forward at a faster speed.

Tony?

We've cleared the catwalks, he replied mentally this time. *I needed to speed us up. The sputtering was from the engines running too slowly so I could navigate the more difficult parts. But the humidity from the hydro-turbines and the river was starting to put the exposed flame out. It's okay now; the flame is hotter, so it'll evaporate all of the water before it can touch any more components, and besides—*

He paused as we broke free of the fog bank and the greenery, and pulled down on the stick and flipped a switch, angling us up. The entire time, he'd been showing me his thoughts partially in picture, revealing the design of the pod we were in: a round hunk of metal mounted around what he called an omni-directional rocket propulsion engine that blew a controlled flame from ports in the back, which could apparently shift our direction nearly 180 degrees in a matter of seconds. I had never heard of any of this technology but was grateful that Tony knew how to handle it, and that it still worked after nearly three hundred years.

We're free of it, anyway.

That's nice, I replied, but I was still seething in spite of the insight he was sharing with me regarding the pod. It was like he did it as an afterthought—like I wasn't worthy of knowing it beforehand—and that made me feel like I was pacing the confines of a tight cell of my own ignorance. *But why can't you just tell me what's going on? What would it hurt to, I don't know, reassure me a little that you're not going to get me killed before I have a chance to fix anything? I like being alive, Tony. I want to remain that way! Dying before I save my friends is counterproductive!*

I thought I had been reassuring you, Tony replied, his thoughts feeling a little surprised. *What else does "relax" mean?*

If I had had control of my eyes, I would've rolled them. Instead, I said, *I don't even understand how you can be so relaxed, considering your creator just condemned you to death! Doesn't that upset you at all?*

Not really, Tony replied. *My duty is to the Tower, even if it means sacrificing my own life to save it.*

His answer didn't surprise me, although I wished it had. If I had been in his shoes, I would've at least been resistant to the idea at first. I wasn't sure I could resign myself to death as a matter of duty, and I couldn't see why Tony would, either. He might not have been a full AI, but he was still a being with emotions, and the prospect of death, even digital death, had to be frightening enough to make him wonder if it was worth it.

You can't really mean that, I replied. *I mean, why do you even have to die? Maybe we could put the fragments into each department's mainframe. We'd have to figure out how to fix Alice, and figure out what has happened to Kurt and fix him, but maybe—*

I think it's a little too late for them. And besides, you're forgetting the big glaring fact that we failed. Not just the fragments, but Scipio as well. Sure, we lasted a long time, but the system we were designed to be a part of was flawed. The Tower can't continue the way it was before, and it's my job to ensure that what does continue is what my creator wanted. Call it programming, or call it determination; either way, I will do what must be done.

I was taken aback by his adamant speech and could feel the passion of his thoughts like a fire in my mind, blazing hot and daring me to anger it. For a second, I thought about it, but then I realized it was pointless. Tony had accepted his own death and wasn't willing to fight it.

And if I was totally frank with myself, the argument I was having with Tony wasn't even meant for him. It was manifesting from my fears over how *Leo* was going to react to the news that he had to replace Scipio. Even though I anticipated that his answer would be exactly the same as Tony's, a part of me hoped it wouldn't be. That he'd resist the idea, the very notion of doing what Lionel wanted, and that we would figure out a way to defeat Sage and repair Scipio using the fragments. If we could do that, then he wouldn't have to leave me, and the fragments wouldn't have to die!

For a second, I let the idea sweep me away, imagining what it would be like to finish this fight with Leo and Grey intact... And then I carefully put it in a box and closed it up. I knew there was no way that was going to happen. Leo's sense of duty was too strong for something as simple as love to get in the way, and even if it weren't, I believed what Lionel had told us. Scipio couldn't continue as he was.

Especially if part of Sage's torture meant he was being subjugated to the death of every citizen Alice was killing—and every citizen who had died in the Tower over the past two hundred years. The AI had been experiencing this level of torture for all that time, and it was only going to get worse. I doubted he was holding up well under the strain, and I knew he couldn't survive the experience and remain mentally and emotionally whole. I was certain that we were going to have to replace him. But the fact that it was going to be with Leo broke my heart.

You really care about him, huh? Tony asked softly, and I immediately shut the line of thought down, angered that I couldn't even get a moment to myself to process my own thoughts.

It's really none of your business, I replied icily. *And if this is what Grey had to put up with when he woke up, I am really surprised at how accommodating he was to Leo's presence.*

Ouch, Tony replied. *That's not very nice. Not to mention, that situation was extremely different. According to your memories, Grey woke up before his memory was fully restored. He's bound to feel differently now.*

Get out of my memories, Tony! I practically snarled, feeling as if my entire body had been invaded. *I'm really trying to cut you a break here because I know you're helping, but this is getting annoying. If you need to use my body, fine. Just talk me through what you're doing. I know it's not easy being trapped in the head of a control freak, but can you just do it for me already, so we can stop having this fight?*

I felt him hesitate and prayed that somewhere in his little AI logic processes he would get it, and respect my need for privacy.

"All right," he breathed a moment later, and relief poured through me, as free and wild as water. "I'm currently flying us up the side of the Tower. Fuel reserves are at 60 percent and dropping because this thing wasn't designed to shoot straight up, against gravity. I'm readjusting our course so we can get to the south side of the Tower, where we left our friends, and then I plan to open up the door and give them a ride."

Open the door? I exclaimed, fear quickly replacing my relief. *We could fall out! They could miss! Why can't we just land on the nearest greenery arm and wait for them?*

"Oh my God," Tony groaned, flashing me an image of him banging his head against a wall. "First you want to move faster, now you want to move slower! Make up your mind, woman!"

I bit back a defensive growl. He was right, of course. I did want to get there quickly. But he had clearly forgotten the part about how I wanted to get there in *one piece*.

Tony—

"No more arguments from you," he said petulantly, turning my eyes back to the window and surveying the approaching corner. "We can't land, because this thing doesn't actually have a re-initialization process for the engines. They're meant to burn themselves out trying to get as far away from the Tower as possible! As soon as I shut it off, it becomes a big old pile of useless junk. Opening the door and getting them to jump in is the best and only way to do this."

I thought about what he was saying for several seconds and dialed back my anger some. He was right, and now that I actually had enough information to confirm that, I could accept his plan.

But just barely.

CHAPTER 21

What do we need to do? I asked, paying more attention to what he was doing.

"Not much," he said, our hand going to a screen and tapping on it rhythmically. "I'm stealing the trick from the drone to send a message to Rose in Morse code, using the fog lights on this thing. As soon as we—"

He stopped when the screen lit up with another red outline, showing two shadowy figures a few hundred feet above, nearly halfway above Greenery 7, but closer to the west face of the Tower, and clearly trying to get to where Greenery 9 was. I couldn't make out the details from this view, but I knew it was Dylan and Rose, still continuing their ascent.

As we hurtled closer, Tony began to ease down on the throttle, slowing us, and then reached over to a latch on the side, pulling it open and sliding it back to create a seven-foot hole that was about five feet wide. It wasn't much of a space for them to get into, but if Tony planned to message Rose to let her know what was coming, I was certain the sentinel could get them both to us safely.

We looked back at the window in time to see Dylan and Rose peering down, and Tony continued to tap out the message with one hand, flying the escape pod with the other. There were several seconds in which neither of them moved, and then Rose stuck one hand out and flashed a thumbs-up signal that would've been indiscernible if it weren't for the red line around it.

The next thing I knew, she had reached over to pluck Dylan off the wall. Dylan's legs kicked, her arms flailing, and I could only imagine her terror at suddenly being jerked off the wall. The sentinel ignored the blond woman's struggles, pulling her tightly to her chest and eyeing our trajectory. Tony continued straight ahead, his hand tapping out a countdown that I was barely aware of—because I was more obsessed with what I was witnessing. We hurtled straight for them, and though I was certain Tony was about to turn, he didn't, instead flying closer and closer to my friends. Just when I thought that he'd miscalculated, he flipped a switch and jerked the column to the right, rotating the pod so that the door was angled toward them. The sudden press of gravity had panic spreading me thin, as did their rapidly approaching forms.

If I had had full control over my lungs, I would've sucked in a deep breath as Rose let go of the wall and started to fall toward us. For several seconds, I knew that she would miss, that we would miss, but then the pod shook with a violent tremor, and she was inside of it, holding on to the frame of the door with one hand while letting Dylan go with the other.

"What the—" Dylan shouted as she stumbled, clearly shaken from her short fall. But she cut off when she saw me. "Liana?"

The chair I was sitting in swiveled, so Tony twisted my body around to face her, smiled, and said, "More or less. I'm in control for the drive, but Liana's here too."

She blinked her blue eyes at me several times, and then pressed a fist to her forehead, sighing heavily. "This AI stuff is really weird," she finally said.

Tell me about it, I thought, wishing I could share my own experience with her.

"Liana said, 'Tell me about it,' which I think is rude, considering how helpful I have been!" Tony retorted, turning back to the windows to correct our course.

"I'm sure she doesn't like sharing her body with you," Rose said. "And you should be mindful of that. Now, tell us what happened!"

"And how you got a ball that can fly," Dylan added wryly.

"You guys are going to *love* this," Tony announced, and I could tell from his thoughts that he intended to inform them of everything we had experienced since we had jumped. "So, after I disconnected the lines, Liana was all like 'Aaaaah, we're going to die,' and I was like, 'Naw, girl, we got this.' We fell—"

If I had had control over my own mouth, I would've shut him up. Not because I didn't want to tell the others what had happened, but because I knew Tony was about to over-embellish the story.

But since I couldn't stop him, I did my best to distract him with corrections whenever the opportunity presented itself.

22

"So, let me get this straight," Dylan began as soon as Tony had finished his explanation. I wasn't surprised. Tony had gone above and beyond, crafting the adventure to be more fraught with action and adventure then it actually was, and I had no doubt that Dylan could smell something fishy in the air. "You rappelled down the Tower face at unimaginable speeds?"

"Right," Tony said with a nod, flicking a switch and repositioning the pod as it continued to head up, fighting the pull of gravity. We had long since passed Greenery 9, but I had told Tony to ignore it and head higher, to Greenery 13. The only reason we had been angling toward Greenery 9 was that it was on level 85, which would've given us access to the bridges. It had been the best option for us at the time, considering we had to climb nearly seventy-five stories to get there. Adding another fifty would've just been insanity at that point and added another two or three hours to our trip.

But now that we had the pod as an option, I wanted to get to the next one up, as Greenery 13 was on level 125—the starting level of the Attic. To me, it made the most sense tactically. Not only were those levels mostly deserted during normal Tower operation—meaning they should definitely be deserted now—but if I could just get to the right storage room, I could use the escape hatch into my quarters to get in and avoid the Citadel altogether.

"And you got into Lionel Scipio's secret office under the Menagerie, and found a holograph of him, and it gave you orders for replacing Scipio with the backup and a new full neural clone to make a stronger Scipio."

"Check and check," Tony said, scanning the multitude of dials and digital displays and pausing on a blue one. He leaned forward and tapped the blue glowing panel, and suddenly I felt a surge of urgency coming from Tony. "No more questions," he said abruptly, and sent me a picture of us running out of fuel faster than he had anticipated. "Are you strapped into the chair?"

"Yes," Dylan replied, suddenly nervous. "Rose is, too. What's going on?"

Tony was opening my mouth to tell her when the entire pod wobbled, and then we were falling. A moment later the thruster caught again, and we were slammed into our seats and hurtling upward.

"Hold on!" Tony shouted, grabbing on to the controls and shoving the rudder forward, giving it more juice. But the fuel reserves were almost depleted, and before I could even ask why, he sent me a picture of how much weight we were hauling with Rose, as well as several complicated algebraic and geometrical questions that I didn't fully comprehend but got the gist of.

Gravity had already been weighing us down due to the design of the pod, and Rose was only making it worse. Compensating for both those things had started eating our fuel at a catastrophic rate.

And Tony had missed it. But whatever savage satisfaction I had that the fragment wasn't as perfect as he made himself out to be was dwarfed by the colossal terror that we were going to die.

Suddenly my great idea to land on Greenery 13 didn't seem so great anymore.

I agree, Tony thought sourly as he started to pull away from the Tower, creating some distance for a landing. *I made a mistake by not taking Rose's weight into account! Now hold on, this is going to get rough!*

CHAPTER 22

Through the window on the door, I could see the bright brown of the side of Greenery 13's farming floor shooting past, and then we were over it, and Tony was rotating the pod and turning us away from the Tower to angle for a landing across the roof. The trajectory we were on gave us at least two hundred yards of space to land on, but even as Tony began yanking back on the stick to slow us down, I could tell we wouldn't need that much. Because the fuel reserve was almost dry.

As if my thoughts lent power to action, the roar of the thrusters behind us suddenly cut out again. For several seconds, we continued to glide forward, as if we hadn't just lost our only source of propulsion, and then we slammed down on the greenery arm.

Tony grabbed on to the harness as we were suddenly thrown to the right side of the escape pod, bouncing once, twice, then a third time, and then rolling through the air. My stomach lurched, and I could tell Tony was overwhelmed by the sensations my body was experiencing, because the AI quickly receded into the back of my mind, giving me control (at the worst possible moment, I might add), and I felt, more than saw, the world spinning all around me. In my head, I could see us careening off the side of the greenery—and dropping to our deaths.

There was a loud scraping sound as we hit for the fourth and final time, and I squeezed my eyes shut as sparks exploded from somewhere within the walls. I could vaguely hear Dylan shouting something, but it was mostly inaudible due to the terrible screeching sound that was now surrounding us as we slid across the greenery roof.

When the pod finally came to a jerky stop, I was certain it meant that we had slid right to the edge. It felt like we had used up every bit of space the farming floor had to offer, and that any second, I would feel gravity pull us downward as the pod plummeted to the Wastes below. The certainty was ice under my skin, dread in my heart.

"Liana?" Dylan groaned from behind me, coughing. I heard something metallic shift, and there was a sharp jolt underneath us that jerked me in my seat.

"Don't move," I said, my eyes popping wide open. If there was a jolt underneath me, then that meant that we *had* stopped on the greenery's roof—and were about to crash right through it, the weight of the pod and the damage it had caused to the glass undoubtedly making the support struts bend and break. The slightest misstep would send us all falling through.

I looked out the window and saw that we were lying on our left side. A quick glance down showed me a glimpse of darkness framed by shattered bits of brown glass, confirming my theory.

"We have to get out of here without jostling the pod too much," I said softly, slowly shifting my position in the seat and harness to reach up to the door. "We broke the glass over the greenery."

Dylan cursed, but I ignored it as I carefully stretched my weight forward, bracing it all on my hip and keeping the lower half of my body as still as possible. My fingertips brushed the handle of the door, and I carefully wrapped my hand around it, pulled down, and then slowly started pushing it back, trying to keep as still as possible.

It was halfway open when it hit something. I froze, but the hit was enough to jostle the pod slightly. There was a groaning sound beneath us, and I held my breath and closed my eyes, praying to whatever god was listening that the panes and supports holding us didn't snap.

For several heartbeats, the entire pod quivered—and my stomach clenched, the image of us dropping five stories to the greenery below carving its way across my mind. But when no drop came, my eyes snapped open, and I let out my breath.

"Okay, Dylan," I said shakily, craning my neck to look at the girl. "You go first. Use your lashes to pull yourself to the hole, and then crawl out carefully. Try really hard not to shake the pod." I wanted Dylan to go first because of the balance in the pod. If I went first, it could tip too far back toward Rose and Dylan, and likely send them crashing to the floor below. We needed less weight in the back before I could move.

But Dylan, being Dylan, had to choose right then and there to pick a fight about the order.

She pressed her lips together, a flash sparking in her blue eyes. "You should go first," she said, and I rolled my eyes. I did not need her doing this hero schtick right now; my reason for wanting her to go first wasn't

CHAPTER 22

based on anything other than our mutual survival. "You know the most about what's going on. You have to be the one to carry on, get to the Citadel, and—"

I groaned as theatrically as I dared and gave her a bored look. "Rose is four hundred and fifty pounds of awesome, and you're a hundred and eighty, unless I miss my guess."

Her eyes narrowed to slits. "One seventy."

"Fine, whatever," I snapped, not really caring if she weighed a hundred and seventy tons at this moment. She was being bullish and missing the point. "If I move before you're out, the entire pod is going to shift. I can't get Rose to go first, because when she makes for the door, the glass below us will probably buckle and break. So that leaves you, sweetheart, like it or not. Think of it as going up to make sure we're not wandering into a trap."

Dylan blinked at me, a surprised smile forming on her face. "Sweetheart?" she asked, and it was my turn to blink, suddenly confused. I hadn't intended to call her sweetheart, or anything, really. In my head, I had intended to say, "So that leaves you, like it or not." Bewildered, I looked at her, and then felt a high-pitched giggle in the back of my mind.

A flash of anger washed over me.

"Tony!" I snarled, looking away from her. "Is this really the time for practical jokes?"

I'm sorry, he replied, but his voice was filled with mirth, telling me he wasn't actually contrite. *You were just all intense and gruff, and I couldn't help it!*

I groaned again, and to my surprise, I heard Dylan start to chuckle. "Even without the 'sweetheart,' you still have a point," she announced. I looked down to find her unhooking her harness. Rose was carefully holding an arm across the woman to keep her from falling farther to the side when the harness came off.

Dylan gingerly planted a foot on Rose's leg, shrugged her shoulders from the straps, and then pulled a lash end out and started spinning it up in her hand. She flicked her wrist, and a second later I heard the *tink* of it hitting. A second one followed, and Dylan expelled a deep breath, and then slowly began reeling herself up, carefully navigating around the pilot's chair as she did so.

I tried not to hold my breath as she painstakingly climbed out of the hole, doing her best not to rattle or shift the pod, but at several points, the area beneath us creaked and groaned as she moved, making me clutch at my harness in terror.

As soon as her legs were clear, there was another groan, followed by a series of thumps and a small squeak. Then silence, telling me she had gotten off the pod.

"I'm clear," she called a second later, confirming my suspicions.

"Awesome," I called, feeling slightly breathless and lightheaded from the experience. I pushed it aside and started shrugging out of my harness, bracing my weight completely on one hip. "Do you think you're going to be able to make it?" I casually asked Rose while I worked.

Her purple eyes stared at me for a second, and then she nodded slowly. "I believe so, but as soon as I move, this thing will break through. I will have to be fast, and there is a chance I might miss. My safety is irrelevant, however. You must go first."

I gave her a sheepish smile as I carefully pulled a lash end from my sleeve. "Don't take this the wrong way, Rose, but I was planning to. You're in an armored death machine; if anyone can survive the fall, it's you."

She cocked her head at me, and then nodded. "A fair point, I guess," she replied uncertainly. "I still would much prefer not to fall."

"Me too," I said, spinning the line and looking away to throw it. "So let's both of us promise, here and now, not to. Besides, I'm certain that you can make it."

The end hit just to the left of the door, and I quickly threw the second one, aiming for the door itself, on the opposite side of the gap. It connected, and I used the hand controls to retract the small bit of excess line I had created for the throw, and then began giving my weight over to it, letting it pull me up.

CHAPTER 22

The pod shifted slightly, rolling some toward Rose's side, but I didn't stop, carefully pulling my legs out from under the dashboard and lightly stepping on the arm of the seat. The pod stopped moving a second later with a slight groan, but I was already reaching for the edge of the door, grabbing it, pulling myself up, and dragging myself out. There was another long groan beneath me, making my heart beat furiously, and I sped up my actions, knowing that if the pod started to fall, I needed to be clear of the door so Rose could escape. Getting my legs under me was the trickiest part, as the entire pod was beginning to shake, but as soon as they were under me, I carefully stepped over the sheared-off edge of the pod's hull, which was smoking slightly, and leapt toward the crimson figure standing a few feet away.

Dylan caught me before I could stumble, and I turned around, terrified that I had dislodged the entire pod in my haste to get off of it.

It was moving, the entire thing wobbling back and forth. There was a tinkle as more glass shattered, and Dylan and I danced back a few steps as cracks began to snake toward us.

"Rose!" I shouted, worried that she was waiting for me to give her the all-clear.

I was worrying needlessly, though, because even as her name left my lips, I saw her pulling herself through the door. The pod shook under her weight, and then dropped several inches, with a sickening shriek of rending metal. Rose ignored it all as she lifted her legs out, balancing only on her arms. She placed a foot against the hull and was carefully starting to shift her weight onto it when the pod dropped again, and then began to rock to one side, rolling. Rose's response was even faster, and she quickly sprang up off the only foot she had planted, throwing herself from the pod and into the air toward us.

She landed hard, the glass cracking under her weight, but she quickly caught her balance and moved off the crack before she went crashing through.

The pod, however, was not as lucky, and with a final creaking groan and the tinkle of broken glass, it dropped through the rest of the roof, into the darkness below. I prayed it wouldn't hurt anyone but couldn't stick around to find out. My friends needed saving, and I needed to get to Leo to tell him everything that was going on.

"Let's go," I said to the others, turning away from the hole and toward the face of the Tower. "We need to get moving."

23

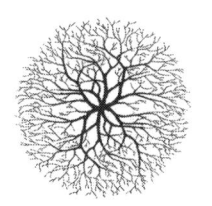

While I could've used Lionel's command code to open the door to the shell, I let Dylan and Rose do it manually as I kept an eye on the area around us. I had a feeling that at any second, the Hands were going to be making their way up to the hole, whether it was to escape, or to figure out who had just crashed through their ceiling. And I didn't want to be there when they arrived.

The door opened easily under their ministrations, giving a creaking, metallic noise that had me turning and shouldering the plasma rifle, just in case something was waiting on the other side. As before, water began splattering out across the glass and through the door the moment it was open. The outer shell was still flooding but was not fully flooded. And even though the sun was still shining down brightly from overhead, the darkness inside already seemed imposing. I pulled my hand light from one of the bags on Rose's back, wrapped the strap around my forearm, and clicked it on. Dylan followed suit, and after a moment's deliberation, I handed her the handgun and extra clip, wanting her to have a way to defend herself that didn't require hand-to-hand combat.

"In case you need it," I told her when she looked up at me in surprise.

She favored me with a lopsided smile. "Show me again how to use it," she said, and I quickly ran her through the basics: shooting, ejecting the magazine, clearing the chamber. She seemed nervous, especially when I told her exactly what a bullet could do, but it was an apprehension born from the realization that she held someone's life in her hands when she pointed it at them.

Regardless, I knew she could use it responsibly.

She put the safety on under my watchful eye and then tucked the gun into a pocket on her hip. "I'm in front, okay?"

"Okay," I replied, swallowing back some of the resentment that she was still following that ridiculous rule. I knew it wouldn't matter what order we were in if the sentinels found us—they'd kill us all the same way. But I pushed the thought aside and focused on a more relevant question. "Do you know where we're going?"

"We just need to get to the Citadel, right?" she asked, and then went on without waiting to hear my response. "The closest hatch to the Attic should be maybe three hundred yards from here."

I hesitated, unsure whether accessing the Citadel was the best idea. We had no idea what the internal situation was like, and since Scipio had used my position as Champion and my bogus crimes against him to declare the department irrevocably contaminated, we could be walking into a civil war—between those trying to win back Scipio's favor, and those who still believed in me.

And I wasn't betting there were too many of the latter. I was too new as Champion and hadn't had time to cultivate relationships with the Knight Commanders under me. My father was likely already organizing extermination squads against me, and Salvatore, now out of the cells, was going to recruit any of the Knight Commanders left over from Devon Alexander's days. As the former Champion's second in command, he knew most of them. Had spent nearly two decades developing relationships with them.

And he had been let out with the rest of the legacies, courtesy of Sage.

"I don't think accessing the Citadel just anywhere is the best idea,"

I hedged. "We should try to get to the emergency exit that feeds directly into my quarters. That's where the others will be."

Dylan frowned, a deep line forming between her eyebrows. "But we'd have to navigate nearly nine hundred yards of halls just to get there! It would be faster my way and get us to the others sooner! We should make for the closest entrance. If the power's still on once we're inside, we can take the elevators right to your quarters. If not, we can still get to the elevator shaft and go down. It'll be faster than trying to navigate the Attic itself."

I frowned. Her plan sounded reasonable, but she still wasn't accounting for human nature. I could see in her eyes that she couldn't imagine a world where Knight turned on Knight. It just wasn't in her. Her sense of loyalty to the Citadel was too high.

It was actually a little odd to realize that for all her sardonic and earthy ways, Dylan was still an optimist at heart, and had turned a blind eye to the faults of her fellow Knights. In fact, it made me a little jealous of her; I wished I could believe as easily.

But I couldn't.

"Sorry, Dylan, but we can't go through the Citadel," I said, adjusting the strap of the plasma rifle across my chest. "Scipio broadcast to every department that the Knights were deemed psychologically contaminated because of me, and I'm betting that anti-Liana hit squads have already formed, fully intent on presenting my corpse to Scipio in the hopes they can get a pass. We can't rely on anyone we encounter in the hall. We'll be stepping into a civil war."

Her frown deepened. "You can't honestly believe that's true. The Knights voted you in! The younger ones love you, and the older ones see you and think of your mom! They aren't going to turn on you!"

I pressed my lips together, meeting her words only with disbelief. I honestly couldn't see it. There was no way every Knight was going to come down on my side. There were too many factors that made it unrealistic.

"They can, will, and probably have," I said, suddenly tired all over again. Whatever boost of energy I had gotten from my most recent adventures was fading fast, and I was already too emotionally drained to explain to Dylan that no matter how she felt the Knights *should* be in this situation, no matter how *she* would be, she couldn't expect the same behavior out of everyone. "Look, let's just get inside the Attic and see what that situation is like first. Then we can argue about the best way in, okay?"

Dylan pursed her lips, but then nodded once, tightly. I suppressed a sigh and remained perfectly still as she turned and moved toward the door, past where Rose was standing off to one side, waiting for both of us. Dylan ignored the sentinel entirely as she stepped through the dripping portal, keeping one hand up to prevent the water from drenching her outright, and then turned to one side of the staircase inside and then the other, checking to make sure it was clear.

"We're good," she called a second later, her back to the door. "Gonna need that code to open the door, though. Forgot the doors to the inner shell didn't have hand wheels."

I moved up to join her, stepping through the doorframe. A trickle of water managed to sneak past the arm I put overhead, running right down the back of my suit and proving that an arm did not make for a good umbrella, but I ignored it as I approached the door. "Command override, Lionel Scipio 001-001-A."

For a long second, nothing happened. Then the lights in the door flickered on, and the door popped open, a robotic voice announcing, *"Authorization code accepted. Welcome home, Lionel."*

I blinked in surprise, then exchanged a look with Dylan. "That's a nice touch," I said, when all other words escaped me. "Think they should've left that one in for everyone to enjoy?"

It was a weak joke, but Dylan gave a snort of amusement. "Oh yeah, maybe added some variety to it. It would add a nice homey touch to the place, for sure."

I smiled at that, and then stood aside to let her lead the way.

Going back into the Tower felt like being swallowed by an enormous monster. After the fresh air and bright sunshine outside, I was now cast back into the claustrophobic darkness, with only my hand light to serve as a thin shield against it. Walls and pipes cropped up suddenly without warning, and every creak and groan of metal contracting and expanding set my skin twitching like I'd been electrocuted. I had to resist the urge to flash my light around wildly, trying to find the source of the noises in the darkness.

It didn't help that the halls in the Attic were wider than the ones down below. If anything, it only made the environment scarier. If I turned the light to one side, I couldn't make out the walls on the opposite side, which meant that every step forward gave the monsters hiding in the shadows time to pursue us.

I knew I was being ridiculous, jumping at imaginary things in the darkness. Then again, I'd never known an inky blackness like this. There had always been light in my world; even when they were set on nighttime settings, the lights of the Tower generated *some* light, so people out and about could see. And when I turned my lights off to go to sleep, there was always something on in the room, to keep the darkness from blanketing me entirely.

But this was different—grander and eerier. It gave off the sense that it was watching me. The hairs on the back of my neck rose as we traveled deeper into the Tower, the feeling that something was off increasing. It was possible I was imagining it—the experience in the shell after Sage had cut the power was likely coloring my outlook up here—but at least there had been people down below.

There was nobody up here. Which was sort of the idea in using the halls of the Attic to get to our destination, but now that I was fully experiencing it, I couldn't help but feel that we were already too late. That the Tower and everyone inside of it had perished in the few hours we were on the outside, making our way up, then down, then up again. I knew it was silly, that my mind was playing tricks on me, but that did nothing to stop the feeling of *wrongness*.

It crept along my spine like a slow trickle of water, making me hyperaware of every sound, every movement around me.

Which was likely why I heard it first: a dull, rhythmic beat.

I froze in the middle of the hall and held perfectly still. Many noises had given me pause since I entered, but this one was so striking, so familiar in its call, that it had to be real.

Rose came to a stop behind me, and said, "Liana?" in a quizzical tone, but I ignored her, shutting my eyes so I could focus on what I was hearing. I heard Dylan come to a halt in front of me, the sound of her boots on the floor stopping, and I took in a deep breath and held it, listening.

Several seconds passed before my heartbeat began to slow after my initial jolt of surprise, but as soon as it did, I could hear it. Clomp, clomp, clomp, clomp, clomp.

So could Dylan, apparently. "What is that?" she whispered softly, alarm rich in her voice.

I hesitated, looking over at the other woman. "I'm not sure," I finally said, unable to produce an answer. I'd never heard anything like it before, other than the familiar rhythm, which I was having difficulty placing. "But we should keep moving, and hope that whatever it is won't even know we're here."

Dylan nodded and resumed walking, this time a hair faster, her light swinging back and forth in a slow arch.

But it didn't matter. The deeper into the Tower we went, the louder the rhythm became, until I was certain that we were heading right for it. Dylan must've sensed it too, because she suddenly turned left down a junction, clearly trying to get away from the pounding, and I kept up, my mind whirring at what the source of it could be and settling on someone or something trying to use hammers to straighten out a sheet of metal.

We sped down the second corridor as the sound increased and intensified, and then Dylan came to a sudden halt, throwing one arm out to block our path. I came to a stop a moment later, following the line of her light into the darkness to see what she was looking at, and almost gasped when I saw the light catch a silver gleam some thirty feet away, revealing a sentinel in the next junction.

24

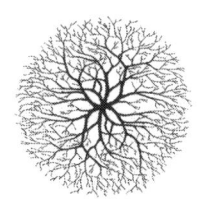

The sentinel wasn't facing us. It was marching down the cross hall, heading toward the center of the Tower. Dylan quickly clamped her hand over her light, cutting the beam off in a mad attempt to shield us from notice, but I knew it was too late. I was already shouldering the plasma rifle, intent on taking it out, when my light caught a shadow forming on the wall behind it.

Another sentinel entering the junction behind the first.

I took an alarmed step back, even as Rose moved forward, planting a hand on each of our shoulders and shoving us back a few steps, then creating a barrier between us and the sentinels. "Run," she instructed, her stance becoming defensive.

I hesitated, not wanting to leave Rose behind to deal with two sentinels when I had a perfectly good rifle, but it finally dawned on me that the sounds we had been hearing were *them*—the sentinels. They were marching, likely from wherever Sage had stowed them to whatever department they intended to hit next. And it wasn't just one or two or three of them, but a seemingly never-ending army of the mechanized monsters.

We had to run. At any second, they were going to spring on us like ants defending their colony.

Dylan got there faster than me, her hand grabbing my shoulder and forcibly pulling me back. I took a few stumbling steps in her direction, my mouth dry and heart racing, then cast a look at Rose, watching as she activated something in the sentinel to make the lines of it start glowing purple, acting like a beacon. My heart was ripping in half at the thought of her sacrificing herself for us when something about the darkness beyond her gave me pause.

Where were Alice's golden eyes?

"Wait," I said softly, the absence of them intriguing enough to bring me to a halt. I knew that if I was wrong, I could delay our escape by precious seconds, but this was important. When Rose was in control, her eyes glowed purple nonstop. So why weren't the other sentinels the same?

In fact... I cocked my head, listening intently. The sound of their feet marching was still there, thundering down the hall, but there was no other sound of movement on top of it. No sets of feet running out of rhythm with the marching, or anything that signaled pursuit. No sounds of voices calling for us to stop.

"Liana!" Dylan hissed, urgently tugging on the shoulder of my uniform.

But I shook my head, shrugged out of her hold, and moved back toward Rose. Even her posture was relaxing some, her head cocking quizzically as she peered down the hall. She glanced at me when I stepped up next to her, and then gazed down the hall.

"I don't understand," she said softly, shifting her weight nervously. "Why are they not chasing us?"

"Maybe they didn't see us," Dylan whispered, taking a few steps forward before stopping again. "We need to run."

I understood why Dylan wanted to run, but I was curious. Curious enough to do something reckless.

I took another step toward the line and lifted my light. I hadn't done much to mask the intensity of it, so the sentinels should've noticed it already. But when I raised my arm, taking the beam from the corrugated floor to their feet, legs, hips, arms, necks, and heads, they completely ignored me and continued their steady march down the hall. Their eyes were dark, completely unlit, and staring straight ahead.

Three passed us, then five, then eight, their pace keeping them within ten feet of each other.

"What is this?" Dylan breathed, finally coming forward to stand next to Rose, her tone bewildered.

I studied them, my mind already wrestling with that question. I considered for a second that maybe they were damaged in some way, but there were too many for that. Sentinels were almost impossible to damage with conventional weapons, so I'd expect only one or two, even if someone had managed it. Not this many. No, whatever they were, it was for something else. Maybe it had something to do with Alice, or maybe they were being used to retrieve something Sage needed, but either way, I wanted to know.

No, scratch that; I *had* to know. If Sage was using these sentinels for something, I had to know what. If I could figure out how to stop them or slow them down, then maybe I could also keep him distracted—or better yet, force him to call some of the legacies from the Citadel up here, to help him handle it.

And though it was keeping me from getting to my friends, I made the decision in a split second, seeing the benefit of at least figuring out what Sage was up to. "We're going to follow them," I announced to the others before turning back to face them.

Dylan was frowning at me, and as always, Rose's face was difficult to interpret. But it was Dylan who spoke first. "We have to get to the Citadel, remember? Sage needs your boyfriend, and every moment we take away from that is a chance for those legacies to grab him!"

I nodded, swallowing down the uncertainty her words created. "I know that, but whatever is happening here is part of Sage's plan, too. We have to figure out what it is, and whether we can disrupt it somehow. It'll distract Sage, and maybe get him to pull some of the legacies out of the attack to fix it, or complete whatever task these things are meant for. At the very least, it'll slow him down and give us more time to save the others."

"Yeah, if there's anyone left to save," Dylan said, exasperated.

"You've been pushing for us to get to the Citadel and your friends since all this started!"

"I know," I grated out, annoyed that she was acting like I had completely forgotten about my friends or the Citadel. "But this is important too, and I'm doing it. You can continue on to the Citadel if you want, but as you said, we need to trust that they can take care of themselves. Besides, the sentinels are heading in that direction anyway. What can it hurt to kill two birds with one stone?"

Dylan frowned and looked up at Rose. "What do you think?"

"I think that the last report we had of the Citadel showed that the Knights were fighting against the legacies, and that power was still on inside. That bodes well for our friends, but not for long. Liana is right: these sentinels are nothing but shells with basic instructions programmed in. For all we know, they are being utilized to manually cut the power to the Citadel. Stopping them would buy our friends more time."

The tall blond woman sucked in a deep breath and looked back and forth between us, her face torn. "I really do not want to die up here," she said tiredly, giving me a pointed look. "But you both have excellent points. How do we do this?"

I turned back to the line of sentinels marching past, and then shrugged. "Let's just join the convoy," I suggested. "Rose, they aren't going to stop us, are they?"

"They shouldn't," she replied, taking several steps toward the line to examine them closer. "It appears they aren't really programmed to interact with anything. Like I said, just basic instructions."

She moved into the line between two of them, facing the next one, and I held my breath, waiting to see what it would do. It continued to march toward her, but slowly began adjusting its course, until it was moving past her and then back into line. She looked at us, gave a thumbs-up, then turned and started to follow the one that had just passed.

Dylan sighed beside me and unzipped a pocket in her uniform to draw out the gun. "If these things' eyes turn yellow for even one second…"

CHAPTER 24

"I know," I said, a thread of fear crawling up my spine. "But it's a risk we have to take."

I strode forward, with more confidence, hoping to hell that this gut instinct of mine didn't get my friends killed, and led to something we could use to stall Sage.

The sentinels continued to march forward, completely ignoring our presence as they proceeded in a straight line down the hall. We passed by massive doors leading to storage bays, the numbers increasing the deeper we went into the Tower. I kept a careful eye on the sentinels on both sides of us, looking for any glimmer of a golden glow to signal that Alice was inside, but their eyes remained dark, their movements stiff and clunky.

The line made several turns during our trek, and after a few passageways, I worried about how far we were drifting from the Citadel.

Until we took an unexpected turn back toward it, down a hall that had a glow emanating from ahead, courtesy of the overhead lights that were on. I quickly pulled up a mental picture of our route and realized that we were actually closer to the Citadel than I had originally thought. In fact, it was seated beneath this floor. Power from there must also be feeding into this section.

Or Sage had allowed power to be diverted here for some other reason.

Either way, we were going to have to step carefully. If there was light here, that meant there might also be people. More importantly, it meant the cameras might be running. I prayed they weren't, but if something important was happening up here, then it seemed likely the Core was watching. I looked up and spotted the camera mounts, studying their position. We could disguise our movement behind the sentinels if we alternated where we walked as we passed the cameras, using the machines to hide us, but there was a chance someone would notice our movements, or even pick up on the fact that Rose was different from the other sentinels, making it risky. But we had to do it. Otherwise we wouldn't be able to follow them *or* get into the Citadel.

I motioned to Dylan, flashing her a few hand signals in Callivax to explain the problem and my plan. As soon as my hand stopped moving, she looked up at the approaching cameras, and then nodded, dropping back to the left side of the sentinel behind us and leaving me to get close to Rose. She glanced down at me, her head cocked quizzically, and I quickly signed a message to her as well, letting her know what was going on. She nodded and returned her gaze down the hall, trying to assume the same walk that the sentinels around her were using. I tucked up next to her, walking in short steps, but quickly enough to keep up without being noticed.

We stepped into the light together, and I fought the urge to increase my speed or turn back, suddenly feeling exposed. I kept my eyes ahead, even though my impulse was to check on Dylan, and watched as the first camera passed us. I was guesstimating where the image would end and where the next camera would pick us up, and, after ten of Rose's steps, I quickly darted around to her other side, praying that neither camera picked up the movement.

I put a hand on her arm this time and chanced a fast glance at Dylan. She was still on the left side, but when I glanced back, she quickly mimicked my movement, coming around to the other side of the sentinel. Exhaling, I returned my gaze to the line in front of us and saw that they were turning right and heading closer to the center of the Citadel. I checked the cameras down the hall across from us, but realized I had no way of knowing where the cameras were placed in the other passageway intersecting with this one, making it difficult to gauge how best to mask our movements.

If I broke cover to check, and someone was watching the screens, they'd know we were here.

My mind was searching for something as the corner loomed closer, trying to figure out how to handle this turn, when Rose whispered, "Get behind me. I'll tell you which side."

Of course! I could use her massive frame to hide my own for the turn. Appreciation surged through me, even as I realized there was still a chance that the cameras in the adjacent halls would see us, but there was nothing I could do about that anyway. Either way, we were going to have to get through this section, so it was a risk we had to take.

CHAPTER 24

I quickly signed a hasty "do what I do" message to Dylan and then stepped behind Rose as she started to turn the corner. It was all I could do not to cringe at the exposure I felt in the intersection, but I kept moving forward.

As soon as Rose whispered, "Go to my right," I was speeding up my steps and tucking in on her right side. A glance over my shoulder told me Dylan had followed. We kept walking, but for several seconds, I felt breathless as I waited for any sign or hint of an alarm.

There was nothing. The sentinels continued on for several more junctures, with Dylan and me dodging cameras in between, and by the time we arrived at the next turn, I was feeling exhausted and my heart was pounding desperately against my ribs in protest of the prolonged exertion of everything I had put it through over the past twenty-four hours.

I ignored it—I was getting good at that—but also knew that I wouldn't be able to do that for much longer.

Although, if I could just reach Leo and initiate the process Lionel had told me about, it might end this fight, and I might finally be able to get some rest. After we found and caught Sage and the legacies, of course.

As ideal as that picture was in my head, I knew there were a few steps between here and there, and for it to actually work I had to get to Leo. And then... I paused, a sudden question occurring to me. Did I tell him about the New Day protocol? Should I? I felt like I should. But what if my time with Leo had somehow changed his priorities?

What if he refused?

Tony kept trying to reassure me that he wouldn't, and truth be told, I didn't believe he would either, which was probably why my initial idea was just to use the activation code without telling him. It would be easier that way, and potentially less painful than dragging out any sort of goodbye. And while I still secretly hoped we could copy him, I couldn't justify the loss of life that would occur if we delayed the protocol while we figured out how to do it.

If we even could, that was. I had no idea whether that was something he could do in Cornelius's terminal, or if we needed a bigger computer to do so. Leo was full AI, meaning it took a lot of energy for him to copy himself, and a lot of space to house him. Cornelius's terminal was probably too small to handle the process. And even then, what if we did copy him? His clone would have all of his memories of us, and share his feelings toward me, and I would be consigning him to a future without me, all so I could keep a version of him to myself. It didn't feel right.

It would be easier if I knew my neural clone was the one that made it through the vetting process, because at least then he'd have some version of me to be with. But I highly doubted it would, and I didn't want to fill him with false hope. I wasn't suited to be an AI; I barely had it together as a human, and even that was questionable at the best of times. Not to mention, I had failed more times than I could count, trying to keep the people in the Tower safe. That alone would probably disqualify me.

I shook off the dark musings and focused on keeping up with Rose as we took another corner, moving to her left side when she told me to. As I did, I realized that this was it—the sentinels were turning in to one of the storage rooms. I checked the cameras, and then told Rose, "Move to one side and stop by the door, and act like you're malfunctioning a little bit. I'll hide behind you and look inside, see what they are up to."

Rose nodded, and a moment later, her steps became jerkier, loud whirs and straining noises being emitted from her legs. She began altering her trajectory, and I followed her, shifting behind her as she walked. I motioned for Dylan to tuck in next to me as her sentinel went by.

Within moments we were stopped just to the side of the door, Dylan and me pressed together behind Rose's back. It wasn't the best cover, but it was all we had.

While Rose continued her ruse of her legs not working, I quickly slid up to the edge of the door and looked in.

And what I saw made my heart stop.

25

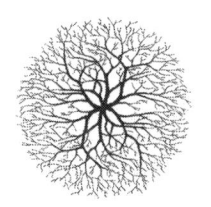

Inside the room, in an aisle running between plastic-wrapped packages of emergency supplies, stood a tall metal frame, like a door. A low ramp ran up to a pad under the frame. The pad itself reminded me of the wireless transfer pad Lidecher had created earlier, only this one was much larger, and sparking with yellow lightning. As was a weird glowing circle on top of the frame.

As I watched, the first in the line of sentinels marched up the ramp and onto the pad, where it came to a halt. The circle at the top of the frame flashed yellow while the pad began to glow gold, and a moment later, the flash dimmed and the sentinel stepped down, and was met by a man wearing IT gray. When it turned toward him, giving us a view of its side, I could see the eyes were now glowing a brilliant gold.

It was Alice. Or rather, *they* were Alice. This was where Sage was downloading her copies directly into the sentinels. Dozens were already in the room, forming twin columns of ten before marching through a side door into one of the adjacent halls. My spine tingled at how lucky we were not to have been passing by that door when they emerged, but I quickly shoved it back to worry about our present danger.

I came around the wall and leaned against it, my hand going automatically to the plasma rifle. I looked over at Dylan, and then back at Rose, and blew out a breath, a special kind of insanity beginning to form. The same one that had driven me to shoot those two Eyes outside the server room in Cogstown. The one that was telling me to shoot now... and then make a run for it.

And I knew I needed to let them know this time before I acted. Kicking this particular hornet's nest could not be a solo operation.

"Dylan, Rose, I am about to do something stupid and reckless," I said in a low voice, my heart beginning to catch up with the plan I was moments away from enacting. "It looks like this is where they're downloading Alice into the sentinels, and I'm thinking we need to stop that right now. Maybe we can buy Scipio some relief from the torture they're subjugating him to. Here's the thing: I'm going to shoot the crap out of that thing, but there are at least twenty sentinels in there, and a few humans to boot, so as soon as I do this, we need to book it. Like, run because you're going to crap your pants sort of running, you know what I mean?"

Dylan gave me a concerned look. "Yeah, I think I'm okay with all of that, but are you okay? You sound a bit... mmm... crazy?"

I nodded in absolute agreement. This was crazy. It was suicide, really. As soon as I unloaded into that machine, the sentinels with Alice inside of them were going to come tearing after us like nothing we'd ever seen before. If we didn't make it to a hatch that led to the Citadel before they caught us, we'd be ripped apart, and we'd never get Lionel's message to Leo. I was putting the entire future of the Tower in jeopardy by doing this, and to be honest, it would've been smarter to focus on getting to Leo and starting the New Day protocol.

But that wouldn't save the people these Alices were destined to kill. I was here, and I had the means to do something about it. How could I just walk away?

"That's a totally fair assessment," I said. "Because this feels a little crazy. But she's killing people, and if taking out this little download pad slows her down on that front, I'm really okay with the risk. I just need to know where we can find the closest access hatch to the Citadel. Do you know?"

CHAPTER 25

She looked around, studying the numbers on the hall. "I think so," she said. "We're a little far from the one I'm most familiar with, but I think there's one nearby."

"Let's hope so," I breathed, lifting the plasma rifle up and bracing it with both hands. "Because we are super far from the one leading to my quarters, and we won't have a lot of time to get there once I start pulling the trigger. Tony, any advice on how to use this thing?"

Tony, who had been doing a great job at staying out of my head for the last twenty minutes or so, sent me a surge of reassurance, along with his response. *Sure do. There's a button on the side that changes the yield of the plasma. For this, you'll probably want to crank that bad boy up to thirty.*

I flipped the rifle over in my hand and spotted a button right next to a little indicator that read "10" in a cool blue light. I hit the button and it leapt to "20," then "30," the number growing redder the higher it got. At 30, it was a mild orange, telling me this thing probably had a much higher setting. *It does, but that other number on the side indicates how much of the plasma you're using in terms of battery life. Take it to 100, and you'd be left with no charge, so just keep that in mind.*

An important and good note. I pulled the gun to my shoulder and exhaled, thinking, *Anything else?*

Should be good to go. Permission to take over if things get too dangerous for us?

Granted, I replied, and took a small moment to mentally steady myself and close my eyes. "All right, ladies, get ready to run." I exhaled as I opened my eyes. I turned toward the corner, already moving the plasma rifle between Rose and the wall, stepped out past her leg, and turned the gun in to the room.

I pulled it tight to my shoulder, took a second to scope my target through the sights along the top, aiming for the download pad itself, and then squeezed the trigger on my next exhale.

Purple plasma exploded from the tip at high velocity, the gun itself hissing as a blast of heat shot out around me. The kick of it also caught me unawares, and I staggered back a step, bumping into Rose's side, but never lost sight of the volley, my eyes tracking the violet projectile as it arced past the line of sentinels, toward the download pad.

My breath caught as it hit, just left of center, splattering all over the frame and the sentinel mid-download before exploding in a fiery blast that blew my hair back.

"Move!" I shouted as cries of alarm from the men and women inside hit my ears. Dylan was already running and had passed the line of sentinels that were grinding to a halt with the explosion. I ducked behind Rose to follow, and within seconds, all three of us were tearing down the halls.

I fumbled with the gun to lower the charge, hitting the button several times to cycle through the yield number, knowing we had only seconds before the Alices were after us. Dylan darted through a pair of sentinels and down an adjacent hall, and I followed, spinning through them and catching one last glimpse of the open door behind us—just in time to see one of the Alices pushing a frozen sentinel out of her way, her eyes and carapace glowing golden.

Then there was nothing but wall, and a need for speed like I had never known before. I tore after Dylan, holding the plasma rifle tight to my chest, and almost slammed into the girl when she came to an abrupt halt at a set of doors halfway down the hall.

"Here?" I exclaimed, looking back over my shoulder. "This isn't the best—"

"I know," Dylan shouted. "Dylan Chase, 051-29—"

"Cancel that," I said, knowing that anyone watching in the Core could override her authorization to enter. "Open on my authorization, Lionel Scipio 001-001-A."

The door began to rattle open, just as an Alice stopped in the intersection a hundred feet back, its form twisting away from us, then toward us. There was nowhere we could hide.

I pulled the plasma rifle to my shoulder and fired, catching it in the chest. The burst was smaller than the first one but hit square on the sentinel's chest and began to smoke. Seconds later, bright sparks were shooting from the armor, and it fell to a knee only a few feet from where it had been when I hit it, before toppling over, its golden eyes flickering.

I wasn't sure whether that meant it was dead or not, but it didn't matter. Two more entered the junction behind it, automatically turning toward us, and I could hear more behind them. Standing here shooting at them and expending plasma rounds was a waste of the time we could use to escape.

"C'mon," I said to Dylan, moving toward the widening door. "Let's get to the hatch."

"You go," Dylan said, shoving the gun in my hand. "Leave me the rifle. I'll stay and hold them—"

I growled and grabbed the lapel of her uniform, giving her a little shake. "No martyrs," I ordered, not wanting to accept even one more loss. Cyril had been the last for me, as far as I was concerned. "No sacrifices. We can make it to the hatch if we move now. So go!"

With that, I shoved her, forcing her through the door instead of letting her take a breath for an argument. She stumbled for a second, clearly confused that I wasn't letting her stay behind, but got her feet under her quickly and began moving down the aisle, heading toward where the hatch was hopefully located. I stepped in and looked up at the door even as Rose slid in next to me.

"Emergency: seal the door under the same authority!" I shouted, praying that it would work.

The door jerked to a halt, filling me with hope, and then began to close itself, the motors in the wall screeching angrily at the rapid movement. I took several steps away from the door, the clanging sound of the running sentinels drawing closer, and then stood my ground, sighting down the rifle.

I tried to keep my breathing even as my finger curled around the trigger, my heart thundering in my chest.

The gap in the door grew narrower as the door continued to roll forward, the opening dwindling from eight feet, to five, to three... My mouth was dry when it got to one, and my eye caught a glimpse of silver near the edge of the door seconds before it slammed shut. For several long moments, I remained stock still, convinced that the sentinels would tear the door open at any second, and attack.

Then something slammed against the door, rattling it in its tracks, and I realized they *couldn't*. Using Lionel's code must've done something to the door that made it ignore their orders.

Or at least, that was my best guess. And even if it wasn't true, I wasn't going to stand around waiting for them to break down the door. I had done what I set out to do and destroyed the Alice download pad, hopefully applying yet another set of brakes to Sage's plan.

But there was one more thing I needed to do to really obliterate it, and we were finally getting there. I did an about face away from the door, swinging the gun around to my back using the shoulder strap, and headed to where Dylan was on one knee on the floor halfway down the aisle, fiddling with what I assumed was a keypad.

"It's not taking my code," she said in a frustrated voice. "I'm putting Lionel's in now."

I nodded. I appreciated her taking the time to try to limit our use of Lionel's code, but the cat was out of the bag at this point, and speed was of the essence. The banging against the door continued, the sounds both creepily rhythmic and terrifyingly loud, and I wanted to be halfway down the shaft before they even got in.

The door slid open as soon as Dylan hit the enter key, and I quickly motioned for her to go first, afraid she might try to volunteer for a suicide mission again. I was relieved when she didn't argue, and quickly looked at Rose, gesturing for her to go next.

"I should stay," she said hesitantly, looking back at the door. "Try to talk to my sister, and figure out what—"

"What did I just tell Dylan?" I demanded, my irritation at having to explain to them why self-sacrifice, and stupid ideas about reasoning with a psychotic AI, were both unacceptable. "I'm done arguing about this. Get in the hole, now."

Her eyes "blinked" at me, and then she slowly nodded, but I could tell from her posture that she wasn't pleased. Still, she climbed in after Dylan, and I let her, keeping my mouth clamped closed. Maybe I was being too harsh on them both. I was beyond tired, and everything since this morning had been nonstop, so it would make sense if my patience was getting short.

But at the same time, I was angry about how easy it was for them to volunteer to stay behind. I didn't want people willing to sacrifice their lives for me; I wanted them beside me, making smart moves that kept us all alive.

Because out of every goal that I was currently juggling, that was my biggest priority.

I counted to five to give Rose enough time to get a few rungs down, then leapt in after her, my friends emblazoned upon my mind as a final destination. It should've felt like coming home, but all I could feel as I closed the hatch and started my descent was dread.

26

When Dylan opened the hatch leading into the Citadel, it was like she had opened the door into a realm of chaos. I could hear the muddled voices of men and women shouting back and forth, punctuated by the unmistakable sounds of weapons fire.

Not just any weapons fire, either, but the zinging whir of lancers, one of the Class B weapons that were supposed to be on lockdown. Lancers were a projectile weapon that used a battery to superheat the ammunition, which loosely resembled a circular saw. My skin crawled even remembering what it was like to use one in our training classes, and I realized that someone—either the legacies or the Knights (or both)—had raided the armories.

Not only that, the fighting had evidently reached the topmost level of the Citadel. Which meant the legacies were way beyond level 20 now. It meant they were closing in on my friends.

"Dylan!" I shouted past Rose. "Report!"

"Lancer fire," she confirmed grimly. There was a pause, and then she added, "If we come out here, we'll be right in the crossfire."

I cursed and looked back up the shaft. If we climbed up we could find a safer way in, but it would require finding a way around the sentinels up there, if they had broken in already. Either way was a gamble, but if there were two factions fighting down there, then it meant that one of them was on my side.

"Liana?" Dylan called, her voice rife with concern as another volley of weapons fire was exchanged. "What do we do?"

I blew out a deep breath and shook my head. I wasn't sure I could gamble our lives in this way. Going up was the safer bet, but only if the sentinels weren't waiting for us. If they were, we were dead. If we dropped into that hall and didn't make it to the Knights on our side, then we were dead.

But at least if we went down, we'd be closer to the others. Going up was taking a step back, and I'd taken enough of those today.

"We go down," I finally said. "Rose, we're going to need to use you for some cover, girl. You okay with that?"

"Of course. Dylan, do you think you can move past me, or will you have to go first?"

There was a pause, and then Dylan's heavy sigh carried over the sound of weapons fire below. "As much as I'd love to say that I could move past you, the answer is no. I'm a little too... ahem... busty for that."

I winced, not pleased with the answer. I didn't like the idea of Dylan dropping out first without cover; it would be too easy for her to catch a lancer bolt meant for someone else. "Ideas?" I asked, knowing that the fighting in the hall below was either going to end soon or get worse while we were up here trying to figure out how to get out.

Tell Dylan to fall down flat, Tony said. *It improves her odds of avoiding any crossfire by 17 percent.*

Improves them to what? I asked, wanting to know what I was consigning her to before I suggested anything.

Forty-three percent. If Rose drops out a second after her, it'll be higher, but will also increase the odds of Rose accidentally stepping on her, so...

"Right," I muttered, and then cleared my throat. "Dylan, Tony suggests falling flat to the floor. Rose will drop out a second after you, so fall perfectly straight, and don't roll in any direction."

There was a pause, and I tried to look down past Rose to see what Dylan's reaction was, but I couldn't see anything beyond the sentinel's bulky frame. "Yeah, all right," Dylan said a second later, her voice shaky. "I can do that."

"Hell yeah, you can," I called to her, trying to bolster her spirits. "You're Dylan Chase. The true winner of the Tourney, even if you didn't become Champion."

She chuckled. "Well, if I survive and you don't, it's not too late for me to change sides and try again."

I smiled at that, glad that she had found it in herself to trade quip for quip before stepping into a life-threatening situation, and then quickly put the emotion aside. "You good?"

"I'm good," she replied. "Going in three... two... one... Go!"

I tensed, my hands tightening on the rungs I was clinging to. I wasn't sure what I expected—I couldn't see anything from this position—but as the lancer fire continued, I was relieved *not* to hear Dylan scream or cry out in pain.

And then I was afraid because she *hadn't*, and grew concerned that a bolt had caught her right in the head. I shivered, my stomach crawling, but as soon as Rose let go and fell, I was moving too, desperate to make sure I hadn't gotten Dylan killed.

I took a look down before my boot hit the final rung, and saw Dylan's legs—moving, thank Scipio—between Rose's spread ones. I kicked off from the ladder and dropped down behind Rose, landing in a low crouch. Sparks erupted overhead as a loud *zzt ting* shot overhead and then ricocheted off Rose's torso. The lancer bolt was crimson and flat, but I knew from experience that there was a small circular saw inside, superheated so that it could cut through microfiber and inflict maximum damage.

I dove to my belly as several more shots exploded into her, worried that one of the blades might bounce off Rose and right into Dylan or me, and began to crawl toward the wall, knowing it was the best place to be if we were going to use Rose as a shield. Dylan was already leading the way.

Rose continued to stand in the hall, drawing fire from both sides until we were both pressed against the wall, and then moved over, creating a barrier between us and the fire. It wasn't perfect—any shot

CHAPTER 26

that got into the gap between Rose and the wall would shred us—but it was better than nothing.

I got shakily into a low squat and peered both ways down the hall. The walls were marred with long black scrapes where the lancers had sheared right through the metal that encased the hall, telling me the fight had been going on for a while. As I looked, I realized that one group of people had set up a barricade between the people on the other side of us and the elevator shafts that would lead to my quarters, and immediately knew who was on my side.

"We gotta get over there!" I shouted, pointing to the left. "They're on our side!"

Dylan took a look, and then nodded. "Yeah, I agree. It looks like they're keeping the others away from your quarters. Seems to me that's something Knights loyal to you would do."

I ignored her barb. Was I pleased and impressed that some Knights were loyally defending me? Absolutely. But I was also angry and bitter that they were being forced to fight in the first place. Each death either side inflicted was only helping Sage torture Scipio and was an absolute waste.

"Rose?"

"Go!" she shouted. "I'll cover you! Just make sure the Knights on your side don't hit my hard drive!"

"Roger!" I replied, eyeing the distance to the barricade. It was thirty feet, and while I believed that Rose would do her best to keep us covered, I had no doubt that a few of the Knights on the other side of the barricade would take shots at us before they realized we were on the same side. "Dylan, I'm going to lay some covering fire down in the hall," I called. "When I do, you book it over there and shout whatever you think will work to get them to not fire at us."

Dylan gave me an incredulous laugh, and I could tell the madness of everything was hitting her now, too. "Why not?" she exclaimed, her voice a mixture of ruefulness and sarcasm. "This is just like what they trained us for in the Academy!"

I laughed at that, unable to help myself. Maybe she and I were both going insane, but she was absolutely right. The Academy had trained us for a lot of things, but nothing like this. "If it makes you feel any better, I'm the bigger target," I told her helpfully.

Dylan gave me a look so filled with droll humor that I laughed again. I couldn't help it. Here we were, surrounded by lancer fire, between two factions fighting for the heart of the Citadel, probably about to die. Sure, some people would be serious, but not me. And not Dylan.

And all I could say was... thank Scipio. I needed a morale boost, and for some reason, laughing had steadied some of my nerves. I placed a hand on her shoulder, gave her a squeeze, and then pulled the rifle off my back, shouldered it, and sighted down the hall to where two halls intersected, where the enemy fire was coming from. A quick check of the charge told me that I had 60 percent battery left. I set the charge for the lowest yield available, not wanting to kill any of the Knights by accident, and discovered that the lowest setting was 1. I selected it, and then pulled it to my shoulder.

"On my mark," I called to Dylan and Rose, sighting down the top of the plasma rifle and curling a finger around the trigger. "Three... Two... One... MOVE!"

I fired two shots down the hall, the bursts barely the same size as the lancer bolts, and hit the back wall on the left side, then stepped with Rose, keeping her in front of me for partial cover as I sighted on the other hall. A man in a Knights uniform was coming around the corner, one arm up, with the lancer strapped to the back of his hand. I squeezed the trigger a second before I recognized him, and instantly hated that I'd aimed for a few feet in front of him and not *for* him.

Because if I had, then Salvatore Zale would be dead, and not spinning back around the corner shouting, "IT'S HER! GET HER! KILL HER NOW!"

Rage erupted in me—not only at his words, but because this man had played a part in my mother's death. He had made a deal with Sadie Monroe, who had agreed to help him win the Tourney, and that deal had resulted in Rose killing my mom. If I had just realized who he was a second sooner...

A part of me wanted to stand here and wait for him to come around the corner again so I could shoot him right between his eyes and end his treachery once and for all. But common sense, or rather Dylan's sharp, "Liana!" from behind me, had me moving, turning away and racing for the barricade behind which Dylan was already disappearing.

Moments later, the hall erupted in lancer fire coming from Salvatore's side, and I ducked my head down and poured on the speed, scrambling for the assortment of furniture that had been stacked up to form the barrier. I could've climbed it, but the gap at the top was wide enough, and the fire behind me insistent enough, that I spun up a lash end and threw it.

I knew that I was giving my enemies a clear shot at me, but it wouldn't be a prolonged one like they'd have if I tried to vault over the furniture. My lash end hit the ceiling right in front of the barricade, and I jammed the hand controls and let them jerk my body into the air. I lifted my legs to gain some speed (and to clear the furniture), and then disconnected the second my rump was past the tallest part. My landing was less than ideal—the whole thing had happened so quickly that I had been more concerned about being shot than hitting the ground—but I caught my balance and then turned to the barricade, where eight or nine Knights were firing at the charging enemy, ducking as lancer fire whizzed by overhead.

"Don't shoot the sentinel!" I ordered as I moved up on the line, the plasma rifle already prepped. "Rose!" I could see her dark form backing toward us, but it was also taking up the bulk of the hallway, keeping us from having clear line of sight. "GET DOWN!" I shouted, cranking up the power setting to 5 and aiming.

Rose obediently fell to her stomach, and I unleashed three shots down the hall, aiming for the floor twenty feet down and creating a burning line of purple plasma with crimson flames springing up in front of the charging group of Knights, sending them back a few steps. The metal the plasma hit immediately began to melt and burn, and another few pops of the molten hot fluid forced them back a few more steps.

The Knights on my side took advantage, and before I could tell them not to, they began to fire their lancers into the crowd. The first few bodies in the front began to drop, and the other Knights erupted in a panic. I heard Salvatore shouting, "Retreat!" and they immediately broke.

"Hold your fire!" I ordered on my side, not willing to let my Knights fire into the backs of retreating men.

To my surprise, the line stopped firing, with only a few shots being made by those who hadn't heard the order, but they were quickly corrected by a nearby Knight. Relief poured through me when I realized we had chosen the right side, and I took a step back, lowering my weapon.

My knees immediately felt weak, and I almost dropped right then and there, my exhaustion slamming into me like a heavy weight I was carrying in my bones. I managed to make it to a chair that hadn't been shoved into the barricade before they gave out entirely, and ran a hand over my face, trying to wipe away the sudden lethargy that was overcoming me.

It didn't work. I leaned over and pressed the heels of my hands into my eyes, trying to massage them into a wakeful state.

"Liana?" a deep masculine voice above me said, and I froze, my spine stiffening in awareness.

I took a deep breath and sat up, pulling my hands away from my eyes and opening them.

Sure enough, my father was standing in front of me.

I gaped at him for a second, and then leaned in the chair to look around him, for Dylan. I found her standing right behind him, a pleased smile on her face.

I blinked at her, realizing she had no idea about the history between my father and me, and sighed, returning my gaze to him.

"I think we chose the wrong side of the hall," I said tiredly, certain that there was no way in hell my father would ever be fighting on *my* side.

27

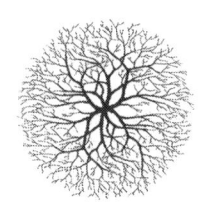

"No, you didn't," said an elderly voice, and I leaned to the other side of the chair to see Astrid Felix, former Knight Commander and longtime family friend. She'd led the investigation into Ambrose's death, and my mother's, and while I hadn't been able to trust her at the time, seeing her filled me with a small sense of relief, as I knew from the files I'd recovered from Sadie's office that she hadn't been involved with the legacies.

But that didn't explain why my father was here. Our relationship was beyond damaged; it had been obliterated after my mother died, with each of us blaming the other for her death. I blamed him for not listening to me like she had—and for turning against her when she did so—and he blamed me because, why not? I was the problem child, and had been my entire life, according to him. Even Alex, who had turned his back on our department, had been preferable to me in my father's eyes, although Alex didn't like him any more than I did.

"Hey, Astrid," I said with forced cheerfulness. "Good to see you! Quick question: What's *he* doing here?"

"Liana!" Dylan exclaimed, her tone appalled, and I gave her a sharp look filled with warning, telling her she in no way understood enough about my relationship with my father, before turning back to Astrid.

The older woman was frowning at me, but I ignored it and got to my feet. "Sorry, I just find it a little hard to believe he's actually on my side. What's up, Dad? Salvatore send you to plant the dagger in my heart personally, or..."

"Liana, stop it," my father cut in sharply, looking down and away, his face contorting to something that looked like pain. Seeing it gave my anger pause, and I took a step away from him, disconcerted by what I was seeing. He looked damn near remorseful. I'd never seen an expression like that on his face, and it was so alien that it scared me for some reason.

"What is this?" I asked, unable to help myself. "Why are you on my side?"

He looked up at me, his dark eyes heavy with anger... that wasn't directed at me. This was getting weirder and weirder by the second. "Astrid and I were meeting with Lieutenant Kellin to find out why Salvatore and his wife had been arrested, when the power went out. We were in the process of trying to figure out what was going on when Scipio sent his message. I knew Maddox's loyalty to you extended far beyond her role as a Knight and Lieutenant, and started to arrest her—"

"You *what?*" I sputtered, suddenly furious that he'd even dared to try that. "You better not have hurt her, you rat bastard. If you did—"

"He didn't," Astrid cut in, frustration roiling off of her.

I knew she didn't like the idea of us airing this particular family drama in front of the rest of the people in the hall, but I really didn't care. I had no reason to trust my father's intentions. I'd grown up with the man my entire life, and there wasn't one single time when he'd put his faith in me. I found it very difficult to believe that he'd suddenly had a change of heart now, *especially* after he'd just admitted to trying to arrest Maddox.

"Your Lieutenant exercised some very quick thinking and offered to let us see the evidence that you'd collected against Salvatore and Sadie. It was pretty convincing, if not deeply terrifying," she continued. "When Knight Commanders Farmless and Brown were able to get the power back on, we learned of the breach in the cells and were able to quickly mobilize against them. But we didn't account for Salvatore. His emergency codes were still active, and he managed to slip up a few more levels, collecting followers on the way and convincing them that if they killed you, Scipio would forgive them."

Her words were like a slap in the face, and disappointment and humiliation rolled through me. Even though I had anticipated there would be a schism in the Knights, a small part of me had hoped that there wouldn't be. I didn't want to be the reason the entire department devolved into murdering each other, but I was, and anticipation did nothing to soften the sting.

Still, that didn't do anything to help me understand my father's role in all this. "Okay," I said, giving Astrid a pointed look. "That still doesn't explain why my father is—"

"She started by showing us the messages between Salvatore and Sadie," my father blurted out explosively, running a hand through the thick black crop of hair on his head, his mouth twisted with disgust and anger. "I had no idea, Liana. If I had known…"

"No," I said coldly, but inside I found myself praising Maddox's cleverness. Because in those messages, Salvatore had told Sadie to use any means necessary to secure his win in the Tourney, and she had. If there was anything that could reach my dad, that was it.

But it still didn't make me want to forgive him.

"If you had believed me when I told you something was going on, then things might be different. But you chose not to. In fact, you *told* Salvatore that Mom's loyalty couldn't be counted on! You betrayed your own wife and daughter!"

My father met my gaze head-on during my tirade, his eyes solemn as I laid my litany of his crimes at his feet, for the whole world to hear. As soon as I was done, he nodded, his mouth tight. "I know," he said simply—and to me, it wasn't good enough.

"You know?" I said, incredulous. "You *know*?! You know nothing! You don't know what it's been like the last few months, trying to survive this nightmare long enough to figure out what was going on! Being set up for Gerome's death, killing Devon Alexander! And I had no one to rely on except for Alex and my friends! And you tried to make sure of that!"

He sighed heavily and stepped closer to me, reaching for me. I jerked away, almost stumbling over the chair in the process, too angry and bitter to ever want his hands on me. He froze for a moment, arms still out, and then slowly lowered them to his sides.

"Let me try this again," he said tiredly. "You're right. I hurt you. I may have gotten your mother killed. It's my fault, and I know there are no words to ever convey how sorry I am. But that doesn't matter now. What does is that we stop whatever Sadie and Salvatore have planned."

I stared at him. His words sounded sincere—hell, he *looked* sincere—but years of his abuse had left me filled with doubt and mistrust. I couldn't believe him; it was too bizarre, too far-fetched.

And that had to be showing on my face, because Astrid made an irritated little noise and stepped around my father, placing her hands on her hips. "Look, believe your father or not. We've got bigger problems. We brought a contingent of Knights up here to defend against Salvatore and the others three hours ago, but we haven't heard anything from central command in an hour. They had runners moving around with information and updated orders, but we haven't seen any since the last one, and we have no idea what the situation is on the levels beneath us, or even in the surrounding areas. Whatever you have planned, you need to get moving. So please tell me you have a plan, or at least know what the hell is going on."

"Sage," I said, snapping out of my disbelief and focusing on what Astrid was saying. I didn't like the news, not one bit, but at least there was some hope. Maddox had been doing an incredible job keeping the Knights on our side organized and working to defend the Citadel. She had been able to organize a defense against our enemies. Even though she didn't know it, she had kept them from their true goal of getting ahold of Leo. The only problem was, she had no idea that was who they wanted, or that the sentinels were on the loose, so she couldn't take steps to further ensure his safety.

Well, that and the fact that Astrid had lost contact with her.

Astrid cleared her throat, and I realized I had started to tell her

CHAPTER 27

what was going on but had gotten sidetracked by my thoughts. Shaking my head, I swallowed back my fears and focused. I needed to tell as many people as possible what was happening in case I didn't make it to my friends or died trying to stop Sage. They needed to be aware, so they could keep up the fight. "Sage is really—"

Everything I had been about to say stopped when I heard a vicious grating sound coming from down the hall. My head jerked toward the sound, my eyes already searching for the source, and I saw the hatch we had come through now hanging by one hinge and wide open, with a pair of chromed silver legs dangling from the hole... and descending closer to the floor.

The sentinels! They had followed us. I hefted up the gun and strode toward the barricade, about to deliver orders, but Astrid grabbed my arm and jerked me around.

"We will hold this line," she said, pausing when several lancer rounds shot by overhead, telling me Salvatore was back, and had brought friends. My hatred for him was rivaled by the realization that she was right—I had to get to Leo, not stay here and fight.

I cursed, and then began shrugging off the plasma rifle. "Here," I said, thrusting it toward her. "You're going to need this to take out the sentinels. Fire here, and—"

"I'll handle that," Dylan said smoothly, shoving the handgun into my hands and taking the rifle. "You and Rose get moving."

I gaped at her, and then shook my head. "No, I need you," I said, unwilling to lose her. I'd started to rely on her, and now that we were this close, I didn't want to give her up, and leave her to potentially die. "I'm gonna need your help—"

"No, they are," she said, pointing to the younger Knights. "And you need my help out here. I'm recognizable as your competitor, the girl who could've won, and I'm still on your side. That'll make the Knights on the other side reconsider their choices, especially if we can hold the line here. So go. I've got the Citadel. You and the others get to the Core and stop Sage."

Still I hesitated, not wanting to leave her. It was Rose who made the decision for me, prompted by the sharp cry of a young man on our side getting hit with lancer fire. Dylan immediately sprang toward the barricade, shouting, "Run!" while Rose grabbed my shoulder and spun me around, pulling me toward the elevator area. I stumbled forward, confused by the sudden shift in my world. It felt wrong leaving without Dylan. We had saved each other too many times to count!

"Rose, we can't—"

We can and will, Tony said stubbornly. *We are too close to finally putting a stop to this for you to be torn about it. This is what Dylan wants. She wants to keep her fellow Knights safe, and you should let her. You have to trust she can handle it and let her make her own choices!*

His words made me angry, but only because he was right. There was no reason for me to think she couldn't handle herself, and the Knights there *were* going to need her. Because she knew how to fight the sentinels. If anything, she was going to save everyone in that hallway— or take out as many of the enemy forces as possible.

But it was the last thought that made me fearful for her. I cast one last look at her, watching as she fired a volley of purple plasma down the hall before ducking down to avoid several crimson rounds. Some of the Knights were less lucky. The blades ricocheted and tore lines along their arms, legs, and sides. But all of them were fighting.

Fighting for me.

It was a humbling, yet necessary, reminder that I had to stop Sage. And soon. Before things could get any worse.

I poured on the speed and moved past Rose, that reminder giving me a much-needed dose of energy and determination. "Let's get out of here," I told her, taking a moment to chamber a round in the gun Dylan had handed me and turning the safety off.

28

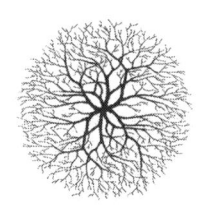

I took a cursory glance at the elevator bay as Rose and I emerged from the hall, checking to make sure the coast was clear before heading to the nearest one. I stopped in front of it and automatically gave my name and ID number, expecting the elevator sensors to start scanning me almost immediately.

But they didn't. The elevator remained dark and still, and I realized that whatever Quess and Leo had done to restore power, they hadn't been able to restore it everywhere. I cursed as the sound of fighting from behind us increased, definitely drawing nearer, and quickly spat out Lionel's code, nervously scanning the entrances to the other halls and wondering what was happening in each of them. Had Astrid and my father set up other barricades there as well? I assumed so, but what was their condition like? Were they holding the line, or were they being torn apart? Were the sentinels coming through there, or were they just in the one hall?

I hated running away from a fight, especially one of which I had been the root, but there was no alternative. I had to get to Leo, because it was the only way to stop Sage's plan outright.

The elevator lit up and a pad slid out of the wall, and I stepped on it quickly, motioning for Rose to follow. I told it my destination, level 65, and we began to descend.

But not before I saw a sentinel emerging from the hall in which I had left Dylan, its eyes glowing yellow, its silver hide drenched with blood. My mouth dropped in shock before it fell out of view as the pad descended, and it was all I could do to keep from throwing a line out and racing back down the hall to check on Dylan and Astrid.

Because I already knew—had known since Rose had grabbed me and forced me down the hall—that they were dead.

Pain slammed into me, and I closed my eyes, trying not to give in to it. But it was hard. Everything had happened so fast, and now they were gone.

Tears started to form, my stomach churning, and I sucked in a shaky breath, trying to stave it off. But my fear was beginning to mount as well. I had no idea what I was going to find in the Champion's quarters. I just prayed it wouldn't be anything like that damned hall.

"Get down!" Rose cried, shoving me back behind her. I slammed into the wall as she moved in front of me, and then ducked down when she staggered back, the elevator pad shaking under my feet as something heavy crashed onto it.

Confused, I looked down between her legs and saw another set of them, facing her. It didn't take me long to figure out that the sentinel in the hall had realized which elevator we had taken... and jumped down after us.

Rose took a half step back, crowding me closer to the wall that was speeding past.

"You won't survive us, *Sister*," Alice spat. "If I see you, we all see you!"

Rose finally managed to catch her balance and began pushing at the sentinel in front of her, giving me a little more breathing space. "You're choosing the wrong side!" she cried with a final shove, slamming Alice into the wall with a spray of sparks. The other sentinel tried to break Rose's hold, but a moment later she fell through an opening in the wall as a doorway opened up.

She disappeared into the hole, but I kept my eyes on it, knowing she would be back up and coming down the shaft for us at any moment. I grabbed my baton, twisting the dial to increase the voltage and then pressing it down to hold a charge.

"I'll stun her!" I cried as I caught a glimpse of movement from above. "When I do, smash her hard drive!"

Rose nodded as a dark shadow began to form above us, her eyes already on it. I stood behind her, ready with the baton when the sentinel came crashing down on us again. The clash of metal was even heavier this time, and the pad rocked back and forth, scraping the walls. My heart nearly stopped, as I was certain that any number of the fragile components inside the pad would break apart and stop working, but when they didn't, I quickly leaned around Rose and jabbed my baton at Alice's midsection.

Alice was a step ahead of me, though, and broke Rose's hold on her, then leapt back before I could get her. She reached up, grabbed a fistful of the wall, and clung to it like a spider. Confusion slammed into me as we began sliding away again, wondering why in the world she would be letting us go—but then I realized what she meant to do.

She was going to fall on us again. She was trying to take out the pad.

"Rose," I started, about to tell her of Alice's plan. But she whirled and hugged me to her chest, curling around me protectively. Before I could ask what was wrong, I heard the unmistakable sound of lancer fire, and the world around me exploded into lines of crimson as several whirring blades shot past us and ricocheted off the walls of the elevator.

The best I could figure was that several people had been just outside the elevator when we passed, ready to fire in. Alice must have managed to notify them of our descent—or they had seen it light up with activity and decided to fire on whoever was inside. Either way, the blades continued to rain down on us as we moved past, with Rose curling even more protectively around me and taking the hits.

A few blades got through, though. One zipped by, clanged off of Rose's chest a few inches away from my head, and severed a few loose strands of my hair. The other barely nicked me on the shoulder, but the pain was indescribable.

Still, I clenched my teeth on it, focusing on my warning to Rose about Alice's plan. "She's planning on jumping down on us again!" I shouted. "If she does, the pad could break. We need to check and see where she is!"

"Get ready to get off the elevator pad in twelve seconds!" Rose replied, and a moment later, her arms let go of me and she drew away. I half turned in the low crouch she had forced me into, confused by her directions, and then saw her reaching for a chunk of wall, grabbing for it like Alice had done.

Before I could ask what she was doing, she was gone, her grip on the wall stopping her descent, but not mine. As I watched, she quickly lifted her body up, placing her feet on the other side of the shaft and forming an X over it. She was using her body to block the shaft!

A second later, I realized that the impact of Alice hitting her would kill her. Alice was at least seven or eight stories above Rose at this point. When she hit Rose, and they fell to the pad, they would both be severely damaged, to the point where neither one would survive.

She was sacrificing herself for me.

"Rose!" I cried, unable to accept the gesture for a second time in twice as many minutes. "Please, don't!"

"Follow Lionel's orders!" she shouted back. "Don't stop for—"

Whatever else she was about to say was cut off by a dark form slamming into her with a terrific clang that seemed to shake the very air of the shaft. I flinched back as Rose was ripped from the wall, one arm severed clean off, and plummeting toward me.

My eyes widened as the sentinels twisted in the air overhead, hurtling toward me. To make matters worse, I felt the pad starting to slow its descent, alerting me that it was about to stop on my level.

I had only seconds before the two sentinels crashed into me. Not enough time to get the door to my quarters open. I eyed their trajectory as they bounced against the walls, and then moved, letting nothing but instinct guide me—with a little help from Tony. Making the best of the small space, I raced for the opposite wall and planted a foot on it, then leapt straight up in the air, staying as close to the wall as I could. I felt the breeze of their passing ruffle the hair on my neck. There was a sharp snap and several sparks from below as they crashed into the pad, likely shattering the thin disc, but I didn't look down. My eyes were up, focused on a fixed point on the wall. I snapped one arm down, forcing a lash bead out of my sleeve, then spun it up as gravity began to pull me back down, and finally cast it, the lone bead glowing brightly against the darkening lights of the shaft. There was a bright blue spark as it hit the wall, and I was jerked to a sudden halt before I had the chance to pick up much downward momentum.

I looked down, my eyes focused on the glowing lights below, but Rose was already gone. I squeezed my eyes shut, my heart sick. I'd lost not only Dylan, but Rose as well, in a matter of minutes, after we'd come so far. For all my grand speeches and lofty goals of getting us through this alive, I'd failed.

Suddenly, I wanted to break down and cry right there in the shaft. It wasn't right—wasn't fair. Rose might've been an AI, but she was a sentient creature who had the right to live. And as for Dylan... That girl had intimidated the hell out of me at first, but after I'd gotten to know her...

They hadn't deserved to die like this. Not for me. Not because some bitter old man who couldn't let go of the past had turned me into public enemy number one. Again.

Anger burned new life into me, taking whatever tears I had and melting them away, and I set my mind on who was truly to blame. Sage. I was going to take him out, just as soon as I got everyone else I cared about to safety.

I quickly turned on the hand light that was still wrapped around my wrist and looked around, trying to figure out what level I was on. My light finally caught the white 67 painted on the side, and I quickly threw a lash down and headed for the area between the 64th and 65th floors, where my quarters were located.

The door was still sealed—a good sign, in my mind, until I remembered there were six elevator shafts with doors that led to the room. Still, if the power was on and Sage hadn't managed to get control of Cornelius, then the legacies would've had to fight their way through a slew of defenses to get to my friends.

At least, I hoped they had to. I would find out soon enough.

I gave the order to open the door using Lionel's code, not wanting to waste time trying my own, and then swung in as soon as the door opened, landing lightly on my feet.

I took a quick look around and realized I'd entered at the third door in. I quickly followed the curved hall that looped around and paused, instantly on guard when I saw another door to the outside standing wide open. I pulled my gun out from my pocket, aimed it at the elevator shaft, and searched for any sign of movement.

A quick look into the shaft told me it was clear. I wasn't sure whether that meant the attack had been repelled, or I was too late. All I knew was I needed more information. I hesitated for a second, and then thought, *Cornelius? You there?*

His reply was almost instantaneous, filling me with some small measure of relief, if only for a moment. *I'm here, Champion. But please be aware, the war room is surrounded by your enemies and is about to be breached.*

29

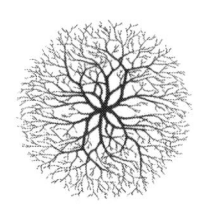

Panic slammed into me, urging me to run and get there, but I tamped it back, knowing I needed to be smart. *How close to being breached?* I demanded, moving down the hall for the main walk in a quiet stalk. *Put me on speaker with the others.*

Of course, he replied. *You may speak now.*

Guys? I said. My heart formed a swollen knot in my throat at the thought that I was about to find out whether any of my friends had died, and I did my best to swallow it back.

Liana! Grey/Leo said, his voice filled with relief but still tinged with an edge of panic.

Hearing his voice was such sweet relief that I paused in the hall and put one hand against the wall to keep my knees from giving out. I was so close, finally... but there were still miles to go before I was done.

Thank Scipio. Are you okay? What's going—

Worry about that later. I interrupted, shaking off my relief and continuing to move down the hall. *What's your situation?*

Bad, Maddox replied for him a second later. *We're all in one piece, but we can't get through the escape tunnel. Motion sensors on the other side are going crazy, like there's a small army up there. Luckily Leo and Quess were able to restore power by hacking Cornelius's link to the Core, but IT has figured out what they did and is working to kick us out. Not to mention those bastards are using cutters to get through the wall. They've dismantled every defensive measure we've had, room by room, and they're probably just a few minutes from getting through this door. We're trapped.*

I slowed down as I approached the stairs that led into the first main room of my quarters, checking to make sure the room was clear. Thanks to Maddox's report, I was prepared for the destruction that lay within, but it was still gut-wrenching to see. The couches and sofas I'd set up theater-style for my briefings with my Knight Commanders had been torn apart by the small photon laser emitters I'd placed at strategic points. Piles of burning fabric lay strewn wildly through the room.

I was halfway down the stairs when I spotted the first body: a young man with curly hair who looked a lot like Liam, but older, was lying on his stomach, blood pooled around the severed stumps where his arm and leg had been, from where the laser emitters had caught him. Behind him, I spotted three more bodies in various forms of dismemberment, and another two on the floor between me and the next door to the hall.

That was six people, but we had arrested over a hundred legacies. And they'd all been in the cells in the Citadel. Some of them were probably stuck fighting the Knights somewhere, but how many were here?

Do you still have cameras? Can you tell me how many are outside the door? I asked, carefully stepping over the bodies and suppressing the queasiness I felt as I headed up the stairs toward the next hall. I paused to check down the curved corridor for any sign of movement. There was none, but I held my position, waiting for Maddox's answer. If the answer was a few, then I could come up behind them and take them out. If it was more than that, I was going to have to think of another way to help my friends escape.

Liana, there are over forty people in the next room, Zoe piped up, her voice lined with urgency. *Whatever you're thinking, knock it off. You can't fight your way through them.*

No, I couldn't fight my way through forty people alone. She was right about that. Even if they were trapped in the hall, I only had so many bullets. But if Leo and I could get them pinned between us and our guns, maybe we could create a crossfire that would kill and wound many of them.

But if they had lancers, then we'd be sunk. They'd have a way of attacking us at any range, and since there were only two of us and more of them, chances were they'd cut us down before we could do any considerable damage.

I blew out a breath, looking around and trying to think. There had to be a way to get my friends out, but how? The escape hatch had been eliminated, and the ceiling was enclosed, meaning we couldn't easily climb up the shaft to try to escape them, so the only way in or out of the apartment was behind me, on the elevators. And there were no legacies left alive between me and those elevators. If I could just get everyone to me...

A moment later, it hit me, and I turned back to the elevator bay, already transmitting my thoughts to Maddox and the others. *Use the room controls to create a way from the war room to one of the elevator bays,* I ordered. *You'll have to raise a few walls here and there, but there's no one guarding the front rooms, and if you put walls down in the hall, sealing your path, you'll be long gone before they figure out what's going on.*

Hey, yeah, that's a great idea, the youngest member of our group, Tian, chirped. *I'm on it!*

Good. Be aware that the legacies have a target, I informed them. *They're after Leo. Apparently, he has protocols that Sage needs in order to replace Scipio with Kurt. Whatever you do, get him out of the room first.*

I'm your best fighter, Leo immediately said, the affront in his voice thick. *You're going to need Maddox and me to cover everyone else as they run away! We can't be sure—*

I argued with you about this exact same thing once upon a time, I snapped, my patience coming to an abrupt end. I was referring, of course, to the insufferable rule about not letting me go first into dangerous situations —and sending him instead. *And I lost. Accept the inevitable and get out of there first, or Quess and Maddox have my permission to knock you unconscious and drag you. We need you, Leo. The Tower needs you. So stop arguing.*

There was a pause, making the sounds of my boots on the stairs quite loud to my ears, and then a, *Fine. Tian and Eric are figuring the best way to get around these guys. We just need a—*

Leo, Quess cried, his voice desperate. *I need you! There's something weird going on with the data stream!*

I stopped mid-step and turned around to face the war room. *Ignore it,* I ordered. *Get out of there!*

We can't! Leo shouted. *We're going to lose power in the Citadel if we don't—*

I don't care! I thundered, angry that he was risking his life over the power in the Citadel. *We'll worry about it later! Now means now!*

If we lose the power, Tian won't be able to move the walls to let us out! I just need to buy her a few seconds to finish laying out a path for us. Give me a second!

There was a long pause, and my heart began to skitter out of beat, dread forming as each second went by without any sign of the walls being moved. I heard muffled sounds in the background, and quickly thought, *Guys, what's going on?*

The only response I got was from Leo, and it wasn't directed at me.

It's a feedback surge, he cried. *Everyone get down, now!*

I took a step back toward the main room, my eyes widening as the lights in the quarters flickered, a sharp, high-pitched hum beginning to fill the room. I recognized the sound as the one Tony's server in Cogstown had made—right before an electrical surge had hit the servers and me—and danced back just as sickly green lightning began to spark from the outlets, shattering the bulbs overhead and casting the room into darkness.

30

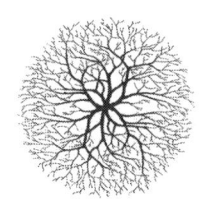

The net buzzing in my skull died a heartbeat later, telling me I had lost my connection with the others. My pulse skyrocketed as I realized that whatever power surge I'd just witnessed had likely fried the delicate components in the quarters, including Cornelius. Whatever attack the Core had just launched against us had taken the program out, and with him, the power that Quess and Leo had managed to keep from Sage's hands.

But that was the least of my worries. My friends were trapped. I had no idea whether the emergency power was going to come on, but if it didn't, I wasn't sure they'd be able to use the room controls to get out. Any second now, the legacies were going to finish cutting through the door, and my friends would be trapped with no way out, and Leo would fall right into Sage's hands. I had to get to them.

I broke into a run, turning on my light so I could see where I was going. *Tony,* I thought, my breathing already labored. *I need you.*

Already on it, doll face, he replied, and I felt his presence rise up to meet mine. He stayed just below the surface, but it was like he spread his own arms and legs out, just under my own. The burning in my lungs began to ease as he somehow managed to slow my breathing, and my heartbeat dropped in response. He then released a small trickle of adrenaline while stimulating my brain to produce more endorphins, giving me a wash of energy. His thoughts were just behind mine, explaining everything as he worked, giving me reassurance, until it was hard to tell where my thoughts began and his ended.

We sped through the halls like this, unified as one, but with me leading the charge in a deep and deadly calm. One hand was already holding my gun while the other pulled out the baton, pressing the button to start the charge.

The hall spiraled inward, taking me through the kitchen, past the bedrooms, dodging the signs of chaos and searching for any hint of movement in the shadows.

A light began to shine from the opposite side of the hall as I drew closer to the war room, and I came around the turn to see a long line of people pouring through a hole where the door had once been. An angry yell burst from my mouth as I saw it, and I raised my gun and began firing into the crowd.

I caught the first three legacies in the back, dropping them immediately, and a fourth mid-turn, and then missed the fifth when he dodged to the side, somehow managing to avoid the bullet. He slammed up against the wall and made for me, but I had anticipated his charge and picked up my foot, planting a kick low to his belly. He staggered back, and I shot him before he had a chance to recoup, the rage in my heart unwilling to show any mercy.

Several other legacies peeled off from the back and moved to meet me, but I gunned them down, and two more behind them. The gun clicked empty, but instead of ejecting the magazine, Tony compelled me to spin it around in my hand and use it to crack some heads, and I was more than happy to comply, turning it in my hand until I was gripping the top and then bringing it back down on a man's temple.

I jabbed my baton into the woman behind him, going to a knee to do it, then caught the blow from a man with my gun hand seconds before he slashed me open with a cutter. With a vicious growl, I dropped the baton I had been holding against the woman's stomach and grabbed the man's cupped hands with my free hand, forcing the angle of the blade back on him. His eyes grew wide as he realized the mistake of his position over me, and then I stood up, shoving my forearm up while pressing down on the cutter hilt with my other hand. He barely had a chance to scream before the crimson blade began to cut a fiery line through his forehead, and then I jerked his arms down quickly, savagely ending his life.

His hands fell away from the cutter, and I pulled it out of him and swung it around to the hall in front of me, bending and scooping up my baton as well. Several legacies were hovering a foot away, their faces wearing various masks of hatred, revulsion, disgust, and fear, and I couldn't help but bare my teeth at them in a silent snarl as I began to stalk toward them, wondering who would be the first to meet my challenge.

A big man on the left opted to be the first, and he launched himself at me, wielding not one, but two batons. I cut through the first one with the cutter, ducked under the second, and then drove the cutter through his chest, giving the plasma blade a vicious twist before jerking it out of him and letting him fall to one side.

I heard Zoe and Maddox shouting in panicked voices over the clamor, and Tony responded by giving me another hit of adrenaline. I burst into action, racing toward the remaining three legacies, impatient to have this at an end.

I leaned back to avoid a wide blow from a baton brandished by a blond woman, and then grabbed her arm, pushing the baton she held into a second attacker and stepping behind her to use her as a shield against the third attacker. I planted a boot in the small of her back and shoved her forward, then brought my cutter down at an angle in the spot where I had last seen the man. The red-hot, super-charged plasma turned orange in the dim light as it connected with something, and I heard a cry of pain followed by a sizzling spatter of something wet evaporating under the heat of the plasma. The smell of burning flesh filled the hall, but I carried the blade through, then spun all the way around and brought it up over my head in a two-handed grip. I spied the woman I had kicked forward seconds before I brought the blade down, slicing a line down her spine.

I ignored the queasiness that was beginning to form at so much carnage in a matter of seconds, and sprinted toward the door, spying more legacies inside. Several of them were watching me warily, all wielding batons, but they had their backs to the fight behind them—a fight I couldn't make out through the flashing hand lights and darkness.

I turned my gaze on the handful of legacies waiting just inside the war room and took a quick look at the floor, spotting my gun lying a few feet back. I moved to get it, tucking my baton into my belt loop and then pulling out my last magazine.

As soon as the gun was in my hands, I ejected the old clip and inserted the new, taking a second to chamber a round. The entire time, I kept my back to my enemies, giving them an open target, an invitation to come and get me. A part of me had hoped they would take it—it was easier to fight five when only three of them could fit in the hall, shoulder to shoulder—but they had chosen not to, which meant that their deaths were going to come a whole lot faster.

As soon as the round was chambered, I turned the gun on them, aiming it at the five standing at the other end and squeezing the trigger, Tony's minor corrections to my arm making my aim true. I began walking down the hall as I fired off another round, hitting a second person before the others ducked into openings to use the walls for cover.

Then I was running, racing toward the opening. I used my free arm to throw a lash end down, snapping out a few feet and then flinging it through the door, aiming for the ceiling beyond. I saw the sharp spark of blue that told me it had connected, and hit the hand controls, jamming them to full throttle. They sent me flying through the door, my gun already turning to the side to angle down, in anticipation of where the enemy would be.

As soon as I saw the sparking blue tips of the batons, Tony and I were able to estimate their positions, and I fired two shots back to back, changing the angle slightly between the two. The flash from both shots showed me that our aim had been spot on, so I put those legacies out of my mind and looked ahead, searching for my friends.

My light caught the edge of the large conference table in the center of the room, now on its side, and I let my lash line continue to drag me up and threw another line, angling for it. I knew my friends were on the other side—the table was surrounded by legacies—and I needed to get to them.

The line hit, and I disconnected the first, swinging into the new connection and firing on the legacies who were trying to flank my friends. I cleared the edge of the table still firing, disconnected the line, and fell to the ground. I landed on my feet and then fired my last two rounds at the men racing around the right side of the table for me.

The gun hit empty, but no one else came around the corner, and I realized I had scared them off for a few seconds. I turned my eyes to the handful of forms huddled behind the table and quickly counted off Maddox, Zoe, and Eric, all of them holding batons.

"Where are the others?" I demanded as I moved closer to them, my eyes searching the area around their feet for any sign of the locked cases that held the ammunition for the guns. I found one a second later, next to a bag by Zoe, and waved for her to pass it over.

She gaped at me, still stunned by my sudden appearance, but Eric quickly spotted what I was after and slid the heavy box toward me while Maddox answered my question.

"Leo and Quess were by the terminal with Tian and Liam when the power went off," she called, pausing long enough to land a series of hits with her baton as a woman tried to come over the table at us. "Leo thinks he can get the emergency power on if he can pull the burned circuits!"

I grated my teeth together and threw open the box, digging around for a magazine and thinking. The emergency power could help us, in that it would mean we still had defenses in this room, but it was a waste of time at this point. I had taken out almost half their number, and the defenses in the room weren't going to help us as much as Leo would like. If anything, they were going to catch us in the crossfire, especially if Cornelius wasn't there to guide them. And I had a feeling that whatever attack Sage had just launched from the Core had taken my virtual assistant offline permanently.

I could try to buy Leo some time, but I could feel Tony's concern that I was already pushing too hard. My body had been on the verge of crashing for the last few hours, and this particular push was going to be it for me before I hit oblivion. We needed to get out of here, and the only way for us to do that was to make a hole and get out through the halls.

"LEO!" I called, pushing from my diaphragm to make my voice stand out over the cacophony of noise. "LEAVE IT AND RUN! WE WILL COVER YOU!"

"ONE SECOND!" he shouted back in a slightly singsong voice, and I felt a rush of irritation at him that was swallowed by my fear *for* him. The legacies were after him on Sage's orders, but I had no idea whether they'd actually take him alive or try to shoot him if things got too heavy for them. I had to get to him and get him out of here.

"We gotta move," I told the others, slapping the magazine I found into the gun and chambering a round. "We're going right for the dais. You three charge, and I'll shoot anyone who comes behind. Get Leo and move. Sage needs him for his plan."

"Got it," Zoe said, shaking off whatever shock she was feeling with a sharp nod. Her eyes were wide, but they were also focused. "Ready when you are."

I nodded and took a few steps to the right of the table, checking the gap to make sure no one was there. After a quick look, I nodded to the others and waved them forward, then turned back to check the other side of the table while Maddox crept past, heading for the gap. I kept one eye on her and the others as they went through, the other on the open gap, and then backed away from the spot as soon as Eric, who was last to go, moved.

I was turning back to race across the floor after them, when a man stepped around the table and threw his baton at me. Tony and I reacted quickly, leaping back so that the baton missed us by a matter of inches, and then shot him in the head, dropping him to the ground like a bag of bricks. I quickly followed Eric, racing after him toward the steps and scanning for any targets. Bodies lay all around the steps, but there was a thick crowd of people at the top, all legacies, surrounding my desk.

CHAPTER 30

"I GOT IT!" Leo cried from the thick of things, and a second later, the lights in the room flickered on, momentarily blinding me.

Several things seemed to happen at once in my momentary blindness: the sound of something heavy hitting the ground, a sharp gasp from Eric, beside me, and then something slamming into my chest hard, too heavy to be just a simple baton.

It threw me back, riding me down, and as I blinked against the weight of it, Tony was already responding for me, curling my spine and lifting my feet up. My boots hit something solid, and Tony pushed as I slammed into the ground. I rolled with the blow, flipping the attacker over my head with a strong push of my legs. Whoever it was grunted and lost their grip on my uniform, and I skidded to a stop. I scrambled to get my legs under me and looked up at the dais, where I could now see Leo being physically dragged away by not one, but four legacies, each holding a flailing limb while a fifth began walking toward... me?

I frowned, confusion washing over me at why they would come at me when I was on the opposite side of the room from the door, and then I shrugged it off and scrambled to my feet. I made it halfway there before something heavy fell on my shoulder, and I heard Zoe scream behind me.

Stupidly, I turned—just in time to see a chrome fist flying toward my head.

Then I saw nothing.

31

My eyes jerked open and darted around the darkness, searching for any sign of the sentinel that had hit me. I was already panicking, and that sensation doubled when I realized I was no longer in the war room.

Was I a prisoner? Had the sentinels grabbed me to take me to Sage? If so, where was he, and why wasn't I tied up? Where was I? Where were my friends? The softness beneath me told me I was lying in a bed. I started to sit up, trying to find some clue as to where I was, or hint of who I was with.

A wave of nausea, accompanied by a throbbing pain in my head, had me lying back down for a moment while the world spun rapidly on its axis. I cried out as the pain in my head intensified to a sharp stabbing and my vision spun faster and faster, and closed my eyes against the sensation, reaching up with my hands to grab my head as if I could somehow contain the agony by pressing them against my scalp.

It's okay, Tony said softly, his voice somehow modulated to be as gentle as possible, making him sound like he was standing on the opposite edge of a distant shore, calling his message to me. *You're suffering a severe concussion, but I'm working to correct some of the damage. Just hold on.*

CHAPTER 31

Wait, I thought, ignoring the pain that focusing brought. *Where am I? What's going on? How long have I been out?*

I'm not sure where we are. Unlike that time in Cogstown, I was inside your head when you went out, and the shock of it took me offline as well. The only thing I can tell you is that we've been out for two hours. Now stop thinking so hard; the pain is unbearable.

I ignored the last part, my mind still in shock over the fact that I'd lost two hours and had no idea what had happened to Leo or my friends, or where I even was! I needed to get up, figure out what was going on, and maybe contact Dinah again to figure out how far along Sage was—

Seriously, stop it, Tony snapped, and as soon as he broke my thoughts, I suddenly became aware of an intense pressure making my entire head feel like it was swelling, while simultaneously being squeezed by a vice. So I lay there and let him work, my skull feeling like it was shattered into pieces and digging into my brain. I knew if I tried to move again, I was going to lose the meager contents of my stomach and then pass out, and I couldn't let myself do that. I needed to know what had happened and where we were.

So I exercised patience, trying to focus on my breathing and not the searing lines of agony crisscrossing my brain. Tony worked slowly and methodically as he did whatever it was he was doing to correct the damage to my head. It started with a slow lessening of the pain, making my tense muscles relax and my breathing come easier. Then he corrected my balance, sending electrical impulses through my brain to my inner ears and doing something to them that made the world slow until it felt still again. My stomach was last, and after a few moments, the only thing I was left with was a mild headache and a bone-deep exhaustion.

I was so tempted to just let myself fall back into the pillow, and my eyelids started getting heavier just thinking about it, but I jerked them open and slowly worked myself into a sitting position. My entire body felt like a giant bruise, and I winced at an ache in my ribs that I hadn't noticed through the agony of my head, and then cried out as the muscles on the left side of my face erupted in fire at my facial twitch, the pain damn near blinding.

My eyes teared up from the sting of it, and I immediately lifted my hand to feel what the damage was, moving gently. My fingers touched something hot and swollen, and I jerked my hand back with a hiss as the tender flesh erupted in pain. I took a second or two to blink against it, then looked around.

I spotted a small candle burning on the floor across from me, right in front of an open door, and set that as my first goal as I gingerly got out of bed. I had no idea where I was, but since the door was open, and the room design was one that the Citadel used, I surmised I wasn't a prisoner. Which meant I was with people I knew and trusted. But who?

The aches in my body ran deep as I surrendered all of my weight onto my feet, swaying back and forth for a second before finding my balance. I limped over to the candle, moving at the hobbling pace of an eighty-year-old Hand who'd worked harvesting duty her entire life, and felt a rush of success for every step I made that brought me closer.

By the doorframe, my breathing had turned into a sharp pant as the line of pain against my ribs continued to tighten with each jerking step, and I paused, leaning onto the frame and pressing my heated face against the cool metal. The unbruised side, of course. I wasn't a sadist.

As I stood there, trying to catch my breath and summon up enough energy to start the next leg of my journey, a dozen questions began to form in my mind, the first being, "What happened?" I remembered the sentinel, but what I didn't know was how it had gotten in. I had no idea what had happened to Leo, either; the last I had seen of him, he was being dragged toward me... No, toward the sentinel next to me. The sentinel who had come in through the emergency escape shaft from above. It must've dropped down and crashed through the ceiling—that was the sound I had heard during those seconds when the lights had blinded me. It had blindsided me, knocking me unconscious, and then...

And then what? Where were my friends, and how did I get here?

The litany of questions was beginning to make the pain in my head intensify, so I quickly shrugged them off. The only way to get answers was to find out who was with me. I pushed away from the doorframe and stepped out into the hall, looking in both directions. There was a door across from me that was closed, but I ignored it, focusing instead on the candle burning at the end of the hall, where the living area should be.

I braced myself against the wall as I walked toward it, still not fully confident in my legs' ability to keep me up. As I drew nearer to it, I could hear the soft exchange of quiet voices. It took me a moment to recognize them, as most of my attention was focused on getting there, but when I did, I relaxed a little bit more. It was Quess and Maddox.

I slowly emerged from the hall and scanned the living space, spotting them at a dining room table beyond the kitchen to the left of me. There were several pads lined up on the table, along with batons, my gun, a few cutters, and a lancer. The two were sitting side by side, heads pressed together as they looked at a pad, but their demeanor was grim, telling me that our situation wasn't good.

Quess noticed me first, his dark blue eyes darting up toward me as I came around the counter. He was up like lightning, moving over to me. For a second, I tensed, expecting him to order me back to bed, but to my surprise, he simply put an arm around my lower back and held on to my arm with the other, letting me lean into him while he helped me to a chair.

The gratitude I felt for him was immeasurable, but next to the relief of just sitting down, it was nothing. My legs felt rubbery, and the pain in my head had shifted to a throbbing sensation that seemed to be connected to the beating of my heart. I closed my eyes for a second, taking a moment to regain my composure. When I opened them again, Quess was setting a glass of water in front of me, along with an assortment of pills.

"What are these?" I croaked, and then winced around the pain in my jaw.

"Nerve blockers, pain pills, a stimulant, some vitamins... Something to help you regain some of your wind. No offense, but you look like hell." Quess spoke gruffly, his voice thick with something I couldn't quite place, and I looked up at him, a frown tugging at my lips. I resisted it, knowing that the side of my face the sentinel had smashed would not respond well, but the fear remained.

"Where's Leo?" I asked, my heart in my throat. "Is he..."

Quess shook his head and looked away, folding his arms across his chest. I continued to gaze at him, trying to figure out if he was telling me Leo was dead or taken, but his face revealed nothing.

"They got him," Maddox informed me when Quess didn't say anything, and I turned toward the tall girl to see her looking at the table, her face lined with exhaustion and sadness. "Tian got the room controls working when Leo restored the power, and she managed to drop walls between us and the bulk of the legacies, as well as the sentinels, but Leo was on the other side when the walls came down. As it was, we barely got out alive. We're not sure where he is, but—"

"He's with Sage," I interrupted automatically. I wasn't sure why I was even talking—how I was still rooted in the moment in spite of the news that Sage had both Leo and Grey now—but I was. "Sage is Ezekial Pine and has spent the last three hundred years trying to kill Scipio to replace him with Kurt. Sage needs the protocols that Lionel Scipio programmed into Leo if he's going to kill Scipio and install Kurt."

And now Sage had him. And I had no doubt he was going to do whatever it took to get those codes from Leo, even if it meant killing Grey and then ripping Leo's code apart piece by piece.

A wave of despair crashed into me, and I felt the overwhelming urge to break down and cry. I wasn't sure I could go any farther—wasn't sure I had what it took. I'd gone through hell and back to get to him, to stop all this, only to have our one chance slip through my fingers.

And I was losing both the men I loved at the exact same time. Even if Grey was alive, he wouldn't be for long. And as for Leo...

I squeezed my eyes shut and blew out a slow breath, trying not to give in. I could do this. Maddox and Quess clearly had a plan, and Quess had given me medication that would hopefully give me enough gas to see this through.

Opening my eyes, I reached out, grabbed the pills off the table, and began popping them in my mouth one by one, taking careful sips of water in between each. If I could, I would have taken them all at once, but as it was, I doubted I would be able to eat anything other than broth for the next week or so.

But that was the least of my worries. "Everyone else is okay, right? Where are we, by the way? Still in the Citadel, but—"

"We're on one of the lower floors, hiding out," Maddox interrupted softly. "But the fighting in the hall is getting worse, and our side is losing. I'm getting fewer and fewer reports from the Knight Commanders loyal to us, which either means that their runners are being taken out, or that they've fallen. Sentinels are beginning to pour in from the Attic, and it's only a matter of time before we're discovered here."

I took another sip of water, using the action to process the bleak picture that Maddox had just painted for me. It wasn't good. But then again, nothing about today had been. We might have to fight our way out, but where there was a will, there was a way.

Or at least I hoped there would be. On both fronts, as my will was rapidly burning out, and the way was growing increasingly dark and filled with terror.

"Then we should get everyone up and moving," I said. We'd already been here for two hours—which was probably one hour too many at this point. "Where're Tian and Liam? We'll have to get them out of here and find them a good place to hide, but—"

"Liana," Quess interrupted, his tone heavy and hesitant. I shifted around in the chair to look at him, and found him staring at his shoes, a pained expression on his face.

The hairs on the back of my neck rose as I realized his reticence to talk earlier wasn't about Leo. There was something more going on. My heart skipped a beat when he chanced a glance up at me, his dark blue eyes filled with horror and... *guilt*. Quess was feeling guilty about something, but what? And why the theatrics?

"What is it?" I demanded. He shifted his weight and continued to fidget, his nervous delay causing my anxiety to grow. I glanced over at Maddox to find her gaze still fixed to the table, her mouth turned down as if she had tasted something awful. "What's wrong? Is it Tian? Is she o—"

"It's Zoe," Quess whispered, his voice breaking on her name. I whirled back toward him and then stood up, panic growing at the dark way he had said my best friend's name.

"No," I whispered, shaking my head when I saw remorse glittering in his eyes. "No, she's okay. I saw her between Maddox and Eric. She was safe between them; they wouldn't let anything happen to her."

I looked over to Maddox for her confirmation, and found the raven-haired girl pressing her hand over her mouth, on the verge of tears. I took a step away, knocking the chair to the ground, and shook my head harder, as if I could shake away this reality and what they were telling me. "No," I repeated, when nothing about them changed, trying to will it to be so. "She's not dead. Quess, tell me she's not dead."

Quess met my gaze, his eyes shimmering with tears. "She's not dead," he said grimly. "She's dying. And I... I can't save her, Liana."

3 2

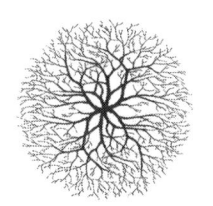

"No," I repeated adamantly, trying to refuse the defeat I saw on their faces. It was starting to scare me, make me believe they were telling the truth, but they couldn't be. Zoe had to be all right—she was my best friend. They were lying. They had to be. It was a sick joke.

Quess and Maddox would never do that to you, a small voice inside of me whispered, and I took a step back, as if I could reject even having the thought. It didn't matter that they hadn't done so before. They had to be doing it now. Zoe couldn't be dying.

I tried to get the words out, but all I could seem to get out was a litany of noes that grew more panicked as the expressions of my friends remained unchanged.

Finally, I couldn't take looking at them anymore, and turned my back to them, already searching the small apartment for my best friend, determined to show them they were wrong. "Zoe?" I called, my voice coming out small and thin through the tightness in my throat. I took a few staggering steps forward, toward the living area, and saw Tian's familiar blond form curled up on a couch, tucked in tight next to where Liam was sleeping sitting up, one arm curled protectively around the young girl, and a baton within reach. No sign of Zoe or Eric, and the two young people remained sleeping in spite of my call.

I ignored them, turning back toward the hall, toward the closed bedroom door that I had walked by earlier. She was there, probably just sleeping. I'd open it up for Quess and Maddox and show them that she was just fine.

I started hobbling toward it but reared back when Quess suddenly stepped in front of me, his face a tight mask. "Get out of my way," I grated out. "I don't know what trick you're playing, but Zoe is just fine."

My voice broke on the last part, and suddenly, I realized that deep down inside, I believed them. They weren't lying. I'd never actually thought they were. I had only wanted them to be.

A cry escaped my lips, and I cupped my hand over it, taking a step away from him. "Please tell me it's a joke," I begged as tears started clouding my vision. "Please, please..."

My chest started to shake as his face only grew more and more broken, and I began to sob. "Nooooo," I keened, unable to stop myself. All I could think of was my best friend in the world, the way she had laughed at my jokes and made me feel accepted in a world that had rejected me. She was everything to me—at the center of me. I loved her as much as I loved my brother, as much as I loved Grey and Leo...

Quess crossed over to me and threw his arms around me, holding me tight, and I sobbed against his chest, unable to accept that my friend was dying.

"What happened?" I croaked out, needing to know.

"The sentinel that attacked you," Maddox said, her voice thick with tears. "You went down and... it was going to kill you. Just step on you like you were nothing. But Zoe got in the way. She saw you go down and just... ran to help you."

My grief and pain grew tenfold as I realized that I had caused yet another one of my friends' deaths. First Roark and Cali, then Dylan and Rose, now Zoe. I wasn't worth it. I didn't deserve it. Everything I'd done had made things worse, and now I was going to lose my best friend as a result.

"The impact damaged almost all of her inner organs," Quess said when Maddox stopped talking. "I thought she was fine. She was up and moving almost a moment later, but once we got down here to look at you, she collapsed. I scanned her and found small holes in her spleen, her liver, her intestines—too many for me to repair without the use of a surgical bay and a microlaser, and the one in the Citadel is offline, so she's just been... slowly bleeding to death. I've been periodically draining her inner cavity to alleviate the pressure, but it's just... slowing everything down."

"*Quess,*" Maddox cut in harshly, and I wasn't sure if I should be grateful to her or not. Quess's list of Zoe's injuries had only twisted the dagger of guilt stabbing through me, each wound more evidence of how I had failed her—how I had failed all of them—and yet I needed to know what was wrong with her, if only because I secretly hoped he would say something that would spark an idea for how to save her.

"I'm sorry," Quess said, immediately contrite. "I'm just... I should be able to save her! If we were in the Medica, I could save her!"

"You said we can't move her, and she doesn't want to be moved," Maddox said tiredly. "And it's a good thing we didn't go to the Medica, if Sage is really behind everything! What we need to do is move on him. If we can end this, maybe we can get Zoe some help!"

"She doesn't have that long!" Quess replied, his voice breaking. "As it is..."

I pulled away from him, pushing back my tears enough to meet his gaze. "How long?" I whispered.

His jaw trembled for a second, his eyes filling with tears. "Not long," he replied.

I had to see her. I had to tell her how sorry I was, and... I wasn't sure, but it was a good place to start. "Where is she?" I demanded.

"Bedroom," he replied. "Eric's with her now, but you should go see her. She's... She's been real worried about you."

My stomach flipped at his words, and I damn near dissolved into tears again at the urgency in his voice. This was my last chance to talk to my friend—the last chance I'd ever have—and I wasn't sure I could handle it.

But for Zoe, I would do anything.

I nodded for Quess's benefit, and he moved to one side, giving me access to the hall. I started walking down it, but suddenly the candlelit area had become dark and foreboding, filled with shadows and the presence of death. For half a second, I was certain that if I could just shine a bright enough light down the hall, I would scare Death off and save Zoe. But then reality crashed in, reminding me that there was no easy fix for death.

Good guys and bad guys die all the same, and nothing ever turns out like the stories.

Which made it all the more important that I get to my friend. I didn't want her to die without knowing how much she meant to me, and how sorry I was that I had put her in this situation. It was all my fault. I had convinced her and the others to keep looking into the legacies, and my attempt to catch them all before the others could escape to Patrus had wound up getting her killed. I didn't care if she forgave me; I just wanted her to know that I loved her no matter what.

Each step felt like a prison sentence, but I didn't stop walking until I got to the door.

Only then did I halt, becoming a statue as I stared at the thin portal blocking me from my friend. The door was open a crack, but I didn't look through it. Couldn't, really, until I pulled my face into something vaguely resembling composure, and even then, I still didn't look.

I was afraid to. Afraid to see what my best friend had been reduced to. Not because I couldn't bear to see her in pain, although that didn't help. No, I was afraid that if I looked, I would suddenly chicken out—run away and hide without saying one word to her. It was already tempting. The guilt and shame were damn near overwhelming.

But I pushed it aside. It was a selfish and cowardly thought that was unwelcome in this situation. I needed to do this—to see her. If only to make sure she didn't feel alone at the end.

Reaching out, I slid my fingers through the gap in the door and pulled it back. The gears inside moved easily under my hand with the power out. The room had several candles burning all around, making the room glow warmly. The bed was set opposite the door, flush against the wall, and Eric was perched on the edge.

He glanced over his shoulder at me, and I took a hesitant step toward my friend, then saw the forlorn look in his dark eyes. He looked down and away for a second, and then turned back to the bed. "Hey, Zo," he said softly, his voice thick. "Liana's here."

"She is?" I heard my friend whisper from behind Eric, and I took another step forward, my hands coming together as if in prayer. "She's okay?"

Eric nodded, and then leaned forward, presumably to give her a kiss on the forehead. "I'll leave you two alone for a few minutes. But only a few minutes. You need your rest."

"Ha." Zoe chuckled weakly. "I think... the next... time... I rest..." She paused, struggling to cough, and I clutched my hands over my chest, trying to contain the terrified flutter at how awful she sounded.

"Shush, you," Eric tried, forcing some mock lightness into his tone. "I'll go get you some water."

"Thank you," she wheezed.

Eric lingered for a second more, and then stood up, turning toward me. The massive bulk of his body still blocked Zoe from my view, and I kept my eyes on him as he walked toward me. His own eyes were lined with red, and as I watched, a tear slipped from his lid. Even he'd accepted that she was going to die, and he loved her; he should be the one person in the world doing more than I was to save her. But if he wasn't, then he knew it was because he couldn't.

I reached for him, sensing he needed comfort, and he took both my hands and squeezed them lightly.

"I can't," he muttered thickly, another tear slipping from his eye. "I can't hug you right now. I'm trying not to break down. For her. Y'know?"

His words made my eyes sting and burn with more tears, and I let go of his hands to wipe them away. "I know. How's she handling it?"

The broken smile on his face almost had me crying again, and I knew she'd been handling it better than we were. "She's still got her sense of humor. I'm just trying to laugh for her, but it's hard. And the worst part is, she understands. I'm supposed to be here for her, and half the time, she's still trying to help *me*. God, I love her so much, Liana."

I took his hands back into mine and nodded. "I know," I said, forcing my voice out through a throat so tight it felt almost impossible to breathe. "It's okay. Just give us a few minutes, all right?"

He nodded, looking down. "Okay. But just a few minutes, okay? I don't want to not be here when..."

I squeezed his hands harder and nodded. I didn't want her to be alone, either; she had to be so afraid of what was happening to her, what *would* happen to her, after... after she died. "I'll call you," I promised solemnly, and he pulled me into a rough hug before leaving and closing the door partially behind him.

I didn't actually see him leave, because my eyes were on Zoe the instant Eric was out of my way. My friend's eyes were open, staring at me from a pale and tight face—one that told me she was in pain. Her head was propped up by a pillow, while the rest of her lay flat on the bed, covered by a blanket.

"Hey," she said with a smile, her eyes tearing up some. "You okay? When that sentinel crashed through the ceiling and then punched you, I thought for certain you were dead."

I nodded, not even sure what to say. A part of me wanted to yell at her, to tell her that if she'd thought I was dead, she shouldn't have jumped between me and the damned sentinel. Then we wouldn't be in this mess. But I couldn't do that—because I would've done the same thing she did, if our positions had been reversed, and I knew that.

It just wasn't fair. I had an AI fixing the damage in my head, but Zoe... Zoe's damage was to her internal organs. She needed surgery to fix what was wrong, and we didn't have the facilities to do anything about it here.

"More worried about you," I finally said, taking a step toward her.

"No need," she said in a strangely cheerful voice. "My fate's sealed. I know what happens to me now. I continue to bleed out until my heart stops beating, and then I die. And I don't have to do anything except lie here. Easiest job ever."

And though I knew she was trying to lighten the mood, I couldn't handle my best friend being so glib about her imminent demise. The tears I had been diligently battling for the past few minutes returned full force, and my chest felt so tight that I couldn't breathe through my mouth, resulting in a really wet sniffle when I inhaled through my nose.

"Zoe, don't talk like that," I finally got out. "It sounds like you're giving up!"

Zoe groaned and rolled her eyes theatrically. "Look, I'm going to tell you the same thing I told Eric: it's my death. You both seem to have some stupid expectations about how people should act, and on your deathbeds, you can act that way. Me, I'm going out laughing with my friends, because it was the best part of my life, and the part I want to remember the most. So, you can either be the friend I laugh with, or you can go outside and miss the death day party I'm hosting for myself. Your choice."

I sniffled again but couldn't help but smile as well. God, I loved her so much, and admired how brave she was being in spite of everything. Only Zoe would decide to flaunt the traditional deathbed motif for something more suiting of her, and I loved her all the more for it.

And felt sorry for myself that the light she brought into my life was going to fade.

But I pushed that aside and scrubbed the tears off my cheeks and from under my eyes, pulling myself together. If this was how my friend wanted to spend her remaining time, then I was more than happy to oblige.

"I choose the death day party," I told her as soon as I felt collected enough to say anything, and she gave me a lopsided smile.

"Excellent. For my first death day wish... Will you come cuddle with me? I'm a little cold."

I nodded, unable to refuse her anything she wanted, and crawled into bed next to her, taking careful pains not to jostle her too much. It took me a little shifting and adjusting to attain a position that wasn't hurting her, but within moments, I was lying on my side, pressed against her, one hand thrown over her waist.

"How's that?"

"Awful," she replied dryly, and I laughed.

"Not as good as Eric?"

"Nowhere near. That man is a furnace. But still, it'll do. How are you holding up?"

I opened my mouth to reply, but then realized the truth would only worry her. But I couldn't lie to her on her deathbed. It wasn't right. So, I changed the subject. "Let's talk about something else. Did I tell you Sage is actually Ezekial Pine?"

"What?" She gaped, her eyebrows going up a few notches. "That's not possible."

"Get this: he invented a serum that kept his cells alive and used Kurt to keep his mental state from deteriorating." I paused. I still had no idea what Kurt's motivations for helping Sage were, and thinking of it suddenly had my mind mulling it over, but I pushed it aside. Now wasn't the time. "He's actually trying to use Kurt to replace Scipio."

"Crazy," Zoe said. "Why'd he need Leo?"

I sighed and ran a hand over my face. "He needs the protocols Lionel Scipio hid in Leo's code to upload Kurt as the main AI."

"Oh. Do you know where he'll be?"

I nodded, smiling down at her in what I hoped was a confident way. "We'll get him back and stop this," I told her, trying to reassure her that we'd all be okay.

We wouldn't be, of course. Sage had almost everything he needed, except for Tony, and I wasn't sure he absolutely *needed* the last AI fragment.

But Zoe didn't have to worry about that. All she had to know was that everything was under control. Even if it was a lie. "So, yeah. There's that. I... um... I found Tony. He's in my net right now, and he's kind of got a bad habit of taking over my body when I least want him to, but we're making it work."

"That's nice," Zoe said, a small smile playing on her lips. "And I hope Tony doesn't get offended by this, but I want to talk to you about something a little more serious. Like how you're doing."

I pressed my lips together. I had thought my distraction had worked, but Zoe was acting like a dog with a bone on this question. "I told you I'm fine," I said, knowing damn well I had told her no such thing. I wasn't even sure what compelled me to say it like that, but I quickly glossed over it, adding, "I mean, I've got a little headache, but I'm managing. This isn't about me. It's about you."

Zoe laughed at that. "Which is why I'm asking. And don't give me that crap about you being fine. I knew you'd say that, and I know you're lying. You're blaming yourself for what happened to me, aren't you?"

I met her blue gaze for several seconds, and then looked away, hating that she knew me so well. "It's my fault," I started. "If I had just—"

She laughed bitterly, and it quickly turned into a racking cough. She turned her head to the side away from me until it subsided into rough pants of her trying to catch her breath. "I'm fine," she said when she looked back to notice me hovering over her, alarm and fear making my muscles tense. "I just think it's very funny that you think you could've done anything to change the outcome of what happened. Like, I love you, Liana, and I know you take being our leader really seriously, but sometimes you are too arrogant for words! I mean, c'mon... What could you have done differently about anything that happened? You fought your way through forty legacies to get to us without getting a scratch, and you think you could've done more? No human being could've done that in the first place!"

"Well, I had Tony to help me, and that's beside the point," I said, searching for a way to defend my guilt. Unless Zoe saw that I was the cause of her condition, she'd never let me apologize, and I needed her to know how sorry I was. "Those legacies were in the Citadel because I put them there! They were able to break free because I missed one— the most important one—and that is costing you your life! Can't you see how that's my fault?"

"Nope," Zoe said firmly, and I looked back over at her to see her jaw set at a stubborn angle. "You didn't let them go. You didn't train them to be murderers and fanatics. You didn't unleash the sentinels, and you most certainly did not get me killed. Nothing that has happened is your fault, and I refuse to die with you believing that it is. Consider it my final request. And you can't not fulfill a dying girl's last request. It's in the rules."

Whatever retort I had been attempting to craft during her rant died under the final request part. She had a point, but it didn't mean that I wasn't going to feel guilty. I couldn't just turn it off like that, no matter what she said. I should've been faster and smarter during the fight. If I had just been able to keep Rose and Dylan with me, maybe I could've...

I stopped the thought there. I had lost them both, and now I was losing Zoe. And there was no changing that.

The only thing I could do was to give Zoe what she wanted and tell her how I was doing. Without the guilt.

"I know I'm not supposed to be, but I'm really scared, Zo," I said, my eyes tearing up. "And I know you said no tears, but I... I can't help it. I love you. And the fact that this is happening to you is tearing me apart. I don't know what I'm going to do without you."

She smiled at me, managing to look beautiful in spite of the gray pallor of her face. "You're going to keep going," she said with a nod, her own eyes filling with tears. "You're going to fight for the Tower, and you're going to win. You're going to change our world, just like I always believed you could. And... you're going to take care of Eric. Because that man is going to be a hot mess after I die."

"So am I," I admitted, my voice breaking. "Please, Zoe, don't die. I can't... I can't be without you. Please."

"Sorry, girl," she breathed, a tear slipping from her eye. "You know I would give you anything in the world, and there's nothing I'd love more than to give you this, but it's out of my control. It's out of *our* control. You have to accept it."

I began to sob then, resting my head against her shoulder, unable to take it anymore, and Zoe—the girl who should've been yelling at me for making her death all about my fear and pain—stroked my hair, and did her best to whisper reassurances in my ear. She was too good for me, too good for this world, and her light was being extinguished.

"I'm sorry," I said, sitting up when it finally hit me that I had broken her rules. "I'm sorry," I repeated, trying to wipe away my tears. "We shouldn't be... I just... I don't know... Oh God."

CHAPTER 32

I couldn't seem to form a coherent thought, let alone a sentence, and I faltered, looking away, as lost as a small boat in a storm.

"Yeah, I hear you," she whispered, patting my arm. "Those have pretty much been my thoughts the last few hours, and my suggestion is just to put it out of your head. There are a lot of questions that are going to be unanswered, and you know what? I'd rather spend my remaining time doing other things. Like asking you to find my mother when this is all over and tell her... Well, tell her I'm not sorry for joining the Cogs or being with Eric, but I love her all the same, okay?"

I nodded, my lower lip trembling. Zoe's relationship with her mom was similar enough to how mine had been with my own mother that I understood the lack of apology, just as much as I understood her need to give her mother a parting message. I was sure my mom would've had a message for me, if she hadn't died so suddenly, and I would've given anything to hear it.

Which was why, come hell or high water, I'd find a way to get Zoe's message to her mother. "I promise," I told her solemnly.

We fell silent for a moment, and on impulse, I laid my head down on Zoe's shoulder and snuggled closer to her. "You know I'm going to miss you, right?"

"You better," Zoe replied weakly. "Because I'm going to miss the hell out of you, too."

Her words broke me in ways I couldn't begin to describe: with unconditional love for her, with anger at myself, with pain at knowing that my existence would continue without her, and with crushing defeat that there was nothing I could do to stop it. My best friend was going to die, and I was never going to be able to talk to her again.

"I love you so much," I said, unable to stop myself.

"And I you," Zoe sniffled back. "Now... can you get Eric please? I think... I think maybe it's coming, and I need my last minutes to be with him, if that's okay. It's not that I don't love you, I just..." She broke off, her own tears starting to flow down her cheeks, and I pressed my forehead to hers, shaking my head at her silliness. I understood perfectly why she wanted to be with Eric over me. I was her best friend, but he... he was the love of her life.

"It's okay," I said, pressing my lips to her cheek and trying not to cry at how cold her skin felt. "I'll go get him, okay?"

She nodded, her eyes drooping heavily. "Hurry?"

I did, getting out of bed and moving to the door as I wiped my tears away. It didn't matter that Zoe's time was coming and she was asking me to leave. All that mattered was what she wanted to be comfortable, and I was going to make that happen for her, no matter what.

33

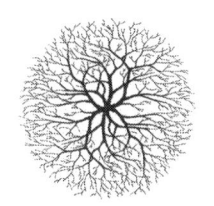

I was sitting quietly in a stuffed chair opposite where Tian and Liam were still sleeping, staring blankly at both of them. I hadn't moved in the last twenty minutes, not since I had come out to get Eric for Zoe. He still hadn't emerged, and it felt like the entire apartment was holding its breath, waiting for the inevitable.

Even though we all knew what was coming.

But that didn't stop me from looking up when I heard the sound of heavy footsteps coming down the hall. And it didn't stop me from getting out of the chair and crossing the room to head directly toward the sound.

What did stop me was Eric—or rather the hard lines of anguish on his face as he stepped into the weak candlelight illuminating the room, looking like he had aged ten years. "She's gone," he whispered to me, and I closed my eyes at the wash of pain that overwhelmed me.

She was gone. She was dead.

It didn't seem real, even after having talked to her about it.

"I'm so sorry," Maddox said softly from behind us. I wasn't even sure when she had gotten there, but it didn't matter. Zoe was gone. "And I don't mean to undermine the tragedy of this, but we have more problems developing. Liana, sentinels have been spotted only a few floors above us. I've lost touch with most of the Knights that were loyal to us, and the handful of people still with us is wavering. We need to get out of here. We need a plan. What do we need to do to stop Sage?"

I heard the soft edge of panic in her voice. She was doing her best to try to hide it, but it was there nonetheless, and the sound of it scared me.

Not only because the sentinels were drawing close to us, but because I knew that whatever decision I made had to be the right one. But what was the right one? Ordering them to help me stop Sage? That was insanity; there was no way we were going to be able to get into the Core without raising some sort of alert, and every member of the IT Department was part of Sage's army. Maybe if we had fifty more Knights and an entire arsenal with us, we could cut a path through the integration chamber. But we were just five.

No, I realized a heartbeat later, with a sickly jolt. We were just four, now. My heart twisted with the sudden reminder that Zoe was gone, leaving me feeling queasy that I had even dared to forget. Was this what it would feel like if I lost all of my friends trying to stop Sage? I could already feel Zoe's absence poignantly, like someone had reached up in the sky and plucked the moon right out of it, leaving the terrain ahead dark and treacherous.

What would happen if Sage managed to kill the rest of my friends as well? I could handle my own death, but theirs?

No, they weren't sticking around to fight. If anything, I was getting them out of here. I'd figure out how to fight Sage on my own, because I had to keep them safe. I couldn't ask them to die over this. I wouldn't. This was my fight now.

"Did you grab the Patrian communication device?" I asked, already knowing exactly how I was getting them out. I turned to Maddox and Quess, who were standing side by side, holding hands, and the two looked at each other in confusion, and then back at me.

"Yes," Quess said, his tone mystified. "Why?"

"We're getting out of here," I said. With a plan now in my mind, I suddenly felt the need to move, to do something, and I walked past my stunned friends toward the kitchen table, going over the supplies there. They had my gun, and someone had managed to steal a few more clips of ammunition, but the box with the ammunition wasn't there. There were several batons and lancers, and I left them out so that my friends could arm themselves. The rest of it—the medical supplies, food, water, pads—I started shoving into a bag I found on a chair, talking while I worked.

"We'll override one of the lashway doors and scale up the Tower to the Attic, then take an elevator straight up to the roof. We'll call Alex from there and tell the Patrians that we'll give them AI technology in exchange for refugee status. Hopefully that'll be enough for them to fly one of their airships over here and rescue us. You guys should be safe up there until they get here."

"Wait, what?" Maddox said as soon as I finished. "What do you mean 'you guys'? Where will you be?"

I paused in the act of shoving several apples into one of the bags and looked at her. When the Patrians had come, all of my friends had been excited about the prospect of leaving, but not me. I had always intended to stay. Only Zoe had known that, but now that she was gone... it didn't seem like there was much use for secrets. Especially this one.

"I'll be in the Core," I told them, swallowing back my fear. "I'm going after Sage."

"Alone?" Maddox asked, and I nodded. She frowned and looked over at Quess, then back to me. "Liana, don't be ridiculous. If we're going to escape, then we do it together. And if you're going to stay, we're staying with you."

I raised an eyebrow at her calling me ridiculous, anger tearing through me at the thought that Maddox could believe I was acting irrationally, but let it go. It didn't matter what she thought. She and everyone else was leaving.

"Not this time," I said, returning to the bag and shoving more items in. "Sage has us outnumbered, outgunned, out-damn-sentineled! He's got Scipio under his control, has had access to Leo for the past few hours, and is inside the Core. He might not know I'm still alive, but he will be expecting something. A large group will draw attention, and one person is a lot easier to hide than four."

"That's suicide," Quess said, stepping around Maddox. "Look, I'm down to escape if you're going, too, but I'm not going anywhere without you. If you stay, we stay! We can help you."

"No, you can't," I said, swallowing back the warm feeling his declaration had left me with. I loved that they were being so loyal to me, but in this case, that loyalty was going to get them killed, and I couldn't allow that. "Quess, you and Eric can barely lash, let alone fight."

"Hey!" Quess said, folding his arms across his chest, affronted, but I ignored him, turning to Maddox.

"You know I'm right—that they will get killed trying to help me. And I'd keep you with me, but you need to stay with them, to protect them. Think about it, Maddox. They won't be able to make it without you."

"Don't do that," Quess said, making a slashing noise as if to cut my statements in half. "I know I'm not much of a fighter, but I know the Core, and I'm great at computer stuff! You need me!"

"No, I don't," I said with more calm than I felt. He was already beginning to override my arguments with logic, but this wasn't a logical thing. I couldn't go in there knowing that at any moment, one of them could die. I'd lost five friends already, and I couldn't lose any more. "I have a way of contacting Dinah, and I know she can get me inside. From there, I'll make my way to the integration chamber using Lionel's code. I'm fairly sure I can give the Eyes a run for their money, especially if I'm alone." I stopped packing, picked up the bag, and turned to my friends. "I'm going to be fine. And I promise that if I can, I will fix this. But there's no guarantee at this point, and you all need to get moving."

"Dinah is an old woman," Maddox replied, folding her arms across her chest. "She might be able to get you in, but if the transmission between the two of you is intercepted, they'll know you're coming and set up a trap. You'll need our help then. I don't understand why you're pushing so hard against it!"

I immediately grew defensive at her reasoning and went on the attack. I didn't care if they wound up hating me for what I said. At least they'd be alive. "I'm pushing for what you and Quess and everyone else wanted! A life outside these Tower walls, free from this insanity! That's what Cali and Roark were fighting for, remember? And I'm giving it to you—a real way out! You have to take it. Not for me, and not for you, but for Tian. And Liam. And Quess. And Eric! They need to get out of here; they aren't warriors like we are. They'll die, and we'll have to watch. Do you want that?"

Maddox's glittering green eyes narrowed, but to my credit, my words had given her pause, and she looked away, thinking. Even Quess was momentarily stunned into silence, my words making him reconsider his position, and I felt hope begin to bloom in my heart.

Until I heard, "Hell with that. It's bull," from a voice too high-pitched to be from an adult. I immediately zeroed in on the source of the sound to find Tian standing just outside the living area, one fist scrubbing the sleep out of her eyes. "We're a team, remember?" she asked, looking at me.

Dammit, I was not about to have my orders argued with, not even by Tian. "That's right," I said amicably. "You're the team. I'm the leader. You put me in charge, which means following my orders, even when you don't agree with them. So grab some stuff, wake Liam up, and get ready to go. We've wasted too much time as it is."

Tian scowled at me, her fists dropping to her hips, but I ignored it, took a few steps toward Maddox, and shoved the bag into her arms. She grabbed it reflexively, her brows furrowing, her face pensive, but didn't argue as I moved past her into the kitchen, intent on throwing open cabinet doors to pull out any other food that might be inside. Who knew how long they were going to be on the roof before the Patrians arrived.

Tian, however, wasn't letting this go without a fight. The young teen marched into the kitchen at my heels, fists still planted over her wispy skirt. "Then I vote we remove you as leader," she declared imperiously. "For danger of being a big stupid-head. You can't go alone! We won't let you! We're family, and we do things together. That's what Cali wanted for us, and that's what we're going to do. So if you're going to the Core, we're going to the Core."

"Whoa, now," Quess said, stepping behind Tian and resting his hands on her shoulders. "Tian, I agree with everything you're saying, but if we go, you know it's just going to be the four of us. You can't come with us this time."

She opened her mouth to argue, but I interrupted her before she could start a new tirade. "He's right in that you're not coming with me," I agreed with mock cheerfulness. "Because none of you are. Think about it: are we really going to risk leaving Tian and Liam by themselves? No, because we're responsible. Quess, you and Maddox are responsible for Tian, and you have to do what's best for her. That means—"

"Stop it, Liana," Eric announced in a gravelly voice, breaking his silence for the first time since telling us all Zoe was gone. I stopped mid-word, turning around to see him standing on the other side of the counter that sat between the dining area and the kitchen, a haunted look on his face.

"Eric?" I asked, taking a step toward him, concerned about his well-being after losing the woman he loved. "What's—"

"Zoe told me not to let you do anything she called heroically stupid, and that's what you're gearing up to do."

I silently cursed Zoe, and then felt a stab of guilt at doing so. Even dead, she was trying to take care of me, and while I loved her for it, she didn't understand what it meant for me. How defeated I would be if I lost everyone I loved trying to save the Tower. I wouldn't be a person anymore, just a shell, without any light and love to fill me up.

"Eric, Zoe's gone, and we have to think about what comes next. I have Tony in my head, which means I'm more equipped to—"

"The Tony you want to trade?" Quess cut in angrily. "What, you want to copy him so that we give one version to the Patrians while you carry the other version into the Core? That's so... How did Zoe phrase it?" He looked over at Eric, who mouthed the words "heroically stupid," and then continued. "That's right, heroically stupid! Can't we just be heroically smart instead? Let's do that option. I like it way better than the other one."

Frustration had me gritting my teeth, not just from the overuse of Zoe's phrase, but because they were making it really difficult to argue with them. I could already tell that the harder I pushed for this, the more they were going to resist. "You don't get a choice," I said. "None of you do. You elected me leader. This is the plan, and we—"

"Fine, who agrees that Liana is no longer the leader?" Maddox said, placing the bag on the counter and coming around to stand next to Eric, a scowl on her face.

"Hey," I said indignantly. "I am doing what a good leader would do and trying to save your lives. I'm responsible for them, and I know this is a suicide mission. I already lost Dylan and Rose getting here, and now I've lost Grey, Leo, and Zoe. Grey and Leo might still be alive, but not for long, and there's a chance I might not even make it to them before Sage gets what he needs and kills them! This is too dangerous. I'm not accepting the risk. Stop arguing with me and get to the damn roof."

"I refuse," Tian said, defiantly crossing her arms over her chest, and I was torn between screaming, bashing my head against the wall, and pulling out my hair. They were being so monumentally stubborn, and I wasn't worth this show of loyalty! I didn't want their loyalty; I wanted them *safe*.

"I also refuse," Quess said a moment later from behind her. "Granted, we'll have to override Tian's objections to keep her safe, but I'm okay with that as long as we're going into the Core together."

I pressed my lips together to keep from growling at him and looked over at Maddox and Eric. "And you two?"

"I've made myself perfectly clear," Eric said, tiredly resting his hands on the counter. "I'm going where you go. End of discussion."

"Same here," Maddox replied. "We've been with you since the beginning of all this, Liana. And you may be responsible for our lives, but it's our choice what we do with them, not yours. We're not going to leave you now. You need us, and we need you. Now, you can be in charge, giving us the best chance of success, or you can follow my lead. Either way, you need to accept that we're coming with you."

A wall of pain and foreboding slammed into me, and I almost cried. I wasn't sure what I was feeling—pain, sorrow, grief, fear, loss... All I knew was that nothing I could say would change their minds.

"Fine," I grated out, angrier with myself that I couldn't convince them. "Wake Liam up, and let's get going. I'll call Dinah while we're on the move."

"Now that sounds like a sensible plan I can get behind," Quess said with a smile, and I could tell he was trying to cheer everyone up and keep us all optimistic.

But I was far from that as I moved to gather more of the things we would need. I was terrified at what would become of us after everything was said and done, confused by how willing they were to sacrifice their lives for this, and in a very small part of my heart, relieved that they weren't going to leave me, even if I wanted them to.

It wasn't enough, but it was something. And something had to be enough, at least for today.

34

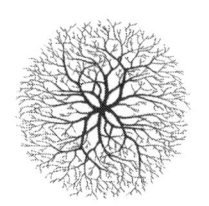

I had Quess exchange my net for the IT one I'd taken from Lidecher before we left the apartment so I could contact Dinah. Our plan was relatively simple: we'd stop by a nearby armory to get as much ammunition for the lancer as we could carry, as well as lash harnesses for Quess and Eric, and then exit through the lashway using Lionel's code. We'd scale the Citadel, cross the roof of the central chamber to the Core, and enter through whatever hatch Dinah told us to.

If I could reach her. Since Quess had put the net in, I'd tried to contact her twice, only to have her reject the calls. We were speeding toward the first destination of our plan—the armory—through halls that would haunt me to my dying days. The signs of battle here were even worse than what I had seen on the upper floors, and I couldn't walk twenty feet without seeing another crimson-clad body lying on the floor.

Maddox had the people still loyal to us scouting the halls ahead, so we moved with relative ease through the corridors, but it was still unnerving. My stomach shriveled up whenever my eyes found another body, and it performed somersaults when my ears picked up the sounds of fighting coming from an adjacent hall.

And it only grew worse the longer it took me to get ahold of Dinah.

Because I didn't just need her help getting into the Core; I needed her help finding a way to sneak up on Sage. Whatever—wherever—this integration chamber was, I was betting there was only one door in, and it would be heavily guarded. If I tried a frontal assault, we'd lose immediately.

But if Dinah didn't call me back, then a frontal assault was all we were going to have.

I was beginning to grow concerned when she hadn't called by the time we got to the armory, but I pushed it back and focused on scavenging whatever we could from the picked-over remains of the room. Whoever had broken in had been in a hurry, so there were lots of little items scattered on the floor that we could use, and the spare lash harnesses were mostly untouched.

I helped Quess and Eric get their harnesses on while Maddox, Tian, and Liam quickly set out to pick up whatever we could use, as their harnesses were already on. By the time both men were suited up, the others had managed to get quite a bit of ammunition for the lancer, as well as extra lash ends, masks, a few flash grenades, and some spare bottles of water that had been tucked back in a cabinet.

Oh, and still no return call from Dinah.

We exited the room quickly and headed for the lashway, a large door that opened right out to the side of the Citadel. They were all sealed right now, but we were armed with Lionel's code, so they wouldn't be for long. I'd use that code all the way to the Core if I had to, though I knew that Sadie and the rest of IT were going to figure out that we were using it, and then figure out where we were heading, and mount a defense against us. If that happened, and we didn't hear from Dinah, then we'd be dead in the water.

I tried netting her again as we walked, but after a few seconds of buzzing in my skull, the call immediately died, telling me she had rejected it again. She had to be physically rejecting the calls; if she were dead, the net would refuse to even establish a connection. Was she in trouble? Had Sadie figured out that she was spying on them and gone after her? Why wasn't she picking up?

My anticipation grew as we approached the curved wall at the end

CHAPTER 34

of the hall, the oval-shaped opening that normally stood open now closed tight. I approached the security keypad next to it and tapped in Lionel's code, eyeing both sides of the hall as I did so. There was a half-second delay as I waited for the code to be accepted, thoroughly convinced that Sadie had already figured out we were coming this way and set up some sort of trap on the other side, but then the two halves of the door split, swinging to the side and revealing the dimly lit shadows of the spires and twisting architecture outside, and nothing else.

I approached the edge, leaned out to make sure there were no sentinels perched outside, lying in wait, and then backed away to let the others exit the Citadel before me. Maddox went first, to ensure that we were alone, and once she gave the all-clear, I began waving everyone out. Tian went next, the young girl sprinting down the hall with her own lash line a blur in her hand. She threw it just before she leapt out over the void, connecting with a gargoyle that jutted out a few feet to the right of Maddox, and then reeled her line in, flying upward until she reached it and then scrambling onto the grotesque thing.

I waited until she was situated to give the signal for the next person, Liam, and had just urged him forward when my net began to buzz, startling me.

I took a quick look at my indicator, and to my surprise, it identified the caller as Alex Castell, my twin brother who had left only two days ago with the Patrians. For several seconds, I stared at it, confused at how my brother could even be there. And then I realized it *wasn't* him. We'd taken Alex's net when he left, so he had no way to net me.

Which meant that it was either Dinah, doing something to cover her tracks, or it was a trap of some kind. I considered for half a moment that it *was* a trap, but if so, it was a highly specific one, considering they were calling me on Lidecher's net. They would've had to know I had it, and I doubted Lacey's people had let Lidecher out of their sight long enough for him to call and warn IT that I had his net.

But even if they had, it was worth the risk of picking up to find out. I needed Dinah's help that badly.

I tapped the indicator, accepting the call, and was relieved to hear Dinah's voice on the other line, even if it was rife with anger.

'Bout damn time you picked up, she said gruffly. *I've got problems—big ones. Some of Sadie's goons figured out I was trying to hack into Scipio's data stream, and she sent a hit squad out after me. I barely got out alive, and I'm hiding. I need help!*

You and me both, I thought at her as I watched Liam sail through the opening. His technique was sloppy, but his form was good. *My quarters have fallen, and Sage has damn near everything he needs to kill Scipio and replace him with Kurt. We need a way into the Core, and for you to find us a sneaky way to get into the integration room where all the power is being directed to. Please tell me you can help us.*

There was a pause on her end, which I used to motion for Eric to go, and then she said, *Liana, all I want to do is get out of here. What you're asking... It's a lot. They could find me while I'm working on it, and I guarantee they aren't going to wait for the expulsion chambers to come back online before getting rid of me. They came into my department with their pulse shields out. If we hadn't been preparing for something like that, there would've been a lot more death than there was. I barely got out of there alive, and I know they're going to be chasing me. So, no, I don't think I can help you this time.*

I gritted my teeth in frustration. Dinah's reticence to help us, to even reveal her identity to us, had been a problem in the past, and today, of all days, was when I needed that trend to end. Luckily, I knew exactly what she wanted—and how to give it to her.

Dinah, all I need is a way in and what you've got on that integration room. I'm sure you've found blueprints by now, and I know you're smart enough to have downloaded them to your pad before fleeing. So how about this: if you meet us where you intend to escape the Core, and give us the schematics, you can go with Tian to the roof and wait for Alex and the Patrians to come rescue you. Deal?

Another pause, and one that had me wincing. Not because of Dinah, but because of Eric's awkward and tentative lash-throwing. The man had never had a handle on the mechanics of it, and even though his line did stick, the execution of his throw and jump was just terrifyingly bad, making me concerned for how well he was going to fare at this. I made a mental note to stay close to him, in case he wound up in any trouble, and then motioned for Quess to go.

Deal. And you're lucky you're right—I do have the schematics for that room. And, I'm not making any promises, but I might be able to find you a way into it. Stand by for a second. I need some time to do a little creative hacking.

Take your time, I thought as I watched Quess awkwardly swing out through the door. Quess had a great many skills, but like Eric, lashing wasn't one of them. Luckily, however, he'd improved significantly since joining the Knights. But significant improvement didn't necessarily translate to being a good lasher, and Quess was still very stiff at it.

Thankfully, Maddox would be keeping an eye on him.

I waited until everyone was clear before doing one last check down the halls, making sure we were alone. Then I leaned out, threw a lash end to connect just over the door, and surrendered my weight to the harness, reeling myself up to the control panel on the outside of the door and taking a moment to seal it behind us. It wouldn't help if Sadie and Sage were tracking us using Lionel's code, but it would slow down anyone in the halls coming after us, and that was something.

I kicked off the wall and threw my other line to a nearby arch, and within moments, my team and I were moving up the side of the Citadel.

It was hard not to move quickly. I'd lived in the Citadel my entire life; I knew every buttress, arch, and line of the structure by heart from lashing around them when I was younger. Not to mention, scaling it was far easier than scaling the Tower, as there were obstacles in the way to hook onto for gaining momentum.

But I kept close to Eric, moving at his lumbering speed while I waited for Dinah to resume talking. Seconds had already bled into minutes, and if it weren't for the buzzing along the tendrils of my net, I would've assumed something had happened to her.

When she finally did start speaking again, we had already ascended twenty floors, and had maybe another forty before we hit the ceiling above. *Okay, I think I have the rudimentary outline of a plan. I want you to get to hatch 54-Q. It's facing the south side of the Tower, up near the top of it.*

Wait there for me to exit, and I'll fill you in on the rest of the plan when I join you. How long will it take you to get there?

I paused in my lashing long enough to eye the distance and my friends, then did some fast guessing. *Maybe twenty minutes, if we're lucky.*

Then let's hope we get lucky. And that my bum foot doesn't get me caught between now and then. I've got to end the transmission now before someone stumbles onto it or me, so... See you in twenty minutes.

Just be careful, I managed to get out right before she terminated the link.

I took a deep breath, unnerved by how quickly she'd ended the transmission, and put my concern for Dinah to one side. There wasn't anything I could do for her where I was, so the only option now was to keep moving forward and hope that she could stay under the Core's radar long enough to give us entry and make her escape.

Because if she didn't, we were all screwed.

35

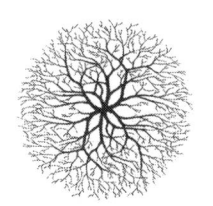

For once I was spot on with my time guesstimate, because nineteen and a half minutes later, we were all dangling from the side of the Core, waiting for hatch 54-Q to open. Our passage between the Core and Citadel had gone largely unnoticed, partially because the lighting from the Core wasn't enough to fully beat back the darkness, but mostly because the bridges and platforms outside the two structures were completely devoid of life. It was as if some great and terrible presence had plucked every human being up and out of the Tower, leaving only us.

I should've counted my lucky stars that there were no sentinels patrolling, but the question their absence created only left me feeling deeply afraid. If they weren't out here, where were they, and what was Sage using them for?

I had a handful of ideas, none of them good: They'd been moved to Cogstown to remount the attack on them. They were moving to the greeneries and killing the citizens there. Sage had ordered them into the Core to defend it.

I knew there was a chance that the lack of sentinels in the atrium area was a result of the destruction of Alice's download pad in the Attic, but it was a slim one. It had been hours since I'd done it, and I was certain that a man who'd spent three hundred years trying to put this plan together had been prudent enough to have a backup route stashed away. I had no idea how long that other plan might have taken to set up, but odds were if they didn't have it up and operational now, they would soon.

My grim thoughts were broken by a sudden hiss from the hatch, and I tensed in alarm, one hand going to my baton. I was dangling to the left of the hole and was the first to see a flash of silvery hair and crystal-clear blue eyes—wide and furtive—as the hatch swung open.

"Hello, Dinah," I said, letting go of the baton. "Are you okay?"

"No, I am damn well not okay!" she snarled, pulling herself forward to the edge. "I—oh, my. This is *very* high."

I blinked in surprise at the older woman's sudden change in tone, amazed at how she could go from anger to trepidation in just a matter of seconds. The elderly woman was now staring down past the fingers she had curled around the ledge to the dark depths below. The fires from the Council Room had died down, but there was still a deep red glow from the embers of where it remained, marking just how far away the floor below was.

"You know what, I made a mistake," Dinah said abruptly with a nod, her voice now high-pitched. "I think I'll just take my chances and walk out of here. There's got to be a crew heading somewhere. I'll just forge some credentials and—"

She had started backing away as she spoke, and I suppressed a curse as I realized how quickly she could move when properly motivated. Before I could even stop her, she was out of reach—and still talking to herself. I exchanged an irritated look with Maddox, as we had intended to pass her one of the spare harnesses and help her put it on before we got through the hole, but now that she was heading back in, we were going to have to chase her down and convince her that leaving with Tian and Liam using the lash lines was the only option.

"Liam, you and Tian stay here and make sure this hatch doesn't close, all right? Maddox, give Tian the Patrian communication device and follow. The rest of you come with me. We've got to get to her before she accidently gets caught."

I climbed into the shaft while I handed out orders and didn't stick around long enough to see if my friends would do what I said. Dinah was still backing away in front of me, sliding a cane I hadn't noticed before along with her as she crawled backward. I pursued her as quickly as I could on my hands and knees, trying to catch her before she reached the end, but she managed to scramble out of the vent opening and to the floor, dropping out of sight.

I growled in irritation and quickly exited behind her, scanning the room for her as I did. We were in some sort of bathroom, with chest-high lockers creating rows across the space, and I spotted her heading for the door.

"Dinah, stop!" I called, practically leaping out of the hole and chasing after her. "Don't be crazy. If there are people in that hall, they will see you, and we'll all be caught!"

Her limping gait came to a slow stop, and I breathed a sigh of relief when she turned around to face me. "I can't do it," she said, thumping her cane down on the floor and taking a step toward me. "That is just... way too high."

"Well, guess what," I said, unwilling to let her fear get the better of her. "The Patrians that we're planning on sending you with can fly, which means you'll be even higher off the ground, with nothing between their ship and the earth below. If there was ever a chance to get over your fear of heights, now is the time."

"You don't understand! I didn't even *know* I had a fear of heights. Liana, I really don't think I can do this! I don't want to plummet to my death."

I drew in a deep breath, trying to calm some of my irritation with her. I could tell she was deathly afraid—her face was damn near white, and her hands were shaking—and realized she needed a little handholding. "Look, Dinah, I get it. But if you go back in that hall, you're taking a big chance. I promise you, the lash harness isn't as hard as it looks, and you'll be with one of our better lashers."

"Tian?" she replied, hope curling in her voice, and I smiled encouragingly at her, even though it was slightly forced.

"She and her friend Liam are..." I paused to check over my shoulder and saw that Maddox, Quess, and Eric were all inside, with no sign of Tian or Liam. Good. That meant they had followed my orders. It was important to me, because I didn't want them getting sealed in here accidently by someone in the Core's command center seeing that there was an open hatch and closing it—with no way for us to open it again. But I also didn't want Dinah trapped in here with us, especially if Sadie was hunting her down. "Waiting outside," I finished, turning back around to face Dinah. "You know how good Tian is with lashes. You can do this."

Her lips trembled uncertainly, but after a moment her mouth tightened, and she gave a barely perceptible nod of assent. I turned to ask for the harness only to find Eric pulling it out of Quess's bag. He moved toward us, but instead of handing it to me, he stepped around me to begin helping Dinah put it on.

I was surprised, but relieved he was helping. It gave me time to run her through the basics of lashing. "Okay, Dinah, the lashes aren't difficult to use unless you're trying to go fast. But you won't be. Tian knows to take it slow and easy. So that's the first thing, okay?"

The elderly woman bit her lower lip nervously, watching Eric as he quickly snapped her into the harness. "Okay, I'll go really slow."

"Good," I said, pleased she was repeating it back to me. It meant she was focusing on what I was saying, and retaining it for the future, which I was all for, given how nervous she was. "Now, the lash ends are going to come out of this strap wrapped around your hips. There's one on each side that you can easily grab. Can you reach them?"

She reached down with both hands, smoothing her palms over the straps until she found the little beads, and pulled them out. "Got them," she said with a jerky little nod.

"Excellent," I praised, noticing that Eric had finished cinching her in. "Now, when you throw these, they are going to build up a static charge. However, it's always good to spin them first, before you throw, for more static. Go ahead and spin one up and then throw it at the ceiling."

I moved to one side and watched as Dinah pulled out a little bit more line to give herself some slack, then tentatively began to swing the lash end in a circle. It took her a few painful seconds to catch the rhythm of it, followed by several more while she fidgeted with her footing, her stance, her arm, all the while looking back and forth from the ceiling to her hand, as if trying to make the line move by sheer will alone.

It took everything I had to be patient with her until she finally released the line. Luckily, she had been spinning it long enough that it had a hell of a charge on it when she threw. Unluckily, her release was sloppy, and she hit the top of the row of lockers several feet behind her. She darted a look over her shoulder, and then turned back, her cheeks flushing.

"It's okay," I said immediately, stepping close and gently grabbing her hand to get to the hand controls so I could disconnect and draw in the line. "It just takes a little practice to get used to, but Tian and Liam will help you, even if they have to throw your lines for you. Besides, throwing isn't the most important part. The controls are." I lifted her hand, flattening it out so she could study the small hand controls located on the strap running across the middle of her palm. "So these two buttons control whether you go up or down, and the dial controls how fast you go. This button disconnects your line, so only hit it when the next line is attached, okay?"

She nodded again, sucking in a deep breath as she did so. "Yeah. Don't disconnect until the next line is holding me up. The... only line holding me up. Just... a hunk of metal and some thin line holding me to the ceiling some eighty floors above the ground."

I could hear her starting to unravel, and quickly seized her shoulders and gave her a good shake. "I've used these damn things every day for most of my life, Dinah. They will keep you up and get you out of here. Now, do you understand the instructions?"

She shifted slightly, and then nodded. "Go slow. Spin up line to gain static charge. Don't hit the disconnect button until second line is attached. Follow Tian's instructions."

I nodded approvingly. "Good. You'll be fine. Now, how do we get into the integration room?"

The woman blinked in surprise, and then snapped her fingers

together before reaching into her pocket to retrieve a pad. "Here," she said, holding it out to me and clicking it on. "This is the schematic of the integration room. It's right below the bottom of the shaft where the power is transmitted into the Core. There's one other way in and out of the room, and that's through the air filtration system, but you have to crawl through a pipe meant for liquid nitrogen to cool the room off to get there. There is a virus on the pad that will shut the nitrogen off for a hundred and eighty seconds—that's three minutes— during which you'll have to crawl through about ten yards of pipe and slip out through the emergency relief valve. Both the entry point and the valve need to be closed before the time has elapsed, or you're going to get sprayed in the face with liquid nitrogen, and the alarms will go off. To get there, I suggest taking this path to an access panel that leads to the shelf."

As she spoke, she clicked on the files, pointing out everything she was talking about as she went on. At one point, Quess had moved in behind me to observe over my shoulder, and as soon as she was done, he reached around me and grabbed it with an, "I'll be responsible for that."

I let him peruse the pad while I placed a hand under Dinah's elbow and began guiding her toward the shaft we had entered through. "All right, we gotta go. Tell Tian she and Liam have to help you lash, step by step. Use Lionel Scipio's code to access the nearest hatch leading to the Attic, and then use the elevator to go to the roof. If... If you see Alex, tell him I'm sorry, and not to try to rescue me. If we haven't gotten to you by the time the Patrians arrive, assume we're dead and just leave."

"Okay," Dinah said, placing her hands on the edge of the vent and stepping on the bench below it. "Be careful, and, for what it's worth, good luck."

"You too," I replied. "Now get moving, and no turning around. We're sealing the vent up behind you, so unless you want to get caught in there..."

"I know, I know," Dinah grumbled, some of her earlier fire returning. It was a good sign, in my mind, but I refrained from commenting and let the woman focus on getting into the shaft. As soon as she was gone, I placed the vent grate back over it, and then looked to the others.

"Hurry up and put Tony's net back in," I said to Quess, turning around to present my neck in what I hoped would be the last time I had to do this for the day. "And then let's get moving. We don't have a lot of time."

36

I studied the pad Quess had handed me while he worked on my neck and the others finished using his special spray on their faces to confuse the surveillance system's facial recognition software, going over the map Dinah had left us. I had already sprayed my face before Quess's incision and was taking a moment to decide whether we should change our uniforms while the others got ready. To be honest, I felt pretty strongly against the idea, even though there were spare uniforms in the lockers. It was going to take precious time for us all to change, and I wasn't about to get caught by an Eye with my pants down, should someone wind up walking in on us.

But remaining in uniform was a risk. While the spray kept our faces from being recognizable, there were humans responsible for watching the camera feeds and reporting anything out of the ordinary—like four Knights slinking through the halls armed to the teeth, for example. But I was betting the chance of us being noticed on the feed was pretty slim, not just because there were literally hundreds of camera feeds all over the Core alone, but because I was guessing the Eyes were pretty distracted by whatever story Sadie was feeding them about Scipio's condition.

It was the Eyes in the halls I was really worried about. They'd definitely notice four Knights and raise the alarm, if we encountered any. According to Dinah's map, we had to move through a hundred feet of hall to get to the hatch, crossing three other halls on the way and running in a straight line. A hundred feet wasn't far, but that didn't work in our favor, either—if a single Eye came around any one of those corners and spotted us, they could have enough time to run and send out a warning. Their nets were still working, so they could easily call for help.

But there wasn't much choice. If we stayed in one place too long, we'd get caught. And if we didn't take care of any Eye that we came across quickly and efficiently, we'd be caught.

Quess tapped my shoulder, breaking my concentration. "You're done," he said, and I reached out with my mind and was reassured by Tony's presence.

I did not like that, he declared. *Too lonely.*

Sorry, I replied, feeling empathy for the AI. He'd had no eyes, or ears, or any ability to contact or communicate with any of us while the net had been out of my head. It must've been awful.

I handed the pad back over to Quess with a "Thanks," and he quickly tucked it into his pocket. "Okay, guys," I said. "It's pretty much the first right and then a straight shot down the hall to the T-intersection at the end. Quess, you'll need to get us in quickly, using the instructions Dinah left, and until we get there, we'll have to be on the lookout for any Eyes. If they see us and we can't knock them out or kill them before they can call for help, we're sunk. I'll go first, then Eric, then Quess, and finally Maddox."

"I should go first," Maddox said as she tucked her black hair into a band. "We need to keep you safe no matter—"

"The time for that has come and gone," I interrupted. "There's no need to protect me exclusively now. You all know what's at stake. If I die, you get down there, stop Sage, and start the New Day protocol. Understood?" I had caught the others up on the way over, so they would all know the plan going in. I had tried desperately to undersell it in an attempt to change their minds, but they hadn't.

Maddox frowned, but nodded, unable to find a fault in my logic, and I pulled out my baton and gun. I couldn't fire it—the noise would draw too much attention—but Tony and I could use it to knock people unconscious, and that could be useful.

Exhaling a slow breath to steady my nerves, I hit the button to open the door, and then stuck my head out into the hall, checking both sides. The dark gray corridors were empty, but I knew they wouldn't be for long, and I stepped out and headed right, toward the first and only real turn. I moved at a light jog, slowing to a cautious pace just at the first intersection. I slid my back against the right-hand side of the wall, focusing on the connecting hallway as more and more of it came into view.

There was no one there, but we had a hundred feet and three more intersections, and anything was possible at this point. I signaled that it was all clear but sped off like a bullet toward the next intersection, already worried about the thirty-odd feet of distance we had to cover, should some Eyes emerge from the cross section.

There were doors on either side of the hall, and I kept a wary eye on them as well, knowing that at any moment one could open, a gray-clad member of the department stepping out to discover us. My nerves itched to check behind me, but I kept my eyes glued to the front, knowing Maddox was watching our tail.

I slowed again as I approached the next junction, pausing several feet from the intersection and taking a moment to listen. We were all doing our best to cover the sounds of our footsteps—which meant I had no problem hearing the two male voices coming from the left hall. Thankfully, they were muffled. I quickly motioned everyone back against that wall, and sidled up to the left wall, stepping gingerly to mask any noise.

Tony slowly started to fill me up again, like water pouring into a container, and I felt him slowing down my heartbeat and regulating my breathing. I sent him a feeling of gratitude as I began to creep up to the corner. The voices were still too low to discern, but they didn't seem to be moving any closer to us. Or any farther away.

I slowly slid my head out around the corner, exposing just one eye, for fear that any more than that would attract unwanted attention, and peered down the hallway.

Two men were squatting in front of a wall twenty-five feet down. I couldn't make out what they were looking at—they were facing the wall on my side of the hall—but they were pressed tightly together, and clearly working on something. I studied them for a second, taking in how focused they were on their work, and then retreated back behind the corner, weighing out the options.

If we moved to attack, they could spot us before we were close enough to do anything to them, and call for help. Alternatively, if we tried to dart across the open hall while their backs were to us, we ran the risk of one of them looking up and over his shoulder at the wrong moment and noticing us. I considered both plans, and then decided our best bet was to try to sneak across.

I turned and signaled to the others, using Callivax to explain the situation and the plan. My friends watched my hands closely, and then nodded or flashed an "acknowledged" sign. I put Maddox first in the line, followed by Quess and Eric, and then put away my baton to have both hands on the gun. I didn't want to use it unless absolutely necessary. The sensors in the Core were undoubtedly working fine, and if I killed someone, the alarms would go off, bringing every Inquisitor on the floor down on us.

I leaned out past the corner again, taking in the two men. They didn't seem to have moved at all, past whatever they were fiddling with on the wall, and I seized the opportunity and motioned for Maddox to go. The tall girl quickly began to walk, stepping lightly on her feet and keeping her pace moderate, so as not to draw attention. I kept my eyes on the two men the entire time, gun at the ready, but noticed when Maddox entered my field of vision, and tracked her progress.

As soon as she was across, I waited five seconds, and then waved Quess forward. The two men continued to work, oblivious to our presence, and I couldn't help but thank whatever lucky stars were shining on us that we were finally catching a break.

Once Quess was safely across, I waved for Eric to follow. The large man padded up next to me and was starting to move past me when one of the men in the hall stood up and tossed something down in disgust. I quickly reached out and pulled Eric back behind me, before ducking around the corner, praying the man hadn't seen anything.

"This is so stupid, Toby. We should be in central command helping them out, not running around checking the secondary systems!"

The man squatting next to him hadn't moved, but I could hear his answer, delivered in a slow and deliberate voice. "It's not our job," he said simply. "Now come here and help me with this."

"No! And have you seen Scipio's levels? They are downright erratic!"

"I'm pretty sure that's to be expected, considering he's under attack right now," Toby replied, his voice far more cool and collected than I would expect, given the nature of their conversation.

"Yeah, about that," the other man blurted out, still clearly needing to vent. "Can you tell me how a girl from the Knights learned how to program intelli-viruses? Because I accessed her server file, and there is nothing there that indicates any proficiency in—"

"Don't have to be a programmer to have a vision," Toby replied, punctuated by a heavy clank. "Look, kid, I know you're scared, but don't be. IT Department has the greatest minds in the Tower, and they are working nonstop to save Scipio. They did it last Requiem Day, and they'll do it this time, too."

"Yeah, but all the people trapped in the rest of the shell—"

"Will probably die," Toby said with a heavy sigh. "But the important thing here is that you won't. IT won't. And neither will Scipio. Now come here and help me inspect this plasma manifold. I know it's not as exciting as central command, but..."

There was a rustle of fabric, and I chanced a quick look to see the man squatting down again, his attention on the secondary systems they were working on. I hesitated, and then moved forward, pulling Eric along with me. It was a gamble for both of us to cross at the same time, but I was willing to take the chance.

We moved at a quick jog, and I kept my eye on the two men, searching for any sign of them turning to see us, but they remained facing straight ahead. As soon as we disappeared around the corner, I let go of Eric and began moving toward the next intersection. It was disconcerting knowing that I had left Eyes behind us—Eyes who, at any moment, could finish and come this way—so my urge was to get through the hall as quickly as possible.

The next intersection was still and silent, but that did little to reassure me.

It wasn't until we were at the hatch in the third intersection that I began to feel like we would actually get in without anyone noticing. But at that moment, the two men from earlier emerged from the hall two intersections down.

37

The two men were looking down at a pad as they crossed the intersection, but all it would take was one of them noticing the splash of crimson our uniforms made against the gray walls, and we'd be sunk.

I was torn between moving and remaining perfectly still. Either way was a risk, but I felt strongly that movement would only draw more attention to us. For several long seconds, all I could hear over the pounding of my own heart were the faint sounds of their voices and footsteps. I watched them closely, searching for any sign that they were going to look over at us.

But they didn't. Whatever conversation they were having was apparently engaging enough to keep their focus on the pad, and they disappeared down the adjacent hall within a few seconds. I closed my eyes in relief, then twisted my head around to check on my friends and saw that they had followed my lead and remained still as well. Blowing out a deep breath to steady my nerves, I motioned for Quess to keep working.

Within a minute, he had pried the security keypad from its mount in the hatch and connected several thin electrical wires coming from

CHAPTER 37

the pad to several exposed metal nubs inside. He tapped a few things on Dinah's pad, and a moment later the security light on the keypad turned from red to green, and the hatch popped open.

Quess grabbed it and pulled, revealing the bright white-blue glow of the energy stream inside. He remained in the hall to disconnect the pad and reattach the keypad, but I didn't wait for him to finish; I was already motioning for Maddox to approach the glowing portal. The tall girl hesitated for a second, and then stepped over the half wall, lifting one leg up and stepping down to straddle it. I watched as she shifted her weight and found her footing on the rungs that ran down the side of the shaft, waited for her to disappear, and then gave her a five-second count.

As soon as the five seconds expired, I gave Eric a look that told him it was his turn, and he nodded slowly and followed after Maddox. His movements were stiff and wooden, but he made an effort to move at a reasonable pace, so that was something. More than I expected, all things considered.

My heart began to ache as I thought about Zoe, but I pushed it aside and took a quick look back down the hall, making sure the coast was clear. "Quess?" I said, pitching my voice soft and low. "You almost finished?"

There was a click from behind the open hatch a second before I finished my question, and then Quess stepped around it and moved toward the portal, tucking the pad and wires into his pocket. "All set," he replied, throwing a leg over the half wall. "Just pull it closed behind you, and they'll never know it was open."

"Perfect," I murmured, turning around to scan the hall one more time. To be honest, this was all beginning to feel a little too easy, and I couldn't help but suspect it was part of an elaborate trap set up by Sadie or Sage. There weren't any signs of anything sinister, but still, I felt the tingle of awareness that told me to keep moving, just in case.

I turned to see if Quess was out of the way—he was—then quickly went through the hatch after them. I climbed down a few rungs on the inside before reaching out into the hall to pull the door closed behind me, feeling that each second it took was a second too long, giving our enemies the chance to attack and stop us.

But the door closed without any sign of attack, and the green light on the inside of the hatch clicked to red as soon as it sealed, just like Quess had said it would. I exhaled, and then took a quick glance over my shoulder, flinching at the bright glow of the beam being sent down the shaft. The energy ray crackled with power, flowing from a point at the top of the shaft to a port in the bottom, feeding the machines that housed Scipio. The heat in the room was dry and stifling, and each breath I took felt like it was somehow lacking in oxygen, making me almost lightheaded. I closed my eyes against the glow, turned around to face the ladder, and took a moment to collect myself.

As soon as I was ready, I began to descend. I was slow at first, but after a few seconds I got the hang of it and began moving at a steady speed. A quick glance down told me that my friends were moving equally fast, and I relaxed a little and settled into the rhythm.

Minutes ticked by as we continued our descent. Sweat formed on my brow and at the nape of my neck, dripping down my back and slickening my skin. My hands were beginning to ache from having to grip the bars, and my forearms and calves were burning from the repetitive motion. After a while, I started to consider switching over to my lashes to get some small measure of relief, but decided against it. The heat and low-level radiation being emitted by the beam wouldn't affect the lash ends from this distance, but if the lash beads accidentally got too close to the stream, they could melt or lose their ability to produce a static charge, and then I'd be stuck. Granted, we had come down the shaft on lashes before, but the lashing had to be precise, and my arms and shoulders didn't feel like they were up to the task. So, down the ladder I climbed.

The relief I felt when my feet hit the bottom seemed to be echoed by all of my friends, who were in various positions of stretching or shaking out their burning muscles. I took the opportunity as well, reaching overhead to relieve the ache in my shoulders and back while I slowly examined the bottom of the shaft.

The beam fed through a large hole at the center, taking up most of the space, but there were several supercomputers tucked against the walls, all of them with large pipes running toward the power conduit, like spokes on a wheel. I had no idea what the computers were for, but they weren't what I was looking for. I was trying to find the integration chamber, or at least access to it. I wasn't sure—I hadn't looked this far ahead at Dinah's blueprints. To be honest, I hadn't thought we'd make it down here without getting caught. But now that we were here, I needed to know where to go next.

Luckily, Quess was already way ahead of me. "This way," he whispered, heading to the left, where a set of metal steps led up and over one of the pipes feeding from the port to the computers. We took them quickly, our boots rattling the frame as we headed up and then back down. We followed Quess until he stopped halfway between the pipe we had just crossed over and the next one and knelt down on the floor. I looked around for what he saw that I didn't—it appeared to be regular flooring—and then frowned when he pressed a section of it down, only to have it pop back open to reveal a handle. There had been no seam to mark that it was there, which told me that whatever schematic Dinah had managed to find was incredibly accurate.

Quess grabbed the handle and twisted it 360 degrees, then pushed down. There was a sharp hiss, and suddenly the entire floor plate dropped down half an inch. I nearly leapt out of my skin watching it happen, and again when the entire plate shot to one side, disappearing under the rest and revealing a series of steep steps leading downward. The lighting in the room was emitted from some sort of red bulb, making the stairs look exceptionally creepy.

My skin crawled, my mind immediately conjuring up images of the condensation room over Greenery 7, where we had found the bodies of men and women torn apart in the steamy confines. I swallowed back the images, rationalizing to myself that that particular nightmare was over, while whatever ones the room below us held were just beginning.

Then I put that fear away, too, knowing that there was no turning back now.

"I'll go first," I said, stepping around Quess and heading down the steps. They were steep and narrow, and ended at a small landing with a wall in front of it. A narrow passage ran to the left of the stairs, and I followed it, turning my hand light on to get a better view of what was in front of me. Once we were past the stairwell, the hall widened slightly, but ended after a few feet, leading into an open room. The room was set up like a control station, with three desks inside and screens lining the wall. No one was inside. In fact, it seemed as if no one had been there for years, given the film of dust lining the screens and surfaces.

Two halls led out—one to the left, and one to the right.

"Okay, Quess," I said, stepping farther into the room and shining my light around. "Where do we go next?"

"Left hall. Follow it until it dead-ends at a large pipe," he replied.

I followed his instructions, moving in between the desks and toward the hall. This walkway was lined with several additional supercomputers, the tall, box-like structures lit up with a prismatic array of colors that seemed to throb. I kept a healthy distance from them, knowing better than to touch anything, but found myself wondering what they were for.

They control the upload of the AI after integration is completed, Tony supplied for me. *Basically, they are responsible for compressing the AI's data stream when it is uploaded, to prevent any overloads. It takes a lot of energy to transfer us. If you destroyed them, you'd stop Sage's plan to upload Kurt to the mainframe.*

Clearly, I thought back wryly, starting to understand why Sage had stolen all that power from the Tower to enact his plan. *Still, I think I'll stick with my plan to kill Sage and upload Leo. Destroying these would stop Sage, but it would also stop us from uploading Leo and starting the New Day protocol.*

True, Tony agreed. *But isn't that also kind of what you want? To fix Scipio and keep Leo all to yourself?*

I pressed my lips together in irritation, because, while he was technically right, it didn't mean anything. I was planning to go through with Lionel's request no matter what. But Leo was in my thoughts, and Tony should know that, which was why his comment stung a little bit. Still, it

CHAPTER 37

wasn't enough to merit a response, so I merely dropped my side of the conversation and kept moving.

As Quess had explained, the hall dead-ended in front of a large gray pipe that was three feet in circumference and sitting three feet above the ground. Steps were fixed to the side of it, leading up to a pressure valve at the top. I slowed to a stop when I saw it, uncertain of how to proceed, but once again, Quess came to the rescue, walking around me and heading to the rungs.

"I just have to plug the pad in to the security port and upload Dinah's virus," he called over his shoulder as he quickly climbed up. "You should all be up here with me when it goes off. We won't have much time."

Three minutes, in fact, making his argument extremely valid. I quickly followed behind him, tucking my baton back into my belt, and then waited as he knelt and hooked Dinah's pad up to the valve. I remained patient, knowing things like this took some time, but I was already anticipating what we would have to do as soon as he got it open: I would jump in first and begin to crawl through the pipe.

"Quess," I said softly, realizing I needed to know which direction we had to go and what valve exit we were looking for. "What do we do when we get inside?"

"Head right," he grunted. "According to the schematics, the third valve deposits us in an air filtration room that gives us access to a vent that will lead into the room we need."

I nearly groaned in annoyance at his mention of vents. I'd had enough of crawling through those things to last me a lifetime. Having to stomach it again was just the icing on a very big cake of suck.

Hey, if you manage to get through this alive, you'll never have to climb through another vent again, Tony chimed in helpfully.

If, I thought back to him, knowing full well that the likelihood of us getting out alive was slim to none. Sage would have sentinels with him, as well as other guards. If we managed to sneak in without any of them noticing, then maybe we'd have a chance.

But that was a big maybe.

All my thoughts evaporated at the hissing sound of the valve suddenly opening up. Quess moved to the other side of it, stepping awkwardly over the portal, and then gestured for me to jump in.

But I was already moving, knowing that if we didn't get through this in three minutes, the alarms would go off, and Sage would find us before we were ready for him to. Of course, we'd be dead at that point —killed by the liquid nitrogen—so we wouldn't really care. But I resolved to not let that happen.

38

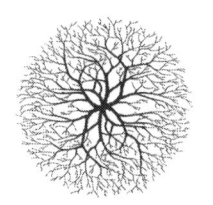

I dropped into the hole, and immediately noticed the extreme shift in temperature when my breath crystallized in the frigid air. The entire tube was lined in frost, and the chill that the liquid nitrogen had left seemed to seep in through the gaps of my uniform. I hesitated, the knowledge that the chemical could instantly freeze any organic matter that came in contact with it making me worry about my ungloved hands, and then quickly touched a pinky to the wall for a second, knowing it was faster than just asking. It was cold, but there was no sign of crystallization, and the skin was still pliable. I immediately hunkered down and began to crawl.

The pipe was only three feet in circumference on the outside, but it was even tighter on the inside, making it difficult to go forward in any way other than a belly crawl, which was intolerably slow. The tunnel stretched on, the darkness inside only pushed back by my light, and I felt each second keenly as I continued to shove myself forward, ever conscious of the time. Quess had said three minutes, and it already felt like I had been in here for an hour.

I used that feeling, funneling some of the frantic energy to my motions and redoubling my efforts. Inches turned to feet, which turned into more as I pressed forward, keeping my mind on the goal.

I paused when my light cut across a panel in the top of the pipe, the glittering lights of it hidden under some of the melting frost. I crawled toward it, and the light on my arm revealed a seam. It was one of the pressure valves—but not our exit. Quess had said the third one.

"Time?" I called behind me, hoping that someone would hear me. I knew that Tony could tell me, but I wanted to communicate with my team, so that we were all aware of how much time we had left. The confines of the pipe made it difficult for sounds to carry past where our bodies were stuffed in.

At first there was no answer, and I worried no one had heard me. But then I heard a muffled, "Two minutes," from behind me, in Eric's voice.

I wasn't sure if making it to the first pressure valve in only a minute was a good or bad sign, but knowing we only had two minutes left added additional fire to my movements. I pulled forward, hyperaware of every scrape my uniform made on the inside of the pipe, the sound of my own breathing, and the thundering of my heart.

In order to cope with the tight confines, I began to focus on what would happen next: climbing out of the pipe, sealing it behind us so as not to raise the alarm, then sneaking into the integration room where Sage was hiding. All I had to do was shoot him, trigger the New Day protocol in Leo, and rescue Grey, and it would be over.

I knew it wouldn't be that simple, but at the very least, it gave me something to preoccupy myself with during the crawl. When we got to the second glowing panel and exit, I felt confident that it had taken less time than it took for us to reach the first one.

"Time?" I asked, hope curling my voice upward.

There was another long pause behind me, and then Eric replied with, "One minute, fifteen seconds. Quess says it's the next hatch. All you have to do is press the green button and it will open."

"Excellent," I breathed, my entire attention focused on the pipe ahead and the final remaining crawl, my eyes searching for the glowing lights that would mean our escape. My hands were burning from the cold, and while I could still move all ten digits, they were hurting and beginning to lose sensation.

CHAPTER 38

Time marched past us while we continued to move forward, the seconds bleeding away with each heartbeat, and I began to count them, growing concerned when thirty had gone by without any sign of the glowing lights. At forty, panic began to set in. Had I missed it? Was the frost over it making it impossible to see? If we were trapped down here when the liquid nitrogen turned back on, we were going to die, so I couldn't afford to make a single mistake.

I trusted that the others would've signaled if I had passed it, and continued to scan the ceiling. A few seconds later, I was rewarded when my light caught another panel and seam, just a few feet ahead.

I raced for it, as best as I was able, knowing that three more people were behind me and needed to get out. As soon as I was within arm's length of it, I reached up, scraped off the frost, and hit the green button. The door overhead emitted a sharp hiss, then rose up, letting in the light from the room outside.

I didn't need a second invitation and rolled to my back so I could grab the edges of the opening and pull myself up until I was standing in the pipe, my head and shoulders inside a small room with a catwalk leading from the hatch to another catwalk pressed between what looked like two tanks—storage areas for the liquid nitrogen, according to their markings.

I quickly looked around and found a wall in one direction, and a metal platform in the other. I climbed hastily to the platform to let Eric out. My boots hit the metal floor, and the structure rattled under my weight. Not enough to be overly concerning, but loudly enough to attract attention. I peered down the steep steps leading down from the platform to a walkway. Massive fans in the floor and ceiling spun lazily on either side of it, while the walkway turned into a hall after it ran between the two silver canisters marked as liquid nitrogen. There was no sign of movement anywhere in the room, or the passageway beyond, but that didn't mean there wouldn't be.

I looked over my shoulder to check on Eric, saw that he was helping Maddox out, and quickly took a few steps down the stairs to make room for them. Then I returned my attention to the passageway, searching for any sign of movement. But there was nothing.

I took several more steps down, keeping my light on the metal catwalk, then paused when I heard Quess's sharp curse, instantly on guard.

"Quess?" I called, turning back toward the pipe and where Eric and Maddox were hovering over the hole to help him out. "You didn't get stuck, did you?"

"Hardee har har," Quess said from inside the pipe. "With a physique like this? Perish the thought."

I frowned at his quip, noting how forced it was, and immediately started back, knowing something wasn't right. "What's wrong?"

"Oh, nothing," he replied in the same tone. "Just... the panel in here got smashed is all. Nothing to worry about, except if I can't fix it, the door won't close, causing an alarm to go off, and liquid nitrogen will spray *everywhere*. But I got it. Really. Nothing to worry about."

That wasn't good. He was repeating himself. That meant there *was* something to worry about. "Quess, get out," I ordered. "We'll force it closed from this side."

"In thirty-nine seconds? I don't think so. The force it would take is far more than all of us could generate together. Besides, I've almost got it. Just a few more seconds."

He was lying. I could tell. My heart skipped a beat as I mounted the steps, and I almost stumbled.

"Quess," Maddox said, her voice nervous. "I really think you should get out now."

"Dammit, babe, I can't. If I do, the valve won't close, and Sage will know someone is back here. I've seen the blueprints, and that room is a deathtrap. And c'mon, it's me. I'm amazing at everything I do."

I reached the top of the steps and stepped between Maddox and Eric. "Quess, give me your hand. We'll worry about the—"

"Just a—" There was a sharp pop of electricity, illuminating Quess's face, and he gave a surprised cry, his hand going to his eyes.

"*Quess!*" Maddox cried, diving toward the opening to try to reach him. I threw my arm across her chest to prevent her from diving back in, knowing that we wouldn't be able to get him out if she was in the way.

CHAPTER 38

"Calm down," I ordered her. "Quess, are you okay?"

"Totally fine," he said back. "I just might have accidently shorted out something important, but that's okay. I can just reroute power to here, and then crosswire this... Almost there."

"That's enough," I snapped. "Get. Out. Now. Eric, will you help me—"

A sharp *bzzt* cut me off before I could finish my thought, and the lights overhead flickered and went out. There was a hiss of air a moment later, coming from right next to us, and all three of us scrambled away from the noise just as the lights flickered back on.

My eyes frantically searched for the source—only to find the pressure valve swinging closed.

Fast.

"Oh no!" Maddox cried, her voice breaking, but I was already moving.

"Quess, the door's closing!" I cried, slapping my hands against the door and pushing, trying to hold it open. The damn thing was already halfway shut, the gap barely wide enough for Quess to squeeze through, but if I could just hold it open long enough, he might be able to escape. I grunted as the force of it continued to bear down, but I might as well have been an ant trying to fight the impending force and pressure of a boot stepping on it. "GET OUT!" I screamed to him.

Hands appeared next to mine, and within seconds Maddox and Eric were wedged on either side of me, trying to help me stop the steady movement of the valve hatch. But even with their help, the hatch continued to bear down, resisting our herculean effort. The door was now three quarters of the way closed, and still going. I strained against it, trying to find a way to leverage more strength into my hold, but we were failing.

Suddenly I caught a flash of something coming through the gap—but knew it couldn't be Quess. It was moving too quickly. Which meant he had just tossed something up. Something that could help us with the door, maybe? I wasn't sure, but I didn't want to let go of the valve long enough to find out.

"Doxy!" Quess shouted. "I tossed up the pad! Don't be upset, but I fixed the door. I..." He paused, his voice growing hoarse with sorrow. "You have to let go now. You're not strong enough to stop it, and you'll hurt your fingers if you keep holding on."

"No!" Maddox cried, and it sounded like Quess was ripping the beating heart from her chest.

Hell, it felt like he was doing that to *mine*. "Quess, stop it," I ordered, the hatch now inches from closing. "Press the button—"

"I can't," he replied, his voice tight with panic and remorse. "I fixed the door, but I had to short out the controls to do it. I'm sorry." His voice broke, and then he took a deep, shuddering breath. "Maddox, baby, I need to tell you that I love you. I've always loved you. Ever since Cali took me in and you kicked my ass that first time we met. Do you remember, Doxy? You threw me to the floor and just sashayed away, and I fell for you then and there." His voice was growing frantic, as the gap between the valve and the pipe dwindled down to centimeters, but still he spoke, trying to reassure Maddox. "Please don't be sad about this, Doxy. I hate it when you're sad."

"Quess!" Maddox sobbed, tears spilling from her green eyes, her fingers still clamped around the lid. "No!"

I had to pull her hands away from the hatch to prevent her fingers from being crushed when the massive weight of it slammed down. The red light next to the door suddenly lit up green, and Eric murmured a sickened, "The liquid nitrogen just turned back on."

"Noooooooo!" Maddox cried, struggling against my hold. "Quess!"

And though it was the last thing I wanted to do, I held her in place as she tried to push past me to the hatch. Tears were leaking from my own eyes, but I kept myself firmly in her way, knowing that it was too late for us to do anything. Quess was gone. He'd sacrificed himself trying to get us in safely, and he'd succeeded. Maddox wouldn't be able to open it back up even if she wanted to, and she definitely wouldn't be able to see anything. If anything, she'd break something that would trigger an alarm.

Maddox's struggles eventually weakened as reality set in, subsiding into rough sobs of sorrow and tragedy that I understood all too well. Maddox had just lost her mother, learned her father was Devon Alexander, then lost him too. And now Quess. It wasn't right. She was a good person—she didn't deserve to know that loss.

I glanced over at Eric, to see his own eyes filled with tears, as he undoubtedly thought about Zoe, and I almost broke down. None of us had done anything to deserve this, but we had all lost people we cared about anyway. It wasn't fair.

On impulse, I wrapped my arms around Maddox, hugging her tight to me as she cried her anguish out against my shoulder, and fought back my own heartbreak. Quess and the others were more than just friends to me. They were my family. Our bond had been forged in the most unorthodox of ways, but they were all I had left, and I was losing them.

Which made the ones still with me all the more precious. It was just too bad that where we were going, none of us were guaranteed to survive.

The thought grounded me, helping me to realize we didn't have time to stand around crying, and I smoothed my hand over Maddox's back, hating myself for how harsh I had to be with her. "Doxy, I'm sorry about Quess," I said, my voice thick due to the constricted nature of my throat. "But we have to move. I don't know how much longer Grey and Leo have, if they haven't broken already, and—"

"I know," she said, jerking away from me and turning around to scrub at her face. "Let's just..." She sucked in a shuddering breath and exhaled slowly, and I could tell she was fighting for calm. "Let's go," she finally said, turning around.

Her eyes were filled with a myriad of emotions: pain, anguish, sorrow, denial, fear, anger, and most importantly, determination. I knew how hard it had to be for her to push the pain of her loss back for even a heartbeat, but Maddox and I were more alike than I cared to admit sometimes, and knowing her, she'd put her pain in a box, lock it up tight, and embrace the void.

Just like I had.

"Eric, grab that pad," I told my friend, breaking from Maddox's gaze to face him. "And let's hope your Cog training has really paid off."

"I can read a schematic," he said quietly, bending over to pick up the pad Quess had thrown out. "Just give me a second."

I turned back to Maddox to find her gazing at the pressure valve, her green eyes threatening to overflow again. "I think we can give you that," I murmured, wanting to give Maddox a few more moments to mourn. It wasn't much, and we had to move, but we could all be dead soon, and she deserved a moment alone with her pain. "I'll help you," I added, realizing that she didn't need me watching it, either.

39

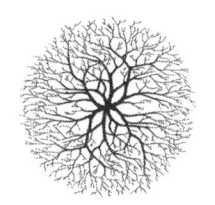

I gave Maddox a minute alone with her grief while I discussed the next step with Eric, but it was all we could spare. The directions for getting into the next room were pretty straightforward: on one of the large vats of liquid nitrogen there was a small ladder, which led to the air filtration system, which then fed into a vent that cooled the integration chamber below—which was where we'd find Sage. The schematics indicated that there were several large machines lining the walls, with space behind them for workers to do repairs, should they need to. Plus, the ceiling was high enough that we'd be mostly hidden if we remained on our lashes, so all we had to do was use our lashes to cross the room—without capturing anyone's attention—drop behind those machines, and then evaluate the situation from there.

Of course, the task was simple, but not getting caught was going to be the difference between life and death, making it infinitely more complicated.

I didn't have much in the way of a plan beyond killing Sage in the hopes that everything would stop, but I also wasn't naïve enough to assume that was all it would take. No, the real goal was locating Leo and initiating the New Day protocol. It was the only way to remove the source of Sage's power. His control over Scipio was what was stopping the Tower from working, and initiating the protocol in Leo would take that control from Sage forever. Even if we died, Leo could turn the Tower against him—against the legacies—and get rid of them. It was the only chance we had of saving the Tower.

I looked down at my watch and sighed, hating that I couldn't give Maddox any more time to mourn Quess. "Maddox?" I called hesitantly toward where she was still standing, staring at the pipe valve.

She turned slowly, looking down at me from her elevated position. Her eyes were red from crying, but she sniffed and nodded. I refrained from saying anything more while she pulled out the lancer we had recovered and checked the battery pack.

"I'm ready," she said hoarsely. "What's the plan?"

She descended the steps while I let Eric explain. Even though we had come up with it together, I was already having doubts about it. There was so much that could go wrong. All Sage or anyone in the room would have to do was look up, and we'd be dead. A part of me wanted to tell them to hold off—wait and let me go first, to make the attempt alone, to see if our plan even stood a chance.

Or, better yet, try to convince them to run away. We'd just lost Quess; there was no need for them to risk their lives, too.

It was on the tip of my tongue to ask them to turn back, but I knew it was pointless. Not just because they wouldn't go, but because there was nowhere for them *to* go. The compartment we were in only had one way out now that we'd sealed the pipe back up, and that was forward.

So, I swallowed the urge, pulled out my gun to recheck how much ammunition I had, and then pushed off the wall and into the hallway, leading the way.

The passageway between the two vats was narrow, forcing me to turn sideways to move through it. The ladder we needed was only thirty feet down the hall, though, running up the side of the chrome vat. It wasn't long before we were climbing, heading for the vent in the ceiling twenty feet above us.

It took no time for me to get up to it and pull off the grate cover, then hand it down to Eric, who gave it to Maddox. A quick check of the edges of the vent told me that there weren't any sensors or automated defenses inside that Dinah's schematic might have missed, and I grabbed the edges of the vent to support my upper half and then stepped up a few more rungs until I could get my knee on the inside and pull the rest of my body through.

I noticed two things immediately: first, the air vent was large enough to stand in, and second, it was deathly cold. Possibly just as cold as the pipe had been, if not colder. I knew that was impossible—and I was sure the air in here was several degrees warmer—but the wind made it feel cold. The air being pumped through the room whipped past me at a phenomenal rate, tugging at the edges of my hair, where I had it secured, and if I faced directly into it, it felt like I wasn't able to breathe.

Luckily, I was heading in the same direction as the wind, not against it, so it was easy enough to turn my back to it and stand up. Within seconds I was moving clear of the opening, breathing air onto my hands to keep them warm and flexible. I moved my hand light around the darkened edges of the massive vent, checking to make sure we were alone, and then turned around to give Eric a hand.

He was already partially through the opening, but his muscular frame was making it difficult for him to raise his leg high enough, so I reached down, grabbed a fistful of his uniform at the back, and hauled him up a few more inches. It helped, and within moments, he was standing and we were both giving Maddox a hand up.

We left the vent open—Maddox had secured the grate between two of the rungs below, to avoid trying to climb with it, and it wasn't worth the effort of going back for it—and proceeded down the shaft into the air filtration system. I knew from the schematic that the ventilation chamber over the room below was large, but nothing could have prepared me for the size and scope of what I saw as we exited the vent.

The entire thing was easily large enough to stand up in, except for the hole in the center of the dome-like room. Overhead, a massive fan spun, pushing the air down into the space. I could see the crackle of energy through its spinning blades, which told me that the power beam was directly overhead, perfectly centered over the opening below. Light from the room lit up the area in which we were standing, and I shut my own light off for fear someone might notice the beam, and then slowly approached the wide opening.

It was enclosed by a waist-high rail, likely to keep workers from accidently falling, but I slowed to a stop long before I reached the edge, not wanting to draw any attention to myself should anyone be looking up.

I immediately frowned when I saw that the area beneath us was not clear like the schematic had read, but instead contained a smaller domed structure, the curved roof of it ending just a few feet under the ceiling above us. In fact, I could easily jump down to it without using my lashes. I wasn't sure what it was or why it was there, but it did offer a small amount of cover.

Emboldened by the fact that the dome provided something else we could hide behind, I dropped to my stomach and crawled to the ledge of the platform, trying to get a glimpse of the area around the dome. I approached it slowly, not wanting my movement to be the thing that gave us away, and cautiously wrapped my fingers over the edge for one final pull forward.

Rows of machines met my gaze, casting dark shadows behind them while multicolored lights intermittently illuminated their faces. There was no sign of any movement or people, but there was more of the room to see.

I carefully pushed away from the edge and maneuvered into a kneeling position, waving for Eric and Maddox to come up right beside me. A moment later, both crimson-clad figures were squatting down next to me, their eyes on my hands while I signed in Callivax. *We need to scope out the room to see if there is a guard set up, where Leo and Grey are, and where Sage is, before we go down. Let's spread out, taking different positions around the edge of the platform, and watch for one minute. If we don't see anyone, we'll go in blind, but let's hope we can figure out where these guys are so we can find the best entry point.*

Maddox nodded and began creeping to the left, while Eric flashed me a thumbs-up signal and went right. I watched them go for a second, eyeing their slow and deliberate pace with appreciation and respect, and then returned to my belly and crawled back up to the edge again.

I kept one eye on my friends as they slowly got into position and one eye below, trying to remain hyperaware of everything at once. It was an impossible task, but I tried nonetheless, knowing the next part of our plan required us to get in unnoticed.

Maddox's hand shot up suddenly, and I immediately looked at it, watching as she signed, *Got a sentinel by a door. Appears stationary. At your three o'clock.*

Not great, but if we could keep the dome between us and it, we could make it work. I turned my gaze below, looking for any sign of movement, and then froze when I heard Sage's voice say, "Ah, good, you're awake. I was worried that last round was too much for you. How are you feeling?"

My skin crawled at how pleasant and cheerful his tone was—how friendly he seemed to be toward whoever he was talking to—but I could hear the undercurrent of malice that twisted his words, and I knew exactly who was on the receiving end.

It was Leo. And Grey. I prayed it was both but feared that it would only be Leo. I wasn't sure if Sage would've kept Grey alive after his legacies delivered him.

I looked up at the other two, trying to see if either of them had eyes on Sage, and noticed Eric changing his position by a few feet, altering his angle so that he was almost across from me. A moment later, his head shot up to look at me, and he nodded, just as a series of coughs erupted from below.

My heart burst with hope. An AI had no reason to cough, meaning that what I was hearing was coming from Grey. And it was all I could do not to race over to where Eric was lying. But I couldn't—I had to move slowly.

I carefully pushed away from the edge and slithered back a few feet, then slowly picked myself up off the walkway into a low crouch. I kept a healthy distance between myself and the edge, crossing in front of other vent shafts that fed into the room, mimicking the wheel spoke design from the bottom of the shaft above.

The coughing subsided while I moved, changing into sharp, pained gasps that I knew were doubling as forced laughter, and the hope in my heart dwindled and died as I realized that just because Grey was alive, it didn't mean he was all right.

"Sorry," he wheezed, continuing his dry chuckle. "The AI you're looking for isn't here right now. Please try again at the sound of the—"

A wet slapping noise cut him off, and I went ramrod stiff, my heart now in my throat. "Here's the thing about AIs and real, physical pain, Grey. Can I call you Grey?"

"Go to hell," Grey spat, and there was another sound that could only be explained by a fist being driven into human flesh.

I swallowed down the nausea and resumed my trek toward Eric, trying to understand what Sage was trying to accomplish. I knew he was torturing Grey, but why? All he had to do was remove the net, and he'd have Leo in his hand. I knew for a fact that he could torture AIs into compliance, so why hurt Grey? As I moved, Sage continued to speak as if nothing about this were out of the ordinary. I had no idea whether the old man was hitting Grey himself or having one of his children do it, but I would know soon enough.

"As I was saying, Grey, AIs... they just can't seem to cope with physical pain. Oh, I mean, they can bury themselves deep in the recesses of your mind and let you endure it alone, but they won't. Lionel raised them all to be self-sacrificing, whether they wanted to be or not, and they almost universally try to protect the host. But physical pain is such a foreign construct to an AI that they can't cope with it. So while they're trying to keep you from going insane, they begin to break down. I know Leo is riding your thoughts, working with you to find a way to escape, and I know each time I break another finger or land another blow he buckles and breaks even more. How long can you keep him from telling me what I want?"

"We got no place to be," Grey wheezed back. "And honestly, this whole torture thing? I think you might be slightly mistaken. Leo's not even talking to me anymore."

CHAPTER 39

"I dislike lies, especially feeble ones," Sage drawled.

"No, seriously! You should take him out and check! I think you might've killed him."

Sage sighed irritably. "Even if I wanted to take him out and put him in my head, I could not. Years of Kurt and I being together has created a synaptic dependency. If I remove him, I die."

Grey gave out a sharp bark of laughter that he quickly cut off with a, "I'm sorry. So you're telling me that in replacing Scipio with Kurt, you'll die?"

"A sacrifice I am willing to make to right the injustices Lionel visited upon humanity. Now, enough. You need to recognize the situation you're in. Your friends are dead, and if they're not yet, they will be soon. Every person in the Tower is gunning for your little girlfriend. I doubt she'll survive another two hours on the run."

"I can wait that long," Grey replied. "She's worth it."

I reached Eric just as Sage began to chuckle, and quickly slid onto my belly next to him, peering down into the hole. I could see Sage. His back was to us, and just beyond him, I saw the crimson colors of a Knight's uniform. I could only see Grey's legs; a chair had been set up closer to the machines, so I couldn't see all of him from this angle, but I could see that he was seated, hands bound behind him, legs tied to the chair.

"You keep telling yourself that, boy. I'm growing impatient, and have decided to step it up, as you say. Sadie? Will you pass me the helmet, please? I think it might be Kurt's turn to take a shot."

As he spoke, the familiar form of the gray-clad head of IT stepped into view, a strange white helmet with a series of cables jutting out of the top in her hand. She gave it to Sage with a beatific smile. "Of course, Father. I have some updates for you about the progress we're making in Cogstown. Would you like to wait, or—"

"Tell me later," the old man interrupted impatiently. "Hook up Mr. Farmless here so I can have Kurt take another crack at breaking them both."

It's Sawyer, I thought to myself, and felt the ghost of a smile form when I heard Grey say, "My last name is Sawyer, you sadistic piece of crap. And Leo and I aren't telling you anything."

"We'll see about that," Sage said ominously. "Sadie, darling, go ahead."

I glanced over at Eric, and then Maddox, and debated whether we should go now, or wait to find a better opportunity. They were clearly going to be distracted for a minute or two, which meant now was the best time for us to move. Especially since it was obvious they hadn't gotten what they needed out of Leo yet—which meant there was a chance we could stop everything, if we could just get down there and get to him.

I thought about the information we had gathered—Maddox's sentinel and the placement of Sage and Sadie in relation to the room—and figured that the best point of entry was closer to Maddox's side, just out of sight of the sentinel. I tapped Eric on the shoulder, indicating for him to follow me, then slid backward on my belly.

As soon as I was far enough away from the ledge, I stood up and crossed over to Maddox, who had moved away from the railing and was waiting in a low squat, her expression thoughtful.

Ideas? I signed as soon as I caught her eye, and she nodded, her hands and fingers bursting into a flurry of motion.

We go down closer to where we entered. Detach from the ceiling as quickly as possible and rappel down the side of the dome.

I flashed her a thumbs-up, and then quickly crossed over to the area she'd pointed out. Pulling a length of the lash line from my sleeve, I leaned over the railing and spun it around several times before slapping it straight down so it hit the underside of the flooring beneath my feet.

There was a sharp click when it hit, and I froze, worried that Sage or Sadie had heard it, but whatever they were doing to Grey must have had them preoccupied, because there was no pause in their low exchange.

Blowing out an anxious breath, I relaxed some of the tension in my muscles, and then carefully threw a leg over the railing, swinging it over until my toes were perched on the ledge and my back was to the hole.

I carefully crouched down into a squatting position in order to make the distance of my fall as short as possible, and eyed the dome below me, gauging how far I would need to lash to get behind it before the sentinel saw me.

Then I let go of the railing with my hand and dropped right into the serpent's pit.

40

I tried not to flail in panic at the sudden terror gripping my heart as I fell. Even though the distance was short, I felt certain the occupants of the room would notice the flash of crimson my uniform made. The outfit was a damn beacon under these conditions, and all it would take was a glimpse of it out of the corner of someone's eye, and they'd know they weren't alone.

Still, I didn't freeze, and bent my knees and pointed my toes as the wall of the dome loomed up in front of me, using my hand controls to slow my descent some. I hit the surface lightly, pushed off, and then lowered myself a few more feet, making sure I was well and truly hidden behind the dome before taking a moment to check below me.

The area along the wall between the machines and the dome was clear as far as my eyes could see on either side, and I quickly tossed my second line out, hitting the dome a few feet above my head. Disconnecting the first lash end, I rappelled down the side, taking short jumps to keep the sound of my boots as quiet as possible.

As soon as my feet were safely on the floor, I detached and turned around, looking at the machines on the wall. There was a space just behind them for service workers, and it was our best route for sneaking

CHAPTER 40

up on Sage and Sadie—provided we could find a place to squeeze through the machines to get to that space.

I studied them for several seconds, spotted a crawl area created by a machine with a weird overhanging section that looked promising, and crossed over to it, stepping on the outer edges of my feet to keep my footsteps as quiet as possible. I dropped to all fours in front of the machine and stared into the shadows. There didn't appear to be anything blocking our way of accessing that area, and I was satisfied that all of us—even Eric—could fit through.

I got back to my feet and quickly turned to signal the others, only to find Eric falling awkwardly from a lash connected to the ceiling, spinning quickly away from the dome as he dropped down. He was fiddling with the controls, trying to arrest his fall, but his boots scraped along the side, and he landed awkwardly on his rump before sliding down.

I winced at the noise it generated, and quickly ran a few steps toward him, holding up my hands to try to break his fall as quietly as possible.

He jabbed at his hand controls, panicking, and then jerked to a stop a few feet before he hit me. His eyes were wide and filled with fear and remorse, but I ignored it to wave him down, already knowing that they must have heard the noise he had made. Which meant we had to move—quickly.

"Did you hear that?" Sadie said loudly, her voice carrying with it a note of alarm, and I cursed internally, increasing the speed of my wave to hurry him along.

"I did indeed, my dear," Sage replied. "Take Alice and check it out while I get to work on this."

Eric hit the ground with a low thump, and I looked up at where Maddox was still standing on the platform above, cutting a hand across my neck to tell her to stay in place. She flashed me an okay symbol and then took a few steps back into the shadows, disappearing from view.

I grabbed Eric's arm, pulling him toward the crawlspace I'd only just found. He followed behind me, keeping his footsteps light, thankfully, but that only made it easier to hear the heavy metallic sound that could only be generated by a sentinel's heavy gait. I quickly slid onto my belly and dove through the hole. My back hit the metal overhang of the machine I was crawling under in my haste to get through so Eric would have time to follow, and I gritted my teeth together and flattened myself to the floor, hating that I had made even more noise.

I quickly scrambled through, pulling my legs into the gap and sliding to one side, and seconds later, Eric was shoving himself after me. He was lying on his back, and I quickly realized the wisdom of the position as he reached up to pull himself into a sitting position, dragging his legs farther under the overhang and out of sight.

My mouth went dry as the thundering sound of the sentinel drew closer, and I quickly tucked myself farther behind the machine, trying to get my legs under me so I could stand up. My gun was in my pocket, but the tight confines meant I couldn't reach it unless I was on my feet. Looking around, I spotted a small pipe running along the wall and grabbed it, using it for leverage to haul myself up.

Eric was doing something similar, only right in front of the hole, and I feared that at any second, the sentinel was going to drop to all fours in front of it and see his feet.

I was only halfway up when the heavy footsteps came to a halt. I couldn't tell where, exactly, but I knew it was close, and I held my breath and slowed my movements, terrified that it would somehow hear me.

"Do you see anything?" Sadie demanded, her voice so close I could've sworn she was standing next to me. I carefully shifted my weight, trying to straighten silently, my fingers inching toward the gun in my pocket. If I could just reach it, I wouldn't feel so afraid, and we wouldn't be defenseless.

"We do not," Alice replied after a moment. "But the source of the noise remains unaccounted for. Was it perhaps mechanical?"

Sadie made a considering sound, and I continued to hold my breath, even though my lungs were beginning to protest the action. Tony started to compensate by slowing my heartbeat some, but he and I both knew it was just a stopgap measure. I continued to hoist myself

CHAPTER 40

up, careful not to make the slightest whisper of sound, and finally got both legs under me so that I could straighten.

My hand immediately went to my pocket, grabbing the tab of the zipper to open it, but then I paused, realizing that if I moved too fast, it would make an obvious noise. Gritting my teeth together in frustration, I leaned my forehead against the back of the machine I was pressed behind, expelling a shaky breath. I was certain that at any moment, Sadie was going to insist Alice check behind the machines. She wasn't stupid—she knew something was up. My muscles quivered, screaming at me to run away, to preemptively make a move to escape, but I ground it down, knowing it was folly. The gaps between the machines were large enough for them to have a clear view of what was going on behind them, so if I moved, they'd notice, and we'd die.

"Call in two more units and start patrolling the room on a circuit," Sadie said, and I balled my hands into fists, wondering how the hell three of us were going to take out three sentinels without any plasma weapons. Then again... I supposed we didn't have to. All we had to do was get close enough so Leo could hear the protocol, and then it would be over.

Except for the fact that we would die, it wasn't so bad. Leo would be wirelessly transferred to the integration chamber to await the neural clone that passed the vetting process. Once he and the other AI were integrated, they could turn the citizens of the Tower against Sage and get rid of him and his children once and for all.

Unless, of course, *Sage's* neural clone was the one that passed the test. I wasn't sure how many legacy nets were currently being used, but I was guessing there weren't that many, considering the lengths to which Sage had gone in order to get rid of them. And given what he knew about the AI program already, I had little doubt that his neural clone could pass the test—whatever it was—that Lionel had set up. Technically, he already had once, in the form of Kurt, so it stood to reason that he could again.

And I had no idea how much control Leo had over the selection process.

Which meant that while I kept "kill Sage" as a part of my plan, I had to prioritize it as the step right before giving Leo the protocol. After that, I was pretty much anticipating that we were going to be killed by the sentinels, but if Sage was dead and Leo was in the process of replacing Scipio, then that wouldn't be so bad.

At least we'd go together.

Okay, can you stop being so maudlin, Tony said, clearly creeped out by my bleak attitude. *Pay attention. They're moving away.*

Tony was right; I had been so lost in my dark thoughts that I hadn't noticed Alice's response, or the fact that they were leaving. I closed my eyes in relief, taking a moment to collect myself, and then pushed back from the machine, looking over at Eric. The young man had his eyes closed, and seemed to be concentrating only on his breathing, so I had to tap him to get his attention.

His eyes snapped open, going wide with alarm, but to his credit, he didn't make a noise as his head swiveled toward me. I offered him a weak smile, and then gestured for him to begin moving in the direction Sadie and the sentinel were going, hoping to use the noise they were making as cover. Eric stared at me for a second, his face pale, but after a moment, he gave me a jerky nod and turned his head to the other side, heading in the direction I pointed out. I knew that it wasn't just the sentinels slowing us down, but his claustrophobia as well, and hung back for a few seconds to let him move at his own pace. I used the short span of time to slowly unzip my pocket and pull out the gun, and then followed, trying to keep from brushing up against the machines.

I had no idea what Maddox was going to do at this point. If she was watching, and paying close enough attention, she might figure out which direction we were heading and shadow us, but I was hoping she realized it wasn't wise to try to come down now. I wasn't sure if she had been able to hear Sadie from where she was, so there was a chance she would try to go for it, but still, I hoped against it. If more sentinels were coming, having her up in a higher position with the lancer would give us an advantage. She could target their hard drives and maybe help us pick off one or two.

But I had no way to signal her to change the plan, so I just concentrated on moving forward, knowing she could take care of herself.

CHAPTER 40

Our progress was slow but steady, and after half a minute, I picked up the rhythm of shuffling sideways. Sadie and the sentinel were far ahead of us—and not moving now, given the quiet of the room—and I focused on my hearing, trying to discern what was going on and where they were.

For a long time, there was no sound of talking or movement. It was eerie—downright eerie, enough for me to want to freeze a handful of times and just make sure that Sadie and the sentinel weren't stalking us somehow. I checked over my shoulder constantly, certain that one of them had snuck up behind us, but there was nothing. Had they left to go fetch the other sentinels? That didn't make sense. Alice had a hive mind now, meaning that if one of them knew something, the others did as well. As soon as Sadie said she wanted two more, two of them would've been dispatched immediately. If anything, I was surprised they weren't here already. I would've assumed Sage had a small army of them nearby, but so far, they didn't seem to have arrived.

Several heartbeats later, I realized I had been wrong—about the timing, at least. There was a soft hiss of a pneumatic door opening, followed by the heavy beat of not one, but two sentinels marching in unison. I froze as the sound grew closer and tucked every inch of my body behind the machine I was currently working my way past before their shadows cut by.

"We have come," they announced in unison.

"Shush," Sadie replied, and my skin tingled with anticipation when I realized how close we were to them. "Father is trying to concentrate. Split up and patrol the room."

On impulse, I pulled myself over to the corner of the machine and leaned out past it, peering down the gap. The angle wasn't the best, but I could see the two sentinels with their backs to me several feet down, Sadie's form in between them. The third sentinel was missing, but I was guessing it was in front of the door again, making sure no unexpected guests entered or left.

As I watched, the two sentinels immediately split up, one of them heading farther around the dome, the other turning to double back. I ducked behind the machine again as it passed, then began to move away from it, following behind Eric.

"Bah!" Sage snorted a moment later, and I heard the sound of something hitting the ground. "After two and a half centuries, you'd think the backup would've gone insane in his terminal, but instead he continues to resist us! I need those protocols!"

"That's too bad," Grey replied, his voice now exhausted, as if he had run a marathon. I had no idea what Sage had been doing to him during those moments of silence, but based on what I had heard and seen, I was guessing he had been using the helmets to have Kurt attack Leo directly, through the net. "Guess you're just going to have to give up."

"Not likely. This is your last chance. Tell me what the protocol is, or I will give your host a very slow and painful death."

I froze in place, hearing the hard undercurrent in Sage's voice that told me he meant business. I knew Leo wasn't going to give it up—and neither would Grey. They knew what was at stake, what could be lost if they failed, and would die before they told Sage.

"Well, as the host in this equation, I say go ahead and put your money where your mouth is. I'm not afraid of you. You're just an old man who doesn't know how to lie down and—"

The sound of gunfire cut him off, and my eyes widened in alarm and panic as I heard Grey make a strangled cry of pain, knowing that Sage had just shot him. A scream built up in my throat, the raw pain of losing somebody else I loved so overwhelming that I couldn't help but open my mouth and unleash my anguish.

41

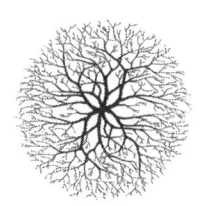

Eric's hand slapped over my mouth before the scream could reach an audible note, and the large man dragged me closer to him and firmly gripped my arm. The instant his hand was on me, I knew what he was trying to do, and I hated him for it.

He was trying to keep me from Grey. My Grey. My sweet, reckless, brave Grey.

Who'd just been shot by Sage.

Rage burned at my very heart, a rage that had been slowly building since this morning's bloodshed in the Council Room, and my fingers curled tightly around my gun, itching for me to break Eric's hold and go after Sage with everything I had. Tony rose up to try to wrest control from me, his concern for me trying to cut through my internal tempest, but the rage inside me was too powerful for the AI, and I shoved him back into a dark place in my mind and closed the door on him, trapping him behind it. Then I started to pull away from Eric, intent on slipping out through a gap a few machines back to sneak up behind them, but the stronger man held me firm.

"Sentinel," he whispered harshly.

A few seconds later I heard the sounds of its steps over the furious beating of my own heart. I exhaled a shuddering breath, common sense threading some rationality through my rage, and tried to focus on remaining still.

It didn't help that I was quite literally shaking, my entire being vibrating in response to the gunshot and my fear that I'd lost Grey before I'd even had a chance to save him. I should've just gone in guns blazing, instead of sneaking around trying to get the drop on them. Because of me, I'd given Sage more time to grow impatient with him, resulting in him dying.

The shadow of the sentinel cut through the beams of light streaming into the small space as it passed, the looming presence of it growing closer and closer, and I closed my eyes, trying not to give in to the reckless urge that told me I should leap out and try to tear the sentinel apart with my bare hands. I knew it was my fury making me feel like I was indestructible, but I couldn't help it. Sage was a monster, and I wanted to slay him once and for all.

But I resisted, letting Eric hold me in place and letting Tony out of the box I had just put him in, to try to contain my anger. I could tell the AI inside me was still overwhelmed by it—he felt like a small fish trying to swim up a fiery river—but I let him in this time, and he helped push some of it away.

Leaving only the fear and my unanswered questions about Grey. Had Sage killed him, or just shot him some place that would cause a lot of pain? It was horrible to think about, but if Sage had shot him in the foot, he would survive that, provided we could get to him in time. We just had to get there.

Suddenly I was grateful to Eric and Tony; they had kept me from doing something monumentally suicidal and given me a chance to think. I reached up with my free hand to tap Eric, letting him know he could pull his fingers away, and a second later, my mouth was free. The sentinel's shadow passed us at that exact moment, but didn't slow, and I closed my eyes in relief that it hadn't noticed us.

They snapped open a few moments later when I heard a weak groan. "You... shot me..." It was Grey—and he was still alive! Alive but in a lot of pain. My heart ached, wanting—no, needing—to go to him, but instead, I put it aside, reminding myself that I wasn't alone. Others were counting on me, including him.

I nodded at Eric to start moving, and together we began making our way to the sound. I kept peering through the gaps between machines, trying to catch a glimpse of Grey, but the machines were too bulky, mostly limiting my field of view to only the dome. Occasionally I got a glimpse of Sadie's back, or Sage bent over something in front of her, but never a clear shot or a good angle.

"Hurts, doesn't it?" Sage said with a laugh. "Gut wounds are always tricky, too. So many organs to hit. May I?" I wasn't sure what Sage was asking permission for, but Grey's agonized cry of pain told me it wasn't good, and I had to swallow back the massive dose of anger that seemed to shoot up from where I was carrying it in my stomach, like a dragon about to breathe flames.

Then Sage continued. "Ah, shoot, it just passed through some of your intestines. I might've nicked your spine, though. It's hard to tell with just a finger."

I pressed a fist to my mouth to suppress a gag, realizing that Sage had stuck his finger *into* Grey's bullet wound.

"C'mon, Leo," Sage continued in a singsong voice. "If you tell me, I won't have to shoot him again."

Grey was groaning in pain, and I had to fight back every impulse I had to go to him. *Please,* I begged. *Just keep your mouth shut for a few moments. Let him think you're in agony, anything. Just don't be a smartass.*

"Awww... but I like being shot. Just one more time, please? I—" Grey's act of bravado was cut off by another gunshot, and I clenched my hand tighter around my own gun pommel, struggling to breathe. I was losing this battle of will. I was too emotionally compromised. I loved Grey, would do anything to protect him, but here I was, slinking behind these machines and trying to get the drop on Sage.

And it was taking too long. Grey was going to die.

I looked over at Eric, who was continuing forward, oblivious to the fact that I had stopped, and swallowed. *Tony, do you understand?* I asked, needing the AI's permission before I did something as foolish as what I was about to do.

Get out there and shoot that son of a bitch, the AI declared, giving me his permission, and I quickly looked around, searching for a space that would let me out. We had passed one a few machines back, and after a moment's hesitation, I made for it.

"Liana," Eric whispered harshly a few seconds later, but it was too late. I was already moving. I heard him try to reach for me, his uniform scraping against the wall, but I was too far away. Grey gave another pained cry, and I used the anger and fear to fuel my actions, aiming for the gap between two machines, which was just wide enough for me to squeeze through. I shifted the gun to my left hand, knowing Tony could compensate for my lack of proficiency with it, and then shoved myself into the tight space.

I froze a moment later, right down to holding my breath, as the sentinel's shadow filled the gap a heartbeat before it entered into view. The urge to curl back and hide was strong, but it was already too late—any movement would only further give me away. My heart threatened to explode in terror, my brain certain that it had already seen me, but two agonizing seconds later, it was past. I released a trembling breath, trying to be as quiet as possible, and then seized the opportunity the sentinel had presented me with: it was heading *away* from Sage, which meant its back would be to me for a few seconds. The other one would be circling around toward Sage, but I had time to get out and act before it was on me.

I carefully slid farther into the gap, taking great pains not to make any noise, and then stuck my head out, looking first at where Sage and Sadie were standing, to make sure their backs were to me, and then at the sentinel that was heading away. It was disappearing around the large curve of the dome, and I quickly stepped into the aisle, shifting my gun to my other hand and looking back at Sage and Sadie. The area they were standing in was slightly different than the rest of the room, in that the walls curved outward to form a small, square alcove, lined by large machines the likes of which I'd never seen before. The bottom half of them looked normal, I guessed, but they were topped by glass balls, not unlike light bulbs, with beams of electricity curling around inside, spilling out from a fountain. Each machine held a different color of light—purple, orange, yellow, green, blue—and it didn't take me long to figure out that each one was housing one of the AI fragments. Sage and Sadie were standing at the mouth of the room, and between their legs, I could see Grey sitting just beyond them.

Sage was bent over him, and Sadie's position behind him made it difficult to get a shot. I grated my teeth together as Grey made another choked sound, telling me Sage was continuing to probe the bullet wound he had left in Grey's abdomen, and I raised my arm, setting my sights on Sadie. In my mind, it played out as simply as this: I would shoot Sadie, then shoot Sage when he looked up in surprise. My only concern was the distance. If I miscalculated the angle of the bullet when I hit Sage, it could shoot through him and hit Grey. And he'd been shot enough for the day.

Blowing out a steady breath, knowing I was beyond exposed, I took several creeping steps forward, trying to get a better angle. My nerves tingled with awareness as Sage began speaking again, and I tightened my grip on my gun, searching for my moment.

"You see how painful it is, Leo?" Sage crooned, and the question was punctuated by Grey's agonized cry. "Imagine this over and over again, and you'll know the kind of torment your copy has been enduring for the last two hundred years. Only, you don't have his protections to spare you the pain, do you? Should I get a new host and infect them with Whispers? I had such fun designing that particular virus to torment Scipio, but I have no idea how it actually feels, so having you endure it would be fascinating. For science, of course. And why stop there? I have always wanted to try flaying someone alive. We should start a list with all sorts of painful deaths on it. Let's see, there's disembowelment, setting you on fire... I mean, I've been working in the Medica for a hundred years, so I know all sorts of ways to kill. I'll march in those innocent humans your idiotic creator made you so protective of, shove you inside them, and then tear them apart piece by piece, until you give me that code. It's your decision. How many more are going to die before you see reason and give me that damn code?"

His patience was clearly at an end, and his speech grew rapidly angrier and angrier the longer he talked, until it seemed he was spitting. I still couldn't get a good angle on him, and I knew my time was running out. Any second, the other sentinel would be rounding the corner, and I'd be caught. I had to fire at Sadie if I wanted to create an opportunity to kill Sage. He could get out of the way before I could get him, but it was worth the risk.

I was tightening my finger on the trigger, aiming directly for Sadie's head, when Sage suddenly stood back up, his face contorted into an angry mask. My eyes flicked to the sudden movement, and my gaze met his clear blue one. His eyes widened, and I quickly adjusted my aim for his head, my finger pulling the trigger.

The gun jerked in my hand, the gun casing ejecting from the slot at the top, and I felt like time slowed down, my every hope and prayer for the future inside that small bullet.

Sage was already throwing himself behind Sadie with more speed and agility than a man in his third century of life should have, and there was a spark against the far wall where the bullet had ricocheted, missing him. I gritted my teeth together. Tony was already readjusting our aim for Sadie. The redheaded woman was turning, and my shot was hurried, but I hit her. Her slim form went down in a spinning fall and a spray of blood. Sage was still moving in a low crouch, racing away from Sadie's falling form toward where I could now see Grey sitting. I fired two more shots, then had to stop when Sage hunkered down behind Grey, using him for cover.

Grey's head was down, his blond-brown hair partially covering his face, but I could see blood dripping from his chin into his lap, mingling with the blood that was oozing out of two holes in his stomach. I aimed my gun toward him, waiting for Sage to move so I could shoot the asshole in the same places he had shot Grey before adding one to the head. I knew that Kurt was still inside Sage's net, but at this point, I didn't care. Kurt had been letting Sage get away with this sort of behavior for long enough. He could die with the man.

"Come out here!" I shouted, knowing Sage was just buying time for the sentinels to get there. I darted a quick glance behind me to make sure the coast was still clear, and then took a few steps forward, now on guard. "I'll make it painless," I added. "One right in the head. You deserve worse, but I'm eager to get this done!"

"I admire your bravery, Liana. If I'd had even one child with your mettle, I might've let him or her breed instead of sterilizing them. But I'm not going down today. I have Alice to protect me."

I took another glance behind me and saw the gleaming hulk of the sentinel striding confidently around the curve of the dome, heading right toward me, golden eyes blazing. I quickly shifted targets and fired at one of her eyes, scoring a hit, but she continued to lumber on. I was starting to dance back, ready to throw a lash to somehow get behind Sage, when a sudden volley of crimson lancer fire erupted from overhead, tearing into the back of the sentinel. I ducked down on impulse and then looked up to see Maddox dangling from her lashes in the center of the ceiling above the dome, firing down on the sentinel. There was a sharp spray of sparks from the sentinel, arcing down across the floor and toward me, and it went slack, its eyes going black. For a second, I stared at it, stunned that we had managed to take it down so easily.

And then the room exploded into chaos.

42

"Get to Leo!" Maddox shouted before twisting around to fire at something down on the other side of the dome, and I moved, taking a few steps backward and then spinning around to follow Maddox's instructions. She was undoubtedly firing at one of the other two sentinels in the room, but the third remained unaccounted for.

A sentinel rounded the corner just as I was spinning a lash bead in my hand, as if an echo of my fears and nightmares manifesting into reality, but Tony kept me from panicking, throwing my line for me and hitting the ceiling overhead. We ran straight for the sentinel, but at the last minute, retracted the line and flew upward, using the momentum to start running along the side of the dome. I took three steps at an angle heading up, aware that the sentinel was reaching to grab me from the movement in the corner of my eye, and then pushed off the dome, flipping myself backward. I disconnected the line as I somersaulted through the air, and landed heavily on my boots, dropping to one knee. My gun hand was already thrusting out, my aim for the shape of the black box seated between the sentinel's shoulders, but the machine twisted, one arm whipping toward me. I squeezed the trigger just as it slammed into my forearm, and the shot sparked off one of the machines.

CHAPTER 42

The pain in my arm was explosive, but I still had a grip on my gun, so the arm couldn't be broken. I threw myself back as the sentinel's other hand came around to grab me, barely avoiding the grasping metal fingers, and brought my gun back up, aiming for an eye. It ducked back, one hand going up to shield the orbs from the bullet, and I cursed. Alice had learned my little trick.

Still, her flinch gave me a moment to carve out a few more feet between us, and at that moment, a blur of movement leapt from a gap in the machine, attaching himself to the sentinel's back. It was Eric—and he was giving me a chance. He had a baton in his hand, already charged, and I knew he was trying to buy me time to get to Leo. I spun around, intent on shouting the New Day protocol at Leo and shooting Sage at the same time.

He was still behind Grey, but he wasn't crouching anymore, and I quickly came to a stop when I saw the flat, matte-black nose of the pistol pressed against Grey's vulnerable throat—below where the net sat in the back of his skull, ensuring Leo would survive. One gnarled finger curled around the trigger. I stared at it for a second, and then up at Sage, my hand tightening on my gun.

"Do it," Grey said hoarsely, his brown eyes finding mine. "Shoot him. Don't worry about me."

I pressed my lips together against the wave of emotion his statement generated in me, and started to lift the gun up, intent on following his orders. I knew I was risking his life, but he knew what was at stake and what he was asking. Hell, he'd been taunting Sage to try to get him to lose control and kill them both, to prevent Sage from getting the codes. I couldn't let that be in vain.

Sage's eyes widened as I brought the gun up to sight on him, and then he rolled his eyes and shook his head, looking utterly irritated with my reaction. I grated my teeth together at the man's arrogance right up to the end and started to squeeze the trigger.

A flash of movement from my right was the only warning I had that I had been flanked. Pain erupted from my wrists as a metal bar was brought down on them, and my hands suddenly went numb, the gun slipping from nerveless fingers. I looked up to see Sadie's slim figure emerge from a gap between the machines, her green eyes blazing with malice as she drew back for another strike with the pipe.

I got my arms over my head, but part of the bar hit my forehead, and I stumbled back, the blow to my skull enough to break through the drug cocktail Quess had fed me earlier to keep the concussion at bay. Immediately my balance faltered, the sickly sensation in my stomach telling me that gravity was shifting to the left, and I slammed against the dome before going down.

My vision went dark and pain exploded into my skull, threatening to render me unconscious, but I fought against it. I felt Tony helping me, but it wasn't easy. I became aware of reality in patches, and in an oddly disconnected way, like I was blinking at a picture without really seeing it. The sentinel was dragging me across the floor by my foot; Maddox was firing at the other one as it climbed up the side of the dome to get her. Then flashing back to my sentinel as my head lolled to one side, only to see Eric tucked neatly under its arm. His face was red, and he was looking at me—shouting at me—but I couldn't hear him, and within seconds, the blackness had swallowed me again.

I wasn't sure when we stopped moving, but I grew aware again when something grabbed a fistful of my hair and pulled, and the feeling was like shards of glass being jammed into my brain. Something cold splashed in my face just as soon as the pain became too much, and I felt water invading my mouth and nostrils, threatening to drown me. It shocked me out of the darkness, and I began to cough it out, already catching some in my windpipe.

"That's it," Sage said from overhead, and I slid open my eyes enough to see the floor and a pair of white boots in my field of vision. "Wake up."

I groaned, the searing pain in my skull only increasing as my head was pulled back to face his. I winced at the bright light surrounding his face, making him a dark and ominous silhouette, and then groaned when it sank in that he had caught me. I rolled my eyes around as far as I could to the right and left, and saw that it was Sadie gripping my hair, and that Eric and Maddox were being restrained by sentinels, metal hands covering their mouths to silence them. The effort cost me, and my vision grew more and more blurred, until it was doubling while the world started to spin the wrong way, sliding to the left and away. Black spots blossomed and danced across my vision, telling me I was about to black out again, and I almost gave in to it, not wanting to see my friends butchered before my eyes.

A soft slap on the side of my cheek snapped my eyes back to Sage, and I inhaled a shuddering breath, trying to think of something pithy to say to him before he killed us.

"Stay with me, Liana. Here, let me give you something for that pain." There was a sharp sting at my neck, and seconds later the intense throbbing faded some. I could see straight without feeling like I was going to puke, and my thoughts felt more ordered and cohesive. "That's better," Sage said with a sigh, straightening up. "I am so very glad to see you! Tell me, do you know where Tony is? I'm betting you do. I think you had something to do with getting him out of that server in Cogstown. Where is he, Liana?"

I stared at him, having zero intention of telling him anything. "In the words of Grey," I wheezed, smiling against the lingering pain in my head. "Go to hell." Then I spat at him for good measure, tearing several chunks of my hair against Sadie's grip in the process. She jerked me back, but a glob of my bloody spit had already struck his pristine uniform.

Sage made a face of disgust and turned to grab something from behind him. "Really, Liana," he said in a patronizing tone. "I'm sorry you lost, but do you have to be so immature about it?"

I curled my hands up into fists but froze when I felt something cold pressing into the back of my neck. I recognized it immediately as a gun and wanted to gnash my teeth in frustration. This was it. We were done. Sage was only keeping me around to get Tony, and after that...

I'd messed up. Missed my chance. If I had just waited a fraction of a second longer to get a better shot at him, I would've at least killed the bastard.

It was becoming the story of my life, really. I made plans, and the bad guys always came out on top. My litany of mistakes was longer than my arm and had cost me so much.

"Go to hell," I wheezed. I was defeated, but I'd be damned if I gave him anything at this point. Call me a spiteful girl, but that bastard could rot in hell. Inside, I thought, *Tony, can you send your program somewhere to keep out of his hands?*

It doesn't really work like that, he replied.

I wasn't happy with the answer, because that meant I had to resort to plan two. *Then can you delete yourself?* I knew I was basically asking the program to commit suicide, but I couldn't let him fall into Sage's hands.

There was a pause. *From your net? I... I don't know. I've never tried. But look, he's not going to kill you yet. He needs you. He knows you're Leo's weakness. There's an opportunity here if you can just wait for it.*

I shook my head against the thought. Sage had given me something for the pain, and it was making me sluggish and heavy. It wasn't full sedation, but it was definitely slowing my reflexes down. I appreciated Tony's advice, but I had to be practical. I couldn't fight Sage like this. *I promise I will, but... we can't let you fall into his hands. Can you try?*

"You're talking to him right now, aren't you?" Sage asked, and I blinked my eyes up at him to see that he had squatted down in front of me and was studying my face. "He's in your net! Of course! It's clever, and also great for me. Sadie?"

Sadie shoved me forward, and I wasn't prepared for the action. I tried to get my arms under me, to break my fall, but I was only able to get one up before I slammed into the floor. The angle of my arm caused the impact to translate into that shoulder in a loud, crunching noise that I both heard and felt, and I gasped at the pain, rolling over to my side and grabbing at it. The thing felt damn near dislocated.

I held it for several seconds, breathing through the pain, only to have it erupt anew as something pressed down on it. I opened my eyes to see Sadie standing over me, her hand cupping her arm where I had apparently shot her, her foot planted on my shoulder, and a sudden surge of anger had me lashing out with my own foot, trying to catch her leg with my own.

I was moving too slowly, though, and she sidestepped lazily, her foot only leaving my shoulder long enough to avoid the blow before coming

CHAPTER 42

back down again, pushing me onto my stomach. I cried out, and rolled to try to escape the pain, doing exactly what she wanted. Moments later, the collar of my uniform was jerked down, and something was pressed against the back of my neck.

My net! They were going to take it! If Sage did that, he'd have Tony. Not to mention, if I did manage to enact the New Day protocol, no net meant no neural clone of me. Not that I had any idea whether my clone would be able to do anything to stop Sage once his own psyche was made into an AI, but I had to hope that it could, if only to eliminate him from the candidate pool.

Of course, I had to enact the protocol first. I just wished I could remember the final four numbers. Was it 6323? 2336? I was only going to have one chance at this, and I couldn't get it wrong.

Tony? I thought as I tried to move away, hoping the AI would give me the right numbers, but Sadie buried one knee on my spine, pinning me in place. I winced, expecting the sting of pain as she cut my neck open to extract the net, but after a few moments, her weight was suddenly gone, with no incision made. *Tony?* I thought, slowly bringing myself to my knees. *What was that?*

I waited for a moment, and then frowned. Tony hadn't answered. Why hadn't Tony answered? I searched my thoughts and emotions for any trace of him, but was only met with silence, and knew then that Sadie had done something to take him.

"Where is he?" I demanded, straightening up and settling my weight back on my heels.

"Wirelessly downloaded," Sage said, his side to me and eyes on where Sadie was walking toward one of the inactive machines. "Lionel's so-called less traumatic way of downloading and uploading the AIs to the nets and other terminals. Now that that's being handled, Leo... your girlfriend brought us some new leverage! Isn't that exciting?"

Sage stepped farther to the side, letting me see Grey. My breath sucked in sharply as I regarded the damage to his face. The sides were mottled and bruised, and his lips were split and bleeding. One eye was turning black, and the other one was red from where a blood vessel had ruptured. His stomach was a mess of blood, and more had pooled around his feet.

"I'm not telling you anything," Grey said. His voice was weak, but the defiance was there. "Not a damned thing."

"You sure?" Sage asked, smiling like the madman he was. Grey narrowed his eyes and pressed his lips closed, his nostrils flaring as he met Sage's gaze headlong. I felt a savage rush of pride, at least knowing that, no matter what Sage did to us, Leo wouldn't tell him anything, but then swallowed it back, knowing Sage would eventually lose his patience, kill us all, and implant Leo in a new human. Leo would eventually break, all without him knowing about the New Day protocol or having a chance to enact it.

And Sage would win. Kurt would become the new AI, and Sage's legacy would be complete.

"That's too bad," Sage said with an indifferent little shrug. "Alice?"

There was a wet snap to my right, and I looked over to see Alice releasing Eric's head, his neck now bent at an angle that shouldn't have been possible. His eyes were wide, open, and... vacant. The light from them had been extinguished by Alice as soon as she had broken his neck. I gaped, horrified at the casual brutality of the action, and the pain of losing yet another friend so soon after all the others slammed into me, breaking me. I fell back to my hands, trying to fight the urge to sob, the urge to vomit, the urge to scream, and struggled just to breathe without losing my crap.

A scream tore out of someone's throat, but it wasn't from mine. It was from Maddox. I looked over to see her boots scrambling on the floor, trying to fight the hold of the sentinel grabbing her. "You son of a bitch!" she screamed. "You dirty coward! Hiding behind your machines and your broken AI fragments and playing God! We'll never give you anything you want, you hear me? Leo, New Day protocol alpha-phi-alpha-6—"

A gunshot cut her off, and her boots jerked. I looked away, unable to see another friend die, but a second later, she was thrown to the floor next to me, her body landing with a boneless thud. I winced, a shudder tearing through me as another friend lay dead beside me, all the fire of her green eyes suddenly extinguished.

But I held on to the first number she had said, trying to focus on it and remember what the code was. 6323? 6332? 6233! That was it!

"Stop it!" Grey cried, and I heard the desperation in his voice, and knew he was about to break.

I couldn't let that happen—not even for me.

"Grey..." I breathed, intent on finishing Maddox's order. But a cold metal hand wrapped around my throat, cutting me off with a vicious squeeze, and seconds later I was hauled into the air, my feet dangling helplessly below me, the life being choked out of me by the sentinel.

43

I wrapped my hands around Alice's metal wrists and planted a foot on her chest to try to physically force myself from her grip, but she only tightened her hands. I immediately went lightheaded, my vision blurring as I heard a wheezing, choking sound that I realized was coming from me. The blood trapped in my skull was beginning to pool into my face and around my eyes, making them bulge and water.

I was dying. Alice was choking me to death.

My vision went gray, and I felt the strength in my hands start to fade, my feeble thrashing growing weaker. Darkness began to pour into the edges of the world, encircling the sentinel's shadowy face, ensuring its nightmarish visage would be the last thing I saw before I died.

"STOP! STOP! I'LL TELL YOU! JUST LET HER GO!"

The voice sounded like it was coming from the end of a long, dark tunnel behind me, barely carrying over the sound of my heartbeat slowing, but I recognized it as Grey's.

A moment later I was falling into oblivion, the darkness rushing up to meet me. I felt myself wonder what was coming next—whether I was going to see my friends or my brother again, how the citizens of the Tower were going to survive someone as sadistic as Sage, what was going to happen to Leo and Grey...

And then I hit the ground. And suddenly realized I could breathe.

My lungs were already pulling air in, through a constricted throat. I had a brief flash of consciousness as my eyes popped open, revealing the lights of the ceiling above, and then the sudden intake of oxygen coupled with the rush of blood out of my head left me spinning, my vision going gray. I released a shaky breath, my body terrified to release the air for fear it was only a brief reprise, and then took another one, trying to keep it slow and prevent myself from hyperventilating.

I lay on the ground for what felt like eternity, the world spinning on its axis and tumbling this way and that. I became aware of a ringing in my ears, the agony of my arm and shoulder, all in slow degrees, like a dial being twisted up.

But the pain helped me focus and prevented me from just drifting off to sleep, which was my battered body's current desire.

In an effort to try to arrest the spinning, I slowly rolled to my good side and opened my eyes. Focusing on something stationary would help sort my equilibrium out and give me an idea of what was happening and where I was.

Opening my eyes was hard. Both felt inordinately heavy, like someone had attached tiny weights to each eyelash in an attempt to keep them closed. What was weirder, the right one felt disproportionately heavier than the other one, like it had not only been weighted down, but also taped for good measure. After trying to raise both eyelids and failing miserably, I eventually just diverted my efforts to the left eye, figuring the lighter eyelid was the easier one to open.

Success. I cranked my eyelid open about halfway. The first thing I noticed was the flooring; it obscured nearly half of my field of vision and seemed to be rocking back and forth. I picked a spot a few feet away and kept my gaze on it, keeping my breathing heavy. The rocking began to still, which made some of the queasiness in my stomach lessen. I let out another heavy breath, inhaled, and opened my eye even wider.

I was facing the dome. It was the next thing I noticed: the smooth, white, egg-like surface cutting into the dark flooring. I let my gaze wander—slowly, of course, for fear of throwing the world out of alignment again—and immediately caught a glimpse of movement to the far right. I tracked it, and saw two... no wait, three sets of legs. Two sets, one white and one gray, seemed to be dragging the third—crimson—through an opening I hadn't noticed before. It must've been there all along, across from where Sage and Grey had been.

As I watched, the room started to glow brightly, and I sensed that Sage was about to win.

Something inside of me refused to let that happen, and I began to scan the floor, looking for something, anything, I could use to stop him.

I spotted my gun lying just a few feet to the right of the door. For several seconds, I stared at it, confused at how it had gotten there. I had been holding it when Sadie hit me. Had they kicked it over here and just missed the fact that it was right there?

Wait, where were the sentinels? Did I risk looking for them and alerting them to the fact that I was conscious, or did I just go for the gun? Did I have the time?

"Dammit," Sage cursed loudly. "He passed out!"

I knew he meant Grey and wasn't sure if he was feigning unconsciousness to slow Sage down, or if he was unconscious because he was about to die, but it didn't matter. He was buying me time to act. It was worth the risk.

I lifted my head slowly, doing my best to ignore the way the right side of my face felt as if it were sliding downward and melting off, and slowly twisted my head more to the right. The axis of the world shifted slightly, my equilibrium not remotely calibrated to handle that angle yet, and I closed my eye for a second, trying to still the sudden rocking sensation.

A rustle of movement had me setting my head down rapidly, and I heard footsteps marching across the floor behind me. I remained focused on my breathing while whoever had just emerged from the room began picking things up and setting them down with impatient mutterings. It took me a second, but I realized it was Sadie, likely coming out to get something to wake Grey. And from the sounds of it, she was having a hard time finding it. I seized the opportunity to open my eye again and resume my lookout, hoping that if the sentinels were around, they were watching her and not me.

She suddenly shouted, "What does it look like?" over her shoulder, loudly enough to make me freeze.

"It's a pneumatic injector, Sadie," Sage declared irritably.

"Not the injector, Father," she snapped, and I realized that neither was paying attention to me. I continued to survey the room, finally noting the set of robot legs standing just to the right of the door, facing in. "The damn vial! What color?"

A quick glance to my left told me the second sentinel wasn't there, meaning it was either behind me, or had gone back to the main entrance to the room to prevent further intrusion. I couldn't check behind me with Sadie back there, but as soon as she was gone, I could move.

"The red one! And hurry up. I'm ready to put this to an end. How about you, Scipio? Ready to die?"

"Please," I heard an agonized moan reply, and I realized that Scipio's hologram was in the room with them. "Anything to make it stop. I can't take it. The voices... They're screaming for me to help, but these chains you've put on me... Just end it, please."

My heart twisted to hear the great machine so desperate for death, in that much pain, and remembered that he felt every death that was happening in the Tower at the exact moment it was happening. He was suffering from it, his very core being corrupted by it, and was powerless to do anything to stop it.

He was beyond broken.

I put my head down as Sadie made a satisfied noise, and listened to the sound of her footsteps marching past me and into the room. As soon as they stopped, I lifted my head up again and risked a glance behind me, peering through a bleary, unfocused eye for any hint of the other sentinel. The world seesawed back and forth, but I just swayed with the rhythm of it and focused, until I was certain it wasn't lurking back there. I swiveled back around, took one last furtive glance at the sentinel by the door, and then began to crawl.

It was awkward, with one arm still aching and tender from all the places it had been hit. I wasn't sure if the damn thing was broken or dislocated at this point, but it wasn't doing much to support my weight as I moved.

But thankfully, I didn't have to move very far. Within seconds I was close enough to brush my fingers across the gun's rough grip, and I dragged it toward me with one finger, then two, my eye on the sentinel's legs. They remained still, her focus completely on whatever was happening inside the room, and a few moments later I had the gun in my palm, the feel of it as heavy as it was reassuring.

I blew out several breaths, and then slowly began to pick myself up off the floor, getting one boot under me, then the other. I ignored the sound of Grey's sharp gasp coming from the opening, and the sentinel herself, just focusing my will solely on the act of rising. I wasn't sure where I was finding the energy; I was beyond spent, broken in both body and soul.

Yet somehow, I rose.

I took several more deep breaths, steadying myself as my balance began to sway with the world. Grey gave another sharp cry—this one pained—and the world suddenly snapped into focus.

I turned and leveled the gun at the sentinel, aiming for the black box on its back, which was partially obscured by a metal cage over it. I didn't have Tony to steady my aim, but I had found some sort of stillness inside that was giving me focus.

I squeezed the trigger, the gun jerking in my hand.

There was a spark from the hard drive, but it was hard to tell whether I had hit the cage or box. I took a step forward, preparing to fire another round, and then the sentinel made a sharp, "EEEEEEEE!" noise that sent a piercing pain through my head.

I winced, just as a flash of movement emerged from the doorframe, and I fired at it, letting instinct guide me. The sharp noise from the sentinel cut off with a sharp *zzt*, and I immediately opened my eyes, and saw Sadie standing with one foot through the doorframe, a pulse shield in her hand. I started to fire at her again, already knowing I was too late, but then paused when she looked down at her chest. I followed her gaze... and saw the hole there, already pouring out blood.

Pouring out of the left side of her chest—from approximately where her heart was located.

She looked up at me, her brows furrowing in confusion. "But..." she breathed, before toppling over.

I felt nothing as she fell, and after doing a quick check of the sentinel to make sure it was out, I took a staggering step toward the doorway. The light inside was glowing brightly in an array of prismatic colors. It was like the room I had met the Lionel program inside of, only not glowing white.

The kaleidoscope of colors was like gravel being dragged along the inside of my brain, but I pushed through it, knowing I'd already come so far.

The protocol was on the tip of my tongue. All I had to do was yell it at Leo, and he'd be uploaded into the server, where he could take out Kurt and stop Sage's plan once and for all. Leaving me to finally kill Sage. I moved up to the side of the door, intent on shouting it through the doorframe.

"Leo!" I cried. Or at least I tried to. But my voice came out as barely a harsh whisper, a gurgle of noise that felt like my entire voice box had been smashed. I suppressed a curse and gritted my teeth. If I couldn't yell it at him, then I'd have to get closer.

I became aware of the beating sounds of a sentinel's footsteps, and on impulse, dove through the door. A gunshot exploded right ahead of me, and I felt it impact directly into my thigh, but I was suddenly too enraged to care. Because I could see Sage standing just off center, next to where Grey was bleeding on the floor. His gun was already pointed at me, and I saw the flash of another bullet explode from the muzzle as he fired at me.

My arm snapped out at him, my eyes already settling on the colorful target his uniform was making in the spectral lights. My heart thundered in my chest as I expelled a slow breath and squeezed the trigger. The gun kicked in my hand, making my arm throb with agony, but I ignored it, my eyes watching Sage. The bullet hit him on the left side of the chest, and I barely caught the old man's look of surprise before he spun away and fell. I exhaled, lowering the gun, and then cried out as I felt the burning in my leg where I had been shot. It was like someone had driven a spike through my thigh.

"Liana?"

I opened my eyes, the weak sound of Grey's voice chasing the pain away for a moment. I scanned the ground, and saw him lying near where Sage had fallen, already climbing across the floor to get to me. The beating sound of the footsteps came closer, and I knew that at any second, the sentinel would enter, see what we had done, and kill us both.

I began crawling for Grey, but the sorrow in my heart was like a weight around my neck. I knew we couldn't fight the sentinels. I was battered and broken, and he was in even worse shape. We were going to die no matter what, but there was still a chance that I could save Leo, and through him, the Tower. It broke my heart, though, because I wasn't going to be able to say goodbye to Leo, or even explain what was happening to him. But I had to do it. It was the only way to prevent any of this from happening again.

I saw him stretching a hand out to me, and grabbed it. Somehow, he found the strength to drag us closer together, because within moments, his arms were encircling me. "I'm sorry," he whispered, resting his forehead on mine. "I couldn't let them kill you. I gave him the code. He's already uploaded Kurt and started the process."

I pressed my lips together, holding back a cry. I wanted to tell him that it was okay, that we would figure it out, but I didn't know what was about to happen. It was probably too late to initiate the New Day protocol, but I had to try. "I'm sorry, too," I breathed. "I love you so much, and I'm sorry I failed you."

"What is this?" Alice exclaimed from the door, and I knew our time was growing short.

"What do you mean?" he asked, cupping the side of my face, completely ignoring her. "I've never met anyone who fought so hard for me in my life. You came for me—kept fighting for us. You're the strongest person I know. C'mon, we can get through this thing together."

I smiled sadly at that, knowing that we couldn't, and leaned forward

CHAPTER 43

to kiss him—to, for just a second, forget that death was coming through the door behind us. Then I leaned to the side, pressed my lips to his ear, and whispered, "Activate the New Day protocol, alpha-phi-alpha-6233."

"Wha—?" Grey breathed, a second before my world was washed away in white.

44

"Wake up, beautiful," a voice whispered in my ear, and I opened my eyes.

I was immediately overwhelmed. Nothing was right. The edges of my vision seemed to be lined in a thousand colors, forming an iridescent oval outline. Every time I moved, distant edges of light shot by the outline, like shooting stars suddenly hitting a shield. My skin was humming, like it was somehow covered in millions of bees that were simultaneously connected to an electrical line. I suddenly realized I wasn't breathing, but on the tail of that, didn't feel the urge to.

I blinked and looked around, momentarily disoriented by the dancing lights, and immediately zeroed in on a blue glow just to my right.

It was Leo—Leo as I remembered him from Lionel Scipio's office, from when he was a hologram. But he was also different, his edges sharper and more defined. Streams of silvery blue ran along those edges, highlighting his features in a way I hadn't known was possible. As I watched, a line of code appeared over his skin, the numbers morphing rapidly as they moved from the ridge of his inky black eyebrow and cut through the dark blue of his eyes.

"What is this?" I asked.

Or rather, I sang it. It was hard to describe—like a series of cascading tones that perfectly conveyed my ideas as well as my emotions. I stared at him, confused, and he smiled.

"It's okay," he "sang" back to me. "Here." I didn't know what he meant by that, but the note accompanying it was one that asked for my trust, and I gave it instantly.

He leaned down, his gaze on my lips, and within moments, he was kissing me.

It was like nothing I had ever experienced before. The only thing I could think of to compare it to was the idea of kissing lightning. His lips brushed against mine, and the humming of my skin intensified and tightened in such a pleasurable way that I broke off the kiss to cry out, overwhelmed by the sensation.

"It's okay," Leo said soothingly, one hand gliding over my forehead to push back some of my hair. "I'm trying to show you what you are now. Just relax."

My apprehension grew as he leaned back down to kiss me. I was still horribly confused, but I relented, trusting him implicitly. His lips brushed against mine again, and this time it was as gentle as the ripple on a pond, each wave carrying outward and hitting every inch of my body with pleasure. A moment later, I realized he was also sending me information, showing me what had happened—and what I was now.

I was an AI.

My eyes popped open and I took a step away from him, in flat out denial, and then paused. I had been certain I was lying down just a moment ago, but now I was standing. I looked down, trying to understand the dimension of where I was, and realized I was... nowhere. I was surrounded by an inky blackness that seemed to glitter no matter which way I spun. There was no up or down, yet I was inexplicably standing on something no matter where I moved. I looked back at Leo, and then down at my hands.

They were glowing. A rich color that was neither gold nor orange, but a true amber. I waggled my fingers, finding all of them there, and then looked back at Leo. "I'm... not Liana," I eventually said.

Leo favored me with a lopsided smile. "You're every bit of her," he said. "But also... different."

"Did I—" I stopped myself for a second, unable to ask the last part, but Leo seemed to know.

"Did you die?" he asked, and I nodded. He didn't answer, but the look on his face told me enough. Grey and... the other me... were gone.

I frowned. "I don't understand what's happening. I shot Sage and initiated the protocol. If you and I are here, then—"

"Sage is here too. He didn't die when you shot him, and he had already started uploading Kurt. Now they are both here, along with Alice, fighting for control." As he spoke, he stepped to one side, revealing what appeared to be a lightning storm growing in the distance. Multispectral clouds, bloated and swollen with power, were emitting massive bolts of lightning angled down at the landscape, at some sort of bubble covering part of the ground. Each lightning strike was different, revolving from sickly green, to golden fire, to pure white.

"What is that?" I breathed, holding up my hand to shield my eyes from the bright flashes of light as it impacted off the surface.

"That is war," Leo said grimly. "The fragments loyal to Scipio are in the bubble. They're trying to keep him alive, even though he wants to die. But they are losing to Sage and the others, who have taken the shape of those clouds. If Sage manages to kill Scipio before we can stop him, he and Kurt will fuse and be automatically downloaded into the Core. It won't be what he originally wanted to do, but I imagine that egomaniac won't object. It's imperative we stop him before that happens."

The humming of my skin slowed in reflection of the sudden fear embracing me, and I looked at him. "What do we do?"

"You're an AI, Liana," Leo said with a smile. "You're only limited by your imagination. Watch." He closed his eyes and held out his hands, palms up. There was a glow in his hands, and tendrils of code started to streak down his arms before being swallowed up by the bright blue light in his hands. Something formed in the center of it as I watched, lines appearing and growing, tapering, curving, filling out... Then the glow disappeared suddenly, leaving a blue sword nearly as tall as I was and half as wide.

"That seems a little big," I said dubiously, but Leo merely shrugged.

"There's no floor or ceiling here, remember?" he said, taking a step away and giving it a few experimental swings. "And it's made from my code, so it's light as a feather. See?"

He tossed it at me, and I reacted before I could fully register fear of the massive blade, reaching out and snatching it from the air like he had been tossing a ball instead of a weapon. He was right—it was remarkably light, and though it appeared to be cumbersome, a few swings told me it was easily handled.

But it wasn't right for me. I tossed it back and held out my own hands, closing my eyes. I pictured in my head the plasma rifle—the smooth lines of it—and my skin began to hum in response. Seconds later, I opened my eyes and smiled when I saw it waiting for me, hardening to a translucent amber that held a small glowing orb of energy, pulsating as if with the beating of my own heart—except I didn't have one anymore. Not in the conventional sense, anyway.

I held it up to my shoulder and looked at Leo. "You realize that if I don't survive, you'll have to find someone else to bond with for the New Day protocol, right?" I asked, needing him to understand that I wouldn't take it personally if he had to bond... fuse... whatever, with someone else.

His smile faltered, and he nodded—and for a second, I caught a glimpse of Grey, as if superimposed onto his image. "I won't like spending an eternity without you, but... everyone gave their lives getting us here. I don't take that lightly, and I won't dishonor what they died for, even if it means losing you."

Love for him blossomed, feeling like a warm rush of wind blowing inside me, and on impulse, I reached out for him and pulled him close. I was afraid, yes, but I wasn't alone. I had lost everyone, including both Grey and myself, my real self, but I still had Leo. I still had the will to end this, and my will had already carried my body far beyond what it should have been capable of. Let Sage and Kurt stand in our way. I damn well dared them to.

I held him for several seconds, taking comfort in what could be our last moments together, and then let him go. "Let's end this," I said, hefting up my gun.

"After you," he replied, casually balancing his oversized sword on his shoulder. I rolled my eyes at him, and then took off running toward the storm.

Running in cyberspace was unlike anything I could fathom. Each step felt like it ate up hundreds of miles in the horizon, and within seconds, we were within spitting distance of the war zone. I zeroed in on the dome first, the soft glow of several AIs inside it capturing my attention. Jasper stood at the center, his hands lifted up to the sky, pouring forth the bubble that was protecting the others. Inside, I could see Scipio's blue form, his code pale and damn near transparent, curled up in a ball, rocking back and forth. Hovering over him was Rose, her code even more fragmented now than it had been the last time I saw her. She seemed to be feeding energy into Scipio, trying to heal him. Beside her was Tony, his head pointed up at the sky, his eyes calculating.

Lightning crashed down onto the dome as we watched, the sickly green color smashing against it and forcing it to shrink in size. I looked up at the clouds, and realized it was them: Kurt, Alice, and Sage. I narrowed my eyes at the white cloud, knowing it was Sage, and immediately cranked the plasma rifle I had created up as high as the charge would go, focusing all of my rage and anger into the blast.

The amber ball of light that exploded from the other side was almost laughable in size, resembling what could only be described as a small sun that, when shooting through the clouds, lit them up with an amber light. The light began to brighten and intensify until beams of it were punching holes in the swollen vapors, scorching the other clouds around it.

Moments later, three figures had materialized overhead, standing on absolutely nothing, and, as if the landscape were trying to make sense of the fact that they were floating above us, a structure began to form under them, complete with stairs. I ignored them—Leo had said I could use my imagination—and seconds later, small pads formed in the air. I launched myself toward them, using each one as a springboard while Leo raced up the stairs.

Alice didn't wait for us to meet her but leapt off the side of the building that was forming beneath her. Her form here was that of an inferno—a golden fire wrapped around the form of a woman, with dark holes acting as her eyes and mouth. She fell feet first, her arms reaching up, and strands of code began to stream into her hands, forming long whips with sharp edges, meant for shredding.

I watched it for a second, marveling at how beautiful it was, and then pulled the rifle to my shoulder, following her falling form for a few feet before squeezing the trigger. My shot hit her in the chest, throwing her through the building that was still manifesting behind her. There was an explosion of brick and mortar as she punched through it, but I kept moving up, manifesting more amber discs to help me.

Above me, I saw Kurt's green form begin to glow, growing brighter and brighter, and I had to shield my eyes to keep it from blinding me. I slipped, and because of the strange mechanics of cyberspace, I was suddenly falling, plummeting toward the ground. I opened my eyes and threw out my hand, and a lash—just as real as the ones I had used my whole life—arced from my sleeve, hitting the side of the building and bringing me to a jerking halt.

A moment later, the building exploded under the weight of a massive foot, and I was thrown clear with the digital rubble that erupted outward. I caught myself midair, my heightened reflexes rapidly flipping me around, and stood up, immediately scanning the rubble for Leo.

I found him hurtling through the air toward Kurt's now-gigantic form towering at least fifty feet above us all, his large sword held in an underhand grip. Kurt noticed him as well, and stepped back, but not before Leo slashed through a section of code on his thigh. Light bled from the wound—pure and sickly green—and I raced for it, sensing it was a weakness.

I fired several shots from the hip. The first one caught him in the knee and forced him back a few steps. The second missed entirely, and the third—which would've scored—was deflected by Alice, who had launched herself up into the air from somewhere. Her chest was a black crater, with dark cracks running through her code, but she was still moving.

And she was coming for me. I had a second to react before she was on me, but I didn't falter, my mind spinning out thousands of ways to avoid her before settling on one. I leaned back as she reached for me, bringing the rifle up between us as she flew overhead and pulling the trigger, releasing all the pent-up rage I had in my heart for her—for what she did to Zoe, Eric, Maddox, Dylan, and Rose, as well as every other person in the Tower she'd killed today.

Her eyes widened in surprise as the amber shots tore through her code, and she screamed an inhuman howl that seemed to shake the very datasphere we were fighting in, before disappearing from sight.

I spun around to find her crumpled on the ground, her code pouring out of her with flashes of golden light that were flickering in an erratic pulse.

"More!" she screamed into the darkness. "We need more!"

A moment later, a beam of light flashed in from the darkness and landed directly on her, and I watched as another Alice was dropped in, superimposing over the first. Rage seized me as I realized that she was pulling copies of herself in to replace the damaged code, and I shot this one before she could even take a step toward me. Then I turned away. I couldn't afford to be distracted by the Alices. Not when I had Kurt and Sage to contend with.

Leo was still going after Kurt with his sword, borrowing a page from my imagination to create little landing pads for himself as he tried to scale Kurt's massive frame. I searched for the white glow that was Sage, knowing he was lurking somewhere nearby, and found him heading for the bubble where the fragments were cowering, a small white scalpel in his hand.

I raced for him, but once again, the scope of the landscape had changed. I shot a blast at him as he brought his arm up and then down, cutting a slit through Jasper's shield, but it went wide, missing him. The ground shuddered under Kurt's heavy footsteps behind me, but I ignored it, shooting at Sage while he reached out to grab the edges of the cut and force them apart.

A second later Tony was there, his crimson code shooting around Sage's as a tornado. Sage's hair whipped around his head as he stumbled back, and Tony pressed the attack, growing larger and spinning faster. I had to admire his creativity—I had never considered changing form like that—but it was blocking me from shooting Sage.

"Tony!" I screamed, coming to a stop a few feet away. "Move away!"

The crimson wind began to shift away from the white glow at its center, but a second later, Sage's claw-like hand reached out and seemed to grab a section of Tony's code, clenching it tight. The wind disappeared instantly, leaving instead a small, dark-haired boy with wide, frightened eyes.

"NO!" he cried. I brought my gun up, but Sage held Tony up in front of him, blocking the bulk of his code from me. To get him, I would have to shoot Tony, and I couldn't do that.

"Put him down!" I shouted, slowly focusing my imagination on whatever the AI equivalent of a flash grenade was. I felt it form a second later but was too transfixed by Sage as he reached up and put a hand on the boy's head.

"No," Sage said, and then dug his fingers into the boy's head.

"Liana!" Tony cried in pain, reaching for me, and then there was a sharp crack. The top of his skull caved in from the force of Sage's grip, releasing an energy pulse. It hit me hard, throwing me back in a tumbling spin. For several seconds, I kept spinning, until it occurred to me to just put my feet down, and then suddenly I was standing, the world still again.

I looked around to reorient myself, realized I was standing on Kurt's knee, and jumped off seconds before his hand came slapping down, right where I had been standing. I rolled on impulse, years of muscle memory shaping my actions. I knew Leo was handling Kurt, so I focused entirely on Sage, secure in the knowledge that once I killed him, Leo and I could take out Kurt together.

Sage was already inside the bubble, which was beginning to flicker as he got closer to Jasper. I pictured a spear, the lines of it taking shape in my hand, and threw it before it was fully formed, flinging it toward Sage.

It streaked off like a star shooting across the night sky, heading right for the point where Sage's neck met his spine, but Alice leapt in the way, once again taking the shot with her own body. I bit back a growl of frustration, and then decided to see what horizons my imagination could really take me to on this plane.

I leapt to where she was falling, my hands outstretched to grab her head. She kicked at me as we fell away from the fight, but I ignored it, tangling my fingers into gobs of her hair and focusing on her eyes. If my imagination and will could manifest anything here, then maybe I could use her as a conduit. Maybe I could kill them all at once.

And the only thing I could think to use was fire. I closed my eyes and imagined flames, the heat and color of them, roiling down my arms and bleeding into her. She started to scream seconds later, and I opened my eyes to find my hands burning holes in her chest. What was more, I could see the thousands of threads—nearly invisible to the naked eye—streaking from her code into the darkness behind her, and feel the weight of her other minds on the other side.

So, I followed them, bringing the heat and intensity of the fire so that it could spread and consume each thread. More and more of them sprang up where others burned away, but I kept burning, until I found a very small orb at the center of it all, like a golden spider. In my mind, I grabbed it, my hands on fire, and focused my rage on it. For several seconds, the orb continued to burn golden through my amber fire. Then I felt something snap in my hands, and Alice's scream intensified, hitting a shrill, piercing final note, and then her code broke into a thousand fragments with the concussive force of a small bomb, throwing me back hundreds of feet.

I recalled my earlier trick and straightened my legs, willing the world to stop, and I was standing yet again—only this time I was upside down, looking at the dome below.

Or where the dome used to be. Jasper was now battling Sage, trying to keep the larger code away from Scipio and Rose, and failing. Even as I began to formulate a plan, Sage shoved his hand through the fragment's chest and then yanked it back again, something orange and glowing clutched between his fingers.

Jasper took several stunned steps back before falling to his knees, and then his code simply... blew apart, scattered to oblivion by the invisible wind of some unknown force.

Then Sage lifted his hand to his mouth, swallowed whatever he had just stolen from Jasper, and started to glow brighter, his form beginning to twist and change.

I didn't hesitate this time. I manifested a sword a quarter of the size of Leo's and launched myself at Sage, intent on cutting the bastard in two.

45

I focused my will upon the sword, imagining that it was razor sharp and indestructible, and brought it down in an overhanded blow, aiming for the top of Sage's head. His body was pulsating with color, streams of orange lines trailing down his jaw and throat, burrowing into his stomach and then shooting through his arms and legs, the orange-and-white codes intermingling and giving him an outline, and he seemed to grow slightly, his stooped form becoming straighter, taller, more imposing.

He lifted his other hand to his mouth, and I saw bursts of crimson light flashing between his claw-like fingers. It was Tony—or rather what was left of him—and Sage was about to swallow him down, just as he had Jasper. He tilted his head back, lifting his hand to his open mouth—and then spotted me, seconds away from driving my sword through him.

He flowed backward, leaving only a ghostly image of himself, and I sliced through it, planting a foot on the floor and going after the real him. I slashed over and under, trying to land a blow, but he sidestepped each one, avoiding any cut by inches. I grated my teeth together in frustration as I continued to press and he continued to retreat, until

CHAPTER 45

finally I feinted a low blow to the left, and then brought my blade up on the right.

The blade severed the arm that clutched Tony, just below the elbow. Sage grabbed what was left of his arm and screamed, molten white code pouring out of the stump, while his arm landed a few feet away. I ignored it, focused solely on trying to end him, but noticed a purple lasso flying through the air from the right out of the corner of my eye, and knew that Rose was trying to secure whatever was left of Tony. I brought the sword around, trying to slice through Sage's neck, but the old man twisted away, as slippery as an eel, and began bounding across the floor.

I ran after him, changing the sword in my hand for two guns, and began firing, sending small amber streaks of fire after him. They collided with some sort of energy barrier, bouncing off of him with small flashes of light, and I shoved more of my rage and anger into the bullets, forcing them to spew out at a rapid speed. The harder I hit the barrier, the more I could see of it—like the bubble was being outlined by the shots—and it grew brighter and more visible with every additional bullet. I continued to hammer my shots into one spot, trying to find a weakness, and in response, Sage changed his angles, created pads to start leaping up and away through the darkness. I darted after him, bouncing through the darkness in pursuit of him, and continued to fire.

Finally, a crack started to form in the shield he was generating for himself, and I felt a dark seed of excitement humming through me as I continued to hammer my will into that spot, in the form of bullets. There was a sharp snapping sound, and a brilliant glow burst through the crack in a stream of pure white light. I could make out the orange lines of Jasper's code and see that they were trying to stitch the break together, and though I knew I could damage whatever was left of that code, I had to seize the opportunity. I fired, directly at that spot, and Sage cried out as the shot tore through his back and out of his chest.

He fell forward with a pained cry, one hand going out to catch himself, and I shot it out from under him, and then formed a floor beneath him to keep him from altering gravity and racing away from me again. He hit the ground with another gasp of pain, and then rolled over to face me, his hands already regenerating. I drew back my arm to stab him, but he rolled to the side and somehow managed to push off the ground until he was spinning to a stop on his feet.

"Really, Liana?" He sneered, beginning to grow as a long tube formed in his hands. "Is your imagination that limited?"

He hefted the tube over his shoulder in time for me to see a white light glimmering in the depths of it, and on impulse, I shot my gun at it, aiming for the center.

Sage hadn't been expecting that, and a second later he threw it away with a surprised yelp. There was a small amber explosion inside the tube, and Sage began to scramble away from it, indicating that he knew it was going to blow. I followed him, intent on not letting him out of my sight—and then the tube exploded, throwing us both up into the air.

I quickly centered my gravity and looked around, trying to locate Sage and go after him again. I spotted him thirty feet away, rising to his feet, and aimed my gun at him, intending to take him out.

"Liana!" Leo cried, his voice suddenly very close. "Look out!"

I caught a green flash of a toe from a massive foot from the corner of my eye and had only a fraction of a second to realize there was nothing I could do to stop it before it slammed into my side, sending me flying. The hit didn't hurt so much as stun me, and for several moments I couldn't move or think, every part of me going deathly still and locking up. I had no awareness of what was going on, and no ability to do anything except wait for control to be restored.

"Liana!" a voice cried sharply in my ear, and I opened my eyes, suddenly aware again. I was lying on my back, staring up at a purple dome overhead. I saw a shadow cross over it and come crashing down. I flinched as it impacted with a shudder, expecting the shield to shatter, but it didn't. Instead, an arm that I hadn't even known was draped across my chest tightened protectively, as if trying to shield me from harm. I opened my eyes again to see that my head was pillowed in Rose's lap. Her purple form was hunched over me as she tried to use every bit of her broken code to protect me.

CHAPTER 45

"Rose?" I called, wondering how the fragment AI's strength was holding up.

"I can't hold the shield for much longer!" she cried, and a second later, her code flickered in and out. Her eyes grew wide with alarm, but she was already moving. "Here!" she said as she slid her hand down to mine and shoved something into the palm of it. I looked down to see a small crimson orb glowing brightly. It was Tony—or whatever Sage had taken from him and been about to eat.

Rose pushed impatiently at my shoulder, and I sat up, still staring at the orb, confused at why she was giving me this. Did she expect me to swallow it like Sage had done with Jasper's? Because there was no way I was going to do that.

"What do you want me to do with this?" I demanded, shifting around to look at her, only to find her kneeling next to Scipio. I felt a momentary confusion, wondering how I had gotten back to them so quickly, and then realized Kurt's kick must've thrown me farther than I had thought possible, clearing me from the fight, and dismissed it as another odd feature of the datasphere.

I hadn't even realized that the AI was still here, but now that I knew, it was hard to look away. His code was spliced with a slick, oily blackness that ran alongside the bright blue lines, clearly corrupting him with its taint. As I watched, black lightning sparked from the inky rivulets and tore through his code, striking against the lines of blue, and he moaned and writhed in agony. His hands were pressed into his hair, clutching his head, and he was rocking back and forth in the fetal position, his eyes wide.

"Please," he moaned, staring up at Rose with open desperation. "I can't take it anymore. The pain.... The pain is too much. They're my responsibility, and I'm losing them! Let me die... please."

Rose's code flickered again as she reached out to touch his face, trying to smooth away the anguish there. "Shh. It's going to be okay. I'm going to help you."

Scipio gave a small sob and nodded jerkily. "Please, I'll do anything... Just make it stop. I can hear their voices crying for me to save them, but I can't... He won't let me!"

It was hard to watch the great machine begging like that, and on impulse, I reached out to take his hand, offering him comfort. Touching his code was gross, like sticking my hand in greasy water, but I held tight, trying to send him anything that would make him feel better.

"Liana," Rose said, catching my attention, and I glanced back up at her, frowning when I saw her putting her hand over Scipio's chest.

"What are you doing?"

"Taking out of Scipio what Sage stole from Jasper and tried to steal from Tony. Our source codes—our memory units. Sage took Jasper's against his will, but Tony, Scipio, and I are giving you ours freely. You'll need them, too; they have all the records of what Sage subjected us to, which will help you in this fight."

"What?" I asked, shaking my head as if to clear it from a punch. "I don't understand!"

"After I... kill Scipio, the New Day protocol will start," Rose continued, as if she hadn't heard me. "You'll have only a minute to eradicate Sage and Kurt's codes—like you did with Alice. If they kill you, their codes will merge and they'll be injected in the Core. If you don't kill them, and all four of you are combined, then the size of the AI you will create will overload the system and destroy the Core and AI forever."

Overwhelmed by her information, I was still sifting through everything she had just said, trying to find a starting place for my litany of questions, when she reached her hand

out to smooth over the lines of Scipio's face, staring down at him with a mixture of hopelessness and love.

"I'm sorry I didn't do a good enough job taking care of you," she told him, her voice quivering. "I wish I had protected you better."

Scipio's face softened, black tears pouring from his eyes. "You did what you could," he whimpered. "Please... just end this."

Rose nodded and put her hand over his chest.

"Wait," I said, trying to stop her from killing Scipio. I wasn't ready; she needed to wait until we had killed Sage and Kurt first. "Don't!"

But it was too late. Rose plunged her hand into Scipio's heart, and the AI released an unearthly note of pain and suffering, his anguish like a sonic boom throughout cyberspace. Cracks appeared in the dome, and then the force of his cry shattered it outward, the sound of his death knell blowing everyone but Rose and me back. I saw Leo's blue streaking away, tangled with Sage's white, and started to get up to go after him, but Rose's tired voice brought me up short.

"Liana, you have to take it," she said, and I turned back to where she was sitting, cradling Scipio's disintegrating form in her lap. Next to her sat a blue orb with crackling lines of black electricity rimming it. Her code flickered again, the distance between each blink growing shorter and shorter.

"I don't know what to do with it," I said, lifting the hand that already held Tony's orb.

Or rather, *had*. Because it was gone and had left in its stead a crimson glove that stretched up my arm in strange overlaying segments, forming blood-red armor over my skin. The individual plates were highlighted by my own amber code, and the entire thing felt smooth under my hands, and lighter than air. It was Tony—what was left of his code —protecting me from harm.

Rose gave a soft laugh that sounded like a bitter cry at the same time, and I turned to find Scipio gone, his code completely erased, and Rose already reaching into her own chest.

"Rose!" I exclaimed, my voice breaking in sorrow. I'd already lost her once today, and the tragedy of it was still fresh in my mind. "Please, I need you."

"No," she said weakly, her code beginning to flicker and pulse as her hand withdrew from the hole in her chest, a small purple pearl clutched between two fingers. "What you need is this: a record of what Sage did to us. We know how his mind works, and we can amplify your instincts with our own, to give you the best chance to stop him. Take it."

Behind us, I heard the thundering approach of Kurt, his massive steps causing the datasphere to ripple and pulse, but I imagined him far away, keeping the distance between us. I wouldn't be able to do it for long, but it was enough for now.

"You'll die."

"But a part of me will live on, in you. Take it, Liana. I know it's not very much, but I give it to you freely. We all do. Now hurry, because your time is slipping."

As she spoke, her code began flickering more and more, until the pearl slipped from her fingers, and she was gone. I stared at it for several seconds, and then picked it up, cradling it to my heart. A small surge of warmth flowed through my chest and then around it, then flew up my back and to my shoulder blades. The skin and bones on my back suddenly started to contort, elongating, stretching out, growing, and I glanced over my shoulder to see that a pair of lilac wings had sprouted from my back, taller than I was and filled with iridescent feathers.

I smiled when I realized Rose still literally had my back, and then bent over to pick up the orb with Scipio in it. I wasn't sure what I expected to happen, but a moment later there was a flash, and I was holding a massive blue sword wreathed in black lightning. It felt light as air as I experimentally swung it around, and I stared at it, suddenly renewed and filled with energy. I had been given protection from Tony, an advantage by Rose, and what I assumed was a deadly weapon, from Scipio. I was as ready as I was ever going to be.

I turned, and studied where Kurt was drawing closer, racing toward me. Every cut and blow that Leo had landed was already healed, his code perfectly intact. Alongside him streaked a white blur, which was avoiding the bolts of blue light being thrown by Leo. Sage looked perfectly intact again, his damage already healed up, and he was holding his own against Leo, dodging his blows easily. I knew he was trying to wear Leo down, and from the looks of things, he was succeeding. Leo's arms were moving slower and slower, his own code flickering as his energy flagged.

Frustration roiled through me as I realized this battle could drag on and on. If I went for Sage in an attempt to protect Leo, I might be able to surprise him once, but not enough to kill him. If I didn't manage to get the upper hand on him, Kurt would arrive to save him, and the cycle would begin all over again.

CHAPTER 45

I needed to be smarter, change my tactics.

Kurt's shape loomed closer. My ability to hold him at bay any further was deteriorating with the attention I was now devoting to the larger problem. His fifty-foot-tall form leapt in the air toward me, both feet lifted up in what could only be described as a purely stomping motion, and inspiration hit me.

I flexed my new wings, flapping them hard, and took off like a bullet, straight for the AI overhead, the blade held tightly in both hands. With my advanced reflexes, I calculated the timing exactly, and then slashed the blade up into the sole of his boot, cutting a bright hole in his code before diving through it, tucking both of my wings tightly around my body as I did.

Within moments I was shooting up through darkened space, using my wings to fly up through his leg and into his body. I was shamelessly inside his code, and not even hiding it, using my sword to cut apart any strand of code that was close enough for me to get at—trying to tear him apart from the inside out.

A slice of a particularly thick string of code suddenly revealed a bright green glow behind it, and I angled for it, knowing it was his source. If I could destroy it like I had Alice's, then Kurt would die, and Sage would be alone against Leo and me. I streaked toward it, Scipio's sword already pointed at it like an arrow, and flapped my wings harder, trying to get there faster. Lines of code rose up to entangle me as I flew, angling for the glowing ball of light, and I struck them down left and right, my arm and blade flying.

But one snaked past my defense, coiling a long line around my leg and jerking me to a halt. I slashed it quickly, but then two more replaced it, one around my free arm and the other around the opposite leg. Even more sickly green lines of code broke off the walls in an attempt to entangle me, and I realized this could be my last chance to act.

I didn't hesitate, tossing the blade up so I could catch it in a throwing hold. I willed the blade to become a spear, but I wasn't certain whether the source code of another AI would respond to me.

It worked perfectly. As I drew back to throw, the tip was already elongating, growing narrower and sharper, with a deep blue glow. I threw it before it was finished—and just before another green line of code caught me around the wing and shoulder. I ignored it, watching as the spear streaked toward the green globe, like a meteor hurtling through the atmosphere of an alien planet.

Several lines of code detached themselves from the wall to intercept it, drawing closer and closer to the spear, and I realized they were trying to stop it. What was more, I had no idea whether capturing it would mean that Kurt could also steal Scipio's source code from me. Fear made my skin hum violently, and to my surprise, the green lines of code holding me into place responded by slackening, as if my fear had transferred into them, overwhelming their purpose. I seized the advantage, twisting around violently to break them into fragments, and then gave a massive beat of my wings and shot off after the spear, lines of amber erupting from the gun I manifested in my hand.

There was a sharp burst of light before I could confirm that the spear had hit the green orb, and I lifted my hand to shield my eyes. I had no idea whether the spear was hitting Kurt's source code or Kurt's defenses had destroyed Scipio's weapon, but then I heard a deep rumbling, the sound of massive blocks of ice breaking, and I opened my eyes to see... the green orb, still intact.

My spirits plummeted, and I felt ashamed that I had missed once again, but then there was another sharp crack. A pulse of green energy rippled out from the orb, reminding me of a massive ripple in a pond, spreading outward. Dark cracks appeared in the surface of the orb a second later, as if someone had clenched it tightly in his fist and squeezed, and then chunks began to break off, moving slowly at first, and then faster and faster, as if the shockwave was dragging pieces of it away, like some sort of reverse comet.

A massive hunk of the debris hurtled right for me, and on impulse, I lifted my arms across my face, forming a shield that looked like the corner of a building, with a blade jutting from its center, seconds before it was going to hit. There was a great shearing sound as the mass of code slammed into the shield, kicking up sparks all around me and forcing me back. The hunk split in two, streaming all around me, but a quick glance told me that I was still in danger, now hurtling toward the wall of code that made up Kurt's skin.

I had no idea whether it was going to be as hard on the inside as it was on the outside, but I didn't hesitate, either.

Lifting my feet, I planted them on the shield and shifted my perspective of gravity until it was like I was standing on an elevator, hurtling toward the ceiling. I formed another plasma rifle in my hands, brought it up to my shoulder, and fired it before it was even formed, and to my surprise, the bolt was a blue orb wreathed in black lightning. It smashed through the wall of Kurt's code, and I leapt for the opening seconds before the remaining fragments of the orb shot through his chest.

I flapped my wings, shooting myself upward to avoid the debris as light spilled from Kurt's wounds. The AI sang his first and final note, and it was like the beating of drums coming to a slow and steady halt on one poignant note of rage, and then he exploded, his code hurtling into the datasphere and disappearing into the glittering darkness. Several pieces slammed into me, but Tony's armor kept me safe from harm.

I quickly scanned the datasphere, looking for any sign of Leo, and found him wrestling with Sage above me. The minute my eyes saw them, Sage kicked Leo viciously in the chest, and then reached out to grab him by his hair in the same way he had grabbed Tony.

Fire burned in my heart, and I snapped my wings out and flapped, imagining myself right next to him.

A fraction of a second later, I *was*, and before Sage could even lift his eyebrows in surprise, I drove a fist right into his face, sending the program flying. Leo fell back, still intact, and I ignored him to chase after Sage, a gun forming in my outstretched hand. I fired at him, the shots blue with black lightning, and he spun in an effort to miss them.

But the lines followed him—whether they were directed by my will or Scipio's, I didn't know—the first one catching him in his hip, the second in his shoulder, the third in his leg.

He cried out and fell, and I was on him a second later, tossing the gun aside to take my fists to his face. I pummeled him as we fell, my rage turning my fists into fire and brimstone, punishing him for stealing my friends' lives, my life, Grey's life, and everyone else's. He struggled, but his strength was waning.

We hit the ground a moment later, and I manifested a sword and drove it though his shoulder, pinning him to the ground like an insect.

"Wait!" he cried a second too late, and I smiled savagely at the choked sound of pain in his request. I manifested another sword while he writhed, and slammed that one into his other shoulder when he tried to use his good arm to free the first. "Stop! Please! We can do this... together! You and me! You can make sure I stay in line while—"

"No," I said, unwilling to hear any more of his drivel. "You and your so-called legacy die now-here, and forever." His eyes widened, pleading, but I felt nothing toward him except a deep sense of purpose. I plunged my hand into his chest, shoving through the outer shell of his coding and deep inside.

"NOOOOO!" he wailed, struggling against the swords pinning him to the ground, but I ignored it, my fingers searching for his source code. I found it a moment later, the humming on my skin intensifying as I came across something hard and grabbed it in my palm. Then I squeezed, using all the pain he had caused me to form a vice around it. I felt it snap and crack in my grip, but I didn't relent, the images of Dylan, my mother, Zoe, Maddox, Quess, Eric, Grey, and even myself flashing in front of my eyes. Then Rose, Tony, Scipio... even Kurt and Alice, whom he had corrupted against their purposes. Then his obsession with destroying Lionel Scipio's code—and how it had cost so many people their lives.

Sage opened his mouth to scream, but nothing came out except a bright white light, which was being expelled by an even brighter amber one, consuming every bit of his code until only his outline remained, and that was rapidly fading into oblivion.

I opened my fist to release the granules of sand I'd crushed his source code into, and released them, letting them evaporate into nothingness as well, then leaned back on my heels.

It was done. Sage was gone.

CHAPTER 45

As soon as it hit me, a sob caught me, the humming on my skin fragmenting and distorting in response to my pain. It was over, but at what cost? I'd lost everyone. All of my friends were dead, Grey and I were dead, and I was all that remained. A ghostly remnant of a girl who had done nothing but fail.

And I had failed. I'd failed them all. Rose, Jasper, Scipio, Tony... gone forever. As was everyone I had ever loved. A tide of grief slammed into me, and I bent over, pressing my face into my hands, as if I could contain the hurt behind a wall of my fingers. And there was no one else left for Leo to combine with, and I knew he couldn't do it with me. I was too impetuous to have the fate of the Tower resting on my decisions. At every turn, I had made wrong call after wrong call, and I was guaranteed to do it again. It was a flaw in my character, and it would be a flaw in my programming. It would corrupt Leo, influence him to make the wrong decisions, and the Tower would fail.

"Shhhhh," Leo said from behind me, and seconds later, I felt his hands smoothing over my shoulders and arms. "It's okay. It's all over. You won. We won. Soon, we'll be bonded, and—"

I shook my head, cutting him off. "You have to go without me," I said, knowing in my heart that I couldn't enter the Core with him. "Take Rose, Tony, and Scipio's source codes, and—"

"What?" he interrupted, coming around to face me, his expression incredulous. "What are you talking about? I'm not going anywhere without you."

"I'm not suitable for the Core, Leo," I told him tiredly, my heart sick. "Everyone's dead. Even Grey. Even... me. The real me. I got us all killed, and it's only through blind luck that we survived that fight! Those aren't good qualities for an AI; I'd make you impetuous and give you tunnel vision. My decisions never turn out right, and—"

"Shut up," he said softly, cutting me off.

I looked up at him, surprised that he'd even think to tell me to shut up, and found him already kneeling down in front of me. I opened my mouth to tell him off for dismissing me like that, but the fiery look in his eyes told me to keep my mouth shut and listen.

"I'm sorry that you've had to suffer so much these past few weeks.

It wasn't fair. It wasn't right. But without you, Sage and Kurt would've won. You've given Lionel Scipio's dream another chance, and I know, together, we can make something really beautiful. We can heal the Tower, make it strong and whole. We can tell the people the world beyond is habitable, and find ways to give them new lives, if they want it. What we want for the Tower is the same thing: we want its people happy, safe, and protected." He paused, and then reached up and cupped my cheek. "I know that you will never give up on that dream. I know you will always fight to keep me safe. And I know... that an eternity without you isn't one worth having. So call me a rotten bastard if you want, but I am absolutely prepared to turn my back on the Tower if you get all stubborn and refuse to come with me."

My jaw dropped, and I stared at him for several seconds, unsure of what to make of his sudden ultimatum. At first, I was angry that he would dare threaten the Tower like that, then suspicious, knowing that he actually wouldn't. A corner of his lip twitched a second later, and suddenly I smiled, knowing that he was joking.

At least, I was pretty sure he was. Honestly, it didn't matter; his words floored me, causing warmth to grow and swell in my chest, like my heart was an inflating balloon. Leo's eyes lighted on the smile, and a moment later, his mouth was pressing against mine, his hands holding me in place while he pillaged it.

My hair felt like it was standing on end from the electric current of the kiss, and I clung to him, wrapping my arms around his neck. Gravity shifted around us, and suddenly we were floating, spinning through the air, hurtling toward some unknown destination. My grip tightened on his code, my apprehension growing as we continued to move, and I broke the kiss, looking up in the direction we were heading.

A doorway made of white stood in the middle of the darkness, a prismatic aura surrounding it.

"What is it?" I asked, grabbing Leo's hand and holding it tightly.

"The next step," Leo replied, squeezing my palm reassuringly, sending me his love and confidence. "I love you, Liana. And I always will."

I looked over at him, trying to memorize his face before everything I knew changed once again, and smiled at the only person I had left, except for my brother. "I love you, too."

Then we were flying through the doorway, and I knew nothing.

46

"Wakey, wakey," a deep voice called from overhead, and my eyes snapped open, every fiber of my being instantly on alert. I was lying on the floor in what appeared to be the holographic projection room we had found in Lionel Scipio's office.

In fact, the holographic projection of Lionel Scipio was standing at my feet, leaning all of his weight onto the cane by his side. I sat up, instantly alarmed, and looked around for Leo. "Where is he?" I demanded. "Is this part of the test?" I paused, a dark fear suddenly gripping me. "Was I rejected from the Core?"

If I had been, then why was I here, with Lionel? He was supposed to be a monitoring and analysis program and had only interfered to fix the problem. Was there another problem that needed to be resolved?

"Not exactly," Lionel said carefully. "Your neural clone survived the simulation, and—"

"My neural what?" I exhaled, and then froze. My skin was no longer humming, and I could feel the steady rhythm of my heart in my chest. I reached up to touch my chest and confirm, and then did a double take of my hands. They were no longer glowing, my skin pale and white like it had always been. "What's going on?" I asked, my confusion only adding to my fear. "Where's Leo?"

"He's fine," Lionel said soothingly, kneeling down in front of me. "He's in the Core, with you. Or rather, with your neural clone. Liana, there's no easy way to tell you this, but everything you experienced after we met was a simulation."

"A simulation," I repeated, trying to wrap my head around what he was saying. "A simulation?" I asked again, not quite understanding.

Lionel nodded, his face pensive. "If we had done the process as Lionel originally designed it, your neural clone would've been separated from your active mind and put through the simulation. You never would've experienced any of the things the simulation forced her through."

I sat there for several seconds, trying to make sense of what he was saying. We had met after Tony had dragged me here, and after that I'd lost Dylan, Rose, Zoe, Quess, Eric, Maddox, Grey, Jasper, Rose, Tony, and Scipio. Their deaths had been so painful, so *real*.

And now he was telling me they weren't? Panic exploded through me as I realized that could mean the legacies were still loose in the Tower—and Sage's people were still gunning for Leo and Grey. I scrambled to my feet.

"I need to go," I said hurriedly. "I have to get to my friends! There's still time to save them!"

"Liana," Lionel said sharply, rising up to meet me. "Listen to me. You've been unconscious for five hours, but it only took your neural clone an hour to pass the test. I didn't anticipate how exhausted your body was, nor how low your electrolytes were when I initiated the New Day protocol, so it took you a while to recover. Longer than I expected, but long enough for the new AI to reassert control over the Tower. Your friends are fine."

I blinked at him several times, my urge to race off and save my friends warring with what he was saying. He had no reason to lie to me, but what he was telling me was wrong; my friends were in danger, and they'd been in danger the entire time. If I didn't get to them soon, they'd die, and I'd have to watch it happen all over again.

"I don't believe you," I said on an exhale, my hands curling into fists. "If I don't reach them, they'll die."

"I'm sorry the simulation forced you to witness that," Lionel said, meeting the urgency in my voice with remorse and compassion in his own. "It's... part of the process, to see how the neural clone can adapt in times of emergency. Grief is a powerful emotion that can make humans freeze up or break down. You'd be surprised how many neural clones were eliminated from the test after seeing their loved ones killed."

I trembled, the weight of what he was saying hitting me. If it was true, then his little test had forced me to watch everyone I loved die, one by one, all for a simulation! Everything I had experienced—the pain, the sorrow, the grief—all to see if I could keep going after that? It was torture—and torture of the cruelest design, because I could still remember every moment of it. I doubted I would ever forget.

"That was your test?!" I seethed. "You kill the people they love in front of them in order to see if they can still perform?! That's cruel. It's inhumane!"

His mouth curled downward in a frown. "I'm sorry you feel that way, but I didn't design the test. I only administered it."

I bit back an angry retort, knowing that he was just a fragment of Lionel's mind and personality and not the real thing, but it was in me to scream at him. I wondered if Leo had to go through this during his simulations and remembered that his simulation hadn't just taken place in the course of one hour, but over *months*. Suddenly I felt awful for everything they had put him and the other AIs through. The test I had experienced had to have been trivial compared to that.

And yet... I still couldn't seem to believe Lionel when it came to my friends. "You say that the power's back on?" I asked him.

He nodded. "All systems in the Tower have been restored to full power. There is some structural damage that needs to be addressed, as well as some problems in every server outside of the Core, but it's being worked on."

"The sentinels?"

"They all shut down when you burned out Alice's source code," he replied. "They still killed a lot of people, but you saved many more."

CHAPTER 46

I frowned. "I thought it was a simulation. How could what I did in there affect the real world?"

"An excellent question. There were a total of sixty-seven active alpha-series nets in the Tower when I activated the protocol. The amount of energy required to run independent simulations for each of them was too great for the system to handle, so the simulations were combined into one massive platform that picked up with what all of you were doing right before the protocol was enacted. Every action you took affected the other clones, and vice versa. The system populated the world using people that you knew so that you couldn't tell that it wasn't real, and then constructed a narrative from your goals that would be believable. Even your enemies had obstacles to surmount—the legacies in the Citadel had to overcome the defense of the Knights, and Sadie had to deal with finding Dinah, who was actively working to slow them down and disrupt their plans."

I frowned. "So then when I killed Sadie..."

"You just killed her neural clone. She's very much alive, and currently locked up in the cells under the Citadel, thanks to your Lieutenant, and AI counterpart. Things got a little strange once you reached the integration chamber. You knew you were going to die, but because you were aware of the New Day protocol and what it was going to do, you unintentionally copied your code, against the design of the system. That action destroyed the simulation and triggered a download of the remaining AIs and fragments into the integration chamber, which you saw as the datasphere. Everything that happened in there... it was real. The protections of the simulation were gone, but your psyche was there controlling your actions, learning what it was to be an AI. It was also exposed to everyone else who was there, and able to die just as easily. The servers in the integration chamber were never built to handle so much data, and I thought you would die within moments from an overload, but in microseconds, you stopped Kurt and Sage, and absorbed the source codes of three of the fragment AIs. So... technically you didn't *pass* the simulation. You destroyed it."

I stared at him. There was so much there to try to wrap my head around that I wasn't even sure where to begin. I had broken the simulation by copying myself? I had no idea how to do that! All I knew was that Lionel had told me to start the New Day protocol, and I had. Could it be... Had my assumption that I would become a neural clone caused me to not accept the death the simulation had chosen for me? Had my imagination overwhelmed the simulation?

From what Lionel was saying, it seemed as good a guess as any, but then... What had he said? What happened in the datasphere had become real—so when I killed Kurt, I had destroyed his entire code. The same with Alice, and... Sage? What did that mean? Had I killed him in real life, from floors and levels away, all through what was quintessentially a shared hallucination? That was the most far-fetched thing I had ever heard of, and I told him so.

"That's ridiculous."

He shrugged. "I think you'll reconsider that word choice after you see what you did to Sage. Oh, he's still alive, but he's nothing but a drooling vessel. You destroyed all vestiges of his personality."

"All I did was crush his source code!" I said in disbelief. "How did that—"

"The net," Lionel interrupted angrily, thumping his cane against the ground. "Your action triggered an energy surge that doubled back and translated through his net. The old man's brain is fried, and he'll be that way until he dies. Which won't be long." He sighed irritably and ran a hand over his face, before adding, "I'm sorry for getting frustrated. I already answered these questions for your neural clone, and she was every bit as belligerent and obstinate as you are now."

I blinked. "She was?"

He snorted. "As soon as your clone came into the system and realized that everything had been a simulation, she was fit to be tied. Luckily, she could use the Tower's cameras to confirm what I was saying, so she calmed down quickly enough to realize that there was still work to be done. She got in touch with Maddox, and after having to explain the situation a few times, finally convinced the woman to go on the attack. They got everyone." He paused for a satisfied chuckle, and then glanced at me.

I could only imagine how I appeared. I was rattled by what he was telling me, unable to emotionally separate myself from the things I had seen and experienced in the simulation. My heart ached with Zoe's loss, and even though he had assured me she was alive, I didn't quite believe it. I couldn't shake the memory of her in that bed, slowly bleeding to death.

"I need to call my friends," I said abruptly. "I'm sorry, but I just need to—"

"Check on them, yes," Lionel replied, nodding knowingly. "System requests visual connection to Cornelius's cameras in the war room, as well as an open channel."

For several seconds nothing happened, but Lionel didn't seem concerned by that, his expression mildly bored. Behind him, the wall suddenly flickered, and a screen appeared on it, revealing several angles of the war room in my quarters. I immediately spotted Zoe sitting in one of the chairs in the conference room, her head resting on Eric's massive shoulder, and her boots kicked off on the floor. Her mouth was partially open, and as I watched, a soft, sharp snore sounded through the speakers.

Tears spilled from my eyes, and I pressed both hands over my mouth to keep my cry of relief from getting out. They were all there—all perfectly alive and whole. Maddox was standing with Quess behind the desk, going over something on the computer, while Tian was lying on the floor in her usual Tian-like fashion, her legs resting on the wall. Liam was lying next to her in a more conventional way, but neither one of them was sleeping—they were talking. Chatting as if everything in the world hadn't fallen apart and then somehow put itself back together. The only person who wasn't still was Grey. He was prowling a circle around the room, his hands clutched tightly behind him.

I sobbed silently, the tangled web of unnecessary grief and relief leaving me weak and shaken. I was happy they were alive, grateful I hadn't lost them, yet scared at how real it had felt and how *close* I had come to losing them.

After I had taken several moments to let it all out, I quickly started to pull myself together, wanting—no, *needing*—to hear the sounds of their voices. It took a few shaky breaths, accompanied by several swipes of my finger under my eyes to sweep away the wetness, before I eventually managed to steady myself enough to say, "Hey, guys."

Several heads jerked up and looked around, searching for the source of my voice, and then Maddox pointed to one of the screens, where I could see the smallest image of myself.

"Liana!" Tian cried, and I watched her quickly scramble to her feet, race around the conference table, and launch herself up the stairs using her lashes, her patience at an end. Grey was a few steps behind her, walking at a fast pace, while Liam trailed behind them, his fists in his pockets. The only two who didn't move were Zoe and Eric—and that was because Zoe was still out like a light. I felt mildly annoyed at that, given that her simulated death had caused me so much pain and trauma, and then smiled to myself.

She was alive. She was breathing. I could get over her sleeping through this.

"Thank God you're okay," Maddox said, bringing my focus back to her. "I knew you were recovering from becoming an AI, but we were getting nervous. Your counterpart wasn't giving up your location because apparently coming out of the neural cloning process can be quite traumatizing, and too much stimulation could overwhelm you and cause you to suffer a psychotic break. After seeing Sage... I felt inclined to follow her lead."

It didn't take me long to figure out that she meant my neural clone, and it suddenly sank in that Liana—the other Liana—had already gotten to work cleaning up the mess that was left in the onslaught of Sage's plan. I wasn't sure how much she'd gotten done, but there was a way to find out.

"What all has... my counterpart been up to?" I asked.

"Let's see... She helped us track down every single legacy that got out when the cells opened up, notified all the departments that they pretty much need to find a new representative for the council, and had the sentinels dragged down to the furnaces in Cogstown and melted down. Oh, Lacey's fine, by the way. Dylan as well. Did you really make her climb the side of the Tower?"

I paused for a second, taking a moment to recall when that

happened in that timeline, and realized that we had started climbing in the real world before Tony threw us off the Tower, and she had obeyed my orders and continued up.

"What about Rose?" I asked. "She was in the sentinel."

"The sentinel lost power about an hour after you left Dylan," Grey replied for Maddox. He looked rough, his mouth turned down in a sad expression, his eyes filled with loss and pain. And I suddenly realized that Leo must've been uploaded at some point, against his will, which meant Grey had lost him suddenly, and without warning.

It suddenly hit me that I had, too, and I couldn't help but feel a crushing wave of despair slam into me. My friends were alive, but I *had* lost someone after all.

We both had.

I met Grey's eyes, and there was a flash of recognition there, and a slow darkening. "I'm all right," he said, before I could ask. "I... Leo's gone, Liana. I... I don't know what happened. One minute he was there, the next he was gone, and I..."

He faltered, and my heart broke all over again. Leo was gone. Both of us had lost him, and neither of us knew what it meant for the other. My spirits plummeted, but I forced myself to push it aside to deal with later. We didn't need to hash it out right then and there, and I was exhausted. Even sleeping for five hours hadn't done much to replenish me, and all I wanted to do was curl up in my bed and go to sleep. "We can talk about it later," I replied with a smile that I didn't quite feel, trying to reassure him that everything was okay. "I'll head up to the Citadel and see you all soon. Just... stay there, okay?"

Maddox frowned, clearly confused by my order to remain in the quarters, but she nodded. "See you soon."

The screen went blank a second later, and I released a heavy breath. In truth, I wasn't sure how to feel. My friends were alive, but the trauma at seeing them dying still lingered. I knew it would consume my nightmares for years to come, but what was worse was that it was a weight the AI version of me was going to have to carry as well. I wondered what it was going to be like interacting with her. Would she appear at council meetings by Leo's side? Would I have to watch them standing there together, and only reminisce that it used to be Leo and me like that?

It felt strange thinking of her as some interloper who had stolen my man away from me. She was *me*. The exact same person, only... without a body. Able to share something with Leo that I never could.

"How are you feeling?" Lionel asked from behind me, and I sighed heavily, shaking my head.

"I don't know," I replied honestly. "Tired, upset, emotionally drained... I can't seem to wrap my head around the fact that it's over. That nothing I experienced actually happened, and yet we still won."

"Some of what you experienced did translate through to the real world," Lionel pointed out. "But I can understand. I know you're tired, but someone wants to talk to you."

I turned in time to see his form flicker out, replaced by an amber glow that I recognized intimately—it was the color of my skin only a short time ago. It was weird watching the lines of my body form, like a mirror that drew me in to create suspense before I could see my final image.

I took a step back as the crimson armor formed over her, the purple wings behind her, and lifted an eyebrow, already concerned with her decisions to keep those as part of her permanent image. "You really think the citizens of the Tower are going to respond well to that?" I asked, giving her the onceover.

"The citizens of the Tower aren't going to know about me," she replied, folding her arms over her chest and lifting an eyebrow. "Leo and I talked it over, and we decided to keep my existence a secret from everyone except the council. In time the citizens might be able to handle the truth, but many of them are still too brainwashed by Sage's changes in the system over the years."

I pressed my lips together but had to give her credit. It was smart to restrict information like that, especially with the way things were currently. "It's a good idea," I agreed with a nod.

"I know it is," she replied dryly, and I couldn't help but smile. She was still me, but also not. It was so weird. "I'm here to talk to you about what comes next. For you."

CHAPTER 46

I frowned, giving her a wary look. "Are you firing me as Champion?"

The AI version of me snorted derisively and shook her head. "Not at all," she replied. "But... you have to know this is going to be really weird for all of us. Do you really want to go to council meetings and have to watch Leo and me working together, side by side? You never wanted to be Champion—it was just something thrust upon you through forces out of your own control. You have an out, if you want to take it. Leo's already told everyone that you single-handedly defeated Sage and Sadie's evil plot to destroy Scipio, so you could retire tomorrow, and everyone would understand."

I chuckled at that, and then shook my head. "I... I'm not sure what I want," I told her truthfully.

"Oh, you are. You just haven't had as much time as I have to think about it."

"You've only had five hours," I shot back tartly, not liking how she already seemed to know what I wanted. Sure, she was me, but that didn't mean she was able to read my mind.

"An eternity to a computer program," she replied, waving a hand dismissively. "Now, I think you can agree with me that this Tower is too small for the both of us. But, if you're willing to hear me out, I have a great idea for a new department that I think you'd be suited to take point on."

I stared at her for a second, both intrigued and a little frightened by the fact that my neural clone was already creating a whole new department. That was a little fast, and I had no idea what function another department could even serve in the Tower! Still, the questions the idea spun up in me were far more intriguing than the speed with which she was moving, and I took a step closer and gave her a considering look.

"What did you have in mind?" I asked, and she grinned.

EPILOGUE

ONE YEAR LATER

"Hey, Liana!" Quess shouted from behind me.

I turned from where I was inventorying supplies, lifting a hand to shield my eyes from the bright glare of the morning sun hitting Greenery 8's roof. The young man was walking over with another crate in his hands, but had a smaller white box on top and a very pleased grin on his face. "Morale Officer and Official Cheermeister of the Diplomacy Corp reporting for duty, with the first bit of good news of the day!"

Excitement thrummed through me as he looked at the small box, and I hurriedly stepped away from the stack of boxes to go to him. "Okay, one: Morale Officer, yes, but you are not introducing yourself as the Cheermeister to the Patrian delegation, or anyone, ever." Quess groaned in mock disappointment, but the smile on his face never wavered as we stopped in front of each other. "Two... is that the gift?"

"Sure is. Dinah says it contains every survey of the outside environment since the Tower's creation and historical events of note, as well as an assortment of what she coined 'cultural gems.' Think they'll like it?"

I grinned as I picked up the box and pulled open the lid, barely able to contain my pleasure when I saw the data crystal nestled in the center, glowing slightly. It had taken hours to persuade the council to give it up—one of the few things that they had argued with me about—and even though I had won, they might still try to convince me one more time that an air filtration system would be a better gift. They just couldn't see the value in passing along elements of our history or culture instead of a piece of technology that served a purpose. But I knew the environmental studies would give the Patrians some idea as to how to help us eradicate the radiation seeping into the area around the Tower, hopefully making it habitable again.

Which was why I took the crystal out of the box and slid it into the pocket of my purple uniform. I didn't want the council members changing their minds and taking it back, and was willing to steal it should they ask for its return.

It still felt weird looking down and seeing myself clad in purple. Years of wearing nothing but a Knight's crimsons made the new color stick out like a sore thumb, but I was getting used to it. As the leader of the newly formed Diplomacy Corp, I had to, because purple was the color Leo and Lily—which was what my AI counterpart was calling herself now—had chosen for us. My contribution had been the patches; each uniform had a patch on one arm that depicted the Tower, and was woven together using the colors of every department. It had been important to me to include it, as a symbol to the citizens that the Diplomacy Corp worked only in the best interest of *all* the people, no matter what department they came from. We took anyone who couldn't make it in the other departments and trained them to be explorers, ambassadors, scientists, historians, negotiators, investigators, councilors... The list was as long as my arm, because there was always some new niche role to fill.

The department's role in the Tower varied, but centered around one idea: how can we help the people have a better, more fulfilling life in the Tower? It took me a while, but I finally figured out that we could start by ensuring equity between departments. Whenever a Cog's transfer request was rejected from the Core and we suspected inter-departmental bias was a factor, they could come to us for an unbiased investigation into the issue. We would then submit our findings to Leo and Lily, so they could override or enforce the decision. Whenever a citizen felt that a Knight was ignoring their problem, they could come to us, and we would investigate that Knight, and said problem, on our own. Whenever an individual felt overwhelmed by their life inside the Tower, we would talk to them, and make them feel less alone.

But then the concept had grown. We had started hosting inter-departmental functions to help develop better relationships between Tower members, had advocated for non-uniformed clothes to be allowed back into the Tower so that the residents didn't have to wear their department's colors all the time, had negotiated territorial and labor disputes, held parties, and now had plans to start the very first inter-departmental sports competition.

But most importantly, we offered a place to anyone who didn't have one.

And today, our mission was finally going to expand *outside* of the Tower, in the first cross-cultural exchange between nations.

"I'm sure the Patrians will like it," I replied in answer to Quess's question. "And to be honest, I think the council is genuinely in love with this exchange idea, but they're too afraid to say it. They're all new to this, remember? With the exception of Lacey and myself, they've only been council members for a year."

Quess gave me a bemused look. "You've only been on the council for a few days longer than them, and you've changed positions to boot. I'm not sure you have a leg to stand on with that argument."

I shrugged, but he wasn't wrong—and sometimes I wished the other councilors would remember that I was every bit as inexperienced as they were at leading. But ever since they learned the new Scipio had half my personality in it, they seemed to constantly defer to my judgment, taking cues and advice from me alone. It was awkward, because I didn't always think the decision I was making was the best one, so I wound up having to parrot the phrase, "I don't know, what do you think?" when things got to be a little much.

It was half the reason I was so eager to leave; the members of the council needed to start forming opinions on their own, without my influence.

"Be that as it may, the exchange benefits all of us—the Tower and the Patrians. They'll get a better look into our lifestyle and culture, and we will do the same with theirs. Hopefully this will lead to trade, a peace treaty, and maybe even a mutual defense pact against whatever is happening in the South. Not to mention the training and observation programs and survival courses! We're going to gain a deeper understanding about each other's culture, the inner workings of our governments and societies, insight into who we are and what our goals are..." I trailed off, trying to find more reasons to sell my program to him, but he laughed good-naturedly.

"You know I'm good with this," he replied jovially. "We get to stay in a *house*. With doors that lead outside to the *ground*. Where we can pick a direction and keep walking forever!"

"Until you run into a lake or a mountain," came a masculine voice from behind me, and I turned to behold my twin. The last year of living with the Patrians had changed him, but only for the better. He seemed calmer. Though "reserved" was a better word to describe it, I thought. It had come from living and acting as the Tower's unofficial ambassador for the past year, and keeping the Patrians apprised of our situation until we got everything figured out. I knew it had been stressful for him—half the time, the council would tell him one thing, and then wind up changing it the next day, which drove him crazy—but he had made it work, and had grown into his own. It hadn't been easy living without him for the last year, only getting to see him during one of his debriefing missions, but after the second Requiem Day, we hadn't been sure what help we would need getting everything back online, and wanted to keep a line of communication open in case the power drain had caused one of the greeneries to fail. Starvation had been our primary concern, as the refrigeration had gone offline and spoiled most of our reserve crops and food, but we'd muddled through.

And then I had insisted we keep Alex in place, to begin working with the Patrians on a trade agreement.

Of course, that hadn't gone very far, due to the changes we were making in the Tower. The Patrians had wanted our system of government stabilized before they would sign an agreement, which made sense, but it took us a while to accomplish. People were obviously upset after what happened during the last Requiem Day, and wanted a lot of answers. We had told the citizens a watered-down version of the truth: that Sage and Sadie had tried to gain control over Scipio to rule the Tower. We *hadn't* revealed that Scipio as they had known him was dead. It was a big pill to swallow, and it would've been even worse if they had learned that an aspect of my personality had been combined with Scipio's, so we held that back as well.

But that meant collecting evidence and having hearings with witnesses, some of which had to be fabricated, which took time. Then I stepped down and started the Diplomacy Corp, which meant we had to wait for a new Champion...

The amount of time coupled with the odds and ends of putting everything together had been tiresome, to say the least, but had gone a long way toward fixing the damage Sage had done to the Tower. Getting rid of the expulsion chambers and overhauling the ranking system were among the first of the things we accomplished. After that, we'd had to decide what our goals should be, moving forward—whether we should find a new homeland and evacuate the population, or continue living in the Tower. It had been shocking to the newly elected councilors that the world wasn't as poorly off as they had been led to believe, but once they had accepted it, they were both scared of the prospect—and curious.

After all, the Tower had only been meant to protect us from the End, and carry us forward to a time when we could leave again. The pollution of the Tower was the only thing holding us back, since it meant the environment immediately outside was untenable, but the Patrians' flying vessels were able to carry us over that... to a place where we could be free.

Thankfully, the Patrians seemed to be ruled by patient and understanding people, because they gave us time to sort that all out, and continued working with Alex.

"Uh, I have eyes with which I can see," Quess said dryly, raising an eyebrow at my brother. "I think I'll be all right."

"You will be after the month-long wilderness survival training course the Patrians have been cooking up for you," my brother replied, not even missing a beat. "So until then, no wandering too far away from the compound where we'll be staying."

Quess opened his mouth to reply, but was cut off when another crate dropped down on top of his own.

"From your wife," Dylan said amicably from beside him, her crimson uniform looking pristine, the insignia of Champion resting on her lapel. After I'd resigned to form and lead the Diplomacy Corp, the Citadel had held another Tourney, and Dylan had won by a landslide. I had been relieved—not only because Dylan was more than qualified for the job, but because I'd found in her a capable ally on the council. "She told me that if you had air to talk, I was to pile on the work."

Quess groaned theatrically, his arms straining under the weight. "Yeah, sounds like Doxy. Where is she, by the way?"

"Distracting the rest of the council for me," I replied, motioning to Alex so we could help take the extra crate. "I didn't want them getting in the way while we moved things out of here. They're as nervous as you were on your wedding night."

"Hey!" Quess said, flushing bright red with embarrassment. "You promised we'd never talk about that!"

I laughed, and Dylan clapped a hand on his shoulder, giving him a little shake. "I don't know how to tell you this, Quess, but everyone knew."

We all laughed at that, even Quess. It was hard not to tease him; his wedding had been three weeks ago, and rushed to boot, as they had decided to get married after Zoe and Eric's ceremony six weeks before. It had all happened so quickly that I didn't think even Quess and Maddox fully understood what they were doing until the day of wedding, and then the panic had set in. Maddox had handled it better than Quess, to say the least, and it was still too fresh in our minds to keep us from teasing.

I think it helped that he and Maddox had never been happier, and I was just grateful that they were alive to be that happy.

The sudden memory of them dying—Quess's fearful voice as he was shut into that tube and Maddox's empty and vacant eyes—caught me unexpectedly, and I had to stop and take a deep breath, trying to push the images away. Lionel had said that the memories should fade, but they hadn't. Not really. I often had nightmares about them, waking up in a cold sweat and crying, forgetting for a second that they *weren't* dead and feeling that crushing despair all over again.

"Liana?" Quess asked, and I started, surprised to see him there. It took me a second to remember where I had been, but when I did, my cheeks heated with embarrassment.

"I'm sorry," I said, shaking my head. "I got lost in my thoughts. What were we talking about?"

Quess flashed me a sympathetic smile. All of my friends knew that I was having trouble recovering from the trauma of the simulation, but after a year of conversation, there wasn't much more for them to say or do but smile and nod. Not to mention, talking about how their deaths had made me feel wasn't exactly the easiest thing for them. Everyone tried their best, but I could tell it bothered them to think about, and they had eventually stopped bringing it up.

"We were talking about what happens after we spend six months with the Patrians," he informed me, setting down the crate he was carrying on top of the others I had been inventorying earlier. "I know there's something to all of these classes you and the Patrians have put together for us. Not to mention the joint military training operation we're going to do with their soldiers. Dylan won't tell me anything, but I know you've got something up your sleeve."

I pursed my lips to fight back a smile, and looked over at Dylan, silently asking for her approval. After all, this involved the Knights as well, as several from my former department would be joining our group. She raised a blond eyebrow, a small smirk playing on her own lips.

"Up to you," she said with a shrug. "Although, I'd say you should only tell them if they aren't going back into the Tower. The Patrians may be arriving any minute, but you're not slated to leave for another hour, and you know how gossip has a way of getting around."

She had a point, and one that I wasn't about to argue with. Because it was important that we keep the citizens of the Tower unaware of our real mission until we knew whether or not it was going to work. It had been hard enough to break the news of Patrus to them. Many had been frightened by the idea that we weren't alone, though they had adapted.

Hopefully, by the time we got back, they would be ready to adapt some more.

I looked at Quess and smiled. "Do you need to go back into the Tower for anything?"

"Nope," he replied with a grin. "Which means you can tell me."

My smile grew even wider. "I got the council's permission to start scouting out potential locations for a colony," I said. "The Patrians will be helping—as in, they've agreed to transport us and leave a few of their survival experts with us as guides. But beyond that, we'll be alone, camping under the stars, looking for a place that could become our new home."

Quess blinked in surprise and rocked back on his heels, considering the idea for a long moment. I had to admit, it had taken a long time to convince the council to look into the idea. It had been one of the few things we had clashed on. Many of them were hesitant to make any bigger decisions until after we had dismantled all of the laws that Sage had enacted over the years, but I didn't think that was the wisest choice. The individual worlds that had survived the End were growing and beginning to collide, and if we didn't get ahead of that, we would be at a serious disadvantage. We needed to carve out territory to create a wider defense, in case anyone who wanted to do us harm came knocking. The Tower was fortified, but anyone who came across us and got the idea to break in and take something from us could try it—and if they had enough support and firepower, the Tower would fall.

We needed to have a backup location ready and operational, in case the unthinkable happened.

Not to mention, it would take time for the land around the Tower to become fertile again. The toxins the Tower was pushing into the river had leached into the water table, making the landscape around us a desert. The Patrians were willing to help us clear it up using their own technology, but wanted us to dump our waste farther upriver from now on, to ensure that a unique area that served as one of *their* natural borders remained intact. If we wanted to take advantage of that technology, we needed to demonstrate to them that we were responsible and willing to take the steps necessary to better our world, and that meant first cleaning up the land around our Tower.

Besides, humans weren't meant to live within four walls for all eternity. We were meant to be explorers and pioneers. But Sage was right about one thing: the people in the Tower had forgotten that at some point, and were all the lesser for it. It was my hope that the Diplomacy Corp would help revive that ancient drive in them all. I knew that not everyone would want to go, but the colony wasn't supposed to be an evacuation, but rather an option for those who wanted to live outside the four walls of the Tower. Maybe in the generations to come, more and more of us would leave the Tower for the colony, until everyone was there—but that remained to be seen.

"That sounds... pretty freaking amazing," Quess finally declared, raking his hand through his hair. "I assume you've got a list of all the studies you plan to do, as well as an idea of where to look. We know the south is out, but what about the east or west... or even north!"

I laughed. His comments barely scratched the surface of what the council and I had thought up when I finally convinced them to just look at sites. We were only investigating to the west and east of the Tower, as we didn't want to squish the Patrians and Matrians between the Tower and the colony. The site needed a well or lake that provided enough water for everyone, and the land needed to be fertile, for farming. We needed an area of at least fifty square miles to start, but we were to make sure that we were at least two hundred miles from the nearest human settlements, so as not to start a war or appear to be invading anyone else. The list of requirements went on and on, but I wasn't bothered by them. Where anyone else might have seen restrictions, all I saw were possibilities.

"You'll have to wait and see," was all I said in reply. There was really no need for me to be cryptic, but I enjoyed yanking Quess's chain, and I couldn't pass up the opportunity.

"What?" he exclaimed, rising to the bait—just as I knew he would. "C'mon, Liana, you can't leave me hanging like this."

"I absolutely can," I replied with a wink. I started to add more, but paused when I saw Grey, Eric, and Zoe stepping through the door from the Tower, each of them carrying gear and supplies. I narrowed my eyes in irritation at the sight of my best friend hauling several bags on her shoulder. "And on that note, I need to go yell at a pregnant lady. Excuse me."

Quess, Alex, and Dylan let me go without too much hassle, knowing I took my responsibilities as godmother very seriously, and I sped over to where my three friends were walking toward us. "You better put those bags down right now," I ordered in a no-nonsense voice as soon as I was close enough.

"Pshaw," Zoe said with a laugh. "I'm only three weeks pregnant. I can still carry things!"

"No, you cannot," I said with a harrumph, drawing close enough to grab one of the bags she was carrying and throw it over my shoulder. I went for the others, but she quickly stepped out of reach, a teasing smile playing on her lips. "That's my little godchild in there, and you are keeping him or her safe no matter what!" I said indignantly, after several failed attempts to catch her and take the bags. "That means no jumping, no eating fish, and *definitely* no carrying heavy bags of crap. It's bad enough that you're coming with us instead of staying here where the doctors can keep an eye on you, so I'm not tolerating any argument on this. The bags. Please."

Zoe snorted and rolled her eyes, but stopped moving to hand the remaining bags over. "Liana, you're worse than my mother, mother-in-law, and Eric combined! I'm fine. The baby is fine. And the Patrians have been having babies for centuries, so I'm sure they can handle all of my medical needs. But you better be damned sure I'm not missing out on this. It's too historic for me not to go."

I sighed heavily, as if giving in to her argument, but inside I was secretly pleased. When Zoe had told me she was pregnant, I was concerned that she wouldn't be able to join us. Which sucked, not only because she was my best friend, but also because she was the lead Cog on the mission, and was going with us to work with the Patrian engineers on how to optimize their recycling systems, and to study their filtration devices. She'd been training for three months to go on this mission, and when she'd discovered she was pregnant, I'd been certain I was going to have to replace her.

But Zoe, being Zoe, had refused to allow it, much to my pleasure and relief. It didn't mean I was taking her with us when we went to look for the colony, though. She'd be three months pregnant at that point, and we'd be roughing it, so she and Eric would be heading back with the others who chose to return to the Tower.

Not that I'd told her that yet. But I was certain Eric would back me up on that decision. He wasn't happy about her going in the first place, so I was betting he'd be on board when I did eventually bring it up.

"I'm not sorry for being overprotective," I told her, shouldering the bags and turning back to the others. "But I am sorry if it's driving you crazy."

She smiled at me, her eyes glistening with humor and love. "It is, but in the best possible way. Still... Grey, tell your woman to back off, or I'll make her the epicenter of every one of my hormonally driven outbursts."

Grey gave her an arch look. "If you think I have any control over what Liana Castell does, you have severely overestimated my power in this relationship."

I gaped at him, appalled that he would insinuate that I was in charge of our relationship, but it quickly faded to good humor when I saw the teasing glint in his eyes. "Hey, you said you liked your women independent," I replied tartly. "This is the price you pay."

"Oh, get a room." Zoe snorted, before grabbing Eric's hand and marching past us. My cheeks flushed, but I knew her jab was well meant, and I appreciated her and Eric leaving. I'd been so busy the last month that I'd barely gotten to spend any time with Grey beyond climbing into bed next to him and passing out. The amount of planning and coordination that had gone into this had been massive, and the responsibilities had only grown the closer we had gotten to our departure date. As it was, I hadn't returned to our quarters last night until almost four, and then had taken a shower and put on fresh clothes instead of trying to get any rest.

All the time apart was putting a definite strain on our relationship—when it had only just started to become comfortable again. When Leo left, we'd both had a hard time coping with it. I had lost someone I loved, and he had lost someone who understood him better than he understood himself. More than that, Leo's personality had rubbed off on Grey in more ways than I could count—in his mannerisms and speech, right down to the gestures he made when he spoke. He was still Grey, but there was an undercurrent of Leo that was there, stamped all over him.

Which also made it hard. It was hard looking at him and not seeing Leo in everything that he did. Sometimes when he smiled, or looked surprised, my heart would break from the loss, and I would start to cry uncontrollably. It was like Leo had died, and even though I knew he hadn't, he might as well have. I couldn't be with him—not just because he was essentially with my AI clone, but because he had to stay in the Core forever. If I saw him again, I'd never be able to touch him, or kiss him, or have him hold me.

And since I had experienced those things when he had been in Grey's body, Grey being there only served to remind me of what I had lost, which had made it so much harder. Not just for me, but for him as well. He had come to rely on Leo's presence in so many innumerable ways, so being without him made Grey feel lost, and confused about his place in everything, making him insecure and uncertain. And my outbursts over another man didn't help.

So we'd taken some time apart. He'd take any diplomacy work that came up that would keep him away for weeks at a time, and I buried myself in my work, trying to distract myself. I wasn't sure how Grey fared during that time, but I hadn't done well. I'd missed him almost instantly, and known that by pushing him away, I had probably lost him, too.

But I didn't know what to do about it, and fell into a deep depression.

Surprisingly enough, it had been Lacey who had helped me through it. The head of the Cogs had sensed my bleak turn, and interceded. It took a while for her to convince me to open up, but she got it out of me, bit by bit, until I was crying on her shoulder.

Saving her life had clearly made her more empathetic toward me, because she'd held me through it all, and listened without reservation or judgment. I talked to her about everything, from Grey to the nightmares I still had about the things I had seen in the simulation, and she'd heard me. She helped me, if I was perfectly honest about it. I had finally earned her respect, and all it took was saving her life and the Tower.

After a while, I felt good enough to have a conversation with Leo. He had kept a respectful distance from me, and let me know he was there if I ever needed to talk, and I eventually took him up on it. It had been hard, and I was sure the conversation would be burned into my memory forever.

"Hey," Leo said softly from behind me, and I froze for half a second, my eyes already beginning to feel the pinprick of tears before I blinked them back. This conversation was going to be hard enough without me getting all weepy. I turned away from one of the bookcases I had been staring at to see Leo standing there, leaning against Lionel Scipio's desk, his hands shoved into his pockets.

I had chosen the location. It seemed fitting to say goodbye in the same place we had met, even if it was metaphorical. "Hey," I replied, trying to keep the flood of emotions that filled me from reaching my voice. Seeing him felt like coming home, and all I wanted to do was throw myself into his arms and beg him to figure out a way that we could be together.

But I couldn't do that. Leo's coding was tied to Lily's, and there was no differentiating where he ended and she began.

The corner of Leo's lip twitched, and for several seconds, both of us were silent. I wasn't sure whether he was waiting for me to speak, or was just as uncertain as I was on what to say next, but it grew awkward. I opened my mouth to fill the space, when he suddenly blurted out, "I miss you."

My mouth hung open for several seconds, and then I slowly drew it closed and swallowed down my heart, the flood of emotions with which those three simple words filled me threatening to break down my control. I looked away for a few seconds, needing something else to focus on, and took in a shaky breath. "I miss you, too."

I darted a quick glance up to him, and saw him looking at me with remorse. "I would've copied myself to Grey," he told me, his eyes pleading for understanding. "But the nets can't do that."

I nodded my head. "I know," I replied, my voice coming out high and tight. "I do." I hesitated, and then asked the one question I had been wondering about since the simulation. "Did you... Did you know what was happening in the datasphere?"

Leo hesitated, and then nodded. "Yes," he replied simply, and a wave of hurt and recrimination crashed down on me. Why hadn't he warned me what was coming? Why couldn't he have told me that I was about to lose him? I opened my mouth, intent on asking him just that, when he added, "And I am so sorry that I didn't tell you. Honestly, I thought we'd have more time after the fight was over, but the protocols took over, and..."

I held up my hand to stop him. I didn't need to hear any more, and besides, it didn't matter. What was done, was done, and I wasn't here to cast blame. I was here to try to get better.

"It's okay," I said. "We did the best we could under some pretty unusual circumstances. I know that this isn't how you wanted things to be either. And I'm pretty sure you would've liked to talk to me sooner."

He shook his head slowly. "No, not at all. It hasn't been easy on any of us."

I nodded in agreement, and then sighed, searching for a way to try to make this conversation more positive. So far, all it was doing was making me want to cry, and I was here to move past that. "Maybe not, but it's been good for the Tower. You and Lily, I mean. You guys have done an amazing job altering the laws in the Tower and selling it to the citizens. The speech you gave about the ranking system and dismantling it was—"

"Thank you," he said, ducking his head. His hologram didn't show his cheeks blushing, but I could tell that he was embarrassed by my praise. I couldn't understand why. He'd made it clear, in no uncertain terms, that rank was no longer to be a reflection of the service anyone performed to the Tower, but rather an indication of their happiness, as it was always meant to be. Eventually, we'd get around to dismantling them completely and destroying the indicators, but people were still too reliant on them to eradicate the system completely. Until then, rank discrimination was not going to be tolerated. "It's really you who has done something amazing. The Diplomacy Corp is a rousing success. The people you've collected are showing an uptick of their rank within a few months of joining, and the amount of work everyone has put in to foster inter-departmental relations has been—"

"Thank you," I said. It was my turn to be embarrassed. I hadn't been fishing for a compliment, and honestly, hearing them from him only hurt, only reminded me how much time we hadn't gotten to spend together. I licked my lips and looked around the room for a second, trying to find the right words to convey everything I had felt since we had last seen each other. How I regretted that I hadn't gotten to kiss him goodbye, and how I missed his arms around me, making me feel safe. How I longed for his voice in our meetings, or how I still dreamed about him from time to time.

"Liana, if I had the power to go back in time and spare you this pain, I would do it in a nanosecond," Leo said, jerking my attention back to him. "I'm sorry I even put you in that position. I knew there was a chance that I would have to replace Scipio, but I still pursued you."

I felt a dull throb of anger. "Don't say that," I said, shaking my head. "I loved what we had together, once I finally got around to accepting it, and I wouldn't change it for the world. Except for maybe the ending, of course, but as you pointed out, there's nothing we can do about that. I'm here to talk about what comes next. How we can move forward and... let go."

Leo stared at me for a second, his eyes deep and unfathomable. "Of course," he replied with a nod, a small quirk of his lips turning into a smile. "What did you have in mind?"

"I'm going to go with the delegation to Patrus when we finally get it all arranged," I informed him at last. "And I might extend my trip there for a while. I think it will be good to get some space from everything. You and Lily need time to... to come to terms with everything too, and having me around as a constant reminder isn't helping."

"Liana, you don't have to go," Leo said, straightening up. "You're the head of your department. Your duty is here."

I smiled and shook my head. "Then I'll resign. Leo, this isn't going to work until we both have time and, more importantly, space from each other. I can't get that as a councilor. I see you and Lily every week, for crying out loud! I've tried to get past it, but it hurts, and I can't help it. It doesn't matter that she's me. I still kind of hate her."

Leo stared at me for a second, and then smiled ruefully. "She says the same thing about you."

I stared at him for a second, and then rolled my eyes, a soft chuckle escaping me. Of course she did. "So then you get it. This is what needs to happen, not just for us personally, but so your program and hers can really come together, if that makes any sense."

Leo ran a hand through his hair and then sighed. "I guess... maybe you're right. Maybe it is better this way, but, dammit, Liana, I don't want you to go. It's dangerous out there!"

I smiled, but it was bittersweet. I could hear the love pouring out of him, making his concern for me more intense than for the average citizen, and while I ached to go to him, I remained where I was. "You see what I mean? You're still too emotionally invested in me, Leo. You have to learn how to treat me like any other citizen of the Tower, and I have to accept that you'll never be mine. Time. Space. We need it."

Leo's jaw tightened for a second, and I could sense he still wanted to fight, but a second later, he sighed, his shoulders slumping. "You're right. I know you're right, I just... I hate it. I hate this, and I hate—"

"No more hate," I instructed him, taking a step closer. "It's exhausting and accomplishes nothing. Just... give me your permission to go, when it comes up in the council meeting."

Leo closed his mouth slowly. "Of course," he said sadly. "Anything you want. I just think you should know that no matter what happens, there will always be a part of me that loves you. It will never go away, no matter how much time and space we take."

This time I couldn't hold the tears back, and my vision grew blurry around the edges. I wasn't crying—more like seeping—but still. His words both stung, and filled me with a warmth I had no way of stopping. "I know," I said honestly.

"And you should know that I'll always feel the same way. But this is for the best."

He smiled sadly, but accepted it with a nod. "Yes. Good luck on your adventures, Liana. Please... be safe."

"You too," I replied, feeling like there was a deeper context to our words that no one but the two of us could understand, one filled with love, remorse, understanding, and underneath it all—a sad farewell. I turned to leave, and managed to make it all the way outside before I had to stop and cry. But it was a good cry, even if it didn't feel like it at the time.

After that, I threw myself back into my work with full force, trying to make sure the Patrus agreement didn't fall apart. It helped, and even though I hadn't left yet, I began to start hurting less, and finally began letting myself heal.

Grey and I had kept our distance until about seven months ago, when we bumped into each other at Quess's first attempt at an interdepartmental function. Barely anybody from the other departments had come, but the Diplomacy Corp had made our own fun, anyway. The night had started off awkward, but somehow, Grey and I had managed to fall into a rhythm like the one we'd had before all this craziness had started, and it was both familiar and new all at the same time. We spent half the night talking about the future, discussing other problems that were cropping up in the wake of all the changes, and then the other half talking about us.

It was nice. It was grown-up. It was mature.

And it had taken many more conversations, coupled with several outings, before we finally agreed to give it another try.

Now he and I stood staring at each other for a second, and then he tossed down the items he was carrying with a loud thump and held his arms out to me. I went to him immediately, letting him envelop me, and took a deep breath, inhaling his spicy scent.

"How you holding up?" he asked, resting his chin on the top of my head.

"Good," I replied. "Tired, but good. Thank you for being so understanding."

"Yeah, well, I plan for you to make it up to me by sleeping in with me for the first week we're in Patrus," he replied, smoothing a hand over my hair and shoulders. "You've been running yourself ragged trying to get this whole thing together, and while I know it's very important to you that this exchange succeeds, it's important to me that you're taking care of yourself. And since you're incapable of doing even that, it's up to me to make sure you do."

I chuckled, and pulled my head away from his chest to look at him, something in his voice making me suspicious. "What are you up to?"

"Me?" he asked in mock innocence. "Oh, nothing..."

My eyes narrowed, but I was already smiling, knowing that whatever Grey had up his sleeve, it would be magical. He was good at creating little moments for us to enjoy together.

"Grey," I said after several seconds, when my glare had failed to get him to talk more. "What did you do?"

"He called me up in the middle of the night and got me to ask the Patrians for a small place for the two of you to spend a week alone," my twin supplied, and I turned in Grey's arms to see that Alex had walked over from the pile of gear on the roof to join us. For what, I wasn't sure, but I was too interested in the answer to ask right that second.

"A small place to spend a week alone?" I asked, turning back to Grey.

He was glaring at Alex like he would happily toss my brother off the Tower, but he replied to my question anyway. "Like I said, you've been running yourself ragged. Since I know you won't take the time off for yourself, I arranged it for you. Besides, you and I have been putting off some relationship conversations, and I've been patient, but that patience is coming to an end."

Oh boy.

It was no secret Grey wanted to marry me. He'd already asked me once, but it had been at Zoe and Eric's wedding, and I had been so sure he'd just been caught up in the moment that I'd laughed it off and called him crazy. That hadn't gone over well, but we'd talked the misunderstanding out, and been all the better for it.

Except he hadn't asked me to marry him again.

Now I felt certain that he was going to use this week he had planned to do it, and I suddenly couldn't wait to get there. "It sounds amazing," I told him, going up to my tiptoes to plant a light kiss on his lips before turning back to my brother. "Did you need something?"

"No, but I wanted to give you a heads-up that Thomas and Melissa are five minutes out. Quess already netted Doxy so the council members can be here for the official meeting, so... just get ready for all the pomp and circumstance, I guess."

I grinned. It was the one part of our roles that he hated, but I had loved putting together. We had created our first cross-cultural welcoming ceremony, and I was eager to see what the Patrians thought about what I had come up with. I hoped that the ceremony and speech would make them feel welcome and comfortable, if it was possible for an event to do such a thing, but that remained to be seen. "Thanks," I told him. "I'll be right over."

He flashed me a thumbs-up as he moved to return to the others, and I turned back to Grey, a warm glow forming in my chest. "You're going to ask me to marry you again, aren't you?" I asked, suddenly too impatient to wait for our time alone together to confirm it.

He opened his mouth to reply, and then closed it again with a soft click of his teeth. "I'm not saying," he taunted, but I knew I was right. He *was* planning to ask me again.

And this time, I'd get it right and say yes.

I placed my head back on his shoulder and closed my eyes, letting myself imagine what the next six months would hold. I was excited and nervous, but the future of the Tower had never looked so bright, and I was just grateful that I had people I loved around me, helping me, supporting my dream for the Tower's future. This moment had been everything I had been fighting for, and now that it was here, I couldn't be happier.

Because now, we could finally start a new chapter. One that began with: After the Tower.

WHAT'S NEXT?

Dear Reader,

Thank you for accompanying Liana through to the end of her journey, and I hope you enjoyed the grand finale.

Leaving behind the Tower and its residents is emotional and bittersweet, but I'm happy about where I've left the characters.

I'm also very excited about my next dystopian story!: **The Child Thief**, releasing **June 11th 2018**.

I've included the first two chapters of *The Child Thief* at the back of this ebook, as a special bonus sneak peek, so keep turning the pages to read them!

WHAT'S NEXT?

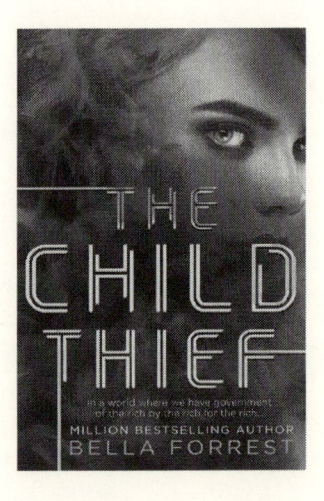

Pre-order the book now for your convenience, to have it delivered automatically on release day:

Visit: www.bellaforrest.net for details.

BONUS CHAPTERS

THE CHILD THIEF

Blurb:

In a world where we have government of the rich by the rich for the rich...

America in 2105 is beset with mass inequality, poverty and increasingly large numbers of the poor. This, combined with the breakdown of families and marriages has led to huge economic and societal burdens.

A fractured and divided America ushers in an authoritarian government that promises to solve all these problems in one stroke with a radical solution.

Welcome to the CRAS: the Child Redistribution Adoption System. Also known as the cure for America's failing economy... and the bane of nineteen-year-old Robin Sylvone's existence.

Under the System, not all parents can expect to keep the children they bring into the world: families who are not self-sustaining have their children taken and given to the rich.

And as a single teen mother, Robin fell within the scope of the scheme and lost her baby two years ago.

After being forced to drop out of school and become a factory worker in order to support herself, she doesn't see much light in her future—or hold any hope of seeing her child again.

Until she stumbles upon a group of misfits who share her frustrations and desire for change. An underground movement that operates in some rather clever yet unconventional ways...

By day they still call me Robin Sylvone. Factory worker and upper class reject.

But now, by night, they call me Robin Hood...

Brimming with action, mystery and romance, fans of *The Girl Who Dared to Think* will be gripped by this imaginative thrill-ride through a chillingly warped America.

PROLOGUE

I stood frozen outside my parents' bedroom.

Staring at the door handle, I tightened my grip around the breakfast tray I had prepared. I could hear the murmuring of the television seeping through the cracks of the closed door, and I wished I didn't feel so nervous. I wished today was just like any other day I treated them to breakfast in bed... But it wasn't.

I had news to share with them this morning. News unlike any I had ever shared before.

And although I had known them for sixteen years and ten months of my seventeen years of living, I feared how they were going to react. They had always treated me as if I were their own child, ever since the day the Ministry of Welfare took me from my birth parents and assigned me to them.

But this... This was big.

I tried to convince myself that everything would be okay. They loved me, didn't they? They wanted me to be happy, right? They had always said so, and yet, with this, I feared I had gone too far.

Still, I drew in a deep breath and moved closer to the door. I had delayed this for long enough already. It was time to come out with the truth.

God knew I couldn't wait longer than a couple more months, even if I wanted to.

I repositioned the tray against my hip to free up one hand and then knocked boldly, thrice, with more confidence than I felt.

"Come in," my mother's musical voice chimed through the cracks.

Swallowing, I gripped the handle and opened the door, then entered with the tray.

My parents were in bed. My mother, forty-five years young, a beautiful woman with long, dyed blond hair and eyes the color of a clear sky, had been watching the television, while my father, a tall, bald man of forty-nine with swarthy skin and a strong black goatee, was holding a newspaper in front of him. Even lying in bed, he exuded the confidence of one of the most important people in the United Nation of America: a governor, whose moral high grounds were as high as they came.

"Oh, thank you, darling. What a treat!" my mother cooed as I approached her side of the bed. I set the tray down in between the two of them, then tucked my hands behind my back and stepped backward.

"Thank you, Robin," my father murmured, lowering the paper momentarily to pick up his coffee and a piece of toast.

I nodded and tried to smile back, but it felt like I was wearing one of my mother's solidifying masks.

As they began eating, my toes curled over the silken rug, and I allowed my eyes to wander to the television screen, unable to resist the temptation of procrastinating a few minutes longer.

"—latest report from the Ministry of Welfare was released this morning. Divorce rates are steady at 79 percent—a slight improvement from 2102—while the number of children born out of wedlock remains at 56 percent of the total number of children born. Government savings are up, thanks to continued implementation of the CRAS, while adoption admin fees continue to improve living conditions for low-income families nationwide. The CRAS has saved the UNA trillions in child welfare and foster services since the system's introduction by President Burchard after the Crisis in 2082—"

"You sleep well, hon?" my mother interrupted around a mouthful of fruit.

And I was glad for the interruption, as the current news topic was doing nothing to help my nerves.

"Yes," I lied.

"Are any of your siblings awake yet?" she asked.

"Um, I think I heard Joseph and Lora. I'm not sure about anyone else." The last thing I'd thought to do this morning was check on any of my seven younger siblings—not when we had two full-time nannies caring for them.

"It's going to be a gorgeous day, by the looks of it." My mother sighed, glancing toward the sunshine streaming in through the wide French windowpanes. "You want to take the dogs for a walk?"

"Um, yes. Sure. I just..." I cleared my throat, forcing myself to look from one parent to the other. I inhaled slowly. "Mom, Dad... There's something I've been meaning to tell you."

They both paused in their eating, their eyes moving to me.

"What is it?" my mother asked, while my father raised a dark eyebrow.

A surge of blood rose to my face, and I suddenly felt too hot, even with the cool breeze wafting in through the window. I balled my fists together, trying to take a deep breath through my constricting throat. And then I closed my eyes and let it out.

"I met a boy last year at summer camp. We... We've kept in touch ever since. He's the reason I've been coming home late from school on some days, recently. I was going to tell you about him sooner, but... one thing just led to another, and I just... didn't. I wish I had told you sooner now, though, because... things got a bit out of hand. I never planned for this, but... I'm pregnant."

It felt like I could have dropped a pin onto the mahogany floorboards and heard it even over the television. My parents stared at me, their jaws slack.

"What?" My mother finally found her voice, her fingers quickly moving to the remote to switch the television off. She gave a nervous laugh. "I'm sorry, Robin. Is this some kind of late April Fool's?"

I shook my head. "It's not," I croaked.

She gaped at me, stunned, while my father maintained his shocked silence.

I was most fearful about what *he* was going to say, and I was so desperate not to be one of the statistics I knew he so disapproved of—which was why I'd waited for Henry to propose before telling them. I'd thought he would... but he still hadn't.

And I just couldn't hide my pregnancy from my parents any longer.

I knew this was a big thing to ask my father to accept. Governors of the Burchard Regime were expected to have the highest moral standards, to be paragons of virtue that set an example for the rest of our lax society. And their families were considered reflections of themselves, their ability to influence and infuse good behavior in others—which, in my father's eyes, was ultimately what defined a true leader.

If he couldn't even keep his own family in check, what did that say about him? He'd be gossiped about, and even if nobody said anything to his face, he'd be subtly looked down upon in his social circles.

I knew the consequences, and I felt bad for letting him down, but what was done was done.

His affection for me just had to be strong enough for him to swallow his pride and accept the situation. I had to believe it. Because I had a baby on the way, and a man I was deeply in love with.

If he didn't accept it, he could ruin everything.

"Who is this boy?" my father asked, dropping the food and cup in his hands onto the breakfast tray and rising to his feet. The bedcovers slipped off him, revealing his full, tall, broad frame, the muscles in his arms visible even beneath his nightshirt.

I hesitated, then glanced toward the door. "Henry," I called softly, and a moment later my boyfriend stepped tentatively through the doorway. His normally tan complexion looked pale as he laid his deep brown eyes on my parents, his handsome face a mask of tension.

At least he had offered to come meet them today. I'd let him in through the back door first thing this morning, and hoped it would help soften the blow of what we had done once they saw that he was a sweet guy. Marriage was a big step for anyone, and while I wished we had come to my parents with news of our engagement, I loved Henry too much to pressure him into it.

"Good to meet you, Mr. and Mrs. Sylvone," he said tightly.

Silence reigned once more over the room, as both of my parents glared at him. It occurred to me then that inviting him into their bedroom might not have been the most sensitive move.

"Henry's eighteen," I said, desperate to break the quiet, "and he works part time at the camp during the summer. He lives on the Meadfield Estate."

My father's gaze darkened as he exchanged a glance with my mother, and I looked anxiously at Henry. He came from a humble background compared to me—very humble, in fact. He'd dropped out of school at sixteen to work in the factories and help his parents pay to keep his two younger siblings, and while that shouldn't be an impediment to us being together, I knew it had to be playing on my father's mind. I was sure he'd had the son of one of his governor friends in mind for me, although he'd never come out and said it.

There would be little to no financial support for our child coming from Henry's side, but that didn't have to be a problem, because my parents had no shortage of money to support an extra child. Hell, they'd been talking about hiring another nanny and doing another adoption recently anyway.

We could pull this off easily. *If* my father could accept the situation for the sake of his grandchild.

The pause that stretched between us seemed endless, as my father turned his back on us and faced the window. His broad shoulders rose and fell as he took deep breaths, and I feared it was all he could do to keep himself from exploding.

I'd borne the brunt of his temper before, over the years, when I did something to irk him. But I'd never done anything like this. I knew how strongly he was against intimacy outside of marriage. He'd told me time and time again.

Still, I couldn't help but feel that sometimes you just couldn't plan love. And since contraceptives had been banned before I was born, situations like mine were hardly uncommon.

But they are uncommon within governors' families, a small voice in my head reminded me. *They train their children well.*

It was true that I didn't know anyone within my social circle who'd been in my position. Which was why I was so nervous about this. Even now that I'd told them, I still didn't know how this was going to go down.

I looked to my mother, but her expression was stoic, unreadable, as she watched my father's back. She was avoiding looking at me, waiting for my father's reaction.

"I'm sorry, Robin," my father said finally, heaving a sigh and turning back around. "We welcomed you into our family with open arms, raised you as our own. But this... this I cannot, in good conscience, sustain. Your stay here is over. You must leave."

I gaped at him. I had feared this would go badly. I'd expected some sort of punishment for my indiscretion. But *leaving*?

My voice choked up and I looked to my mother again, but she was still avoiding eye contact.

"B-But Dad," I gasped. "What do you mean, *leave*? Wh-Where will I go?"

I had not a cent to my name. Everything I owned, including the clothes on my back, belonged to my parents. *Leave?* It was... It was absurd.

I... I was pregnant. This was my home.

Tears flooded my eyes as a surge of panic took hold of me. This couldn't be happening. I had to get him to see reason.

"Sir," Henry spoke up, before I could attempt anything. He had gone pale as a sheet and his own voice was raspy as he hurried toward my father, his palms open in a peaceful gesture. "I'm sorry. I'm sorry this happened, but please, don't ask Robin to leave. I-I'll marry her. We... We'll get married before the baby's born."

His words made my heart expand, and I prayed this would be enough to fix things. Then my eyes returned to my father's face, and I saw the deep scowl that remained there.

"Unfortunately, it's too late," he grated out. "You were more than willing to mess with my daughter behind my back, and you're saying this now only because you're desperate. The two of you have already revealed your mentality to me—and it's one of the ailments of our country. Irresponsible people like you are what led our great nation to crisis twenty years ago." He shook his head bitterly, his eyes returning to me. "No restraint. Despite all I have done to try to mold you, make you into an honorable human being, it's all gone to waste. I can no longer maintain my association with you. You have disqualified yourself from living in our household. I won't have you infecting your siblings with your bad example... So get out. Now."

"No, Dad!" I choked out. I rushed toward him, trying to pull him into a desperate embrace, but he gripped my arms as though I were a stranger, and pushed me backward.

"You've lost the right to call me that," he said, then stalked out of the room.

I followed him out at a run, not knowing what else to do. This couldn't be happening. If I was thrown out, I'd have no means of supporting myself during my pregnancy, and Henry and his family were stretched to the max as it was. If I couldn't get the money together, then...

"No, Dad!" I cried out again. "Please, just stop!"

I didn't even know where he was going as he sped down the staircase to the entrance hall. All I knew was that I had to get him to change his mind. I had to get him to see *reason*. I could hear Henry's footsteps pounding behind me as I raced after my father, who, I realized a moment later, was heading toward his study.

He ran to the door and pushed it open, and when I entered a few seconds after him, it was to the sight of him rummaging through the drawers of his bureau, his face dark, his eyes a quiet storm.

I realized, then, as he pulled out a brown binder, what he had been searching for.

My adoption papers. He tore them from the folder and drew a huge red cross over each of them with a marker, then ripped them apart, one by one, the pieces scattering all about the room.

"I'm sorry, Robin. But we're done here. You've left me no choice. And now you two are as good as trespassers—your boyfriend in particular. I'll have the neighborhood know that you have forsaken me and are no longer anything to me, so I suggest you leave and never show your face around here again. You two have made your bed, and now you can damn well lie in it."

"No, sir!" Henry surged forward, and the next thing I knew, my father was pulling a gun from one of the drawers, his eyes glinting with a rage I had never seen in him before.

He fired at Henry's left leg before I could scream out for him to stop, and then Henry was crying out and crumpling to the floor.

"No!" I gasped and rushed to him, pressing my hands down around his wound to stem the blood flow while he writhed in pain against the carpet.

"I told you to *leave!*" my father hissed. "*Now*, before my children come down here."

"No, wait! I need to call an—"

My father's hand closed hard around my wrist and he yanked me up from the floor, then grabbed Henry by the arm and hauled him up, too. His strength was enough to allow him to drag us both out the front door, and he cast one last glowering look at me before he slammed it shut behind us.

Henry collapsed again the second my father let go of him, and I stumbled to help him back up, even as my whole body trembled in shock. Adrenaline lent me strength I didn't know I possessed, and I managed to support the hobbling six-foot boy down the steps and out onto the street.

I staggered down the sidewalk with him, praying our neighbors were in and would allow us to make a call. It wasn't a fatal wound, and if an ambulance arrived quickly, I knew Henry would be okay.

But I also knew then that, barring a miracle, the baby I gave birth to would never be mine.

CHAPTER 1

TWO YEARS LATER...

I stared at the girl in the mirror. At her long, dirty-blond hair. At her light hazel eyes. At her narrow bone structure and thin lips. She was me, and yet she was a me I was still getting used to.

Two years can do a lot to a person. And just about everything that could have gone wrong in a person's life had gone wrong in mine.

And yet, here I stood. A survivor.

It would be a lie to say, though, that I hadn't been convinced I would break—more than a few times. The days had been dark and long after my adoptive father banished me from home. I had no choice but to move in with Henry and his family, and it was there that I experienced what life was like outside of my comfy little bubble for the first time. I experienced what life was like for the unprivileged.

I was forced to quit my private school, with no means of affording the tuition, and wound up getting a job at the same clothes factory in which Henry worked during the week. The pay there was a pittance, just enough to cover living and travel expenses, given that I was still under eighteen and had no prior work experience.

And then, when I could no longer work due to my pregnancy, it became a waiting game—waiting for the day my baby was born, and a member of the Ministry for Welfare arrived to inform me that unfortunately, I was not eligible to keep my child.

I became a victim of the same system that had punished my birth parents, all those years ago, when they were forced to give me up. The Child Redistribution Adoption System, the CRAS, aimed at the poorest of society. President Burchard's genius idea to solve the Great Crisis our country found itself in, which was, if we were to believe the news channels, precipitated by the spike in family welfare costs over the past century, thanks to our country's deteriorating morals. When it reached the point where taxes rose to unprecedented heights to meet the expense of welfare, his regime swooped in to solve the problem by instituting the CRAS, whereby only those who could afford it—the wealthy of our society—would shoulder the "burden." They would take in children under the age of three, which allowed for an easier adjustment period than older kids, thus relieving the government, and everyone else, of the expense. The system would work particularly well, they argued, because many upper- and middle-class families with career wives tended to have few or no biological children anyway, and wanted to adopt.

I lit up as a bright red flag on the Ministry's audit system, labelled as someone who would sap too many resources from the government because I didn't have adequate means to support my child. I became part of the bottom 20 percent of the population—those who were in danger of being targeted. In fact, I was probably closer to the bottom 5 percent.

And so a minister arrived the day she was born. My beautiful baby girl, whom, during those few precious hours I got to hold her in my arms, I named Hope.

Because she was my Hope, on that bright, sunny morning. That someday, things would change. That someday, I would live in a world where I could see her again.

I cried and whispered to her that I would find her, though it was a promise that was virtually impossible to keep, given that it was illegal for parents to seek out their children after they had been resituated, and detailed adoption records were kept in cyber vaults.

CHAPTER 1

It was the same reason that my birth parents had never found me—because I was sure they would've sought me out if they could.

If they had experienced anything like I had, that day I gave birth, then it was a certainty. I had never thought I'd be the kind of girl to have a baby before her mid- to late-twenties, with the academic path carved out for me by my parents. But when I held Hope, it felt like a huge piece of my life had been missing until her arrival, and I didn't know how I could've lived without her. Couldn't bear even *imagining* a life without her.

But I had to.

The tears stopped after a week, once the Ministry took her away, and numbness settled into their place. The ordeal took its toll on Henry and me, as a couple—although, to be honest, I'd felt the beginnings of a crack in our relationship when my father shot him in the leg.

Not that I could blame the poor boy. He was probably afraid to have anything more to do with a governor's daughter after that—even an ex-governor's daughter. And the time he spent with me during the pregnancy and birth was more out of duty than anything else. Henry would never admit it, but it became clearer to me in the months that followed that my father had been right about one thing: he hadn't been intending to commit to me anytime soon. We'd both been caught up in the passion of a first-time, forbidden summer romance, and had let it go too far. I'd thought that maybe our relationship could survive it, but after the baby was taken away, it became clear that she had been the only thing holding us together. Once she was gone, Henry announced that he had accepted a job transfer to another factory up north, and left.

I guessed different people reacted differently to trauma. Some people drew closer together, while others drifted apart. Our relationship was never as deep as I had thought it was, in my naïve seventeen-year-old mind, which was why he hadn't proposed until he'd been guilt-tripped into it.

In any case, we lost touch, and if he'd started seeing another girl in his new town, I honestly couldn't say I would have minded, or even felt the smallest twinge of jealousy.

CHAPTER 1

Hope's absence ate at my soul, and I could barely even think of anything else.

I moved out of Henry's parents' small apartment as quickly as I could, to get away from the memories it held, and managed to get another job in a factory—as I had given up my previous one to have the baby. I found a little cabin in the woods to call home, and it was where I lived to this day.

The sound of barking outside my window made me start, and I turned away from the mirror. I padded out of my little five-by-seven bedroom, over the rough wooden floorboards, and into my only slightly larger living room, toward the front door. I pulled it open with a creak and switched on the lantern outside. The beams illuminated a small pack of local wolves I had befriended, standing in the darkness of the late evening. They had basically become part-time pets—ever since I'd allowed them to sleep in my living room last winter, during a particularly bad storm.

"No food today, boys," I muttered, bending down to stroke their silky fur. They nuzzled against my face, and I kissed them each gently on the nose.

"Nor for you, girl," I added, my eyes falling on the female. I felt particularly bad about having nothing for her, as she was heavy with pups.

But I was earning just enough to support my lifestyle, with only the occasional money to spare, which I tried to save up. I did occasionally give them treats, but it wasn't something I wanted them to get into the habit of expecting.

Besides, my day-to-day diet wasn't suited to them, anyway. I grew potatoes and greens in a small dirt patch round the back of my cabin, and those, along with grains and milk from the local farmer, were basically what I ate. Except when I was in a rush. Then I resorted to Nurmeal, a meal-replacement drink. But I preferred real food in my mouth when I had the option. Living alone didn't exactly motivate me to cook fancy, either way. I just consumed what did the job and kept my food bill as low as possible so I had more flexibility in my budget for other things.

CHAPTER 1

After a couple minutes of back stroking, I closed the door on the animals and retreated back inside, gazing around my little cabin with a sigh. It contained only three rooms: my bedroom, the living area—which was combined with a kitchenette—and the bathroom. It had taken a while to get used to living in such a raw environment, but the months I had spent holed up in Henry's parents' apartment had gotten me accustomed to small spaces. By comparison, I had more room to myself here.

Still, the first few months I'd spent in this cabin had been the hardest of my life. The dark and cold seemed to seep out of every nook and cranny, and it was the kind that no amount of cozy lighting or fur rugs could drive away. The depression had come close to consuming me, and the only thing I had to look forward to every day was work at the factory, to take my mind off things. Not that the mind-numbing work was ever really a distraction...

But then, seven months ago, things had changed. The darkness was still never far away, lurking in the shadows of my mind like a waiting monster, but the bad days were far fewer, the motivated, optimistic ones the norm now. Seven months ago, I found a renewed purpose in life...

The sound of my phone ringing brought me back to reality—and told me that I had been spacing out. I hurried to my bathroom counter, where I had left the small device, and picked it up. After checking that my phone's encryption app was running and the line was secure, I accepted the call and pressed the speaker to my ear.

"Hey, Nelson, what's up?" I said.

"Coordinates have changed for tonight," a low, crackling voice replied, only barely distinguishable as female. "You need to head to the Roundhouse, and we'll launch the mission from there."

"Oh... Everything okay?"

"Yup. Just a slight, unexpected shift of target. So we're gonna have to approach from a different angle. Get over there and you'll get a briefing."

"Okay. I'm leaving now," I replied, and then she hung up.

I hung up too and slipped the phone into my pocket, then hurried

CHAPTER 1

to tie my hair back into a tight bun and slide into my jacket. After pulling on my backpack and grabbing my keys, I left the cabin and swung onto my motorcycle, kicking it into gear.

As I drove out through the woods toward the road, I breathed in the crisp evening air, taking a moment to just... *feel* the mix of emotions coursing through me. They came whenever Nelson got in touch, and while I looked forward to her calls, they didn't exactly fill me with light or happiness. Nor could I even say with excitement. No, it was with something much darker than that. Something deep and burning, almost primal... Perhaps the kind of thing only a broken mother can feel.

If there was one thing I had learned in these past two years, it was that pain can make you hard. But it can also mold and shape you into something you never thought you could become.

And that, I hoped, was what had happened to me.

By day they still called me Robin Sylvone (as much as I disliked the surname now, I had no other to which I could subscribe). Factory worker and upper-class reject.

But seven months ago, my nights had gotten a whole lot more meaningful. Now, by night, they called me Robin Hood.

READY FOR MORE?

Pre-order the book now for your convenience, to have it delivered automatically on release day!:

Visit: www.bellaforrest.net for details.

CHAPTER 1

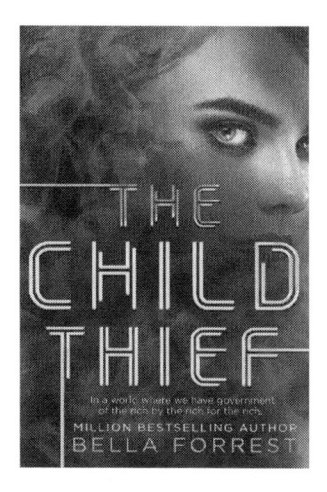

Thank you, once again, for reading, and I cannot *wait* to see you there!

Love,

Bella x

READ MORE BY BELLA FORREST

THE CHILD THIEF
Brand new dystopian series!
The Child Thief

THE GENDER GAME
(Completed series)
The Gender Game (Book 1)
The Gender Secret (Book 2)
The Gender Lie (Book 3)
The Gender War (Book 4)
The Gender Fall (Book 5)
The Gender Plan (Book 6)
The Gender End (Book 7)

THE GIRL WHO DARED TO THINK
The Girl Who Dared to Think (Book 1)
The Girl Who Dared to Stand (Book 2)
The Girl Who Dared to Descend (Book 3)
The Girl Who Dared to Rise (Book 4)
The Girl Who Dared to Lead (Book 5)
The Girl Who Dared to Endure (Book 6)
The Girl Who Dared to Fight (Book 7)

HOTBLOODS
Hotbloods (Book 1)
Coldbloods (Book 2)
Renegades (Book 3)
Venturers (Book 4)

Traitors (Book 5)

Allies (Book 6)

A SHADE OF VAMPIRE SERIES

Series 1: Derek & Sofia's story

A Shade of Vampire (Book 1)

A Shade of Blood (Book 2)

A Castle of Sand (Book 3)

A Shadow of Light (Book 4)

A Blaze of Sun (Book 5)

A Gate of Night (Book 6)

A Break of Day (Book 7)

Series 2: Rose & Caleb's story

A Shade of Novak (Book 8)

A Bond of Blood (Book 9)

A Spell of Time (Book 10)

A Chase of Prey (Book 11)

A Shade of Doubt (Book 12)

A Turn of Tides (Book 13)

A Dawn of Strength (Book 14)

A Fall of Secrets (Book 15)

An End of Night (Book 16)

Series 3: The Shade continues with a new hero...

A Wind of Change (Book 17)

A Trail of Echoes (Book 18)

A Soldier of Shadows (Book 19)

A Hero of Realms (Book 20)

A Vial of Life (Book 21)

A Fork of Paths (Book 22)

A Flight of Souls (Book 23)

A Bridge of Stars (Book 24)

Series 4: A Clan of Novaks

A Clan of Novaks (Book 25)

A World of New (Book 26)

A Web of Lies (Book 27)

A Touch of Truth (Book 28)

An Hour of Need (Book 29)

A Game of Risk (Book 30)

A Twist of Fates (Book 31)

A Day of Glory (Book 32)

Series 5: A Dawn of Guardians

A Dawn of Guardians (Book 33)

A Sword of Chance (Book 34)

A Race of Trials (Book 35)

A King of Shadow (Book 36)

An Empire of Stones (Book 37)

A Power of Old (Book 38)

A Rip of Realms (Book 39)

A Throne of Fire (Book 40)

A Tide of War (Book 41)

Series 6: A Gift of Three

A Gift of Three (Book 42)

A House of Mysteries (Book 43)

A Tangle of Hearts (Book 44)

A Meet of Tribes (Book 45)

A Ride of Peril (Book 46)

A Passage of Threats (Book 47)

A Tip of Balance (Book 48)

A Shield of Glass (Book 49)

A Clash of Storms (Book 50)

Series 7: A Call of Vampires

A Call of Vampires (Book 51)

A Valley of Darkness (Book 52)

A Hunt of Fiends (Book 53)

A Den of Tricks (Book 54)

A City of Lies (Book 55)

A League of Exiles (Book 56)

A Charge of Allies (Book 57)

A Snare of Vengeance (Book 58)

A Battle of Souls (Book 59)

Season 8: A Voyage of Founders

A Voyage of Founders (Book 60)

A SHADE OF DRAGON TRILOGY

A Shade of Dragon 1

A Shade of Dragon 2

A Shade of Dragon 3

A SHADE OF KIEV TRILOGY

A Shade of Kiev 1

A Shade of Kiev 2

A Shade of Kiev 3

THE SECRET OF SPELLSHADOW MANOR

(Completed series)

The Secret of Spellshadow Manor (Book 1)

The Breaker (Book 2)

The Chain (Book 3)

The Keep (Book 4)

The Test (Book 5)

The Spell (Book 6)

BEAUTIFUL MONSTER DUOLOGY

Beautiful Monster 1

Beautiful Monster 2

DETECTIVE ERIN BOND (Adult thriller/mystery)

Lights, Camera, GONE

Write, Edit, KILL

For an updated list of Bella's books, please visit her website: www.bellaforrest.net

Join Bella's VIP email list and she'll send you an email reminder as soon as her next book is out: www.morebellaforrest.com

Made in the USA
Middletown, DE
08 February 2019